**Also available from Rhenna Morgan
and Carina Press**

*Rough & Tumble
Wild & Sweet
Claim & Protect
Tempted & Taken
Stand & Deliver
Down & Dirty
Guardian's Promise
Healer's Need
His to Defend*

Coming soon

Mine to Keep

Also available from Rhenna Morgan

*Unexpected Eden
Healing Eden
Waking Eden
Eden's Deliverance*

HERS TO TAME

Rhenna Morgan

carina
press

**carina
press®**

Recycling programs
for this product may
not exist in your area.

ISBN-13: 978-1-335-96264-5

Hers to Tame

This edition published by arrangement with Harlequin Books S.A.

For questions and comments about the quality of this book,
please contact us at CustomerService@Harlequin.com.

Carina Press
22 Adelaide St. West, 40th Floor
Toronto, Ontario M5H 4E3, Canada
www.CarinaPress.com

Printed in U.S.A.

For my daughters. Watching you grow and become your own unique selves is a beautiful thing to behold. I love everything about you both—exactly as you are.

HERS TO TAME

Chapter One

White siding, rickety brown shutters and a pecan stained front door. Not a single bit of it matched and the combined effect made the 500-square-foot hut on Mandeville Street look like it'd been pieced together from salvage scraps, but as of twenty-four hours ago, it was officially home sweet home.

Cassie couldn't be happier.

Aunt Frieda's tired footsteps and heavy panting sounded behind her a second before her favorite relative trundled past Cassie toward the faded painted stoop with its rickety iron railing. At fifty-six, Aunt Frieda was still one heck of a looker. Dark brown hair cut in a messy pixie, green eyes with a wealth of knowledge and mischief behind them and curves that made young girls want to weep. But even more than that, she had a personality that naturally swept people up and took them along for a wild ride.

Today her outfit was almost as sassy as her demeanor—cutoff jeans, a sleeveless white button-down, red Keds and a matching bandana tied like one of those old Rosie the Riveter posters. "You know, if you want to get this move done before your vacation is over, you're gonna have to stop grinning like a loon and finish unloading boxes."

"I'm not grinning like a loon." Okay, maybe she was, but after three years of scrimping and working her butt off at New Orleans's highest rated television station, Cassie had good cause. She hefted the last box from her back seat and kicked the door to her hand-me-down Honda shut. "I'm admiring with deep appreciation."

Aunt Frieda grunted and nudged the front door open with her hip, but there was a sly, knowing smile on her face when she did it. "You and your wordplay." She paused with one foot over the threshold and jerked her chin toward the row of even more ramshackle houses down the street. "Whatever it is you're doing, hurry it up. The less your neighbors get a look at how cute you are, the less nervous I'll be leaving you here tonight."

Oh, God. Not that again.

Cassie hurried in behind her aunt and closed the door before any of her precious cold air could slip out into the bright summer day. It might only be June 1 and barely in the nineties, but the humidity was already rivaling August, which meant her baby air conditioner was working overtime.

The layout of her rental wasn't much—a living room right as you walked in, a postage stamp for a kitchen with no walls to separate the two and a bedroom in the back. But the coral walls, white trim and yellow painted cabinetry had wowed her from the get-go. She dodged the unpacked clothes, dishes, pots and pans stacked haphazardly everywhere and aimed for the fifties diner-style table where her aunt had already unburdened herself of her own box. "Marigny isn't *that* bad of a neighborhood."

"Not bad, no. Just butted right up to the Quarter where you can count on all kinds of trouble, and you know what they say about shit running downhill."

The harsh *scruuunch* as Cassie ripped the packing tape from the cardboard filled the tiny space. "I did my homework and there's very little *shit*. The only crimes they've had reported near here in the last year are a few robberies and a domestic dispute incident. And it's not like I haven't had my share of dealings with shady people in skeevy parts of town."

"You say that like you're a cop instead of a reporter." Frieda pulled the pink stuffed dog she'd given Cassie when she turned three from the box and studied it. Back in the day, Frieda had lived in Houston where Cassie's parents and older brother still lived, but she'd escaped the stuffy and opinionated confines of her family for the spirited life of New Orleans years ago. After she seemed to overcome her shock that the old stuffed animal was still around, she promptly shook the dog's head at Cassie. "And don't act like you're out there doing those stories on your own. You've got a camera guy and an engineer everywhere you go who, thank God, make sure you stay out of trouble."

"You're preaching again, Aunt Frieda."

"No, I'm not." Frieda kept unpacking items onto the table, but peeked up from beneath her lashes long enough to show even she wasn't buying her bullshit. "I'm vehemently advocating for your well-being."

Cassie snickered. An indelicate sound that was somewhere between a giddy witch and a piglet that, knowing her luck, was undoubtedly going to end up happening on camera one of these days. "Now who's wielding wordplay?"

"Touché!"

The laughter that followed was easy, and the conversation while they worked toward the bottom of their respective boxes even easier. Two peas in a pod, fencing with words and debating everything imaginable one minute and fangirling over musicians and actors the next. For as long as Cassie could remember, it had always been that way between her and her aunt, no matter the fact that Frieda was more than twice Cassie's age.

Her aunt stacked her now broken down box on top of the others like it on the floor, planted her hands on her hips and sighed. "This place does have a certain bohemian charm to it, but I still don't see why you didn't just keep living with me. You had your own entrance. Privacy." Her gaze swept the chaotic room. Clothes piled high on the plush maroon couch Frieda had found for her at an estate sale. Dishes stacked on the cerulean and red painted coffee table Cassie had found at a secondhand store. The mound of oversized gold, burgundy and jade pillows that would hopefully work for extra seating if Cassie ever had more than three guests. "You certainly had more room to spread out."

"Your house is amazing, but it's *yours*." Done breaking down her own box, Cassie opened the handful of kitchen cabinets. She didn't have a ton of dishes, but with the limited storage, good planning and effective stacking was going to be a priority. "I'm twenty-five years old. I've got no family of my own, and the only way you can move up with my kind of job is to change markets. Renting instead of buying makes sense, but the fact that I've never actually lived alone is kind of embarrassing."

Behind Cassie, the *whoosh* of her aunt taking a load off in the pile of brightly colored pillows was broken only by her tired sigh. "Is that you talking, or your parents?"

It was a gently delivered question. One offered with both heart and concern, but it struck deep.

Cassie stared at the empty cupboards. The outside of the cabinets had been painted a cheery yellow, but the original dark stained wood remained inside. It stared back at her like the black hole of disappointment that seemed to characterize every conversation she'd had with her mom and dad.

She shook off the dreariness and got to work transferring dishes from the coffee table to where she wanted them. "You know how Mom and Dad are. Logic dictates everything. If what you do for a living doesn't make you enough to provide for a comfortable and predictable life, then you're doing the wrong thing."

"They said that?"

"Not in those exact words. I think Dad used something more eloquent like, *'A professional should be able to cover the expense of a reasonable dwelling and the basic costs of living.'"*

Frieda chuckled at the overly deep voice and enunciated words Cassie had used to mimic her father. "You sound just like him."

"Well, I've listened to enough of his lectures to pick up a nuance or two." Cassie paused long enough to figure out where she was going to put various pieces of cookware still waiting for a home. "How I ended up in a family full of scholars is beyond me. If it weren't for you, I'd swear there was a switch up at the hospital."

Frieda grunted a bittersweet *hmmff.* When she spoke, her voice was a mix of fond memories and sadness. "You know, once upon a time, it was your mother who felt like the black sheep of the family."

The statement halted Cassie mid-path to sliding a stack of mixing bowls onto the last shelf. She twisted to see if Frieda's face showed any signs of the usual razzing she was known for. "You're kidding, right?"

Frieda shook her head. "Nope." Her gaze softened and grew distant, and she smoothed one palm against the top of a pillow's silk surface. "Our mom and dad were loud and boisterous. Loved going places and experiencing things. I mean, they wanted us to get good grades and expected us to do our homework, but they encouraged us to explore the arts. To follow our instincts and enjoy life." Her gaze sharpened and zeroed in on Cassie, a soft smile playing on her lips. "Your mother struggled with playing and letting go the same way you struggle with all things science and math."

Well, that wasn't hard to imagine. What was hard to grasp was that her mother could have felt as ostracized as Cassie had growing up and not been able to show *some* kind of understanding to her youngest offspring. In the end, it had been the rigidity and lack of support toward Cassie being her own person that had spurred her to leave Houston and chase a career as a news reporter in New Orleans.

Done creatively stashing her meager kitchen things away, Cassie shut the cabinet doors. "I didn't struggle in math and science. I just don't like them."

Frieda mock gasped and splayed her hand above her heart. "Cassie. How *could* you?"

"I know, right? The shame of not pursuing a higher and more educated calling." She meandered to the couch, plopped down between two piles of clothes and plunked her feet on the now mostly empty coffee table. "I tried. I really did, but I've been so much happier living here."

"And yet, you moved out of a perfectly comfortable suite that would have provided more financial cushion when you didn't have to simply to prove yourself."

Ugh.

Straight to the heart.

Leave it to Aunt Frieda to make a point and do it with the touch of a fairy godmother. "Are you telling me you'll help me pack all of this back up and figure out a way to get me out of my rental contract?"

"No. You'll stay the six months you signed for and give me time to paint your old space in some of these gloriously wild colors. Then we'll find a couple of hot men to help you move everything back. That is, unless you find some galleries for your pictures, make a million bucks on 'em and shuck that reporting gig. Then you can buy a fancy place of your own and I can move in with you."

"Ha! That's a nice dream. Not realistic, but a nice dream."

Frieda somehow managed to ace a motherly scowl even though she'd never had children of her own. "That's your father talking again. Your pictures are fabulous. Just because someone else tells you you can't do something, doesn't mean it's true." She huffed out a sharp, exasperated breath and nodded to the stack of framed pictures leaned up against the wall and the boxes with all of Cassie's carefully stored camera equipment. "Speaking of—where are you going to set up your stuff?"

A good question, and one she still didn't have a decent answer for. By moving out of her aunt's ranch-style home on the eastern edge of New Orleans, she'd willingly surrendered a whole lot of extra storage space. "Maybe I'll save up and find an antique armoire. Something I can put in here and store my laptop in, too."

"You know, I saw a cabinet over at Miss Margery's shop a few months ago. A vintage-looking armoire that had been reworked to have a hideaway desk. I'll swing by there the next time I get a chance and see if it's still there. That would make a nice housewarming gift."

"You already chipped in on half of this furniture and all of my dishes. I don't think I need any more house-warming."

"Little girl, I paid off my mortgage five years ago, and I've got no kiddos to spoil but you and your brother. If I want to buy you a cabinet and call it a housewarming gift, you'll let me." Her gaze slid to the stack of portfolios in front of all of Cassie's other photography gear. She slid the top one off the pile, positioned it on her knees and started perusing. "Besides, you need to get your savings built back up. You never know when you're going to need money for an aww-shit moment."

"*Now* who sounds like my dad?"

"I am nothing like your daddy. There's a distinct difference between making sure you can pay the bills and having a cast-iron rod wedged up your butt." She turned the page and a stack of photos Cassie hadn't mounted yet slid onto her lap. "Oh, are these new?"

Cassie leaned to one side, but still couldn't get a good view of them from the couch. "Which ones?"

"The French Quarter at night… Jackson Square vendors… Lake Pontchartrain…" she said, studying each one then moving it to the back of the stack. "And…ho, ho, ho…what do we have here?" She angled her head to a considering angle and an appreciative grin crept onto her face.

Cassie scrambled up and tried to grab the stack.

Frieda slid the lot of them out of reach before she could, but angled them so the top picture was in full view. "Who's this guy? He's hot."

Oh. Holy. Hell.

Of all the pictures Frieda absolutely did not need to

be looking at right now, it was the one she'd snapped of Kir Vasilek a month ago. "Aunt Frieda, give me that."

"Why? When a man looks like that, the last thing I need to do is let go. Especially when he's in a suit, has a mouth that could kiss you stupid and looks like he commands the world with a snap of his fingers. You ask me, suit-wearing men are an endangered species. We should protect them at all costs."

Lord help her. If Frieda only knew. The man she was advocating protection for was, according to her colleagues, a killer. Too bad Cassie hadn't known that particular detail *before* she'd learned he could kiss every bit as good her aunt suspected he could. At least then her libido wouldn't be at war with her common sense every time her mind went strolling down memory lane—which lately seemed to be too often.

"You're my aunt. Aunts don't call men *hot*. Especially when they're half their age."

"Um, this aunt does!" She pulled the picture in for another, closer gander. "And there's no way he's half my age. I'm only fifty-six and he's gotta be at least mid-thirties."

"He's thirty-five," Cassie said, making another grab for the stack and coming away successful.

"See?" Frieda said. "Totally legal. And I betcha he'd appreciate an older woman." She paused all of a second, watching Cassie stuff the prints back into her portfolio. When she spoke again, there was a whole different glint in her eyes. "Then again, I'm guessing from your reaction, he already *appreciated* you. Do tell!"

"No way. I'll tell you a lot of things, but dishing about my sex life isn't in the cards." With that, she stood and carried the wide leather-covered book to the dinette.

"Um, hate to tell you this, sugar plum, but I'm the

woman who gave you detailed dos and don'ts before you ventured out to buy your first battery-operated boyfriend."

The pillows shuffled and Frieda's Keds squeaked against the faux wood floors. While she didn't make a grab for the portfolio, her aunt did pull out a chair, sit and prop her chin on her hand, clearly ready for all the details. "Now, tell me all about Mr. Hottie and why you felt compelled to keep him a secret."

Cassie let out a tired exhale and dropped into the chair next to Frieda. Beneath her palm the navy-blue leather cover was buttery soft and cool, a welcome relief to the heat creeping up her neck. "He was the one who gave me the leg up on all the stories that got me so much good feedback at the station."

"The ones on that mobster? What's his name?"

"Stephen Alfonsi. And yes, those." Cassie opened the book, the pages easily falling open to where the pictures sat wedged against the spine. "If it hadn't been for Kir, I'm not sure I'd have had such a good run. Or any run at all, for that matter."

"Kir?"

Cassie plucked the photo off the top and held it between her fingers. The composition of the image was amateur at best, but with Kir as the primary focus, nothing else really mattered. Her aunt wasn't wrong. The man wore a suit extremely well. Though, with him seated behind the iron and glass patio table, you couldn't really appreciate how well it fit his six-foottwo frame. But what really captured the attention of pretty much any woman who met him were his features. Blond hair worn just long enough to show he'd inherited cherub-like curls from someone in his family line, a sharp aristocratic nose and an equally strong jawline. "Kir Vasilek."

"*Mmm.* You say his name the way I say *Häagen-Dazs.* Either you've got a doozy of a crush, or you had a taste and are eager for another."

Oh, she'd had a taste.

Twice.

Now here she was seven months later, and she still hadn't shaken the impact he'd had on her.

"He's quite charming," Cassie said. "Confident and educated. Very well connected. He gave me all the information I needed to start a steady roll of stories when Alfonsi disappeared."

Frieda snorted. "Girl, everyone knows Alfonsi's dead. *Disappeared* is just the politically correct way of avoiding saying he finally pissed off the wrong person. And good riddance, if you ask me." She motioned to the picture. "So, you took this when you met him?"

The same slimy disgust she'd felt the day she'd taken the picture slithered down her spine. "No." She tucked the picture back in place, closed the book and stood. At the rate she was going at work, she was either going to be out of a job, or working for some smarmy gossip rag. "Have you seen my phone anywhere?"

"Whoa. You just changed the subject on me."

"I did not." Cassie shifted the clothes on the couch and checked behind the cushions. "I just need to check the anchor schedule for next week."

"Bullshit. You were looking at that man like he was the cat's meow."

"No one says *the cat's meow* anymore."

"I do. And when I look at a man like that, I keep him."

Under normal circumstances, she'd agree with her

aunt. But Kir wasn't just any man. Rumor had it he was the right-hand man for another up-and-coming mob boss in New Orleans. A fact she hadn't known until after she'd had her second toe-curling tussle with him. "Kir's not the kind of guy you want to have a relationship with."

"Why? Did you sleep with him?"

Cassie ignored her aunt and checked behind the pictures.

"Mmm-hmm." Frieda stood and ambled to the kitchen counter. "I'll take the lack of answer as a confirmation. So, does he suck in bed?"

No-no-no-no-no-no. No thinking of Kir in bed.

But it was too late. The same pleasant swirl she'd felt that first night he'd sauntered up to her at Bacchanal Wine and aimed that devastating grin at her took root low in her belly. If she dared to think about the way his body had felt against hers—how his low and graded voice had sounded in her ear, thick with a Russian accent and muttering all number of deliciously naughty things he wanted to do with her—she'd be daydreaming and sleeping restlessly for weeks. "I could have sworn I brought it in here. Maybe I left it in the car."

"*...and* he's stellar in bed. Good to know!" Frieda lifted Cassie's purse from the white Formica countertop. "It's right here."

Thank God. Sweet diversion.

Cassie marched the handful of steps to her purse and rooted around the massive hobo bag for her phone.

Of course, Frieda showed no mercy. When it came to *seizing life by the balls* (as she put it), the woman was a veritable hound. "If you're out taking pictures of him, you're clearly interested. Why not just go up and start talking to him?"

"I wasn't taking pictures of him because I want to sleep with him. I was tailing him."

"Why?"

"Because all of my leads have dried up and I need a story!" The admission burst forth a whole lot more forcefully than she'd intended. What was worse was the guilt she'd somehow stuffed for the last month crowding around her like a malevolent ether out to choke the life force from her.

Frieda studied her for long seconds, concern and caution etched across her face. "I'm confused."

All the fight, worry and conflicted emotions she'd wrestled since late last year bled out of Cassie at once, leaving her deflated to the point she was lucky there was a chair right behind her. She sat and stared up at her aunt. "Me, too."

"Okay, so break it down for me. Tiny bite-sized chunks."

Right. Tiny bite-sized chunks. The same way she pieced together her stories until the message came together and made sense.

"We met at Bacchanal last year. He was charming and hot and seemed like a really good guy. We slept together and it was *exceptional*. We're talking *Oh my God, this is what I've been missing my whole life* exceptional. When he called me to go out on a real date, I was giddy. Euphoric. And the time with him in and out of bed was everything right out of an insta-love story. But that's when he gave me the leads on Alfonsi. He called me after to go out for a third date, but I never returned his calls."

"Why? By all accounts he's amazing and those stories got you a raise at the station, right? That sounds like a damned fine reason to go for date number three and then some."

"It's a bad idea because while he might be smart, witty, gorgeous and stellar in bed, the guys at work say he's also a mobster."

Frieda's eyes got wide and the comprehension in them likely mirrored the same shock in Cassie's own eyes when she'd figured out who Kir worked for. "Oh."

"Yes. *Oh*."

"He's like Alfonsi?"

"No. Alfonsi was the boss of his organization. Kir works directly for the boss of his family. A guy called Sergei Petrovyh."

"And this Sergei guy is a jerk like Alfonsi, but Kir is a good guy?"

Such a straightforward, simple question. But for all the digging she'd done in recent months, she couldn't corroborate the information she'd been given. "The truth is, I don't know. Rumor has it Kir and Sergei moved here with another friend of theirs about a year and a half ago and that they've got deep Russian *mafiya* roots, but I can't find one shred of evidence that ties them to organized crime. Honestly, I can't even find a source that will say a single bad thing about either of them. I can't tell if Sergei's just got them too scared to talk, or the rumors are all wrong."

"And you know this because you've been working on a story about them?"

"I wouldn't say I was working on a story."

"Well, what would you call it?"

"I don't know. Considering a story? Maybe?"

Aunt Frieda stared down at her, an eyebrow cocked high and one side of her mouth screwed up in a rare show of consternation. No doubt, that agile mind of hers was going warp speed and closing in on the very thing that had stuck in Cassie's craw for months. "So, basically, you thought this guy had the potential to be *the one*, but he's got a mobster label on him, so you cut him off."

"Right."

"Now, half a year later, your boss is nagging you to pick up the pace on some new stories, so you've started digging hoping you'll find some juicy story, but you can't. You feel like shit because you actually thought about crossing this Kir fella when he not only helped you out, but is still ringing your bell."

Cassie slunk a little deeper in her chair, hung her head and fiddled with her phone. "The whole scenario didn't sound that bad when it was stalking around in my head."

"It never does. And the truth is, you might have been smart to dodge this guy. Just because you haven't proven the rumors, doesn't mean they aren't true. Nothing wrong with being cautious." Frieda's voice softened and she stepped a little closer. "But I've never known you to be the type to undercut someone who helped you out."

Engaging her phone, Cassie thumbed up her email account. "Easy for you to say. My editor hits me up nearly every day for what I'm working on next. If I don't come up with something soon, they might give my weekend anchor slot to someone else. It took me two years to nail that seat."

Her emails filtered in one after the other, the last of which was a message from her editor, Ed.

While her aunt's voice rolled in the background, the content of what Frieda said didn't register. In fact, the only thing that registered was next week's weeknight schedule beaming back at her and the volcano-size eruption bubbling up from her belly.

"Fuck!" Cassie tossed the phone to the table, shot to her feet and started pacing.

Frieda planted her hands on her hips. "Now what?"

"One of the main anchors is out on Tuesday." Cassie spun, started a trek back toward the table and flicked her hand toward her phone. "They gave the fill-in to Lizbet."

"So? You're on vacation. Last time I checked, that precludes you getting called into work unless it's some kind of massive crisis. And besides—I've seen that girl's work. She's got nothing on you. You'll get back to work and things will go back to normal."

Before Cassie could turn for a fresh loop, Frieda snagged her by the arm and whirled Cassie so she was face-to-face with her aunt. She grabbed Cassie by both shoulders. "Baby girl, you've got to stop this. You can say it's your editor pushing you all you want, but we both know that's not the case. You have *nothing* to prove. You're doing a job you're good at even if it isn't the one you really want. One you have an uncanny knack for. Don't ruin it chasing your parents' approval."

"It's not about approval. It's about being a grown-up."

"Really? Because the Cassie I know and love wouldn't undercut someone to get ahead no matter how good the story might be. When it's time for you to find a story, you'll find it. But if you keep chasing and trying to force things to happen, one of these days you're going to end up with more regret than you can stomach."

A two-by-four to the gut couldn't have had more impact. And the truth that rang in the wake of her aunt's comment was as loud and resonant as a giant gong.

You already have regret.

A lot of it.

She'd known the second she'd conducted her first interview about Sergei that she'd knee jerked by avoiding Kir when she should have simply asked him questions directly. Knew that, while living with her aunt at the ripe age of twenty-five might make Cassie a financial hanger-on, moving out had left Frieda alone when all she wanted was love and company.

On the table, the leather portfolio sat slightly askew, the tip of Kir's picture poking out of the top.

Cassie slid back into her chair and opened the book. In the picture, Kir's face was just slightly in profile, his attention and laughter aimed at a giant of a man just out of view. This she'd learned was his partner in whatever it was they did, Roman Sokolov.

Yes, there were times when she'd been with Kir that he'd been demanding. Commandeering, the way a mobster might be. But for the most part, she just remembered how comfortable it had been to be with him. How engaging he'd been. How attentive and focused.

Especially when things had gotten physical.

She ran her finger along the edge of the picture. "What would you do?"

Easing into the chair beside her, Aunt Frieda leaned in for a better look at the image. Her voice was full of tenderness and sympathy. "I don't know, kiddo. But what I do know is that life is short." She covered Cassie's hand with her own and waited until Cassie met her gaze. "Maybe it's time you stopped worrying about what everyone else thinks and whether or not they approve of your life, and just slow down and enjoy the life you have."

Chapter Two

If anyone would have told Kir three years ago that he'd be celebrating his thirty-sixth birthday in the United States complete with a homemade cake and a family of his own, he'd have either laughed or punched them. But here he was—joined not just by the two men he trusted most, but by his *pakhan's* wife, Evette, and the son Sergei had claimed as his own.

Happy Birthday, Uncle Kir!

The message Emerson had written in bright blue icing against white frosting was only marginally legible and smeared in places, but for the life of him, Kir couldn't remember receiving a gift that meant so much. Hell, now that he thought about it, it was the *only* cake he'd ever been given. Which was rather sad for a man his age.

All around him, the customers crowded into Bacchanal's patio chattered and laughed while the lively notes from the Zydeco band playing inside the restaurant filtered out into the pleasant night. Even the little white lights strung overhead seemed a little brighter than on his normal visits. As if Evette, Emerson, Sergei and Roman had conspired to make them a part of the celebration as well.

Beside him, Emerson shifted from one foot to the

other and stared up at him, his dark blond hair long enough it slightly shadowed his keen eyes. "Do we have to sing the birthday song first? Or can we eat it now? Olga wouldn't let me steal a bite before we frosted it."

"Boy, don't go telling fibs to your uncle Kir on his birthday." Seated next to her husband of almost six months, Evette was the epitome of casual class—short dark hair cut in an artfully messy style, sharp hazel eyes that always seemed to hold a wealth of laughter and a spunky grace that fit her petite stature. She shot Kir a conspiratorial wink then propped her chin on her hand and eyeballed her son. "You and I both know I had to make a second pass at the icing before we left tonight to cover up a suspicious hole on the backside of the cake."

Most kids might have balked or tried to talk their way out of it, but Emerson was nothing like other kids. More of a grown-up with a razor-sharp wit trapped in a rapidly growing body. He grinned right back at his mother and lifted his chin. "You can't call that a bite. That was just a taste of the icing with a few extra crumbs along for the ride."

Kir barked out a laugh along with everyone else, but directed his words to Sergei. "He's a clever one, *moy brat.*" He shifted his attention to Emerson and ruffled the boy's hair. "I should make you suffer and force you to wait through the song."

"But you won't," Emerson said. "You like good food and good music too much to sit through all of us singing off key, and everyone knows Olga's cakes are the bomb."

Roman's low chuckle sounded on Kir's opposite side. While his friend of many years was never long on words, his voice was menacingly deep and the growl as intimidating as his size. "He has you there."

"Indeed," Sergei said, the pride behind his dark eyes as he gazed upon Emerson unmistakable—even to a man who'd never known the pleasure of receiving such a look.

"Well, then. It seems we're all in agreement." Kir stuffed the depressing reminder of his youth back down to the bowels of his memory, grabbed his Stoli Elit and raised it in salute. "Let us cut the cake and eat."

He'd expected something simple—either a vanilla or chocolate center. He should have known Sergei's cook—imported directly from Mother Russia when they'd relocated to the States—would do the unexpected and bake something indescribable.

"That's good," Roman grunted after shoveling in his second bite. "What's in it? Tastes like almond."

Evette licked a dab of icing off her lip and nodded. "Almond cake, gold cake and devil's food all mixed together, plus raspberry jelly and rum."

"She's a genius," Emerson said with a mouthful, earning him a sharp look from his mother. He dutifully swallowed before he kept going. "You should open a bakery, Dad. We'd make a fortune with Olga's cooking."

"Nyet," Sergei said between bites. "If she cooks for everyone else, she cannot cook for us."

The wide eyes that came with Emerson's quick comprehension were comical. "Oh. Right." He forked up another bite and shook his head. "Bad idea."

For only five people, they put a significant dent in the cake in no time, the sheer gluttony of the night and the sugar rush from their dessert slowing the conversation considerably. Even Emerson, who usually seemed tireless, was a little heavy-lidded by the time everyone pushed their plates away.

Evette noted her boy's fatigue and leaned in to Sergei, whispering something in his ear.

Sergei nodded, stood and motioned for Emerson to do the same. "Come. It's time to get you and your mother home."

Kir and Roman got to their feet as well.

"But it's Uncle Kir's birthday! The guys said we're doing more birthday stuff after dinner."

"No, *they're* doing birthday stuff later." Evette scooted her chair under the glass-topped table and laid her napkin beside her empty plate. "The places they're going don't let eight-year-olds join the fun. You'll have to stay home and keep your momma company."

"Just wait," Kir said to Emerson. "When you turn twenty-one, all the men will take you out, and you don't have to go home at all if you don't want to."

Evette might have been a foot shorter than Kir, but her playful sass was giant-sized, and everyone loved her for it. "Shut your mouth, Kir Vasilek. It's bad enough all the ideas he gets from you and your guys. He doesn't need a thirteen-year head start planning all the trouble he'll get into when he's legal."

Kir pressed his hand to his overly stuffed stomach and gave her a mock bow. "Of course, *madám*."

She snorted and waved him off. "God save me from all the testosterone."

Sergei chuckled and pulled her tight against him. "Say the word, *liubimaja*, and we'll start working on evening out the scales with a baby girl."

To that, Evette merely rolled her eyes, but also grinned in a way that said she didn't mind practicing for such an outcome in the least.

"Give me forty-five minutes to drop them off and I'll circle back," Sergei said to Kir and Roman.

Kir eased back into his seat, the fit of his suit pants more uncomfortable than he cared to admit. "Take your time. I need vodka and a rest before more celebration can begin."

"Spoken like an old man," Roman said, taking a sip of his own Stoli. "You sure you don't want to call it a night now so you can get a good night's sleep?"

Evette giggled and snuggled in closer to Sergei, her head resting naturally against his chest. "Poor Kir. And you've got a whole night full of those verbal slingshots to endure."

Sergei shook his head, but the fond smile on his face as he turned his wife toward the exit said he loved his woman's shenanigans.

Craning herself around long enough for a wave, Evette called out. "You two have fun and be safe."

"Happy birthday, Uncle Kir!" Emerson added just as loudly.

And then they were gone, the happily-ever-after threesome disappearing into the sultry shadows of the bar's main building.

"She's good for him," Roman murmured. "Grounds him."

It wasn't surprising his old friend had zeroed in on Kir's thoughts. The two of them had been banging around the more dangerous neighborhoods of St. Petersburg for as long as Kir could remember. Roman had been one of the few people he'd known to stand by him despite his father's betrayal.

"Sergei has always been grounded." Kir stared at the now closed door a moment longer, then turned back to his empty plate. He anchored one ankle over the top of his knee and grabbed his Stoli. "Though, I admit her presence has been a good one."

"Hmmff." Roman matched Kir's drink with one of his own. "A hard thing for you to admit by the sound of it."

Not so much now, but at first he'd been heavily resistant to the idea of Sergei getting close to anyone. At least until he got to know Evette.

Kir set his tumbler on the table in front of him and ran his finger through the sweat that had formed along the side. "She's not like most."

"You act like anyone with a pussy is not to be trusted."

"You act like you've met a lot who can be."

Rather than answer, Roman kept his silence. A particularly odd reaction considering the two of them had been sparring about the same topic off and on for years.

Kir looked up from his ruminating and found Roman frowning at someone or something in the crowd behind Kir. Before he could turn and follow his gaze, Roman shifted his attention back to Kir. "Just because your mother was a bad seed doesn't mean the entire gender is lacking." He finished off his vodka, clinked the glass back down on the table and changed the topic. "So. How fast do you plan on settling yourself between a woman's thighs tonight? Or should we just call one of the men and have them drive you to the retirement home early?"

Kir took the out and let the dig on his mother stay in the past where it belonged. "You're just jealous you're too much of a brute to appeal to the ladies." He raised his drink and offered a mock salute. "Besides, now that Sergei's settled down, one of us has to pick up the slack and keep the balance."

"Is that what you're doing? Keeping the balance?"

Kir shrugged, but he'd have given a lot to be free of the confines of his suit. "And enjoying myself."

"Interesting." Roman scanned the crowd again, his gaze sharper than normal. "Looks to me like you're a man desperate to avoid the truth."

Something wasn't right.

While he wouldn't exactly say Roman appeared uneasy, he'd also lost the relaxed demeanor of moments before. "What truth?"

Roman's focus settled across the room for the briefest of seconds and his frown disappeared. He zeroed in on Kir. "That maybe Sergei had the right idea about settling down."

A scoff ripped up Kir's throat. "For me? Not a chance. Evette is a rare find. Our *pakhan* may have gotten lucky, but there's no way in hell I'd risk what I have today for a woman."

Roman cocked his head, and his voice dropped to that of a man edging close to a ticking bomb. "I seem to recall you breaking one of your precious rules for that reporter late last year."

Kir studied the crowd around him. Loads of beautiful people out to celebrate the weekend's arrival with good food, good drink, and good company.

Cassie McClintock was one of those beautiful people. Tall, short platinum-blonde hair and a lithe body with a megawatt smile that disarmed everyone. She was also funny and alluringly intelligent. The intoxicating mix had thrown him for a loop.

"I don't have any rules," Kir said.

"You've never given a woman your time or attention more than once, but you did for her. Now that I think on it, your eagerness to bed every woman in New Orleans increased shortly after your second round with her. Perhaps she scared you."

Okay, maybe he did have rules. Carefully crafted

protocols to ensure he never fell prey to the schemes he'd seen so many of the men he'd worked with succumb to. "I'm not interested in relationships. I only contacted her a second time to further our plans with Alfonsi. Not because I wanted anything more." And never-ending summer would come to Russia before he ever admitted that he'd reached out to her repeatedly and been firmly shut out.

For the briefest of moments, Roman's gaze cut to a space just over Kir's shoulder before it locked back on Kir. He smirked and picked up his glass. "Is that so?" He stood just as Kir sensed someone behind him. Roman said in Russian, *"Remember, brother. The worst lies are the ones we tell ourselves."*

Before he could process or ask what Roman meant, an unmistakable feminine voice sounded behind him. "Kir?"

He should have stood.

Should have at least turned around and faced her, but the manners he'd had deeply ingrained since the day he was born couldn't fight their way free of the shock and foreign panic seizing his muscles.

Roman gave him a barely perceptible nod, the silent dare behind his gray eyes conveyed loud and clear. He lifted his attention to Cassie and his stern glare shifted to something bordering on approachable. "Miss McClintock. It's good to see you." With his empty glass in hand, he motioned to Kir. "Please, take my seat and keep my brother entertained. I need to see about getting another drink."

He left without another word.

Cassie, on the other hand, didn't budge.

But she was still there. Kir could feel her. The weight of her stare on his back and the same prickling awareness he'd felt the first night he'd laid eyes on her. He forced his muscles to relax and motioned to Roman's vacated chair. "By all means, sit. I doubt a conversation with the back of my head would be very gratifying."

It took another few hesitant seconds before she moved, the energy pulsing off her like that of a doe face-to-face with a rifle.

The second she stepped into view he regretted the invitation. Realized he hadn't braced appropriately for the skirmish that lay ahead, because time had clearly muted his memories. Maybe it was a survival technique of the mind. A way to ease past hurts and allow for his lungs and heart to keep working after she'd cut him off.

Because she was beautiful.

Not some cut and paste, unoriginal model-type beautiful, but unique and vibrant. Blue eyes. A pert little button nose that matched her bold personality and full lips that felt like heaven against his own.

He could still taste her on his tongue.

Hear the throaty sigh she made whenever he found a sensitive spot on her body.

She stood in front of Roman's chair and gripped her tiny purse with both hands in front of her. The coral leather matched her nails and the whimsical flowers printed on her white sundress. Definitely dressed to catch a man's eyes. "You sure you don't mind?"

He cleared his throat and sipped his vodka to chase away his bitterness. "Is there a reason you think I would mind?"

"Maybe because I was a shit and never returned your phone calls?"

He chuckled despite himself. "Your directness was always something I appreciated." He dipped his head toward the chair and set his drink on the table. "Please. Sit."

She set her purse on the table and scanned the empty plates and remains of his birthday cake as she sat. "You had more people here when I came in. Were you celebrating something?"

"My birthday."

"Oh. I didn't realize." She smiled, though it lacked its usual power. "Happy birthday."

He nodded in lieu of a thank-you.

"Were they relatives?"

"Not by blood, but family nonetheless."

Her smile faltered and she ducked her head. "Well, it looked like you were having a good time."

Odd. He'd only been with her on two exceptional nights, but he'd never seen her hold herself so rigid. As if she was braced to bolt at a moment's notice. From someone in his crosshairs, he'd expect such a behavior, but coming from her it was unexpected.

She's afraid of you.

The second the thought whispered through his head, he knew it was true. The question was why. "I followed your stories after we last saw each other. It seems you got a good deal of traction from Alfonsi's downfall."

She peeked at him from beneath her lashes, then lifted her chin. "I got a good deal of traction because you got the ball rolling. I'm not sure I'd have had the same success if it hadn't been for you." She hesitated all of a heartbeat, and her lips curved in a soft, but sincere smile. "I never really thanked you for that, but it was very much appreciated."

Interesting. A thank-you and fear all rolled into one visit. "Is that why you're here tonight? To thank me?"

She shook her head and wrinkled her nose. An adorable gesture that made him wonder what she'd looked like doing it when she was little. "Not exactly. I mean, I am grateful and wanted to tell you so, but…" She clasped her hands tighter in her lap and took in a long, slow breath. "I wanted to apologize, too."

"For?"

The shy hesitancy disappeared in a blink and she cocked one eyebrow high to match the dry humor in her voice. "Really? I ignored at least five voice mails from you. You have to ask what I'm apologizing for?"

There it was. The spunk and wit he'd so enjoyed for too brief a time rising above everything else. "I would have preferred something less evasive, but a rebuff is hardly something that requires an apology."

"It is when the same person calling me did a lot to help me get a leg up."

The chatter, music and early weekend energy around him never wavered, but everything inside Kir got eerily still. "I merely assumed you got what you needed from our…acquaintance."

A flush crept up her neck and she pursed her mouth like she'd bitten into a sour grape. "I suppose it would look that way. And believe me—you really did help me a lot. Not just with my job, but with my family, too. But no. That's not why I didn't call you back."

He forced himself to keep his face impassive. To hold himself completely still even though his instinct was to lean forward and demand she get on with her explanation.

She swallowed so hard it looked like it hurt, but she held his stare. "I didn't realize who you were."

"Who I was?"

"Who you work for." She circled her hand in front

of her as if that might hurry the words out of her head. "What you do. For a living, I mean."

She's afraid of you.

Why the thought hurt so much more the second time around he couldn't say, but he also couldn't blame her.

"I started digging into the details you'd given me," she said, "then one of the guys asked me who my source was. I told them your name, and they told me you work for Sergei Petrovyh." She grimaced as though uncertain how to continue. "It's intimidating, you know? Frightening. When you called, I didn't know what to do. Then the follow-up stories started pouring in and my editor took note of my work, so I ran with them. For the first time in my career, my father actually used the word *impressed* in a sentence about me." She paused to take breath and studied him. "Looking back, I think I just used all the momentum and activity to ignore the fact that I was an ass, and…well, I'm sorry."

She wasn't lying. Not about a single word. He'd been reading people his whole life, often banking his survival on reading them correctly, and she was absolutely sincere. Not to mention offering him a glimpse into her life for the first time. "I thought you didn't like to talk about your family."

Her head jerked back as though his comment had come out of left field. "Excuse me?"

"The second night we went out. I asked you about your family and where you were from, and you deftly changed the topic. And yet, twice tonight you've mentioned your family. Were you being coy before, or cautious?"

She huffed out a tired sigh and her shoulders drooped. "Honestly, I don't normally talk about them. Dealing with them is exhausting and depressing enough as it is. Rehashing the details with anyone else is just salt in the wound."

"Exhausting how?"

She considered him for long seconds, reluctance swimming behind her stormy blue eyes. Whether it was her guilty conscience riding her, or that she'd decided to face her fears, he couldn't say, but something made her decide to open up. "I'm kind of the black sheep of my family." She wrinkled her nose again, though without the smile she'd paired it with before, the action was a bit sad. "More like the black, black, black sheep."

"How so?"

She shrugged. "I've got a neuroscientist for a mom, a nuclear engineer for a dad and an experimental physicist for a brother. I tried for years to get into the heavier stuff like them, but in the end, my niche was reporting. It doesn't matter that I finished my BA degree with Honors. Dad just says it's a degree in bankruptcy."

"Not very supportive."

She snorted. An adorable sound he'd first heard her make on this very same patio surrounded by her girlfriends. "That's a polite way of saying he's a jerk. The truth is, he's just wound a little tight and doesn't seem to be capable of comprehending things outside his own world. Life is a textbook to him and, if you don't line up with the black and white on the page, then he keeps his distance."

"Textbooks are often filled with lovely illustrations. Focus on the words only and you miss some of the more beautiful messages."

The smile his comment earned him felt like the first rays of sun after a cold and gloomy winter. "I like the sentiment, but I'm afraid it would be utterly lost on my father." Her gaze shifted to the space just behind Kir's shoulder and her smile slipped.

A moment later Roman stalked to Kir's side, his voice low and calm but his words delivered in their mother tongue. *"We have a problem."*

One thing his brother in arms wasn't known for was drama, so if he said there was a problem, it had to be a sizable one.

Either Cassie surmised the urgency through Roman's tone alone, or his intimidating size and presence jump-started the nerves she'd finally shaken, because she grabbed her purse and shot to her feet. "I'm sorry. I didn't mean to keep you, but I do appreciate the time to talk."

Kir stood as well and buttoned his suit jacket.

Before he could say anything, Cassie stepped out from in front of her chair, aimed an unsteady smile at Roman, then met his stare. "Thank you, again." For a moment, he thought she'd add something else. Instead, she nodded and offered a nervous wave. "I hope you have a happy birthday."

Her stylish heels weren't as tall as women often wore to the club, but carried her in long strides toward the bar's interior and the exit beyond.

"She draws much attention when she moves," Roman said with a mix of appreciation and humor. "All hips and attitude."

It took a minute for what his brother had said to truly sink in, his attention still rooted to the door she'd disappeared through. When it finally did, he faced his friend. "Why are you looking at her hips? I thought you were saving yourself for Mrs. Right."

"You said you were not interested, and a woman with grace and courage is very attractive."

"You don't know if she's courageous."

"She talked to you, didn't she?" Roman waited. Ready for another comeback.

God knew, Kir wanted to give him one. His daily banter with Roman was one of the many joys of his life, but it was damned hard to generate a retort when he could only agree with his friend's analysis.

Roman smirked, clapped Kir on the shoulder and turned him toward the door. "Come. Mikey's waiting." The seriousness in his tone crept back into place. "It's good you got a few good surprises tonight, because you're not going to like the next one."

"Then perhaps it might be wise for you to warn me in advance?"

Pulling open the door to the bar's interior, Roman shook his head. "*Nyet*. I'll tell you in the car." The door shut behind them with a stern thud that echoed in Kir's gut, and Roman's voice dropped another notch. "I like this bar, and they won't let us back in if they're introduced to your ugly side."

Chapter Three

One thing about New Orleans—it catered to nearly every walk of life. Young. Old. Rich. Poor. Boisterous or somber. The sinners and the saved. Everyone had a place, and each of the many neighborhoods that made up the city had their own flair and feel.

Kir stared out Roman's passenger window. Up and down Tchoupitoulas Street, bright lights, music and laughter from bar hopping patrons beat back the cloud-shrouded night, but the Mississippi River rolled dark and murky in the shadows not a tenth of a mile away. A deathly black ribbon of whispers more appropriate for his mood.

Roman steered them down Washington and into the heart of Irish Channel toward the Victorian-style house his computer whiz, Kevin, had sealed the deal on just four months ago. It'd been the first property he'd ever owned.

As of tonight, it would also be his last.

Four men stood out front, two on the raised wood porch and the others just behind the knee-high wrought iron fence that fronted the tiny yard. Every one of them zeroed in on Roman's Ford Raptor as he parked directly in front. The beast of a truck was black and as gritty and intimidating as its owner.

An *avtoritet* didn't lose their composure. Didn't act without purpose, or speak without thought. Especially when those he led looked on.

But Kir wanted blood. Wanted to let loose the furious howl building behind his sternum and deal the killing blow for whoever had dared to touch one of his own.

Roman killed the engine and unbuckled his seat belt. "They will watch you. Whatever tone you set, they will echo."

He forced himself to speak. Willed the air in his lungs to give voice to the mantra he'd repeated to himself the whole drive over. "I will not dishonor my *pakhan*, or the peace he's created, and move without reason." He met Roman's stare. "But this injustice cannot stand. You know it. Sergei knows it. Kevin will have his vengeance."

Outside, the scents of cigarette smoke, moss, and freshly laid mulch hung thick in the air, held trapped by the oppressive humidity with no hope of a breeze to sweep them on their way. The fine weave of his button-down rubbed uncomfortably against his skin, and his suit jacket hung heavy on his shoulders, but the weight of his Glock stashed in his holster was a comfort.

His men fell in beside him and Roman as they strode to the door, each offering a nod, but keeping their silence. Mikey waited by the front door, his mouth clamped tight and his gaze bright with rage.

Kir met him on the porch. "How long ago did you find him?"

"An hour." Mikey opened the ten-foot-tall wood door, stepped back for Kir and Roman to go through, then followed. "Reggie and I were gonna pick him up and meet the rest of you at Cure. We found him in his bed. Knife to the heart."

The home might have been a classic, but the interior was clearly that of a bachelor. The living room mostly consisted of a huge flannel couch that several of their men had crashed on in recent months, an oversized leather chair beside it and a state-of-the-art flat screen mounted on the wall. With little else to absorb the sound, their combined footsteps on the restored wood floors ricocheted off tall ceilings. "Forced entry?"

"None."

"Struggle?"

"No."

Kir kept moving. Past the half bath in the hallway and the mostly restored black and stainless steel kitchen to the staircase at the back of the house. "The police?"

"Haven't been notified. The men have combed the streets and are keeping an eye out for anyone suspicious."

"There will not be anyone." The finality behind Roman's quietly muttered words was absolute, fueled by a lifetime of experience. "No struggle. No forced entry. Whoever did it—Kevin knew them, and their act was planned."

The upstairs was simply laid out. Two small, plain bedrooms that overlooked the meager backyard, and a nice-sized master suite that fronted the street. Kir strode toward the master, his gut roiling higher even as his muscles braced for the visual impact of what waited inside.

He paused at the threshold, as did Roman, years of detached experience pushing past his anger. The gold curtains that had been left behind when Kevin bought the place were drawn shut. The unremarkable painted gray dresser and space-age computer desk seemingly untouched. The only things out of place were the discarded T-shirt on the floor, the pooled blood on the rumpled comforter and the bare-chested dead man staring up at the ceiling.

"He hasn't been moved," Roman murmured in Russian. *"He could have been caught sleeping."*

Kir shook his head and prowled deeper into the room. *"Nyet. The lamp beside his bed is on. It would not have been if he were asleep. He was also fastidious. He would not have thrown the shirt aside unless something else had his attention, or he was told to."*

"A woman?"

"Perhaps." Kir stopped at the foot of the bed and studied his slain soldier. Short messy brown hair and a tall, yet lanky body that came from too many hours behind the computer and forgetting to eat. He was only twenty-five and, unlike the majority of his men, had always had a childlike innocence about him. A goofy smile usually graced his face, but tonight that smile was gone, his mouth slack and his skin void of life. *"Or a woman as a diversion."*

Kevin's computer sat open on the desk, the front edge of the laptop perfectly horizontal to the edge.

Odd.

Where Kevin might make sure everything was in its perfect place the vast majority of the time, his computer was seldom out of reach.

Kir turned to Mikey and Reggie both waiting just inside the doorway. "Has anything been moved?"

Reggie dipped his head toward the far side of the bed. "Just that piece of paper on the floor. I knocked it off when I checked for a pulse. Everything else has been hands-off."

Kir rounded the bed. At the far side was a simple piece of white copy paper that had once been folded into quarters lying facedown on the hardwoods. Grasping it by one corner, Kir flipped it over.

Alfonsi's Downfall stretched across the top of it, topped only by the television station that had sourced the picture and the author who'd penned it—Cassie Mc-Clintock. The picture was a candid one of Sergei walking on a neighborhood street, his gaze aimed over one shoulder as though he sensed a camera on him. The quality of the print job was grainy at best, but the frown on Sergei's face indicated he hadn't been in the best of moods when the picture had been taken.

Kir knew the article intimately. Had seen the original broadcast that went with it and read Cassie's print version many times over.

Roman studied the paper over his shoulder. "A message."

"So it seems," Kir said. "And not a very subtle one at that." Carefully setting the paper aside on the desk, Kir pulled the chair out of his way and swept his fingers over the laptop's mousepad to activate the screen. His young soldier had been one of the most enthusiastic and creative hackers he'd seen in a long while. He'd even hinted to Sergei's brother from Dallas, Knox Torren, that Kevin would give him a run for his money one day. To give him that chance, Kir had been more than willing to finance whatever technological request he made. The one thing that had been a nonnegotiable term from the get-go was a full share of passwords, infrastructure and data storage.

Mikey inched closer to Roman. "What message?"

"Someone knows we're responsible for Alfonsi," Roman said. "Whoever it is isn't happy about it."

"Can't be a huge number of people in that camp," Reggie murmured from the doorway.

"More than you think." Kir checked one directory after another, every one of them coming up empty. "Alfonsi had a lot of side businesses. Our direct competition and those he blackmailed might have been happy to see him gone, but those on his payroll are still reeling."

"What are you looking for?" Roman said.

He checked the last directory, exited the DOS prompt and faced his old friend. "Whoever was here wasn't just sending a message. They wanted information."

"How can you tell?"

"Because Kevin had a failsafe on this laptop. Any more than four attempts on logins destroyed any data stored on it, along with any connections to our shared drives. There's not a thing on this machine." Beside the computer, the photo of Sergei sat waiting, the scowl on his *pakhan's* face likely matching Kir's own expression this very moment.

Alfonsi's Downfall.

Kir focused on the author's name beneath it.

Cassie McClintock.

So zeroed in on the text in front of him and the thoughts spinning through his head, he didn't sense Roman closing in until his lowered voice sounded right behind him. "What are you thinking?"

That he couldn't find the person who'd killed Kevin fast enough. That when he found them, they would pay in the most gruesome fashion possible.

And that while death might have taken one of his own, it had also delivered a tool to ensure vengeance.

He twisted enough to commit Kevin's corpse to memory. To let the coppery bite of so much blood imprint itself on his lungs. "I'm thinking the fastest way to find who has the biggest motive is to talk to the person who's already done most of the footwork."

Chapter Four

What the hell was wrong with her? Cassie knew better than to rush her segues from the forecast or sports back to the news, but she'd been disconnected and bordering on dismissive with her peers tonight. Enough so her editor had caught her coming off set to ask her if something was wrong.

On the bright side, he didn't mention the three different times she'd butchered names she'd gotten right several times before.

She strode down the hallway toward her desk in the newsroom, the sharp raps of her heels with each step showing about as much mercy for the stained concrete floor as she showed her performance.

God, the newsroom was hot today. If she'd known it was going to be this stuffy, she'd have forgone the ice-blue suit for something a little more lightweight. And what was that smell? She'd swear someone left a tuna salad sandwich lying out overnight again.

An overly cheerful voice shot down the hallway. "Hey, Cassie! Wait up."

Fuck.

Fuck, fuck, fuck.

Tempting as it was to ignore Lizbet and her fake *let's*

be besties routine, Cassie slowed her steps, pasted on a professional smile and turned. "Hey, girl. What's up?"

"Well, I was going to ask the same thing of you." Lizbet's smile was perfect—an ideal blend of concern and kindness—but there was definitely calculation behind her brown eyes. She slowed as she got closer. "You seemed a little angry on set tonight. Everything okay?"

Ding. Dig number one.

Cassie waved her hand and snickered. "Oh, yeah. I'm fine. Just got a little distracted. There's a new story I've been noodling and a few angles popped in my head. Bad timing, but you never know when you're going to get good ideas."

"True." Lizbet cocked her head just enough the tips of her dark bob played around the edges of her perfectly painted red lips. Cassie couldn't pull off a harsh red like that if her life depended on it, but Lizbet could and did frequently. She'd swear half the men on staff fantasized about what it would take to get her lipstick stains on some very tactical body parts. "If there's anything you want to bounce off me, I'd be happy to brainstorm with you. I think it'd be great if we teamed up."

Right. Because that wouldn't be an idea that would come back to bite me at all.

Cassie at least tried for a decent smile to go with her playful response. "Wow. Could you imagine? The two of us working together? That'd be a dangerous combination, for sure!" Dangerous as in a cat fight, or an all-out bloodbath, but at least she hadn't lied or blindly agreed to something she'd never actually do. She checked her watch, knowing perfectly well it was only ten minutes past six. "Oh, shoot. I've got to run and get something to eat across the street before my seven o'clock. You staying for a bit, or are you done for the day?"

"Oh, no. I'm done. Running down that last story wore me out. I'm headed home for Netflix and ice cream, but I'll be sure and watch you at ten."

Watching and jabbing her Cassie McClintock voodoo doll was probably more like it. Cassie hustled to her desk midway into the newsroom for her purse, but kept talking. "Well, have some extra for me. Especially if there's chocolate involved."

"Oh, that's right. I forgot you were a chocoholic." Lizbet leaned one shoulder against the wide opening that led from the hallway to the newsroom and crossed her arms across her chest. "Maybe you ought to stop at the store on the way back from dinner and grab a bar. That might perk you up a little for the ten o'clock."

Ding. Dig number two.

Slinging her purse over her shoulder, Cassie forced a casual pace and a carefree attitude. Better that than swinging her overstuffed hobo bag at the bitch's head like she wanted to. "Nah. A little Mexican food and time to flesh out my ideas should do it." She strolled into the hallway, casting a polite wave back at Lizbet. "Have a good night."

"You, too."

Just a few more steps and she'd be in the lobby and well out of killing distance.

"Oh, Cassie?"

Fuck.

Cassie paused at the glass door and looked back to Lizbet.

Her nemesis hadn't budged an inch, but her smile was all smug satisfaction. "Don't let the bungled names in the last newscast get to you. The higher-ups rarely pay attention to things like that—unless they happen a lot."

Ding. Dig number three.

Be classy, Cassie. Do not stoop. Do NOT stoop.

"Thanks for that. Always good to get the wisdom of someone who's been there many times before." She pushed open the door and took one step across the threshold, silently reveling in the flash of irritation on Lizbet's face. "Have a good night!"

The door whooshed shut behind her and the iceberg conditions of the reception area rushed in to cool her flushed skin. "Good grief," she said to the part-time woman manning the front desk. "Now I know why it's so hot back there. They've got all the good air directed up here."

"You think that now, but you wouldn't if you were up here for more than an hour," the woman said. "At this rate, I'm gonna end up with work-related frostbite."

Cassie giggled and paused at the double doors that led outside. The woman wasn't the perfectly coifed mannequin and soft-spoken variety they usually hired to man the front desk. Rather, she had ruler straight hair to her shoulders that bordered between dark brunette and deep auburn and wore almost no makeup. Then again, with her pale blue eyes, adorable freckles and pretty features, she really didn't need it. "You're new here, right?"

"Yep. Just started last weekend. My temp agency sent me over on a last-minute deal. I guess the person before me got a better offer and quit without notice. Probably found someplace with a better thermostat."

The sharp bark of laughter the new girl's comment drew out of Cassie did a lot to erase the lingering grime from her interlude with Lizbet and the bumbles in her newscast. "Well, nice to have you here. I'm Cassie Mc-Clintock."

"Bonnie Drummond. Glad to have a paycheck."

Yep. She'd definitely called Bonnie right. Spirited, funny and right to the point. "Are you here because you're looking to work in broadcasting?"

"Aww, hell no." Bonnie paused and checked either side of the desk like she half expected a profanity censor to tromp out and kick her out from behind the desk. "I mean, *heck* no. This place is a little uptight for me, but it also beats standin' on my feet for twelve hours waitin' tables, so I'll take it as long as I can get it."

Cassie jerked her head toward the street. "I'm heading over for cheap Mexican food. You want anything?"

Bonnie's gaze slid to the restaurant across the street and her smile dimmed. "Nah, I'm good." She lifted her chin and pinned her attention back on Cassie. "Got a gourmet PB&J chillin' in the break room fridge. No way I'm passing that up."

Cassie knew that look. Had felt the stark want and hunger painted all over Bonnie's face before she'd wiped all vestige of her reality away and put on a brave mask. If she was truthful, she'd put herself at risk to be right back in those shoes by moving out of her aunt's house. All to prove a freaking point. "I've got one of my own waiting back there, too, but after the day I've had, I need a little indulgence. You sure you don't want some? When I say they're cheap, I mean I'm willing to swing for a few tacos as a *welcome to the party* gift."

For a second, Cassie thought she'd refuse. In the end, Bonnie swallowed hard and dipped her head. "I'd appreciate that."

Definitely good people. "Deal. See you in a few."

Two minutes and a walk across the street later, she was second-guessing her urge to leave the television's air conditioning behind. She was definitely going to have to give her hair and makeup one heck of a touch-up before her next round in front of a camera.

The bite of spices and simmering sauces hit her the moment she opened the door, followed by the urgent chatter of employees behind the counter racing to fill orders. With no drive through, crazy reasonable prices and decent food, El Torro was almost always busy. The post-bar crowd was especially fond of the long-time family-run restaurant, though how anyone dared to eat Mexican food after a hard night of drinking, Cassie couldn't fathom.

Three deep in the line of customers waiting to order, Cassie studied the menu. If she scrimped and stuck to the dollar options, she and Bonnie could both pig out on a twelve-pack of tacos, but what she was really craving was the monster platter that gave her a taste of everything.

At least that was one thing she had on Lizbet. Never once had Cassie seen her eat anything but a salad. Cassie, on the other hand, could eat junk food morning, noon and night and still feel like a twig. One of the upsides of having a high metabolism.

A presence registered behind her a second before a rich masculine voice with a delicious Russian accent rumbled near her ear. "I'm not at all confident this establishment passed its food handling inspections."

Good grief, that man was dangerous inside reaching distance. Even without physical contact, he'd sent goosebumps out in all directions and stamped out all the other sensory inputs clamoring for her attention. Rather than turn, she kept facing toward the counter. She'd have liked it better if she could have kept her smile in check, but she lost that battle entirely. "Mr. Vasilek. I didn't take you for the El Torro type."

"Mr. Vasilek, is it?" He moved in to stand beside her and considered the menu as well. Per usual, he was decked out in an immaculate suit—this one a light gray and paired with a crisp white shirt and charcoal-gray tie. While his tone was conversational, the volume behind it was markedly discreet. "I'm fairly confident we've gone far past the point where formalities are required."

"Is that so?"

"Well, we have seen each other naked, and I find once I've heard my given name on a woman's lips mid-orgasm, my surname loses all of its appeal."

No, Cassie. Don't go there. That's dangerous terrain.

But it was too late.

The intoxicating way he'd touched her—how he'd leisurely savored her skin like it was the most divine indulgence and taken time to build her anticipation—was burned in her memories. And the feel of him next to her without any barriers between them? She'd never felt anything like it in her life. It was electric. A connectedness beyond any imagining or explanation.

She cleared her throat and glanced at him. "I don't think this is the best location to discuss our past…interludes."

"I agree." He faced her and motioned to the door. "Let us go someplace more palatable and we can talk about any number of things. Our…interludes…included."

Oh, no. Thinking about them was risky enough. Talking about them was tantamount to building a bonfire at a gas station. "I think it's a much more feasible plan for me to stay within my budget and eat something quick so I can get back to the station." As soon as she mentioned the station, two and two finally added up in her head. "And what are you doing in this part of town anyway?"

"I followed you."

"You what?"

"I followed you. I was sitting in the parking lot hoping to catch you after your last newscast. I saw you walk across the street. So, here I am."

No subterfuge. No clever ploys. Just the cold hard truth.

The last of the customers in front of her slid their trays off the counter and left them face-to-face with the flushed girl manning the register. "Hi there. What can I get you?"

Go for the tacos.

Less messy.

And cheaper.

"I'll have the monster platter for here and three crunchy beef tacos to go, please."

And there went the opportunity to duck out of work later this week for more cheap Mexican food. Shaking off the self-recrimination, she opened her billfold and started pulling out ones. "Can I get the to-go order in about twenty minutes?"

"You bet." The cashier looked to Kir. "Anything for you?"

"Nyet." Kir stuck his hand in his pocket and pulled out a silver money clip pinching a decent stack of bills. He popped the clip off, peeled off a twenty and handed it the lady. "That will be all."

Cassie looked to the money disappearing in the register, then back to Kir. "I can pay for my own food."

"I am certain you can, but you will not with me." He dipped his head toward the ones folded in her hand.

"Put that away. Save it for another daring excursion of the intestinal variety."

"But—"

"We could argue the point, of course, but this is a nonnegotiable issue for me. Consider it a behavior too ingrained for me to change at this juncture in my life."

Cassie glanced at the rotund woman avidly watching the interplay behind them. She cocked one eyebrow that pretty much said she thought Cassie was twenty kinds of stupid if she argued.

Ducking her head, Cassie stuffed her bills back in her billfold. "Thank you."

"You're very welcome."

While waiting for her order, Kir kept his silence and openly studied not just the goings on behind the counter, but the patrons seated in the red Formica booths behind them.

By the time she got her food, there were only two seating options available—a booth in the far corner and a two-seater near the door.

Kir made the decision for her and steered her to the two-seater.

She set the paper bag with the to-go portion of her order aside and tugged a few napkins free of the dispenser against the glass wall. "So, what did you want to talk to me about?"

"You assume I have an agenda."

"Well, you said yourself you were waiting on me in the parking lot. You seemed awfully indifferent to me last night, so I'm assuming you were waiting for a more professional reason."

Kir reclined between the corner of the chair and the window, one arm on the table in front of him and the other on the chair's back. "I wouldn't use the word *indifferent*."

If she hadn't been ready to eat her own hand, she'd have likely engaged in some verbal back and forth. Instead, she dug into her food and gave him what Aunt Frieda called her *I don't have all day* look.

The boyish grin he gave her in return was utterly disarming. The kind of smile leveraged by ornery boys who well knew their allure and used it every opportunity they could. "You have an amazing spirit about you. I suspect there are very few who dare to challenge you."

"You haven't met Lizbet yet."

"Who?"

Cassie waved the topic off with her fork and prepped another bite. "Never mind. Just answer the question."

"What question?"

"If you weren't *indifferent*, what would you call it?"

His smile faded. He studied her intently for several moments. "Angry." With that, he let out a slow breath and the tension that had crept into his shoulders eased. "However, once you explained your reasons, your actions were understandable."

Cassie snagged a tortilla chip. "Yeah. Not exactly my finest hour." She lowered her voice and leaned in. "But, in my defense, it's not every day you find out the guy you're sleeping with is connected to the mob."

His mouth twitched. "That sounds like something out of a suspense movie. And, for the record," he said clearly mimicking her prior statement, "you don't know that I am *mafiya*. Nor, I suspect, do you have any real-world experience with what such a designation would mean."

"You're denying it?"

"Am I being interviewed?"

Oh, it was tempting. Terribly tempting.

But it felt all wrong. "No." She scooped up another bite. "I'd just like to know who I'm dealing with."

The comment sobered all sense of verbal play in an instant. While he didn't move from his relaxed posture, there was an intensity behind his sky-blue eyes that unsettled her. "I am an honorable man, and—no matter my line of work or present affiliations—you will always be safe within my care."

Within my care.

On the surface, it sounded deliciously romantic and stirred all those knights in shining armor ideals she'd once entertained. But that couldn't be what he meant. Probably just one of those odd meanings that didn't translate well from Russian to English. "So, you're willing to let bygones be bygones, and you're here to… what?" *Pick up where we left off?*

Did she want that?

Could she?

Just because he wouldn't affirm what he did for a living didn't mean he was innocent as the wind-driven snow.

He studied her. A deadly predator who clearly didn't perceive her as a threat, but still might eat her for lunch just for fun. "You mentioned our last encounter proved to be beneficial for your career. I believe we may have more opportunity to work together for our mutual benefit."

The greasy food in her stomach threatened to push its way back up her digestive tract, and she'd swear her lungs shrank to half the size they'd been ten seconds ago. Which was utterly stupid, really. A business relationship was a whole lot better than anything personal. Or it would be as soon as she figured out a way to expunge all memory of how he'd kissed and touched all the common sense right out of her.

She pushed her refried beans around on the plate and tried to rally her appetite. "Say more about that."

He sat forward and crossed his arms on the table. "I need someone to help me formulate a list of individuals most impacted by Alfonsi's disappearance, and you've spent a considerable amount of time dealing with those people."

"Why?"

"Not a specific enough question. Elaborate."

"Why do you need information on the people impacted by Alfonsi's disappearance?"

His expression didn't change, but there was steel in his voice. An uncompromising edge that said someone had crossed a line they should have avoided. "Because angry people tend to take rash actions. Rash actions aren't good for my family."

Roman's stern expression when he'd returned to the table last night flashed in her mind. She might not have been able to understand his words, but there'd been a growled urgency in his message. While she'd quick-stepped her exit from the bar to avoid any further awkwardness or embarrassment, she'd spent a good ten minutes letting herself cool down in her car. Roman and Kir had left all of three minutes behind her. "Does this have something to do with you and Roman leaving right after me last night?"

"I have many responsibilities. You'd be surprised how many times my employees call me away."

An answer, but not a direct one. Which meant she'd either at least brushed the truth, or nailed it entirely. She pushed her tray away enough to mirror his pose. Helping him after the way she'd treated him would be a far better apology than mere words. Then again, being around him would be a delicious torture, and God only knew what would happen if people found out she was working with him. "A lot of people trusted me with their thoughts and emotions in those follow-up stories. Why would I risk their trust by sharing those thoughts and emotions with you?"

His grin was instant, and his eyes glinted with the satisfaction of a man who knew the fish was nudging his hook. "Because one never knows when and where they'll pick up a new story."

Well, she'd give him one thing—he certainly knew which button to push. At the rate she was going story-wise, she'd be fighting Bonnie for a spot behind the reception desk. If he was going to at least open up some new avenues for ideas, she certainly wasn't going to let a good chance slide by.

She checked her watch and snagged the to-go bag from the edge of the table. "We can have an initial talk and see how things go, but we can't do it now. I've got to get back. How about if we meet at a coffee shop or something?"

"I'd rather our conversation take place someplace private. I'll meet you at your house."

"No."

The calm, yet firm directness of her answer seemed to take him aback. "Why not?"

"Really?"

For a moment he truly appeared to struggle with her response, but then comprehension registered behind his gaze and his lips curved in a pleased grin. "You're afraid of being alone with me."

"Ha!" The sharp bark of laughter paired with the annoying snort she was prone to bounced off the windows, drawing several stares. She straightened her spine then stood, but lowered her voice. "You wish."

His smile never wavered. Not for a second. But there was also a dangerous curiosity growing in the way he studied her. "Perhaps I do. And with the flush creeping up your neck, I don't think I'm the only one."

He stood and motioned her to the door.

Cassie took the out and reached for the bar across the glass door to push it open, but he beat her to it and held it wide. She probably should have let the whole topic go, but her pride wouldn't cooperate. "Not having you at my house has nothing to do with sex."

At least not primarily with sex.

He walked beside her through the parking lot toward the street beyond. "Then perhaps you could elaborate on your concerns?"

"Really?"

"Please. I'm utterly at a loss."

With a huff, she focused on the station's sprawling single-story design across the street. Very little had been done to update the buttery yellow brick so popular in the late sixties and early seventies and the box hedges were exceptionally bland, but the giant American flag waving atop the building at least gave a touch of color. "Please take this in the spirit it's intended, but you work for a man who's suspected of leading a growing crime family. I don't think me telling you where I live is a good idea."

"1023 South Franklin Avenue."

Cassie stopped so hard she wobbled slightly in her heels. "How did you... I mean, I only just moved in there."

His smile softened and his words were offered with gentle deliberateness. "I'm a very thorough man, Cassie.

You can't possibly think I wouldn't learn everything I could about a person before I shared important information with them."

Very thorough.

Frighteningly so.

She shook the foreboding off and resumed her trek to the station, albeit on slightly less stable legs. "All the more reason for us to meet someplace public."

"All right. Then I'll pick you up and take you somewhere."

"Not necessary." She checked both ways on the street and hurried across. "Just tell me where you want to talk, and I'll meet you there."

"I'm afraid my retrieving you and escorting you is nonnegotiable."

She frowned at him, but kept going. "You've got a lot of points you won't negotiate. Tell me why this one's one of them."

"Because while I'm very much interested in hearing what you have to share, I'm not interested in anyone else hearing. The best way to ensure our privacy is to make sure no one else knows where we're going—including you."

She stopped just six feet from the station's front door. "You don't trust me?"

"Should I?"

Hmm. He did kind of have a point. And given how she'd stiffed him after their second date, he still might be wondering if she'd simply used him. "Fine. Pick me up at my place tomorrow at eight. But don't pick any place fancy. A coffee shop, or someplace simple. And not Starbucks either. It's criminal what they charge for coffee."

His mouth twitched as if it were all he could do to

keep a wisecrack trapped behind his lips. "You seem determined to expose me to establishments with limited standards." He nodded, the picture of gentility and confidence. "I'll endeavor to pick a location that suits your expectations." He held out his hand, palm up. "Until tomorrow, then."

He had great hands. Not too smooth like someone trapped in an office, but a man's hands. Slightly calloused, with long fingers and blunt fingertips. Of all the things she'd replayed from their time together, his touch had been the most frequent. Which was exactly why she'd be smart to avoid any and all physical contact with him going forward.

Glutton for punishment and well-mannered Texas girl that she was, she slipped her palm against his.

Oh, yeah.

Still amazing.

Electric and warm. Supercharged and bristling with promise.

And that was just her hand.

"Thank you again for the dinner. It wasn't necessary, but I appreciate it all the same." Hating the breathiness in her voice, she tried to release her hand.

Kir held it tight, the pad of his thumb subtly moving over the tender spot between her thumb and her forefinger. As if he were remembering other, more intimate places he'd touched her. "I assure you. The pleasure was all mine."

He gently released her, turned without the least amount of hesitation, and strolled toward the parking lot like he didn't have a care in the world.

Watching him was something to relish. An indulgence she didn't even realize she'd taken until he stepped off the sidewalk and turned to open the door to his car.

Great. And now he's busted you ogling him.

She swung one of the double glass doors open and strode into the arctic reception area.

"Girl, that dude was hot," Bonnie said before Cassie's eyes could adjust from the blinding sunshine outside. "He your boyfriend?"

"Oh, no." She set the paper bag on the counter and shook her head. "Just a contact that helped me out on a few stories a while back."

And ruined me for other men, but why quibble over details?

Bonnie took the bag and opened it, but the look on her face and her answering chuckle said she didn't buy a word Cassie'd said. "Uh-huh. Looked to me like he was plotting how to peel you out of your professional getup."

Yeah, it'd felt like that, too. But she wasn't going to think about that now. Or ever, if she could help it. "Nope. Just talking business." She waved toward the bag and headed back toward the newsroom.

"Good business, or bad business?"

Cassie swung the door to the hallway open and cast Bonnie one last look. "I haven't decided yet. Could have been the lottery, or the biggest wrong turn of my life."

Chapter Five

The worst lies are the ones we tell ourselves.

It'd been two days since Roman had uttered those words to Kir. Two days, one murdered soldier and two perplexing encounters with Cassie to be precise, and Kir still couldn't shake them.

At close to eight on a Sunday, the streets around Cassie's neighborhood weren't nearly as busy as they would be on a weekend. A fact Kir appreciated given his drifting thoughts. Less foot traffic meant less need for concentration as he navigated Marigny's neighborhood and more time to cement his plan of attack.

He wasn't lying to himself. He accepted his attraction to Cassie. Could allow himself to appreciate once more the exceptional chemistry between them now that he understood what had driven her to ignore his calls. It was also apparent her attraction to him hadn't dimmed either.

But that attraction wouldn't rule him.

His father had made that mistake with Kir's mother and had not only paid with his honor and his life, but had left his son to bear the shame. The only thing that mattered now was protecting his family. Living up to the position and privilege he'd been given when he moved to American with Sergei.

Kir steered his Audi into a prime spot on the street just across from Cassie's address, the throaty purr of the A7's engine one that never failed to soothe him. Reminded him how far he'd come from the frightened and disgraced nine-year-old his mother had essentially sold to save her own ass.

Across the street, Cassie's matchbox of a house sat waiting. One of many such tiny homes that lined this neighborhood's streets and still went for two-hundred thousand and up merely because of their proximity to the Quarter. Most were charming despite their limited size, but Cassie's was a ramshackle mess.

He popped the door and unfolded himself from the driver's seat. Only a minimal swath of sunset remained on the horizon, leaving the skies overhead a deepening blue. For the first time in days, the humidity had lifted, and a light breeze caressed his face, neck and forearms as he strode across the street.

Her home was a break-in waiting to happen. The windows were thin enough they could shatter with little more than a tap, and he'd bet his prized album collection he could break the front door in with a halfhearted kick.

A heaviness weighted his chest, and a chill out of place with the summer night danced along his shoulders. A woman like Cassie shouldn't live alone in a neighborhood like this. At least not without proper protection. If she'd been smart, she'd have stayed at the house she'd lived at before. At least it was distanced from the drunks and trouble that plagued this part of town.

He jogged up the stoop and lifted his hand to knock.

Before his knuckles could make contact with the faded wood, it swung open and Cassie stepped across the threshold, crowding him out of her way as she closed

the door behind her. "Hey. Sorry I didn't see you sooner.
I could have saved you the trip across the street."

While she'd been dressed conservatively the day before in a light blue suit that accented her beautiful eyes,
today she'd gone casual. A stylish white linen button-
down with rolled-up sleeves and fitted jeans that perfectly showcased her fit body. She'd cuffed the hems
to midway up her shins and added tan heels that gave
him all too many tempting, yet inappropriate thoughts.

Most striking though were her flushed cheeks and
overly bright eyes. Suspicious to be sure. But then, perhaps the inside of her house left even more to be desired
than the exterior did. Either that, or she had something
tucked away inside she didn't want Kir to see.

Or someone.

The thought shouldn't have bothered him as much
as it did, but the reaction prodded him like a dagger
between his ribs. "For future reference, it's not only
unnecessary that you watch for me and meet me at my
car, it's undesired."

"Why?" She pulled her keys from her purse, slid one
into the lock and threw the bolt. "It's not like we're dating or anything."

Another jab that took the dagger deeper. Whether
she'd intended to was beside the point. "Dating or not,
I find the idea of a man not calling on a woman at her
door repulsive."

"Repulsive?" Spinning back to him, she dropped
the keys into the black hole of her enormous purse and
tucked her hair behind one ear. He couldn't exactly
call the expression on her face a frown. More that of
a woman thoroughly confused. "That's a bit strong,
don't you think?"

"Failing to personally meet a woman at her door is

lazy and ignoble, both of which are repulsive traits in my book. So, no. I don't think it's too strong at all."

Her instant smile was disarming. A bright moon-beam shining on an otherwise black velvet night. "Did you just say *ignoble*?"

"Are you unfamiliar with the word?"

"Are you kidding?" Not waiting for him, she flounced down the steps, but glanced back at him at the bottom of the stoop. "Impressed is more like it. I'd say more than half the men I know don't have that word in their vocabulary and English is their native language." She waited until he reached her on the street level then added, "Aunt Frieda says I've got a word fetish."

"Is that so?" He cupped her elbow and checked the street for oncoming traffic before he guided her across.

His touch startled her for a moment, but she re-bounded quickly and stayed in lock step the rest of the way. "Well, I do have a love for writing, and I come from a family full of people who require three-syllable words, minimum, for most conversations, so you can't be too surprised."

Actually, he was. Pleasantly so since he found it dis-appointing how little most people availed themselves of the options available in the English language. But then, every time he'd been around her, she'd found some new and interesting way to leave him awestruck.

He opened the passenger door and motioned her in. "An articulate woman who insists on frugal outings and strictly platonic relations." He waited until she was seated and looked up at him. "You do keep me on my toes, Miss McClintock." With that, he threw the door shut, got himself situated and pulled out of his park-ing spot.

Cassie made it all of two blocks before she rubbed

her palms against her jean-clad thighs and studied the neighborhood out her passenger window. "So, where are we going?"

"Ever the seeking and curious mind." He turned onto Rampart Street. "Nowhere extravagant, I assure you. How about you share how the remainder of your evening went yesterday and leave our destination as a surprise?"

Her features pinched in a mix of dismay and consideration. "I'm not especially good with surprises."

"Ah, but I'm quite fond of the expressions you make when I keep you guessing, so I suspect this surprise won't be the last. Besides, you're a reporter. The vast majority of your job centers around new discoveries."

She *hmmphed* and faced forward again, but the look on her face said she couldn't really argue his point.

"So? How was the rest of your night?" he prodded.

"Well, I didn't mispronounce anyone's name for the ten o'clock newscast and actually managed some decent banter with my colleagues between segues, so Lizbet won't have any new ammunition to shoot me with on Tuesday."

"Your nemesis again?"

"Mmm." She might have meant the response to be matter of fact, but the tension in her mouth and the way her fingers tightened against her thighs made him wonder if she was imagining choking someone. "Dark hair that belongs in a Miss Clairol commercial. Five-three. Lots of curves and knows how to use 'em."

"You don't sound like you care for this person."

Cassie shrugged and kept her gaze trained on the shops sweeping past. "I don't trust her. She flirts with the guys on our team to get 'em to help her with things

and seems to get off on cutting people down just to un-
dermine their confidence."

"She's done this with you?"

She scoffed. "It's her favorite pastime."

"Does it work? In undermining your confidence, I
mean."

Quiet filled the car's interior, only the soft hum of
the Audi's engine breaking the silence. While her face
was in profile, her mood seemed too dim. "It didn't used
to, but lately…yeah, she gets me every now and then."

"And the difference between now and before?"

She let out a long, heavy sigh, then swiveled her head
to meet his gaze. "She's gunning for my weekend spot.
I know it. She knows it. And unfortunately, she's the
one killing it with stories lately."

"I don't think I've seen this woman on your station.
What's her last name?"

"Montlake. Lizbet Montlake."

An easy enough name to track down and research
if a man were so inclined. Given the way the woman
upset Cassie, Kir was suddenly very inclined. "Sounds
like a soap opera character."

Cassie snickered at that. "Oh, drama is her middle
name. Particularly, if she can use it to high-jump to the
next rung on her career ladder." She huffed out an *I'm
done with this topic* breath and stared at Kir. "Enough
about me. Tell me about your night. Have you recovered from your birthday weekend?"

Considering his birthday weekend had been spent
dealing with the death of one of his men, that answer
was a resounding *no*. But she didn't need to know that.
Instead, he recounted of the uneventful hours he'd spent
well after midnight running through the varied finances
of the businesses he and his crew were responsible for.

"Not at all the way I'd picture a man like you spending a Saturday night," she said as he pulled up in front of the unpretentious establishment he'd chosen on Common Street. Located in the street level of a gray high-rise building, most people would walk right past Merchant coffee shop if not for the simple white sign hung above it. Their reputation, though, was solid and the destination remote enough on a Sunday that he wouldn't have to worry about too many patrons to overhear. "Is this where we're going?"

"It is." He nodded, exited the vehicle and rounded for her door.

Not surprisingly, she already had it open and was halfway out before he could get there. "You are aware that custom dictates a man open a door for a woman, correct?"

"I'm aware custom traditionally dictates such an action for a man on a date with a woman, but this isn't a date."

"Perhaps it is a behavior relegated to dating for other men, but I think we've established I am not the average male." He shut the door, palmed the inner crook of her elbow and gently steered her toward the entrance.

"Well," she murmured slightly under her breath, her gaze locked on his hand. She let out a slow and steadying exhale then lifted her gaze to him. "I don't think I can argue with that one."

Inside, the air was comfortably cool and the red swivel stools that lined the bar at the front all thankfully empty. A few individuals manned the more casual chairs and sofas near the front, so he motioned her toward the contemporary white tables near the back. "Why don't you tell me what you want, and I'll order it. If I recall, you're fond of sweets and theirs are exceptional."

She quickly scanned the menu overhead and shook her head. "No. No sweets. I've got plenty of those stashed away at home." Her gaze narrowed on the coffee selections. She frowned a second later and started digging in her purse. "Just give me an espresso."

Stubborn woman. At some point he was going to have to break her of the notion he'd ever allow her to use her own money when she was with him, and as they said, there was no time like the present. "If you're reaching for money, you can stop."

Her head snapped up. "But we talked about this."

"No, you intimated you would pay, and I ignored it. But it seems that I need to make my intentions for this and all future outings very clear. Paying for anything when I'm escorting you will not happen. Such a prospect is untenable to me."

"Untenable?"

"Are you unfamiliar with the word, or have I struck on your word porn fetish?"

Her grin was instant, and her eyes sparkled with mirth. "Word porn. I like it. Aunt Frieda will have a heyday with that one." The smile slipped almost as fast as he'd earned it. "But it's not fair for you to pay all the time."

He moved close enough she had no choice but to crane her head to hold his gaze. He lowered his voice. "It's not about fair, *milaya*. Where I come from, a man with any semblance of honor will always look out for the woman he is with."

Her eyes were so wide. Filled with wonder. And her lips parted perfectly, ready for his kiss. That first night at Bacchanal he'd done just that. Even with her friends looking on, he'd been tempted to drown in her taste.

But that wasn't what she wanted.

Wasn't what he needed.

"If it's any help," he added, "remember that I'm a very wealthy man, and the odds of anything you order here or anywhere else putting even a dent in my income are very small. Consider it a challenge to do your worst."

She swallowed hard and managed a dazed nod. "Fine." The rasp in her voice moved over him like a soft caress, and her shy smile made him want to wrap her up and keep the rest of the world far away from her. "Then make it a mocha latte and add one of those almond croissants."

His hand was at her cheek before he could check the motion, his thumb tracing a path against her delicate skin. "Well done. There's hope for you yet."

He placed the order, adding a macchiato and a lemon burrata cheesecake for himself. Rather than finding her waiting for him at a table, she stood near the farthest wall staring up at the many photos mounted in a haphazard pattern, her hands firmly planted on her hips.

"I recall you mentioning a love of photography." He slid the tray onto the tabletop and stood beside her. "What interests you about these?"

Her gaze moved slowly from one to the other, a soft wonder he'd never seen before etched on her face. "They're very evocative. Candid, but captured at a time that shows a depth of personality or emotion." She faced him and, for a moment, that beautiful softness was aimed solely his way. Her wry grin crept in, though, and swept it away. "It's harder to master than you'd think."

"I suspect you've got a knack for it."

She shook her head and pulled out a chair. "Not really. I wish it were, but composition and lighting are more my specialty."

He waited until she was seated before he followed suit. "I'd like to see your work."

"Oh, it's just a hobby," she said as she gathered her items from the tray. "Something I do to unwind or give my brain a chance to untangle something difficult." Whether she realized it or not, her voice took on a melancholy tone and the smile on her face was disconcertingly sad.

Neither sat well with him, but before he could find a way to dig into the reason for the change, she seemed to shrug the response off and lifted her head. "So, I know you want me to help you figure out who's been the most impacted by Alfonsi no longer being around, but I need something from you before I can do that."

Interesting. Definitely not the direction he'd anticipated their conversation to go. "Is this a negotiation?"

"More of an assurance so I can sleep at night."

Reasonable. And indicative that his feisty reporter had been thinking a lot about what he needed since yesterday. "Then by all means...tell me what you require."

She sipped her coffee, her gaze trained on the table. Even once she set the mug back on its saucer, it took her a handful of seconds to seem to find the words. Once she did, she directed her attention squarely on him. "I need to know what you plan to do with the information I give you."

If it weren't for years of dealing with powerful and sometimes hotheaded *vors*, he might have flinched at the request. Or at least shown some subtle surprise or concern that betrayed his hesitancy.

Instead, he forked up a bite of his cheesecake. "I don't believe I ever commented on the need to take a specific action. Only that I sought to learn the names of people significantly impacted by Alfonsi's disappearance."

"And then you said, *'Angry people tend to take rash actions. Rash actions aren't good for my family.'*"

He had said that. Almost word for word. "You have a very good memory." Setting aside his fork, he retrieved his phone from the interior pocket of his suit and pulled up a picture one of his men had taken at Sergei and Evette's holiday wedding just six months ago. Much like the pictures Cassie had appreciated on the walls, the image was beautifully uncontrived and was one of the few photos he'd allowed himself to be captured in for years. He showed it to her. "These are the people I seek to protect."

Cassie leaned in, the softness he'd glimpsed returning as she zoomed in the screen to better absorb the details. Sergei and Evette stood in the middle with Emerson centered in front of them. Roman and Kir flanked the trio. As always, Evette was all class, done up in a form-fitting strapless ivory dress that hit just above her knees and heels that accented her legs in a way that left Sergei's eyes hungry. The men were in classic black suits, but it was the smiles on their collective faces that made the image.

A family.

However oddly they'd come together, they were his base. His smiles. His peace. His escape from a world of shame and lack.

She lifted her gaze to his, a silent question in her eyes.

He answered it the best he could without giving her

more than she needed to hear. "It's better to prevent rash actions before they occur. Wouldn't you agree?"

Sitting back in her chair, she peeled off a bite of croissant. "You won't use the names I give you for anything bad?"

Lying should have been easy. But for some reason, the dispassionate words he'd have easily used on others wouldn't come. "I promise you that my only purpose is to protect those I care for and those that serve me. I will take no action that isn't fully proven and warranted."

The gray blue of her eyes seemed to darken. A color closer to storm clouds than a dusky sunset.

She knew.

She might not want to admit it, or acknowledge the truth out loud, but her conscience accepted who he was and what he was capable of should those within his care be threatened.

Breaking his stare, she dropped the last bite of her croissant back onto the plate and dusted off her fingers. Her voice was low and shaky. "What exactly do you want to know?"

He slid his cheesecake closer to her, along with the extra fork he'd requested. "Let's start with his businesses. You did several follow-up stories on the fallout after Stephen and Stevie Jr. went missing. Did anyone seem angrier than others? Someone who suffered significant financial loss?"

"Hundreds of people had financial losses." She eyed the cheesecake then shrugged and picked up the fork. "Half of the restaurants went under when the estate attorneys couldn't find buyers. All of the construction crews had to find new jobs, and his casino interests have been on shaky ground for months. I think the only people who didn't lose money were the lawyers."

"No one that stood out?"

"A few." She set her fork aside. While her attention was zeroed in on the table, her gaze was distant. Thoughtful. She frowned a second before she trained her eyes on him. "Probably the worst were the two guys running Alfonsi's real estate and construction company. Bob Townsend and Mack Reynolds."

"How so?"

Cassie crossed her forearms on the table and leaned in. "Not many people deal well with losing money, and both of them were making a lot of it with Alfonsi's schemes. The Feds found out how many homeowners had been duped into buying shoddy homes or had paid for closing services they never received and locked down both of their bank accounts. Lots of reporters tried to get interviews with them after the fact and none of them went well."

"They lost their cool?"

"That's an understatement. Townsend took a swing at a female reporter, and Reynolds thought it'd be a good idea to tackle three cameramen. Kind of reminded me of a Jerry Springer episode."

Loss of money. Damage to reputations. Add volatile tempers to the equation and either of the men could be accountable for Kevin's death. "Anyone else? Anyone who might have flown under the radar?"

She pursed her mouth and cocked her head. "You know, the people I always wondered about were Alfonsi's wife and daughter. Three days after she reported him missing, the wife cleaned out the bank accounts and disappeared with the daughter. No one ever called it out in a story—my guess, because they couldn't blame her for getting out of Dodge—but it always felt like a loose end to me. Rumor has it, she's at a house they own in Belize."

Actually, it was exactly what he'd expect of Alfonsi's wife. No doubt, a plan he'd arranged for his family in the event anything happened to him. One of the first things Sergei had done after moving Evette and Emerson into his home was ensure they'd always be cared for and protected in his absence.

For another thirty minutes, Cassie shared her insights. Nuances of the conversations she'd had with prosecutors. Details on which businesses were still fully functional and those who'd closed their doors for good. Not surprisingly, most of her stories highlighted the individuals most negatively impacted in the aftermath.

Kir made note of every one of them to share with Sergei later. If the outcome of the class action lawsuit and the insurance payouts didn't take care of them, he had every confidence another, more silent benefactor would.

She yawned, covering her mouth as she tried to shake the obviously unexpected reaction off. "Sorry. I don't need a ton of sleep, but the last few nights have been short on hours even for me."

"Lots of hours at work?"

"More like lots of hours trying to comb up some work."

He nodded and stood. "Then I'll get you home so you can get some rest."

In the time since they'd arrived, the skies had turned full black and more patrons had filtered in to take advantage of the casual venue with its intimate lighting and comfortable seating areas.

Logic dictated that distance was the wisest course of action, but with the narrow aisle between the tables at the back of the shop, he found himself moving in tightly beside her and placing his hand low on her back.

Her breath caught on a subtle hitch and, for a few steps, her body swayed nearer to his. Such a simple connection, but fiercely palpable. Natural and powerful to a degree he still couldn't quite comprehend. Just walking beside her felt right, an innate synchronicity that somehow made him feel more balanced than when he walked alone. Which was surprising considering he'd never found strolling side by side with any other woman even remotely appealing.

He felt more than saw her glance at his face. Tempting as it was to meet her gaze, he forced himself to keep his attention trained on the exit ahead—until her steps slowed and the muscles in her back tensed. He followed her narrowed gaze.

In the corner of the coffee shop, a girl with long black hair in pigtails sat curled up in one of the suede chairs studying something on her computer. The dim pendant light streaming overhead made her heavy makeup and gothic black attire even more dramatic. "Do you know her?"

Cassie shook her head, and the frown on her face relaxed. "I thought so, but maybe not." She smiled up at him, but it lacked its usual strength. "Job hazard, I guess."

Maybe it was the lack of sleep, but even once they got back in the car, she was less talkative than normal. Pensive as though something plagued her mind with no ready solution in sight.

If he was smart, he'd simply let the silence reign. Take the information she'd provided, see what it turned up and let her get back to her everyday life.

But he didn't want her to get back to her everyday

life. Didn't want to be out of excuses to spend time with her, even if it did make him the most foolish man alive. "I want you to help me research Townsend and Reynolds."

His statement shook her out of her daze and brought her sharp eyes to his. "Excuse me?"

"You know these men. Your observations, insight and experience would help me research them more quickly."

She smoothed her hands up and down her thighs and sighed. "Yeah, I don't think you and I working together is a great idea."

"Why not?"

"Because if some of my other sources see me with you, they might not be sources long. Not to mention any story I write will be questioned on credibility and bias if I'm seen with you."

A reasonable argument. Not one he liked, but reasonable. "Then you can partner with me silently. Counsel me on my findings and make suggestions."

She considered him for long seconds, the scrutiny of her stare more challenging to bear than the *vor* who'd all but bought him from his mother all those years ago. "Why would you want that? I treated you badly after you helped me, and I can absolutely understand you wanting my help in exchange, but I just gave you what you wanted. Why spend any more time around me?"

Because she was smart. Funny. Compassionate and gorgeous. And for some reason he couldn't properly categorize or comprehend, being around her brought a rare peace to his thoughts. A calmness he couldn't remember having since well before his father changed their lives forever.

He focused on the turn into her neighborhood and

used the task of paralleling in a spot just down from her house to formulate his words. He put the gearshift in park, shifted in his seat enough to brace his hand on her seat back and met her stare head-on. "We have a commonality in our respective jobs. Both of us rely on healthy relationships to stay abreast of what's happening in our world. Fostering ours to our mutual benefit makes sense. To cut you out at this juncture would cut us both short, and I'm not a person who walks away from beneficial arrangements. Are you?"

Her lips twitched and a smile twinkled behind her eyes, but her wry tone was just as sharp as Roman's. "You sure you're not in sales? Because I'm pretty sure you could move some snake oil with lines like that."

Snake oil. That was a phrase he'd have to look up, but the sentiment was clear enough. "I like to think of myself as an opportunity engineer."

"Ha!" Her sharp laughter rounded the car's interior. "Smooth *and* creative." Her laughter dimmed, but her smile remained. "All right, fine. Silent partners. You let me know what you find, and I'll give you my feedback. But you gotta let me know if you come across any leads I can use. Deal?"

"Deal." He popped the latch on his door and, surprisingly, Cassie waited for him to round to her side.

Of course, the first words out of her mouth as he helped her to her feet were "You know you don't have to see me to the door. I can find my way there just fine."

"You can, but you won't. We've discussed this."

"You mean, you dictated."

"There are some things a man cannot compromise on." He guided her across the street, her soft perfume mingling with the night's breeze. It was a pleasant scent.

Nothing cloying like some women favored, but light and crisp like petals scented on a spring morning.

At the door, she dug her keys from her purse. "When do you think you'll know something about the names I gave you?"

Most likely, before she even got out of bed to go to work in the morning, but sharing the level of urgency behind his search would only further pique her interest. "A few days, I'd expect. Perhaps sooner."

She nodded and slid the key in the lock.

The space behind his sternum grew tight, and the urge to inch closer nearly drew him from his steady stance. Lingering was foolish. An invitation guaranteed to welcome further disappointment.

But he'd enjoyed the night. Sparring with her. Listening to her. The stolen touches and subtle responses they'd garnered.

She faced him, but her gaze was rooted to his chin. "Well...thank you for the coffee and desserts."

"You're very welcome."

Just one kiss.

One taste to see if her response was as powerful as he remembered.

Ducking her head, she played with the keys still in her hand. "I'm glad we did this. I hope I was able to help."

A single step forward and he could feel her against him. Feel her heat and the way her lithe body moved with his.

"If not, we'll try again." He nodded to the open doorway, but when he spoke his voice was ragged. "In you go. I want to hear the bolt thrown before I leave."

She nodded, but averted her gaze as she did. "Right. Good night. Thanks again."

The door slipped shut with a soft thud, and the tinny chink of a too-small lock slipped into place. A soft white light flared behind the curtained windows, and soft footfalls sounded on wood carrying her farther away.

Slowly, he made his way down the stoop and across the street, hating the emptiness beside him.

He slid behind the wheel, fired up his Audi and pulled onto the street, casting one last glance at the light behind the window.

Leaving was the right thing to do.

Certainly safer.

For both of them.

Chapter Six

The bad thing about math? Two plus two always equaled four. Or, in Cassie's case, five hundred and fifty in disposable income minus a four-hundred-and fifty-dollar car repair bill equaled trouble.

She huffed out a frustrated sigh and shifted to the edge of her couch, plunking her laptop onto the coffee table. Surely she could make a hundred dollars stretch for a month. Or, if she got creative with her grocery list, she could bump her expendable cash by fifty or so dollars. She certainly wasn't a stranger to living on toast and peanut butter and jelly sandwiches.

Yeah, but you were a college student then. So much for showing everyone what a grown-up professional you are now.

Three quick raps from the door rose above the background chatter of *Dr. Phil* on the television.

"Who is it?"

"Well, who do you think it is?" Aunt Frieda bellowed in her singsong voice from the other side of the door. "Because if you're expecting a fella, that means you've been holding out on gossip."

Cassie yanked the door open and frowned at her aunt. Not many women her aunt's age could wear faded Levi cutoffs, a vintage Led Zeppelin T-shirt and sparkly flip flops, but Frieda managed it easily. "You know, for someone who's worried about my safety, you sure don't hesitate to announce my single status to the neighbors."

Loaded down with at least four plastic grocery bags in each hand, Frieda glanced up and down the street then grimaced. "Oops?"

"Oops, indeed." She motioned to the bags in Frieda's hands. "What are those?"

"Provisions. I've got chips and everything we need for homemade guacamole, queso and margaritas."

Oh, thank you, Jesus. It wouldn't keep her from relying on PB&J's for the next month, but at least she'd have the tools necessary to deny what lay ahead for a few hours or so.

Cassie waved her aunt inside. "It's official. You're forgiven."

Treating the kitchen like it was her own, Frieda scanned Cassie from head to toe and got to work on unpacking the bags. "Boy shorts and a T-shirt before five o'clock on a Wednesday night?"

"Don't judge. At least I've got on pants. For a few minutes when I got home, even the boy shorts were debatable."

"Where's your car? I didn't see it out front."

"That's because it's in the shop. Do you have any idea how much it costs to pay for a tow truck?"

"Bad day, I take it?"

"Not the best, that's for sure." Cassie pulled the tequila out of the bag closest to her and lifted it in mock salute. "Definitely a good night to spend with Cuervo."

"You know what's wrong with it yet?"

"Something about a timing chain?" Cassie pulled the blender parts from the top shelf and got to work gathering drink essentials. "I didn't even know cars had a timing chain. What I do know is, they're expensive to get fixed."

"How much?"

With more force than was necessary, Cassie plunked the blender's pitcher into the base. "Four-hundred and fifty freaking dollars."

Frieda glanced over her shoulder and grunted, but otherwise kept her silence and went back to prepping the avocados.

Cassie chuckled. "Go ahead. Say it."

"Say what?"

"I told you so."

Frieda shook her head and sighed, but it was one of those understanding ones rather than the long-suffering variety her parents specialized in. "I'm not gonna say I told you so, sweetie. We all make our choices and do the best we can living with them. The last thing you need is someone rubbing your nose in the first hurdle that hits you." She set her knife aside and rummaged around in the lower cabinet until she found the cutting board, then straightened and smiled at Cassie. "What I will do is make sure we do at least one big dinner at your place once a week until you get over this hump. At least that way I can make sure you've got some decent leftovers."

The tension that had been riding Cassie's neck and shoulders released in an instant and, for a moment, her knees got shaky. She wrapped her aunt up in a fierce hug. "Thank you."

"Oh, kiddo." Frieda's answering embrace was pure acceptance. Comfort and understanding without a single word spoken. "It's just food. Not a big deal."

"No," Cassie murmured. Fighting back tears took everything in her. "Not for the food. Or the tequila. I could live on almost nothing if I had to, but having your support means a lot. A whole lot."

Frieda gripped Cassie by her shoulders and urged her back for a good look at her face. "You're always going to have that, Cassie. I may not always understand or agree with the things you do, but I'll always be here when you need me."

Tears blurred Cassie's vision and a single one slipped free despite her best efforts. "I love you. You're like the only real friend I've got in this world and you're definitely the only person who gets me. Honest to God, I don't know what I'd do without you."

"You'd probably still be clueless on clothes, makeup and highlights and possibly chasing a master's in something you had zero interest in doing. But hey, what are aunts for?" She pulled Cassie in for another quick hug, then steered her back to the blender. "Now get to work, missy. Those margaritas aren't going to make themselves."

It was a classic Aunt Frieda move—take a desperate situation and somehow turn it into not just a moment Cassie could be grateful for, but would remember for a lifetime.

Cassie worked the blender.

Aunt Frieda worked the guac and queso.

Through it all, they bantered back and forth about everything from the gossip in Frieda's neighborhood, to how Cassie might wedge some cute shelves into her closet of a bedroom. Within twenty minutes, they were splayed out next to each other on the couch with the five o'clock news playing in the background and the first round of drinks nearly polished off. Between the laughter and the tequila, she was breathing easier than she had been all day.

Or was until Lizbet popped up on the screen. In a short-sleeved ivory silk shirt, tan pencil skirt and matching heels, she was pure classic sophistication walking down one of the Seventh Ward's more dangerous streets. Of course, she had not one single hair out of place and walked like she'd been born wearing those shoes. "Ugh. How can anyone look that fresh when the humidity's at nearly ninety percent?"

"Oh, no," Frieda grumbled. "Do we need another round already?"

"Shhh." Cassie leaned in and thumbed up the volume. Beneath her nemesis the caption read, *The Darker Side of New Orleans.*

"Not so long ago, the success of a certain erotic romance series brought significant light and no small measure of interest to the practice of BDSM. Movies followed. The genre flourished with other stories quickly gobbled up by eager readers, and research indicates that adult toy sales surged as individuals explored practices they'd read about or seen in the movies.

"But what about the lifestyle itself? Is it accessible to the average person? And if so, what are the venues and the people like?

"Tonight, I'll share with you a conversation I had with an individual who became a part of the BDSM lifestyle long before it became a mainstream curiosity."

The video cut to a movie clip of an elaborate dungeon, the camera panning to depict red leather benches, walls covered with crops and paddles, all accentuated in sensual lighting. Lizbet's voice was edited in underneath.

"The movies and books all paint dungeons as very glamorous locations. But do they really exist?

"Absolutely." The image on screen cut to a silhouette

of a woman's face, though her voice had obviously been altered. Even with the attempts to disguise the woman's identity, it was obvious she had full lips, and her cute little upturned nose added a uniqueness to her image.

"Most dungeons don't look like what you read in books. Some in bigger cities do, but most are more functional spaces. Clean and tidy with well enforced rules, to be sure, but not the opulent settings you see in movies."

"And how do you fit in with this lifestyle?"

"I'm a Dominant. A Pro Domme to be exact."

"But you're a woman."

"I am. But a Dominant role isn't relegated to only men any more than submissive roles are relegated to females."

"And a Pro Domme—what does that mean?"

The mystery woman hesitated, but when she spoke anyone watching could have heard the smug pleasure in her voice. *"It means those seeking submission pay me to Dominate them. Sometimes in the form of a tribute, but most often for money."*

"Do you have sex with them?"

"Sometimes. If it's something that's negotiated."

The question must have caught Lizbet off guard, because there was a slight hitch before her next question came. But it was a damned good one. *"But isn't that technically prostitution?"*

"Yes, which is why I'm very, very careful with those I interact with. But it's still a need, and one I very much enjoy filling. So, I do it. Often."

"Do you make a living at it?"

Even without the benefit of seeing the woman's face, a certain tension crept into the interview. *"I didn't have to for a very long time. Now...it helps."*

The camera feed cut to Lizbet, back live on the streets of New Orleans. *"My source went on to share that the BDSM and other less traditional lifestyles are far more prevalent within New Orleans and the United States than many people realize. While she refused to share the actual location of any dungeons within our own city, she did confirm they exist. So, while the stories penned by authors paint far more elaborate pictures, it appears there is fact beneath the fiction.*

"Over the next few weeks we'll explore more myths and legends purported to take place in our beloved city's shadows. Until then, I'm Lizbet Montlake, reporting live from New Orleans's Seventh Ward."

Cassie punched the mute button and tossed the remote on the coffee table. "You have *got* to be kidding me."

"What?" Frieda said. "What's wrong with it?"

"It's a fluff piece. On a Wednesday night! There's no news there. Everyone knows that stuff goes on. Maybe…*maybe*… I'd buy it on a ten o'clock newscast, but the five o'clock spot?"

"Yes, but it's interesting. And, as she said, it's much more mainstream these days."

"It's sensationalism, not news. And whose side are you on anyway?"

"Yours. That's why I brought alcohol." Frieda stood, grabbed Cassie's now empty margarita glass and marched to the kitchen. "And apparently, we're gonna need a refill, STAT."

"What I need is a story. And for Lizbet to get a job offer outside of New Orleans."

"Well, we both know the latter is a long shot. It took you a year to land the job here. I'd imagine it's even harder finding something in a bigger city."

"It is."

"Okay, so how do you find a story?"

"I've never had to find one before. They always find me. Usually when I'm goofing off, or working on something else."

With Cassie's glass refilled clear to the top, Frieda rounded the dinette. "Then start goofing off. Spend some time on your photography. Sleep late. Do something to your apartment."

"I went on a shoot yesterday." Cassie took the glass from Frieda and took a long drink. "Not going to be doing that for a while. Too hard without a car."

"Did you print your stuff from yesterday yet?"

Nodding, Cassie shifted, grabbed the stack off her makeshift end table made from an empty cardboard box then handed them over. "Not a bad collection this time around, but no story ideas."

She sipped her drink and halfheartedly watched her aunt move from one picture to the next. Rather than take the time to really appreciate her work, she rushed through the stack. "What are you looking for?"

"More pics of the hot guy."

Cassie grunted and sipped another gulp through her straw. "I didn't get any of him."

"Well, that's too damned bad. He's a looker."

Boy, that was the truth. She'd caught herself losing the thread of her conversation with Kir way too many times Sunday night simply from absorbing how good he looked. And when he'd touched her? Yeah, thinking wasn't an easy task anytime he got close enough for contact.

For a second, Cassie considered keeping her mouth shut and shifting topics. But this was Aunt Frieda. The one person in the world who'd never once judged or tried to control her. "I did see him, though. He wants me to help him research something. I'm hoping I might get a lead there."

"A lead from what he's researching?"

Oh, she was 150% certain the cause for his research would be a zinger of a lead.

That said, it might also mean her ending up being the focus of a missing person story if she ran with it. Assuming she ever found out what was driving Kir. "Not exactly. More likely from someone he knows, or something he hears. He's got a lot of connections and plays things pretty close to the vest."

"So, when are you going to see him again?"

"Don't know." Truth was, she'd expected to hear from him Monday or Tuesday, but her phone and text messages had been complete radio silence. "For all I know, he's gotten what he needed."

A knock sounded at the front door, the strength behind it significant enough to rattle the wood. Not that rattling the wood was a difficult thing to do, considering the door had probably been the cheapest option available ten years ago.

Frieda frowned and got to her feet before Cassie could even fully comprehend anyone coming to her place on a weeknight. "You expecting someone?"

"There are literally two people in the world who know where I live, and one of them is already here."

Duh, Cassie. Two people.

Cassie shot upright and tried to get to the door before her aunt, but it was too late.

Frieda was already beaming up at Kir. "Well, hello there, handsome."

Every time she'd seen him before he'd been in a perfectly tailored suit—not counting the two times he'd been deliciously naked in his bed. Tonight, though, he was in casual charcoal-gray slacks and a lighter gray Oxford with the sleeves rolled up to his forearms, and her aunt was openly appreciating every single detail.

Cassie pried the door a little wider and cut her aunt off before she could engage any further. "Kir. I wasn't expecting you."

"I see that." His gaze took a long, leisurely pass down her torso to her very bare legs. When he lifted his head, there was an undeniable heat behind his blue eyes that made her feel like she was standing in front of him completely naked.

He shifted his attention to Frieda and held out his hand. "I'm Kir Vasilek, and you are?"

"This is my aunt Frieda," Cassie blurted.

Frieda volleyed a heavy amount of consideration between Cassie and Kir, way too many dots appearing to connect inside that head of hers. A second later, a sly smile curved her lips and she accepted Kir's outstretched hand. "Frieda Shalaway. Cassie and I were just decompressing from a big day with comfort food and margaritas. Care to join us?"

"Comfort food?" Kir took one step inside, surreptitiously scanning the interior of Cassie's tiny living room and the contents covering the coffee table.

"Nothing fancy," Frieda said as she waved him deeper into the room. "Some homemade guacamole, chips and queso. Can I get you a margarita?"

Ugh. Definitely not a good idea. With the scheming gleam in Frieda's eyes, she'd not only caught Kir's response to Cassie's casual attire, but probably had fifty or so matchmaking ideas lined up in her head. "Actually, I think we're almost out of margaritas—"

"Oh my goodness!" Frieda threw up her hands and

hurried to the kitchen. "I completely forgot I was supposed to swing by my neighbor's house and let her dog out before it got dark."

"Wait—what?" Cassie said.

"My neighbor. She's out of town for the week, and I have to let her dog out twice a day. I completely forgot."

Forgot my ass. More like wanted to increase her niece's probability of hanky-panky.

Frieda anchored her purse over one shoulder and hustled toward the door fast enough Kir had no choice but to step out of her way. "Kir, there's plenty of margaritas left for another round. You stay and keep Cassie company. She needs it after the day she's had."

Kir's attention swiveled to Cassie, his expression darkening. "Something happened?"

"Car troubles." Frieda paused over the threshold and jingled her car keys. "You just never know when they're going to turn persnickety on you, right?" She aimed a sly wink at Cassie and wiggled her fingers in farewell. "You two have a good night."

Cassie stared out the now empty doorway.

Two quick chirps sounded from the street and parking lights flashed in the darkness.

Kir faced her. While he kept his expression somewhat sincere, there was still mirth and a decent amount of curiosity dancing behind his eyes. "It seems I've broken up your evening."

Sighing, Cassie closed the door. "Kind of depends on whose view you're looking at it from. I'm pretty sure Aunt Frieda is already planning an early stakeout to see if she can catch you leaving in the wee hours of the morning, looking thoroughly rumpled and pleased with yourself."

"Is that an option?"

A playful, yet husky question that made every square inch of her skin bristle in anticipation. With the hungry way his gaze lingered on her bared legs and the tequila loosening her good sense, she was halfway tempted to say yes just to see what happened. "I highly doubt you dropped by for a booty call."

"No, it's not the reason for my visit. But I must confess, seeing the casual side to you does inspire me to make more unannounced appearances." He sat on the couch and rested one ankle on his knee. "The view is exceptional."

Good grief.

He'd been here barely more than two minutes and he not only looked utterly at home on her second or thirdhand couch, but had her body fired up and her brain frazzled.

She cleared her throat and motioned toward the kitchen. "Do you want a margarita?"

"*Nyet.* Tequila isn't to my taste. However, I would like to hear more about what happened to your car." He nodded toward the open space on the couch next to him. "Please. Sit."

Said the spider to the fly.

With her couch being more of a longish loveseat than a full-size sofa and his considerable size, the two and a half feet left for her to settle into would make for cozy confines. Not exactly the best arrangement when her traitorous hormones were whispering of coups on her common sense. Then again, it wasn't like she had a wealth of seating options beyond pulling up a dinette chair.

She opted for the sofa, but grabbed her margarita off the table as she rounded it and stayed perched on the edge. "Something about a timing chain. All I know is the mechanic shook his head and grimaced when he came out with the diagnosis."

"How are you getting to work?"

"One of the guys dropped me off this afternoon. I figured I'd take a bus tomorrow, or walk to the street-car and ride it in from there."

"That's a long stretch from here to the station."

She shrugged. "I don't mind. If I had research to do on a story it'd suck, but if my editor sends us out for assigned gigs, my crew and I can take the station rigs." She took another sip of her drink, set it back on the table and twisted so her back was to the sofa arm and her leg was bent in front of her. "Speaking of stories, how'd the names I gave you turn out?"

He shook his head. "Neither of them are a concern. Townsend has been out of town for some time and, from all accounts, Reynolds's hype is all talk and no carry through." His gaze dropped to the hem of her T-shirt for all of a second, then he seemed to catch his distraction and refocused on her face. "Have you had any other ideas?"

Oh, she had lots of ideas. Just not the kind that had anything to do with angry people that might want to cause anyone trouble. "No. But it's hard to guess when I don't know what you're trying to guard against. Has there been a threat of some kind? Something stolen?"

All trace of sensual distraction disappeared in an instant, and his eyes got laser sharp. "It would be best if I keep that information to myself."

"Why?" The question was out before she could soften it, the prickling instinct that always came with the promise of something worth digging into sparking in an instant. "Would you be implicated in something?

Or are you afraid there's something there worth reporting and don't want it to be common knowledge?"

"I'm not worried about being implicated in anything. I'm merely taking steps to protect my family."

"Protect them financially, or protect them physically?"

"Why do they have to be mutually exclusive?"

"Well, if you think there's a need to protect them physically, the police should be involved."

"I prefer to do my own work."

"But you're not doing your own work. You've asked me to help, and if someone gets hurt, then I've contributed to their injury."

His instant smile was warm and appreciative. "You're very clever. And observant."

"I'm also smart. And while you've never actually admitted what it is you and your *family* do for a living, not reporting to the authorities if there's potential danger certainly indicates operating outside the law."

Kir cocked his head. While he didn't seem angry, her words had fired an edge in him she'd never seen before. "You used the word *family* quite mockingly. Do you have any comprehension of what you're referring to?"

Okay. Maybe he *was* angry.

She paused long enough to take a solid breath and weighed her response with a cautious and reasonable tone. "I think the information my colleagues gave me months ago was probably closer to the truth than you'd like me to believe. That you're deeply entrenched with a crime family. If my tone was mocking or aggressive, I apologize. That wasn't my intent. But I'm more than just a reporter. I'm a law-abiding, single female, and I'd be foolish if I didn't call out my concerns or think twice about how deep my involvement goes with you."

He studied her for long seconds, his summer sky gaze steady and considering. As though he were taking his time replaying the words she'd shared and analyzing every detail. Finally, he broke his stare and casually perused her apartment, his voice as calm and matter of fact as if they were discussing the weather. "When I think of those I seek to protect, *crime* is the last word I'd choose to describe them. Protective, yes. Driven and loyal, absolutely." His gaze landed back on her and his words, while still gently delivered, strengthened. "What we are not is the stereotype portrayed in American movies."

Oh, she'd definitely struck a sour chord. One that touched him deeply. A fact that, for some reason, eased much of her immediate fears. "I don't doubt that you appreciate the people you work with and are close to. I don't doubt or question your desire to protect them. But think of it from where I'm sitting. If you had a daughter and she was right here—in this moment—would you want her to take your word for it?"

Something in his expression shifted. Eased to the point it seemed she'd caught him off guard. "No. I wouldn't. I'd expect her to exercise the caution you're demonstrating, but to see and explore what is the truth for herself. Which is why I'm going to show you the core of my life."

All of a sudden, her living room felt more like a portal to an alternate realm she'd inadvertently stumbled into. "Show me? How?"

"Dinner. With my family."

"We're talking about the people in the picture you showed me, right? Not a Sunday afternoon thing with your mom and dad and maybe some siblings?"

"My father is dead, and I haven't seen my mother

since I was nine. Though I do consider Sergei and Roman to be my brothers in every way that counts."

Whoa. Talk about a trip into unknown territory. The reporter in her was practically salivating, but the single gal from Houston was thinking she was twenty kinds of crazy for even considering accepting the invite. "And these people are just going to agree to sit down with a television reporter and have a grand old time?"

"No, they'll agree to welcome my *guest* to their table. My only stipulation—you will not write about anything you see there. You will go for exposure only. For the experience and the perspective."

"And you trust me to honor that request?"

"Can I?"

"Of course."

He lifted one eyebrow.

"Don't look at me like that," she said, suddenly feeling as offended as he'd looked before. "I can be trusted."

"Good." He stood and stared down at her. "I know you normally have a shift on Sundays. What time are you done?"

Rising as well, she stood well within touching distance. A fact that suddenly made her simple T-shirt and boy shorts that much more inconsequential compared to his full attire.

She tugged the hem of her shirt a little lower. "Not until after seven."

"Good." He turned and ambled for the door with all the confidence of a man who'd obtained exactly what he'd come for. "I'll pick you up here at 7:30."

"Wait!" She scurried around the coffee table.

Kir paused just as he opened the door and looked back at her.

"I don't know what to wear. What kind of event it is, or what to expect."

His mouth quirked and the gentleness that had ridden his expressions until their conversation had taken a darker path returned. His gaze slid down the length of her then lifted back to her face. "Just be yourself, Cassie." He dipped his head in farewell and resumed his exit, but added one last quip before he pulled the door shut. "But do prepare to be surprised."

Chapter Seven

Cassie sat at her newsroom desk, headphones on and eyes glued to her monitor while an unedited interview she'd done months ago streamed by like white noise.

What did a girl wear to a mobster's house? A suit? A dress? Something more casual? If she'd been smart, she'd have pushed Kir for an answer to her question last night, but it'd taken a good ten seconds after he closed the door behind him before her brain had fully reengaged.

Texting was an option, of course, but stubbornness and pride had waylaid her more times than she could count.

Now, if she had a new lead to share—some viable excuse to text him that might open up a chance for her to ask a clarifying question or two, that would be different.

Except you're not going to find any clues if you don't actually listen to your interviews.

Huffing loud enough to make Lizbet glance at Cassie from her own desk, Cassie backed up the interview to the last time her mind had wandered off and tried again.

It was a candid conversation. One where she'd cornered one of Alfonsi's bodyguards coming out of a pub only three days after his boss's disappearance.

"How long have you worked for Mr. Alfonsi?" Cassie said.

The man shrugged. While none of the men photographed with Alfonsi over the years looked anywhere near as polished as Kir, Roman or the men that spent time with them, this particular man had already ditched his chinos and plain white Oxford for slouchy jeans and a ragged gray T-shirt. "About a year. Maybe a little more than that."

"Do you have any idea where he is?"

The question seemed to take him aback for all of a second, then he scanned up and down the street. "No more than anyone else."

An evasive answer. One that bugged her now just as much as it did then.

"But you spent a considerable amount of time with him. Surely you have some idea of places he frequented. Have you offered any clues to authorities?"

"I talked to 'em, yeah."

"Can you share that information with me?"

He frowned and planted his hands on his hips. "I saw him Tuesday morning, November 13 when I got to work. Then he left with his son and one of his captains a little while later. Never saw him again."

"But you're his bodyguard. Wouldn't you have escorted him to work?"

"Not always."

"Because you're not his only guard?"

"No, because sometimes he didn't want a guard. Said he'd see to himself."

"You don't think that's weird?"

"What?"

"Not having a bodyguard wherever you go. I mean, if you need a bodyguard, shouldn't they always be there?"

The man shook his head, clearly as exasperated with Cassie as Cassie was with his answers. "Look, lady. I didn't get paid to think for or second-guess my boss. Only to make sure no one laid a hand on him. What he does—or did—isn't my concern."

Someone circled the edge of Cassie's desk and startled her out of focus.

No. Not someone.

Lizbet.

And she was in rare form today, too, sporting a snazzy pair of deep emerald green capris, a matching yet stylishly cut blazer and a marigold silk shirt. The pewter heels she'd paired with the look would've had Cassie limping inside thirty minutes.

Cassie peeled off her headphones. "Cute outfit."

See? She could be nice. So what if what she really wanted to know was how anyone could afford so many clothes on a reporter's pay?

Lizbet straightened a little taller and swayed her hips from one side to the other. "Isn't it fantastic? The lady who's been the go-to costume designer for some of the biggest Mardi Gras floats and drama productions just started branching out into custom clothing. Fell on hard times and had to diversify. She's over on Canal Street. We should go together sometime."

Um. No.

Never.

Orange didn't suit Cassie's coloring and there was no way she'd make it through a shopping trip with Lizbet without ending up in a prison jumper. "It'll be a bit before I'm doing any shopping. Too much catching up from deposits and furniture for my new place. But thanks."

"Money woes, huh?"

"Something like that," Cassie said, moving the slider on the video back to the beginning of the recording.

Lizbet leaned in for a good look at the monitor. "You rehashing those old interviews again?"

"Just trying to figure something out," Cassie murmured. Whatever it was that bugged her about the talk with the bodyguard she still couldn't put her finger on, but it had all the discomfort of getting two miles into her daily commute and wondering if she'd left the iron on at home.

"Mmm." Lizbet watched the monitor a second more, then lowered her voice. "Listen, I know we're not super close and you haven't asked my opinion, but I feel like to be a team player, I really have to point something out."

"Yeah, what's that?"

Lizbet nodded toward the screen. "The stuff with Alfonsi—it's over. I know you got some good headway with it, but it's time for something fresh. Not just for the station, but for you. Don't you think?"

Yes, she did think. Had beaten herself up more times than she could count for even considering another story that had anything to do with Stephen Alfonsi.

But she also wasn't in the mood to have her nose rubbed into the obvious by a woman who'd flirt or shake her ass in a man's face to get him to do something for her, either. "Just because I'm looking at an old interview doesn't mean I'm doing a story, Lizbet."

"Oh." The response seemed to leave her momentarily nonplussed and knocked off course. "Well, why else would you be digging through them?"

"To find something for a friend."

Lizbet blinked.

Then repeated the act.

Then glanced back at the screen and shrugged. "I guess I just thought—"

Cassie's phone rang, the number on the screen vaguely familiar even though it wasn't programmed in her directory. Not that it mattered. If it meant having an excuse to end her conversation with Lizbet, she'd have answered Satan's call.

She picked it up and held up her finger. "I've got to get this."

Lizbet frowned, but backed away from the desk. "Sure. Let me know if you need help finding whatever you're after."

Mindful of other eyes on them, Cassie fought glaring at Lizbet's back and answered the phone instead. "Cassie McClintock."

"Um, Cassie. Hey. This is Rodney."

"Rodney?"

"From Farley Mechanics. You brought your car in yesterday?"

"Oh! Rodney! Right!" Cassie peeled her headphones from around her neck and reclined in her desk chair. "Everything going okay on the repairs?"

"Yep. All done."

She shot upright so fast her seat back rattled. "Already? I thought it was going to take a day or two at least."

"Nope. Got it all knocked out, and it's ready to go."

Maybe it was just her imagination, but it sure sounded like Rodney was as relieved as she was. "Did the cost end up where you thought it would?"

"Oh, no. Just fifty bucks should cover it."

"Fifty? For a timing chain? You said it'd be at least four-fifty."

"Uh..." Papers rustled in the background followed

by what sounded like a metal file cabinet slamming shut. "It wasn't a timing chain. It was…a belt. Those are cheap. Just charging you for that and a little labor."

"Really?" She let out a shaky laugh and anchored her elbows on the desk in front of her. "The way you were looking at my engine yesterday, I thought for sure I was in for some whopper repairs."

"Yeah, well, sometimes that first look we get it wrong." Something muffled the background noise on his end of the phone. A second later he was back on the line, the sound of a power tool causing a pretty significant commotion. "So, listen, if you're gonna be home in the next hour, I'll drop it off."

"Excuse me?"

"I'll drop it off." He hesitated a beat then hastily added, "I can make it in thirty minutes if that's better."

"No, no. An hour is fine. I just—well, fifty dollars and delivery to boot, that's a great deal. I'm really grateful. Let me give you my address."

"No need. I've got it on the paperwork."

The papers stacked on her desk and the insulated tumbler of water she'd brought from work blurred while her mind scrambled for snippets from yesterday. "I don't remember doing paperwork."

"Yep, got it right here. I'll see you there in an hour."

With that, the line went dead.

Cassie pulled the phone away from her ear and studied the screen.

"Weird," she said to no one. Though, as far as weird calls went, that one had to have been one of the best of all time.

She shut down her computer, packed up her stuff and started the cumbersome trip home via public transportation. On the bright side, bus rides made for great rumination time. By the time she'd made it to her house, she'd at least narrowed down to four or five attire options for Sunday dinner with Kir. The whole bodyguard interview, on the other hand, was still needling her from the inside out.

She started to unlock the front door, but got sidetracked when Rodney pulled her car into an open slot right behind her. A ragged blue truck with a magnetic Farley's Mechanics sign on the side pulled in right behind him.

Cassie waved to them both and jogged down to the sidewalk. "Hey, guys. You almost beat me here."

With the door to her car already open and one leg out on the pavement, Rodney rolled up the driver's side window and killed the engine. "Traffic was better than I thought. Plus, Amos has a truck that he's got to have done tonight, so we had to hustle." He handed off the keys. "Here you go."

"Thanks very much." She took the keys and dropped them in her purse. "You two want to come in while I write the check?"

"No need," Rodney said, high-stepping it to the passenger side of the truck. "We'll send you a bill."

A bill? Who sent bills these days? Especially when you had a client willing to write a check on the spot?

Rodney lumbered into his seat, slammed the door and waved from behind the windshield.

The man she assumed was Amos had his window down and his left elbow hanging over the edge. He saluted Cassie. "Nice working with you, miss."

"Right," Cassie said. "Nice working with you, too."

And with that, they were gone, the only reminder they'd been there being her now-functioning car parked perfectly in a spot right in front of her house.

Hold up.

Was her car clean?

She padded closer and peeked in the window.

Holy crap.

She opened the door, threw her purse to the passenger's seat and slid behind the wheel. Her car wasn't just clean. It was spotless. As in cleaner than it'd been the day she'd bought it.

"I am *so* going to them for every tune-up for the rest of my life." She smoothed her hands over the faded leather steering wheel, the lightness whispering beneath her skin the first time in days if not weeks. Maybe this was the turn of luck she'd been hoping for. A shift that would trigger her thoughts and ideas back into motion.

Inspired and suddenly free of the debt she'd braced for, Cassie shut the car door, dug her keys and her phone out of her purse, then fired up the engine. She thumbed up Aunt Frieda's number, tucked the phone between her ear and shoulder and pulled out of her parking space.

Aunt Frieda answered on the second ring. "Please, sweet Jesus, tell me you're calling with lurid details on what happened last night instead of needing bail money for killing the reporter."

"Neither. But I am giving you a heads-up—I'm on my way over."

"You are? How? Your car's on the fritz."

"Not anymore it's not. And better yet? I only owe fifty bucks for the repairs. Now what I need is a cocktail, a sounding board for something I'm trying to figure out, and someone to help me hash out outfit options. You game?"

As she'd hoped, Aunt Frieda shifted gears on a dime. "Sweetheart, I'm always game. I'll be ready before you get here."

Chapter Eight

The parmesan chicken and mushrooms had been cleared away. Only one serving of the blackberry cobbler remained on the dining room table's whitewashed surface and everyone but Emerson was on their second cup of coffee. Kir traced the line of his mug's handle with his thumb, nuancing the words he'd tossed around in his head all day and waiting for the right time to drop his proverbial bomb.

Emerson, who'd been on a roll for thirty minutes about the big mid-month competition in his archery class, snatched his sweet tea off the table. "Bobby thought for sure he had the whole thing wrapped up and was gonna get first prize, but then this girl, Maggie, swooped in and got three bull's-eyes in a row. She was amazing!"

Roman grinned.

Sergei chuckled.

Evette just shook her head. "Mmm-hmm. See what happens when you underestimate the women? We slide right in outta nowhere and catch you with your pants down."

"She speaks the truth," Kir said. Unfortunately, there must have been a little too much sarcasm in his tone, because every head snapped his direction.

Kir picked up his coffee and tried to play it off. "What? It is a very truthful statement. Women should never be sold short. Nor should you assume you know what they're thinking." Especially witty, funny and charismatic ones like Cassie.

Evette pursed her mouth, just a touch of a wry grin tugging the corners. "You say that like a man who's recently had a brush with one, Vasilek." She planted her elbow on the table and rested her chin on her hand. "Do tell."

It was the opening he needed and an easy one at that. All he had to do was walk right through it.

He cleared his throat and set his mug on the table. "Cassie McClintock."

Roman, who'd been mostly silent all night, finally let loose a satisfied snigger.

"Oh, now this sounds juicy," Evette said.

Emerson smiled big enough to show teeth and scooted close enough to the edge of his chair it was a wonder he didn't fall off. "Oh, yeah. For realz."

Sergei's gaze narrowed on Roman then shifted to Kir. "The reporter?"

Fuck.

Not the particular detail he wanted his *pakhan* to home in on first. But then again, Sergei was as shrewd as they came. "Yes." He glanced at Emerson. While they never talked of business in Sergei's son's presence, they'd been known to hint at issues a time or two when necessary. "She provided much coverage several months ago on a topic we were following."

"He broke one of his precious rules for her," Roman added.

Evette cocked an eyebrow. "You have rules?"

Kir scowled at Roman and shook his head. "No."

"Yes, he does," Roman said. "Never sees the same woman twice."

"And how many times did you see this one?" Sergei asked.

The thickly padded dining room chair beneath his ass suddenly felt riddled with hot tacks. "Twice. But the second was business related."

Roman sipped his coffee. "And the third, fourth and fifth?"

Sergei cocked his head, a silent demand for clarification.

Kir sighed. "She was at Bacchanal when we celebrated my birthday last week. She approached me after you, Evette and Emerson left, and we've resumed a business connection."

Sergei barely waited a full beat. "A business connection?"

"Is that why you paid a visit to the mechanic working on her car this morning?" Roman said.

Bastard.

He should have known better than to run that particular errand with Roman along for the ride. "She's less efficient doing research without a functioning vehicle. Ensuring the repairs happened expeditiously only made sense."

"And you paid for those repairs as well."

"The better we take care of people, the better they take care of us."

Sergei's attention drifted from Roman to Kir. "This business connection—are we referring to family endeavors? Or is this a side venture I'm not aware of?"

Evette giggled, the evil glee behind it the type reserved for women everywhere who'd just uncovered a deliciously decadent secret. "Oh Sergei, quit giving him grief. Anyone can see the guy's got it bad. If he wants to lie to himself and call hitting on a girl *business*, then let him." Her smile got bigger. "I personally like the idea of seein' New Orleans's most eligible player swimming toward the deep end."

All of a sudden, her eyes widened, and she splayed her hands on the dining room table. "Oh my God!" Her gaze bounced from one man to another. "Do you guys realize what this might mean?"

The men each cast clueless looks from one to another.

"Gah!" Evette said to the ceiling. She righted her attention and threw her hands up in the air. "*It means* I won't have to fly to Dallas to be with my posse, or fly one of them here to have another female at dinner anymore." She zeroed in on Kir and leaned in. "When can I meet her?"

Silence stretched long and uncomfortable between the five of them.

The opportunity was right there.

So easy to take.

And yet closing the loop felt tantamount to self-inflicting a fire brand on his flesh.

He swallowed hard, wishing like hell he had a glass of Stoli to ease his parched throat instead of watered-down tea or coffee. "As a matter of fact, I invited her to dinner on Sunday." He met Sergei's stare head-on. "It was presumptuous of me to do so without asking you first. If you'd rather, I can rescind the invitation."

"No!" Evette spun to Sergei and planted an urgent hand on his shoulder. "You don't want him to take it back, do you, babe?" She faced Roman and Kir. "We want to meet her."

While Sergei's stare never once wavered from Kir's

face, his features did soften, just a hint of the deep
amusement he often wore in Evette or Emerson's presence lifting to the surface. Finally, he took his napkin
from his lap and set it on the table beside his plate.
"Well, *moy brat*, it appears we want very much to meet
her." He stood, leaned over and gave his bride a kiss,
then stepped away from the table. "I would, however,
like to hear more about this reporter. Why don't you
join me on the patio for a cigar, and you can tell me
what you know."

Evette grinned huge, the apples of her cheeks practically on fire with excitement.

Emerson snickered. "Sounds like you're gonna get
a lot of questions."

It did sound that way, and with how the initial introduction had gone down, Kir wasn't altogether sure
they were going to be the type of questions he was up
for answering.

"Good luck, my brother," Roman said in Russian.
He stood, slid his chair under the table and grabbed his
plate. Before he headed to the kitchen, he added, *"For
what it's worth. I think this one's worth it."*

Kir stood as well and reached for his plate.

Evette waved him off. "I'll get it. You go talk to the
man."

Funny. He'd had countless conversations with Sergei
over the years and not one of them had left him feeling
like a school boy waiting outside the principal's office.

But this one did.

He nodded to Evette and Emerson and strode toward
the back door and the patio overlooking the pool and
gardens beyond.

Evette's voice halted him just before he stepped outside. "Hey, Kir." Where her expression had been full of

glee and orneriness before, now soft compassion and understanding swam behind her warm hazel eyes. "It's okay, you know. To want someone, I mean. Sergei, of all people, will understand that. You just need to tell him the truth."

Such a good woman. Honest. Kind and loving. Full of fire and strength that had greatly augmented Sergei's leadership and vision. Kir couldn't even fathom what it would be like to have such support. His brothers, yes. They were always there. But to have the gentle, unwavering solace of a woman like Evette was beyond his comprehension. "My *pakhan* will always have the truth from me."

Her smile deepened. "Well then...maybe you could let yourself in on it while you're at it."

Emerson peeked over the back of his chair, the mirth in his gaze a mirror image of his mother's.

On the bright side, their amusement had done much to ease his trepidation. Now that he'd had the benefit of having them in his life, he wouldn't trade them for anything. "You're meddlers. Both of you."

Their laughter followed him out into the darkening evening. The rich bite of his *pakhan's* cigar already hung on the night air, mixed with the crisp scent of freshly mowed grass and soft touch of magnolias.

Not waiting for direction, Kir pulled the padded patio chair next to Sergei out from under the glass-topped table and settled in. Since Sergei had moved into the restored historic home in the heart of New Orleans's Garden District, Kir had spent many evenings with Roman and Sergei just like this. Quietly enjoying the night, the stars if the clouds allowed it and the soft reflection of the heavens on the majestic pool's reflection.

Sergei drew from his cigar then leisurely expelled the smoke overhead.

Quiet settled between them.

Under normal circumstances, Kir would have either enjoyed it, or filled it with business observations from the day. As it was, he was clueless on how to proceed.

Dipping his head toward the leather cigar case on the table, Sergei made the decision for him. "Help yourself."

It felt wrong. Too casual and familiar of an action for a topic that felt quite formal riding between them. "I'll pass tonight. *Spaseeba*."

Sergei smirked at that, though his peaceful focus on the pool beyond never wavered. "Tension rides your shoulders and you've never once sat so straight in that chair." He swiveled his head toward Kir, a trace of mischief moving behind his dark eyes. "You can relax, *moy brat*. There is no gun pressed behind your head, nor have you done anything to earn my anger."

The muscles in his belly eased a fraction, but he kept his posture upright and respectful. "I should have asked your permission before I included an outsider in one of our affairs."

With a chuckle, Sergei resumed his perusal of the manicured landscape. "It's a Father's Day dinner. Hardly anything where I expect we'll discuss real business. And if she belongs to you, then you need no permission to bring her."

"She doesn't belong to me."

The comment earned Kir a quick look and a raised eyebrow from Sergei. He decided to let it go, though, and took another drag from his cigar. "Cassie Mc-Clintock. Sounds a bit like a gun-toting barmaid from an old western movie." He exhaled hard and reclined farther into his chair as though preparing for a good tale. "Tell me about her."

Kir cleared his throat. "You already know what she looks like from the stories she did on Alfonsi—tall, graceful, blonde. A model's figure, similar to Darya's. Her personality is bright, her intellect quick. She has keen observation skills I can't help but respect, and she has a tirelessness about her. I sometimes wonder where she gets her energy."

"Mmm," Sergei said, nodding his head. "This I understand. Evette can be the same." He aimed a conspiratorial grin at Kir. "Unless, of course, I've given her good reason to be relaxed."

Kir shifted his attention to his hand resting on the chair's arm. Talking with Roman, or even Sergei, about women in general was one thing. Talking about his *pakhan's* bride was a barrier he wasn't comfortable breaching.

Sergei must have sensed his hesitancy because he kept going. "I've decided it's an American thing. They have a harder time sitting still and simply enjoying the world around them."

"Perhaps. But for Cassie, I suspect it's driven more by her family."

"How so?"

Kir shrugged. "Cassie tells me her family is quite learned. All scientists of one kind or another. They consider her to be a black sheep of sorts."

"Unfortunate."

"It is. She's very driven and talented. Why they don't see that, regardless of her career, I don't understand."

Sergei nodded and tapped the ashes from his cigar into the standing ashtray between their chairs. "And how is she helping you?"

And that right there was why Sergei was their *vor*. His stealthy ability to loosen the tongues of those he dealt with and then slide seamlessly to the heart of a topic was a gift he'd honed over many years. "She interviewed many people after we dealt with Alfonsi."

"So?"

The memory of Kevin's death-shrouded body leapt to mind, the same stinging outrage he'd felt that night igniting right behind it. "She has insights to those who might have a grudge against us. Have some clue we might be aware of as to who might want revenge for our actions."

"And does Miss McClintock know the extent of what she's helping you with?"

"Nyet."

"Why not?"

The question caught him off guard. "Because she's a reporter. I wouldn't risk her reporting on what's happened at this juncture. It's better we keep that information to ourselves. More than that, I wouldn't want her drawn into anyone's line of fire."

Sergei's mouth twitched. "And what would you do if someone were to act against Miss McClintock?"

A white-hot fury blasted through him, stealing his breath and locking all of his muscles tight. He knew he needed to speak. To say something—anything—rational or logical.

But the words wouldn't come. Couldn't get past the fist-sized knot in his throat.

Twisting his head, Sergei smiled. Not a smug action, so much as one of abiding patience and understanding. "Tell me again, *moy brat*, that she is not your woman."

Fuck.

His muscles ached to move. A violent roar that desperately needed release seemed to swell and ricochet behind his sternum. He didn't want a woman. Didn't trust them. Couldn't afford to. Not now. Not when he finally had the respect and opportunity he'd craved and been denied his whole life.

"Our pasts do not define us," Sergei said as though reading his thoughts. "Nor do our parents. If that were the case, I'd be a drunken sot eking out a meager existence on the docks in Russia."

"Your situation was different."

"How? My father was a wastrel. Your father betrayed his *vor* trying to satisfy the needs of a woman he loved and paid for his actions with his life. How are they not the same?"

"Because your mother didn't sell you to save her own ass and buy a new life!" The raw and painful admission ripped up his throat with the tenderness of multithreaded barbed wire. His breath sawed in and out in the aftermath, and his grip on the armrests left his knuckles straining and white.

Sergei waited, somehow knowing Kir needed the time to reconcile the violence coursing through him. When he finally found his voice, it was ragged and broken. "I'm sorry."

"Don't be. You needed that."

Bit by bit, Kir's muscles relaxed.

Sergei went back to his silent study of the stars and the crescent moon overhead. By the time he spoke again, a good minute or two had passed and, from the pondering in his tone, he'd spent it revisiting his own past. "I never thought I would keep to only one woman. Never thought I would enter any type of relationship, let alone marry. Not with what we do for a living. There was too much risk. Too much to lose." He paused a moment and his gaze narrowed on the sky. "But Evette made the risk worth it. Showed me I was worth another's love and trust."

It was the last statement he'd expected from Sergei. They'd navigated countless treacherous situations together. Faced down hardened enemies with all manner of weapons and borne the scars to go with them. But never once had he shared something so personal. So vulnerable. Even if he demonstrated how much he loved his new bride and son on a daily basis.

"What are you trying to tell me?"

Sergei lifted one shoulder in a negligent shrug, stubbed out his cigar and stood. "There is nothing to tell. Just sharing the benefit of what I have learned. What you do with it is up to you." He stood, nodded to Kir and strolled toward the back door. "I look forward to meeting your woman Sunday night."

Your woman.

If Kir hadn't already been shaken to his core, he'd have likely scoffed out loud at the parting remark.

Behind him, the door opened.

"Kir?"

Kir lifted his head and stared back at his *pakhan*. His brother in arms. One of two friends in the world he knew he could always count on.

"You are worth another's love and trust as well. Don't let your parents' past rob you of it." With that, he closed the door, leaving Kir alone with the darkness and his jumbled thoughts.

Chapter Nine

It was official. Aunt Frieda was a veritable genius when it came to wardrobe selections for tricky situations.

Cassie turned from one side to the other in front of the full-length mirror, appreciating the cherry-red romper her aunt had suggested at their impromptu get-together Thursday night. The spaghetti straps and gathered waist gave the outfit a playful look, while the flowing pant legs paired with taupe heels added an elegant flair. A perfect compromise for either a casual or more elegant venue.

She grabbed the matching tan clutch with the delicate shoulder strap that Frieda had loaned her and double-checked for her license, phone, keys, money and lipstick. At least Kir had finally texted her this morning with a reminder of the time he'd pick her up along with a note to expect a big meal. Up to that point, she hadn't heard a word from him since he'd last walked out her front door, which had made her wonder more than once if she'd just imagined his invitation.

A powerful knock on her front door at exactly 7:30 p.m. nearly startled her heart from the confines of her chest.

It was no big deal.

Just a dinner.

She'd interviewed several powerful and influential people. Dangerous ones, too. This was just a meal with people important to Kir. Nothing more, nothing less.

Yeah, keep telling yourself that, sister. You never spent nearly an hour soaking in a tub and another hour afterward dolling yourself up for an interview.

She made her way to the door on shaking legs, let out a slow, steadying breath and opened it.

Wow.

Of all the suits she'd seen Kir in, this one was the finest. A rarely seen double-breasted affair that was perfectly tailored and paired with a light blue shirt. He'd forgone a tie, as usual, but rather than make the overall feel more casual, it gave him a dangerous appearance. A modern-day rogue dressed to conquer whatever or whoever crossed his path.

His gaze traveled the length of her, a slow and deliberate assessment that left tingles in its wake. He stepped closer, slowly took her hand and pressed a warm, lingering kiss to the back of it. "You look lovely."

"Thank you." With her lungs struggling to function properly and her heart off for a healthy jog, getting that much out was a miracle. Especially, when he retained his grip on her hand and crowded closer than was appropriate for colleagues. "You look pretty awesome yourself."

Ugh.

So lame.

Juvenile and uninventive.

As if he'd heard her thoughts, his mouth crooked in a lopsided grin. "Thank you, *milaya.*" He lowered their joined hands and fanned his thumb along her knuckles. "Do you have everything you need?"

Oxygen would be good, and maybe a time-out for a quick shot of leftover tequila.

She nodded and used her free hand to adjust her purse's strap on her shoulder. "Yes. All good."

"Excellent." He held out his hands. "Your keys, please."

"My keys?"

"Yes, to lock the door."

Oh.

Right.

For the door.

She jerked into motion and snatched them from her clutch. "I've got it."

He tugged her forward before she could reach for the door's handle and easily slipped the keys from her fingers. "Allow me." He pulled the door shut, threw the bolt, then tested it to ensure it was locked. Considering his demeanor thus far, his frown when he faced her was unexpected. "You need a more secure entrance."

"What's wrong with it?"

"It's insufficient as a means to keep a determined person out of your house." Rather than guide her gallantly down the stairs with a hand at her elbow as he had before, his arm slipped easily around her waist, and his hand rested on one hip. "At a minimum, your door should be made out of something stronger and your bolt more difficult to pick or break completely."

"Well, even changing those two things isn't foolproof. If someone really wanted in, they could break a window."

"Which is why I'd ideally like to see a security system installed." He opened the Audi's passenger door. "We'll discuss options later."

"Options?"

"Indeed."

"For what?"

"Security." He dipped his head toward the car's interior, but otherwise refused further elaboration.

She was missing something. What it was, she couldn't quite put her finger on, but there was definitely a different air to him tonight. A subtle sub-context or missing plot point that had slipped by her between last Thursday and now. "Is there a reason I should have stronger security?"

His expression shifted. Still as determined and intense as ever, but also somehow vulnerable. "Yes, *vozlyublennaya*. There is a reason, but not one you should worry about." He motioned to the seat. "Please, let me take you to dinner."

Okaaaaay.

She slid onto the soft leather seat.

He shut the door and rounded behind the car.

Not a reason she should worry about? What did that mean? Typically, if a person needed better security there was *every* reason to worry.

Folding himself into the driver's seat, he quickly glanced in her direction and ensured her seat belt was in place. He must have noticed the death grip she had on her clutch, because the humor he'd sported at the front door made a comeback on his face. "Relax, Cassie. Everything is fine. I'll make sure of it."

"See, but that statement alone makes me think there is something I should be concerned about."

He fired up the engine and pulled the car away from the curb. "You're a very beautiful woman. One who spends much of her time in the public eye. Is it so shocking that a man would make your safety his concern?"

Well, put like that, it sounded fine, but she still

couldn't shake the sense that something else was going on. "I can take care of myself."

"I have no doubt that you can." He glanced her direction then refocused on the road in front of him. "That doesn't mean that you will."

Her brain went completely silent. No counter questions. No clues as to what he was talking about. Just that stunned lack of cooperation that came when a person had been caught completely off guard. She finally opened her mouth to ask him point-blank what was going on.

He cut her off. "How is work?"

The about-face in topic rattled her rationalization skills a little more. "Um…it's been fine. With the rash of robberies reported in the Seventh Ward this week, I haven't really had time to work on any feature stories of my own, but the assigned gigs were good."

"Your newscasts yesterday and today seemed to go well also."

A fresh rush of adrenaline flared beneath her skin, and her cheeks warmed. "You watched me?"

"Of course I watched you."

"Why?"

While he didn't take his eyes off the road, a small smile was still evident. His voice was low, but purposeful when he spoke. "Because I wanted to."

The flush beneath her skin turned to pure heat, and as short and shallow as her breathing was, she didn't dare speak right away. She traced the latch on her clutch and scrambled for something neutral to talk about. Anything to get them back to some semblance of normal to keep her mind from dangerous thoughts. "I tried to do a little more research between newscasts this weekend. Went back through some old interviews to see if I could dig up any other ideas on who you might be concerned about."

"Did you?" He briefly looked her way then went back to navigating to wherever they were headed. "And how did that go?"

She shrugged. "It didn't, really. All the conversations and people were pretty much the way I remembered it. Although, there was a man I interviewed that seemed off to me. Both when I interviewed him the first time and again when I watched the recording this time."

"What man?"

"One of Alfonsi's bodyguards."

For a moment, Kir was silent, considering. "What bothered you about it?"

Hmm. How to put into words something she still wasn't sure made sense? "I guess I just always assumed that, if a person has a bodyguard, they have a guard all the time."

"And his guard said something to imply Alfonsi didn't?"

"More than implied. He said the day Alfonsi disappeared, he'd first seen him at his office that morning. When I clarified and asked if he'd been the one to drive Alfonsi to work, he said that sometimes Alfonsi drove himself. That sometimes he didn't want a guard."

Kir nodded. "It's true. Sergei nearly always has protection, but not always."

"Hmm." She sighed and studied the tall brick buildings that lined North Peters Street. "I guess it's not as big of a deal as I thought."

Kir cocked his head. "It might be. If Alfonsi had protection the majority of the time, but opted to forgo it, there could be something he was doing he didn't want his men, or anyone else, to know of."

"Well, if he was smart enough to keep his own men in the dark, I'm not sure how we'd figure out what he was up to."

Rather than comment on her statement, Kir swept into a shallow circle drive that fronted a crowded restaurant.

No, not just any restaurant.

André's Riverfront—the newest expansion to a long-standing New Orleans tradition. While she hadn't done any stories on the Trahan family's newest endeavor, there'd been no secret that Sergei had been a major player in the new and super posh development. While she'd never dreamed of stepping foot in the place, she'd heard people scrambled for months to get a reservation.

She stared up through the passenger's side window at the elegant lighted marquee overhead and the swank entry with its smoky windows and black carpet. "I wish you'd told me we were coming here. I'd have gone for something a little dressier."

"Nonsense," he said, putting the gearshift in park. "You look exceptional."

He got out of the car just as a valet opened her door. To his credit, the valet tried to help her out, but Kir cut him off before the eager young man could fully extend his hand.

As soon as he had her outside her door, Kir settled a possessive hand at her hip and guided her right through the lobby, tipping his head to the maître d' as they passed.

Where the exterior was everything bold and showy, the interior was pure midseventies class. More black carpet. Crimson velvet chairs and rounded corner booths. Gold detailing and crystal chandeliers. The people in the lobby and seated at the tables might have been wearing contemporary attire, but it was all too easy to imagine women wearing dresses with flared skirts and suit-clad men smoking cigarettes.

"Wow," she murmured low enough only Kir could hear. "No wonder everyone's clamoring to eat here."

"Wait until you taste the food," Kir said equally low. "The first time Sergei visited the original *André's* was when he decided to enter the restaurant business."

Sergei.

The main person she was here to meet.

To come face to face with every dire or frightening scenario she'd played out in her head.

A large rectangular table sat isolated from the rest of the crowd at the back of the room. Several people were already seated, but the person situated at the end of the table and already staring at her was unmistakable.

Sergei Petrovyh.

Pictures didn't do him justice, either in looks or in intimidation. Dark hair. Dark eyes. Dark demeanor. And every ounce of his fierce attention was lasered on her.

Her heart, already fatigued from the night's unexpected thrills and highly visceral responses, stuttered as though it was tempted to stop altogether. Her throat constricted to the point she couldn't breathe. She gripped Kir's hand at her hip and her steps faltered. "Kir—"

He spun her around before she could finish and moved in close, the warmth of his body coiling around her and melting the sudden chill against her skin.

She braced her hand atop his sternum. Beneath her palm, the fine cotton of his button-down was cool, and his heart thrummed a steady rhythm unlike the riotous beat of her own. "I'm not sure my being here is a good idea."

"Look at me, *vozlyublennaya*." Soft words. Comforting ones that matched the strength of Kir's arms around her.

She lifted her gaze.

"You are exactly where I want you to be, and you are safe," he said. "Never more safe than you are in this moment. You have my vow."

The particular wording was puzzling. Something she might have dug deeper to sort out if her mind hadn't rerouted and coughed up a mental replay of her behavior. She shook her head and hung it on an ironic laugh. "Well, that had to have made a particularly poor impression, didn't it?"

"Why? Because you showed you are anxious about meeting my family?" He gently nudged her head upright with his fingers at her chin. "Relax. Forget what you think you know. Forget what you've heard and what you've been told to believe. Spend the evening with me. Enjoy yourself and get to know the people I call my own."

The mysterious undercurrent that had woven through all of their interactions thus far blossomed larger. Bolder and sparking with an energy that fueled a sense of anticipation.

"What's going on?" The question came out as little more than a whisper.

"We're eating dinner, having drinks and hopefully laughing a fair amount before I take you home."

It felt like he'd edited a portion of his agenda from the tail end of his statement, but given the shaky emotional terrain she was already bumbling through, she opted to let it go. "You know what I meant."

He studied her for long moments, the message behind his warm, confident gaze one she wasn't sure it was even wise to try and comprehend. "I do. But there is nothing for you to do tonight, save enjoy yourself. The rest will take care of itself."

Inhaling slowly, he inched back and raked her head to toe. "Now, are you steady enough to resume your grand entrance? Or do I need to do something more drastic to unplug your mind?"

She cocked one eyebrow and shot him her best mock frown. "Oh, no you don't. I know what methods you use to distract women, and I need my wits about me tonight."

He dipped his head, all gallant formality. "As you wish." He turned her toward the table and slid his arm back around her waist. "Though, I can't make any promises about what happens after dinner."

He couldn't have timed the suggestive hint any better, the proximity of the table decreasing swiftly enough with each step that she had no choice but to brace for introductions rather than remind him of their platonic relationship.

Thankfully, no one appeared to monitor the rest of their approach. Not even Sergei, whose sole attention was now focused on the young boy seated to the right of him, the one she'd seen in Kir's picture days ago.

The second they reached the far end of the table, though, all bets were off.

The petite dark-haired woman with an amazing pixie haircut at Sergei's left homed in on them first.

Then the boy.

Sergei was the last to turn his head, but the moment he pushed back in his chair and stood, every other man at the table stood as well.

Kir led her directly to Sergei, the proprietorial weight of his arm around her back surprising for such a gathering, but one she appreciated all the same.

Sergei glanced at Kir's hand at her hip, and his mouth twitched. A string of complicated-sounding Russian words rolled from his tongue, every one of them aimed toward Kir, but the wry humor behind them was unmistakable.

Across the table, Roman chuckled.

Kir didn't seem the least deterred by whatever was said. Merely cleared his throat and lifted his chin a notch. "Allow me to introduce Cassie McClintock. Cassie, this is Sergei Petrovyh."

Sergei extended his hand. "Miss McClintock. We're very happy to have you join us."

Cassie took the hand he offered, his grip firm, yet not frighteningly so. "Please, just call me Cassie. Miss McClintock is way too formal for me."

"You sound like my bride. Though, I must confess, I enjoy the formality now that she carries my surname." Sergei motioned to the woman beside him. "Cassie, my wife, Evette."

Before his introduction could fully die out, Evette was on her feet, her beautiful hazel eyes bright with excitement. "Girl, am I glad to meet you!" She wrapped Cassie up like she'd known her for years rather than seconds then stepped back and motioned to the open seats to her left. "I saved you both a spot so I can hear all about the girl that's got Kir so kerfluffled."

Kir? Kerfluffled?

Surely, they weren't talking about the same guy. And what kind of mob wife used the word *kerfluffled*?

Evette motioned to the other people around the table, starting with the big guy in the chair next to Kir. With loose auburn hair to his shoulders, a big build and attire to rival Kir's, he looked like a Scottish warlord turned fashion model. "This is Axel McKee, and next to him is his wife, Lizzy Hemming."

"Oh my God!" She quickly shook hands with Axel and offered him an old-fashioned how-do-you-do, but the majority of her attention was on the brunette rock-star who rose to her feet beside him. For the last year, Lizzy Hemming had all but dominated the charts, her powerful voice and exceptional music casting a wide net for followers.

Cassie held out her hand. "I'm thrilled to meet you! I'm a huge fan."

Lizzy accepted Cassie's outstretched hand. "Glad to meet you, too. Always good to meet a fellow music lover."

Keeping the introductions moving, Evette motioned to an older lady across the table. "This is Dorothy. I've known her as long as I've been alive. My momma worked at her diner in Mid-City when I was little."

"Diner as in Dorothy's Diner?" Cassie said. "That was one of the first places my aunt Frieda took me when I moved here. I had two helpings of blackberry cobbler and that was after I'd already gorged on pork chops and potato casserole."

A proud smile curved Dorothy's thin lips. Despite her gray hair and wrinkled face, there was an undeni-able strength in her demeanor. "That's the one, child. You and your auntie come visit again, this time you ask for me. We'll get ya fixed up with something extra special."

Evette waved at Roman next to Dorothy. "If you know Kir, I'm gonna guess you already know Roman." Her gaze locked on the young boy next to Sergei and her smile deepened. "And this handsome boy is my son, Emerson."

Cassie tipped her head. "Nice to meet you, Emerson."

"Likewise." His attention shifted to Kir, and an ornery smirk crept across his face. "She's pretty, Uncle Kir. I think you did good."

The *Uncle Kir* hit her first.

The next realization was the staggering fact that everyone apparently thought they were a thing.

Well, duh, Cassie. His arm is still around you. What else would they think?

Thankfully, Kir interjected to cover her fluster. "Of course, she's pretty. And smart and funny, too. After all, I have exceptional taste." With a knowing wink, he motioned Cassie to her seat. "I think you'd best have a seat, *vozlyublennaya*. They've been building their list of questions for you since Thursday, and the restaurant only stays open so long—even for their boss."

Cassie took her seat and the familiar comfort that had seemed to grip everyone before their arrival resumed, each person commenting on different options on the menu, or taking up their previous conversation. She leaned closer to Kir as soon as he'd settled and murmured, "What's *vozlyublennaya*? You've said that a few times tonight."

Clearly, Evette wasn't paying any attention to whatever Dorothy was saying to her son, because she chuckled and answered before Kir could. "It's an endearment. Sweetheart, I think. Right, babe?" she said to Sergei.

Sergei grinned. *"Da."*

Sweetheart?

She twisted her head to Kir, a silent question and probably a healthy dose of surprise plastered all over her face.

"All their endearments sound sexy, if you ask me,"

Evette added. "*Malyshka. Daragaya. Zolatka. Milaya.* Russians don't mess around with their sweet talk."

"That last one," Cassie said, taking advantage Evette's chattiness, "what's it mean?"

"Milaya?" Evette said.

"Darling or dear," Roman answered. "A term of affection I'm not certain I've ever heard cross my brother's lips."

The glare Kir aimed at Roman wasn't exactly one of irritation, but held a warning all the same. "Perhaps there would be more opportunities for me to share endearments with my woman if my family didn't give her cause to run after only one dinner with them."

My woman.

Had he just said that?

In front of everyone?

Part of her wanted to duck under the table and shake herself until she woke up. Another part wanted to punch him in the arm and demand he fess up with whatever the heck was going on.

Lizzy snickered and plucked a slice of sourdough bread from the napkin-covered basket between her and Roman. "And here I thought the Dallas branch of our peculiar family was the only one with meddlesome people in it."

"Are ye kiddin' me?" Axel said. "The second my mother and Ninette got their hooks in Sergei, the New Orleans crew was done for."

Cassie scanned the table, for the first time since the introductions had started fully comprehending no one outside Sergei, Roman, or Kir looked even remotely like what she'd expected, and not a one of them looked like blood kin. "I'm confused. You're all related? Really?"

"Might as well be," Evette said. "It started with

Axel's mom, Sylvie, and her best friend, Ninette. Axel and Ninette's boy, Jace, ended up being best friends, too. They picked up a few brothers they claimed as their own over the years, and now the brothers all have wives. Imagine one huge family with a whole lot of big personalities and even more heart, and you'll get the idea."

"And Sylvie and Ninette basically rule the roost." Lizzy pointed the knife she'd used to slather some butter onto her bread at Dorothy. "Though, I gotta say, you're the first person I've ever seen them defer to, so it could be there's a new alpha in town."

Lizzie frowned at her husband a second later and lowered her voice. "Don't tell your mom or Ninette I said that."

"My lips are sealed, pet," Axel said with a wink.

Cassie looked to Sergei. Then Roman. Then Kir. "How does that figure in with the three of you?"

Kir dipped his head toward Sergei. "The mothers essentially adopted him when a woman he's close to from Russia ended up married to one of their own. Darya and Knox Torren."

Evette's chuckle was low, but full of understanding. "Don't try to understand it all at once. Easier to just roll with it."

"Amen to that," Dorothy added.

The waiter wandered up to the table, thankfully offering Cassie a minute or two to get her bearings. Another respite came in the form of a gift for Sergei from Emerson in honor of Father's Day—two tickets to a superhero movie Cassie had never heard of, but that practically made Emerson bounce in his chair.

"Mom said she can get two more if Roman and Kir wanna go," Emerson said. He cast expectant glances at each of the men.

"Nyet," Roman said with a shake of his head. "Movies are better at home."

"Nuh-uh," Emerson argued with all the indignation of a young boy. "You gotta see it on the big screen with the awesome sound system." He looked to Kir. "You wanna go?"

"I think a Father's Day gift is best spent one-on-one with your father." On the surface, Kir's response was both diplomatic and thoughtful, but Cassie could have sworn there was a bitterness behind it, too.

"He is correct." Sergei tucked the tickets inside his suit jacket. "I spend too much time with those two as it is. Better for you and I to make a night of it on our own."

He meant it, too, the words offered with the utmost sincerity and an unflinching gaze. Mob boss or not, Sergei Petrovyh had a soft spot for his boy. And his wife.

And from the way he studied each person around the table a second later, maybe even for everyone else. "Thank you all for joining me today. I'm blessed to have Emerson for a son and to have each of you to help me celebrate my first Father's Day."

Lizzy smiled and elbowed Axel. "You better not let your momma hear anything like that. They'll be hijacking my birth control pills."

Axel's grin was pure wickedness. "And how do ya know I haven't already been monkeyin' with 'em myself?"

"You wouldn't?"

He lifted both eyebrows. A playful *Oh, wouldn't I?* conveyed without a word.

Lizzy rolled her eyes and zigzagged her attention between the women. "God save me. I've got four more months on tour and a new album to cut after that, and he's hinting at kids."

And that was how it went through the salads and most of the entrees. Lighthearted jabs or witty comments shared from those listening. Questions asked and answered. Laughter that ranged from easygoing to all out hilarity.

Absolutely *nothing* like the scenarios she'd imagined.

Kir had been right. They *were* a family. Not the blood-linked kind that suffered through a Father's Day dinner because they had to, but people who came together and genuinely communed because they wanted to. Because they enjoyed everyone's company.

The experience was exceptional. On par with the one-on-one time she spent with her aunt but had never experienced with anyone else.

And wasn't that sad, considering she had a family of her own? Dinners with her parents and brother were brief. Rigorous in manners and filled only with professional chatter carried on politely modulated voices. Honestly, she'd reported on town council meetings with more personality and warmth than meals with her family.

Tears stung her eyes, and a sharp discomfort nudged her heart.

Oh, no, Cassie. You will not cry. Not here. Not now.

"So, Cassie," Evette said. "How'd you end up as a fancy TV news reporter?"

Cassie ducked her head and smoothed her napkin across her lap to buy herself a little time. Her first words were a little rough, but by the time she lifted her head and finished her answer, she'd shaken most of her melancholy. "It was an accident, really. I started photography in high school and a friend who worked on the school paper asked me to take some pictures for her.

The process seemed fun, so I tried it for myself and ended up I had a knack for it."

"Yeah, but that's newspaper, not TV," Emerson said. "How'd you end up there?"

"That happened in college. I was one year in and planning on sticking with the newspaper routine with a Bachelor of Arts in Journalism, but my aunt Frieda said I'd be shooting myself in the foot if I didn't shift to television."

"Good girl," Dorothy said. "You listened to your auntie."

Cassie chuckled. "Not exactly. Not at first, anyway. She basically ended up daring me to go for an internship at a Houston television station. I think we were both surprised when I got it."

"You're very good at it," Sergei said. "Natural. People respond to you."

Goose bumps lifted along her forearms, and for some stupid reason, the urge to sit up a little taller tugged at her spine. "Thank you."

"Do you still do photography, too?" Lizzy asked. "Axel's gone through about fifteen different people so far trying to get good shots of the band in action and hasn't settled on one yet."

"That's a damned fine idea." Axel shifted his focus to Kir. "We've got a show here in New Orleans in late September. Ye should bring the lass and let her work her magic."

"Oh…" Cassie shook her head. "It's just a hobby. I'm not a professional."

"But you're very good," Kir stated firmly. "I saw the pictures you've hung in your home. When we met for coffee, the passion you felt for photography was evident, and you mentioned the first night I met you that you'd once wanted to pursue it as a career."

"Of course, I did. When I was sixteen. But it's not realistic."

Lizzy barked out a sharp laugh. "Who cares what's realistic? People told me I was stupid for slogging from one bar to another for years, but look at me now."

Roman nodded, his gaze uncomfortably keen and locked on Cassie.

"Ye want something, ye just do it," Axel said. "Anyone who tells ya different can bugger off."

Seven people around the table.

All of them strangers but one.

And they'd shown more kindness and acceptance in little more than an hour than her own family had shown in years.

A slow burn fired along the bridge of her nose, and her gaze blurred. "Thank you." She fixed her attention on the mostly empty plate in front of her, fought to keep her breathing steady and prayed the tears wouldn't spill over. "It does sound like fun. I'll definitely think about it."

Her bottom lip quivered, and her lungs hitched. She leaned close to Kir and whispered. "Would you excuse me just a minute? I need to run to the restroom."

She didn't wait for an answer. Just rose, nabbed her clutch and tried to nonchalantly navigate her tear-blurred way through the restaurant toward the restrooms at the front of the building.

It took a good five minutes hiding in a stall and focusing on nothing but slow steady inhalations before the threat of a full-on crying jag subsided. Another two or three before she trusted herself to step in front of the mirror and repair what she could of her makeup.

She'd been so wrong about these people. Kir was right. Somewhere along the way, she'd painted them all as dangerous, self-serving people who sat around figuring out ways to take advantage of others. The truth? They were kind. Personable. Fiercely loving and loyal to each other.

Behind her, the bathroom door opened.

Evette stepped through, scanned open stalls, then locked on to Cassie in front of the ornate vanities. "Oh, thank God." She pressed a hand to her heart and strolled toward Cassie. "For a second or two, I was worried I was gonna have to come out of this bathroom without you and send Kir on a full-scale search."

She rested one hip on the marble ledge and cocked her head. "You took off mighty quick out there. You okay?"

"Embarrassed more than anything." Cassie jerked her head toward the dining room beyond. "You guys caught me a little off guard. Actually, everything tonight's caught me off guard." She shook her head and let out a shaky, ironic laugh. "Maybe I'm pre-menstrual, or something."

"Oh, girl. If you are, I'll totally volunteer to sit in for an ice cream eating binge. Do you have any idea how long it's been since I could stuff my face with some good 'ole Ben and Jerry's and not have a string of men look at me like I'm crazy?"

Definitely good people. Every freaking one of them. "I think I owe you an apology."

Evette straightened to the very height of her petite frame. "You do? For what?"

How could she say what she wanted to without looking like an idiot? Or worse, digging a hole she'd never crawl out of? "I misjudged you. All of you." She scanned the room and ensured no one was there to over-hear. "People told me stories at work. About Kir. About Sergei…"

Comprehension settled in Evette's sharp eyes, but with it came an unexpected lightness. A knowing humor as bright and bold as her personality. "Oh, that. Thought you were gonna show up and find a stiff crowd with all of us packing heat, huh?" She laughed and waved it off. "I get it. I was knocked off-kilter the first time I came around these guys, too. And trust me, there are some aspects to being around them that will make you abso-lutely bonkers—like when Kir finally decides you're not allowed to so much as cross the street without a bodyguard with you. But for the most part, they're the best damned family a girl could ask for."

"Why would he do that?"

"Do what?"

"Put a bodyguard on me."

Evette's head snapped back. "Seriously?"

Cassie nodded.

Gaze narrowing, Evette pursed her mouth for a sec-ond. "How about if I ask you a question first."

"Such as?"

"How serious would you say you and Kir are?"

"We're not. I mean, we were…something. Intimate, I guess. But that was a while ago. Then I went and screwed it up because I listened to what everyone at work was telling me about…well… Sergei, so I didn't return Kir's calls. Then, after I apologized a few weeks ago, he asked me to help him do some research."

"Some research." Not a snarky clarification so much as that tone your mom got when she absolutely could not believe you'd asked her for money one day after she'd given you your allowance.

"Mmm-hmm."

Evette cast her a sidelong look. "You know, when you two walked in here tonight, Kir was looking mighty possessive of you."

"I know. That's one of the things that's thrown me off tonight. He's always been very gentlemanly. Opens doors and holds my elbow when I'm walking to the car, but tonight he was…different. Much more attentive and very hands on. And secretive, or something."

"And you haven't asked yourself *why* he was different?"

"Well, yes. But I only had the drive here to ponder it, and then I got here and got distracted by everyone else."

While Evette didn't outright laugh in her face, her eyes sure did spark with delight. "Yeah, I can see how we'd throw a girl for a loop." Still smiling, she studied Cassie for a second or two. As if she wanted to let Cassie in on a secret, but wasn't altogether sure it was a good idea.

"What?" Cassie prodded.

Evette snickered. "It's just funny—being on the outside and watching the things I experienced happen to someone else."

"Such as?"

"Such as seeing another woman be the sole target of a Russian man's attention. I was there once and let me tell you—Cinderella got the short end of the stick compared to these guys. When Russian men decide who they want, they'll move heaven, hell and the big bad wolf all at once to make them theirs."

"But Kir and I aren't like that. We agreed to just be partners."

That was right, wasn't it? They'd said they'd be silent partners. Just two people helping each other out.

Evette rolled her lips inward for a second then cleared her throat. "Don't know how to break it to you, sister, but from where I'm sitting, the *partnership* you thought you were in has escalated to a very serious committed relationship."

No way.

Things like that didn't just happen. Not with as little history as they had between them. *Especially* with the kind of history they had between them.

But Kir had been much more attentive. Possessive and protective. Had used those sexy Russian endearments more times than she could count tonight and been concerned about her home's security.

You are exactly where I want you to be.

The muted thrum of her pulse grew louder in her ears, and her legs shook as though she'd sprinted up three flights of stairs.

"Don't be too hard on him," Evette said as though she hadn't just completely upended her world. "My guess on the reason Kir hasn't said anything is the fact that he hasn't fully admitted it to himself yet. But he'll get there. And when he does, you're gonna have to hold on for all you're worth, because he's gonna be a hell of a ride."

"I don't…" Cassie licked her lips—or tried to, considering how dry her mouth had become. "I don't know what to do with this. With him. I don't know that I'm cut out for him."

Evette cocked her head. "Do you like him, Cassie? Not what he does, or what you've heard from your friends, but him. The man. The way he treats you and how it feels to be with him."

She did.

Always had.

Even beyond the stellar physical interactions they'd had, spending time with him was easy. Uncomplicated and fun the way it was with her aunt, but on a more intimate level.

She nodded.

"Then don't do anything except enjoy yourself. Be who you are and let Kir be him. The rest will take care of itself." Evette cupped her shoulder and urged her to the door. "But do it out there, because if we don't make an appearance in the next few minutes, we'll have Kir, Sergei, and maybe even Roman in here, and I don't think you're up for that much testosterone right now."

How Cassie put one foot in front of the other without toppling off balance, she couldn't say. The plush details in the hallway were little more than a blur, and the growing murmur of those in the dining room like thunder rumbling in the distance.

Surely Evette was blowing things out of proportion. Yes, it was possible Kir was interested in something more, but no one went from platonic to serious in three days. And three very silent days at that!

A yelp and the quick scuffle of feet ripped her from her distracting thoughts in time to see a man and woman laughing off a near collision at the bar.

But it was the woman perched on a barstool and nursing a martini opposite them that made her heartbeat slow and her senses sharpen. The woman's eyes were downcast, and her profile partially obscured by a thick wave of auburn hair as she stood and grabbed her purse, but she looked frustratingly familiar.

"Cassie?" Evette's voice ripped her attention away from the woman. "You okay?"

"Yeah, fine." She motioned to the man and woman

who'd somehow turned their near collision into a conversation. "They just startled me."

"Well, good. 'Cause you've got about five seconds to brace." She dipped her head toward Kir who was stalking their way. "I'll leave you to it. Take all the time you need."

Well, shoot. She needed more than five seconds. More like five hours just to steady herself. And it'd be a whole lot easier if she had a wingman to keep things balanced.

She glanced over her shoulder, but the woman was gone, the seat she'd vacated already filled with another waiting patron.

Kir moved in all of a heartbeat later, his hands easily sliding to her hips and his body nearly touching. "Everything all right, *milaya*?"

Darling.

Now that she knew what it meant, she couldn't stop the shiver that moved through her. Especially when paired with the husky rasp of his voice. She nodded. "I'm fine. I just got a little overwhelmed, that's all."

"Overwhelmed at what?"

"At everything. You. Your family." She swallowed hard, uncertain what to say next. As locations for frank discussions went, standing beside a crowded bar wasn't ideal. "I just think we need to talk."

His gaze roamed her face, his scrutiny so intense that holding his stare was a challenge. When he finally spoke, there was an implacable determination in his voice. "We will have dessert, and then I will take you home. I will let you ask me whatever you want, and I will answer what I can."

Her breath rushed out on a sigh of relief, and her

shoulders relaxed for the first time since she'd headed for the restroom. "Good. Thank you."

"But Cassie?"

"Hmm?"

He cupped one side of her face and leaned in close enough his warm breath whispered across her face. "You should understand upfront. We'll be doing much more than talking."

Chapter Ten

Cassie was quiet. Too quiet for Kir's liking. Quiet for her meant she was thinking, and the outcome of her thoughts had already derailed things for them once.

Kir exited off the main roadway onto the backstreets of Marigny, the only sound to break the silence between them the low strains of Nothing But Thieves' "Last Orders."

It didn't matter. No matter what obstacles she threw at him, he would overcome them. The three days since his conversation with Sergei had given him much clarity. Time spent facing his fears from the past and coming to grips with what he wanted for the future. What he believed in, and what he was willing to do to change his life.

And he was starting with Cassie.

"It was you, wasn't it?" Cassie said. From the perplexed frown on her face, he surmised that the last few miles had indeed consisted of an internal debate she'd finally decided to make him a part of.

"I've taken many actions in my lifetime, but I'm afraid you'll need to be more specific if I'm to accept responsibility for the one you're referring to."

She faced him, her gaze sharpening. "My car. You're the reason it got fixed so quickly."

Ever his reporter, piecing together details even when they were best left untouched. He'd be wise to be mindful of that as they moved forward together. Particularly where details of his business were concerned. "I paid them a visit and inquired as to the problem, yes."

"How'd you know where I took it to get fixed?"

"There was a receipt by your sofa when I visited. I noted the business name and followed a hunch."

Her mouth parted, the surprise on her face unmistakable.

"You aren't the only person capable of investigations, Miss McClintock. I've been known to track down a clue or two on my own."

She sat back in her chair and stared out the windshield, her hands clasped around her purse. "And the cost…did you fix that, too?"

A tricky answer. In Russia, a woman would expect such an action. Men demonstrated their ability to provide and care for them by any means necessary. But in America? Not so straightforward.

He opted for the blunt approach. "I did. A timing chain is very expensive, and you've just incurred the cost of moving. To have you field repair costs as well when I'm more than capable of covering them was unnecessary."

She twisted her head his direction. "The guy told me it was something to do with a belt."

"There was a problem there, too. I only paid for the timing chain." He paused a beat and forced some levity into his voice. "You see? I didn't totally absorb the expense."

Whether she decided to accept the response, or was merely holding further arguments until they were inside her home, she kept her silence while he parked and helped her from the car.

At her doorstep, he held out his hand. "Give me your key, Cassie."

For a moment, he thought she'd balk, the tight pinch of her lips and death grip on her purse indicating a hesitancy that made him bristle. She opened the tiny clutch instead. "We definitely need to talk."

"I made you a promise, and I intend to keep it." He took the keys she offered, opened the door and motioned her through. "Let me get the lights."

He closed the door and locked it, flipped on the single lamp for the living room, then located an under-cabinet light in the kitchen and turned it on as well.

Still watching him from the far side of her tiny living room, Cassie dove right in. "You were right. About your family, I mean. They're not at all what I expected them to be."

Kir rounded the kitchen counter, but did so slowly to give her time to say what she needed to say.

"Don't get me wrong," she said. "Sergei's a pretty scary-looking guy when he's not smiling, but tonight went much different than I thought it would."

"I'm glad you see them as I do."

"I do. I get it now." She stepped a little closer and laid her purse on the coffee table, the gesture tentative. "But you still can't tell me that Sergei and those of you who work for him play by the rules."

There it was. The truth of the matter laid bare, yet with care and deliberation. Which was fine by him. "We play by the rules—our own."

"Kir, your rules don't count were the law is concerned."

He inched closer, more aware than he'd ever been in

his life of the importance in how he traversed the next few moments. "You report on reality every day. How often does the law get it right?"

Her gaze shifted to the side and grew distant, that agile mind of hers clearly evaluating the question he'd posed. Given the frown that deepened with each subsequent second, he'd struck a powerful point.

Kir closed what was left of the distance between them and cupped the sides of her arms. Beneath his palms, her skin was pebbled with goose bumps. He smoothed his hands between her elbow and shoulders and lowered his voice. "My family helps those who need help. Yes, we also further our business interests whenever and wherever we can, but we do not do it on the backs of those who want no part in our work. We do not hurt innocents or force people to our will—not unless their actions threaten those under our protection."

"And what happens to the people who threaten those under your protection?" The way she whispered her question it seemed as though she wasn't entirely sure she wanted the answer.

"It depends on the transgression."

"Your own brand of justice. Judge, jury and executioner."

He anchored his hands at her shoulders, held her stare and gave her the truth. "You met Sergei tonight. You met his wife. The child he's accepted as his own. The kind of people he surrounds himself with. I followed him to this country because of who he is. Because of his vision—not just for personal success, but for bringing back old traditions that once served communities in a positive way.

"Yes, we are *bratva*. *Mafiya*, if you want to call it

that. But, in the right hands, who's to say that our brand of justice is wrong?"

She held her silence and studied him. A bit of shock at his boldness definitely painted her expression, but there was consideration, too. A woman reevaluating decisions made and future possibilities.

He slid his hands inward, teasing the line of her collarbone with his thumbs. She had amazing skin. So soft. Like the softest powder and silk combined. Never had he enjoyed touching a woman so much as when he'd lain with her. The feel of her beneath his hands and her uninhibited response.

"I understand your fear," he said. "All you've known are the movies you've seen and reports in the news. But my family is not like any other." A few more inches inward and his thumb grazed the fluttering pulse at her throat. His was just as ragged. Unsteady and quivering at the mere thought of the words still poised on his tongue.

He forged ahead anyway. Honored the instinct pushing him to take and claim what was his. What something in him had always recognized on the most primal level. "You are a part of it now."

She trembled, and her breath hitched, eyes widening like that of a startled doe even though hunger and need burned behind them. "That's the part we need to talk about. We were just supposed to be partners. I was going to help you and look for stories along the way."

"I changed my mind. You will not help me on this matter any longer. We will not be partners." He couldn't help himself anymore. Didn't want to. Had kept himself in check and lied to himself and her long enough. He slid one hand upward and cupped the back of her head, the other coasting down her spine and pulling her flush against him. "You will be mine."

He kissed her. Swallowed her startled gasp and reveled in her taste. In the sweet give of her lips beneath his as she slowly surrendered, and the soft press of her body.

This was why her denial had cut so deeply. No matter how his mind had spun it to cushion his ego after the fact, their connection was electric. Powerful as only something this natural could be. There was no awkwardness. No feigned response or tepid reactions, but an intrinsic connectedness that both rattled and awakened him.

He fisted his hand in her hair, the barbarous need to feel her bare skin against his and her arms and legs coiled around him as he took her more incentivizing than a gun pressed against the back of his head.

But he couldn't go there with her. Not yet. Not until he knew she was with him. That she understood what she was stepping into and who and what he really was.

He broke the kiss and rested his forehead on hers, praying for control. For the right words and actions.

"Kir." His name on her lips was a plea, her breath just as ragged as his own. She pulled her head away from his and met his gaze. "We need to talk about this. What you're suggesting…it's too fast. We barely even know—"

"Did you feel that?" His lips hovered close to hers. "How it felt to have your mouth against mine? How your body's still shaking from a simple kiss?"

She licked her lower lip, a hesitant yet deliciously tempting act that stoked his barely contained control. If the subtle move hadn't given away her thoughts, the wide dilation of her pupils and how heavily her eyelids hung would have answered for her.

"I know that I have never felt that response with any other woman," he said, rather than give her what they both wanted. "I know that we see eye to eye on many issues, and that you are as driven as I am to succeed at whatever you do. I know that we both have pasts that fuel our desire to prove ourselves. That I find your mind as intoxicating as your body, and that I could listen to you talk about anything for hours. Time will fill in the details for me, but right now, *you* are clarity enough."

A shaky breath whispered past her parted lips. "You can't mean that."

"I never say anything I don't mean." He pulled back enough to make sure she saw every bit of his expression. The truth of his words echoed behind his eyes. "I made a mistake letting you walk away from me the first time. I will not make that mistake again and I will not stop until you agree. You and I will be. The only unknown is how long it will take for you to accept and surrender to what is inevitable."

Her fingers dug into his shoulders, the barrier of his jacket doing little to disguise the uncertainty and fear behind her grip. Her gaze shifted from one side to the other, distant and yet frantic. As though her mind desperately sought steady purchase. A foothold to keep her from plummeting into the unknown.

He gentled his arms around her. Skimmed his thumb along her nape and teased his lips against hers. "It's all right, Cassie. You have nothing to fear. Not from me. Not from my family. Not from anyone." He pressed his mouth to hers, the fit as perfect and intimate as their bodies once had been. As they would be again.

"I'm not afraid of your family," she whispered. "Or you."

"Then what?"

Her eyelids lifted slowly, such honesty and vulnerability shining from behind her blue-gray eyes. "I don't know how to be a part of something like you have. My family is nothing like yours. I don't know how to be anything but single Cassie figuring out how to do things on her own."

He cupped her face. "You don't need to know, *vozlyublennaya*. All you need to do is let go."

He should have waited. Should have given her time to voice whatever concerns lingered.

But the tentative hope and need written on her face was too great. His own fears and impatience too powerful to risk logic taking the upper hand. He claimed her mouth. Kissed her with all the determination in him. Willed her to understand all the unspoken fears and faith now laid at her feet with each sweep of his tongue.

Bit by bit, she relaxed within the circle of his arms. Sighed into his kiss and slipped her hands inside his jacket, her palms eagerly stroking his chest.

It was all the acquiescence he needed. At least for now. If he could touch her—stoke the embers that had burned between them from the very start—it would give him all the time he needed to teach her. To court her the way she deserved.

He covered one of her hands with his and forced himself to relinquish her mouth. "No more talking." He lifted her hand and kissed her palm. "Not unless the words coming from your mouth are to ask me for more, or say my name when you come."

Gaze rooted on the spot where he'd kissed on her hand, a tremor moved through her. "For a man who speaks English as a second language, you're way too good with words."

"Am I?" He tried to fight what he was sure was a devious smile, but it was pointless. His beast had had enough of waiting and wanting. He stepped backward, using his grip on her hand to pull her forward. "I seem to recall you were quite fond of my verbal skills in the bedroom."

Another step.

Then another. Down the short hallway toward her room, all the while maintaining his hold on her hand.

"My oral skills, too."

While she didn't fight following where he led, her steps slowed, and the sway of her hips grew slightly more pronounced. Her lips curved in a sly grin, and her eyes sparked with fun and mischief. "I never said anything about your bedroom skills."

"No? I could have sworn you commented on them." Clear of the doorway and within a foot of her bed, he tugged her off balance and spun her so the back of her knees met the mattress. He stopped her momentum with a steady hand at her back. Only the glow from the lights in the living room and kitchen broke the darkness. "I guess I'll have to a do a better job of making an impression tonight then, won't I?"

Whether it was her gasp he stifled crushing his mouth to hers, or a clever retort, he couldn't tell. He also wasn't about to stop and find out. Her taste was too potent. Her passion and the greedy way her hands roamed his chest, belly and back too enticing to do anything but forge ahead.

He sampled the skin along her neck and peeled the delicate straps of her romper over her shoulders.

She shoved his jacket past his shoulders and threw it aside.

Her shoes.

His shirt.

Her romper, and his belt.

Every item that stood in their way went the way of the floor in a flurry of quick, impatient movements until all that was left were his pants and his briefs beneath.

He teased the line of her collarbone with his tongue and skimmed his hands from the tops of her thighs, over her hips to her waist. "Lie back for me. I want to see what's mine."

"You've already seen me." Head dropped back and eyes closed, her voice was breathless, but the husky confidence was utterly delicious. She lifted her head and slowly opened her eyes. "And whether or not I'm yours is still open for debate."

Bozhe, she was sexy. A sensual goddess that appealed to him on every level. "A challenge is it?" He toppled her backward, but caught her head before it hit the mattress, his knees braced on either side of her and one hand anchored beside her head. "I do love a challenge. Especially when the prize is as exquisite as you."

She hooked her fingers in the waistband of his slacks and worked the fasteners. "Kir, stop talking. Start doing."

"Oh, no." He stilled her hands and backed off the bed. "Getting you naked quickly was one thing, but rushing the rest of it? That will not happen."

A tiny sliver of moonlight cut between the drapes closed over the windows and highlighted a small lamp on her nightstand. Kir clicked it on.

Soft white light further dimmed from the lamp's dark shade cast the room in a comfortable glow. Like the rest of the house, the room was a riot of color—pillows the color of a mango, drapes to match Caribbean waters and walls painted a comforting shade of green.

But the real focus was Cassie. With the bold red silk comforter beneath her, her silvery-blonde hair, blue-gray eyes and smooth, porcelain skin were even more pronounced. Like an ethereal goddess sent straight from heaven to save him from his past.

She rolled to her side, cocked her elbow and rested her head on her hand. While her figure was more that of a runway model than pinup girl, the sexy way she drew one of her knees inward accented the curve of her hip. "One of us has too many clothes on. If you're going to stare, the least you can do is balance the equation."

Balance? There would never be real balance between them. Not so long as the impulse to see to her needs and keep her for his own burned as bright as it did in this moment. As it had since the day he'd laid eyes on her.

And that had been the biggest fear he'd had to face. His father had shown no limits with his mother and paid the ultimate price.

You are worth another's love and trust as well, brother. Don't let your parents' past rob you of it.

Cassie wasn't his mother. Wasn't greedy. Wasn't a liar and didn't use people. She'd proven her character the day she'd shown up at Bacchanal, offered her humble apology and the truth behind her actions.

"Kir? Is something wrong?"

So much warmth and concern behind her voice. He wanted to hear it every day. To have those inquisitive and caring eyes aimed at him as he crawled into bed at the end of the day. To have the same unwavering support and partnership Sergei had earned with Evette.

"Nyet." He pushed his pants and briefs past his hips

and kicked them aside. "Everything is exactly as it should be."

Her gaze locked onto his straining sex, and her lips parted. "Well, it's definitely better now." She lifted her attention to his face. "Though, I could appreciate the moment a whole lot more if my hands could get involved."

"Only your hands?" He planted one knee in the bed, guided her to her back, then stretched out on his side beside her. The warmth of her body and light, sexy perfume enveloped him. Tempted him to close the scant inches between them and add the sweet press of her silky skin into the mix.

He teased the sensitive stretch just beneath her belly button with the backs of his knuckles, but stopped just short of the pale trimmed curls atop her sex. "The way you were staring at my cock, I thought perhaps you were planning something more treacherous."

She whimpered and flexed her hips into his touch. Her eyes slipped closed and her voice dropped to a husky rasp. "If you keep teasing me and taking forever, I might find a way or two to torture you, and it won't be the pleasurable kind."

He chuckled at that and continued his unhurried exploration. Up the line of her sternum. Along the lower swell of each breast. Circling each nipple until both drew to a taut peak. "There is no reason for you to be impatient, *milaya*. I have every intention of seeing to your needs." More than she probably yet comprehended.

But he'd get her there.

One day—one touch at a time.

She rolled to her side, facing him. "What if my need is to feel you?" She coasted her fingers from his forearm to his shoulder, a featherlight touch that sent shockwaves out in all directions. "To feel your skin against mine and your weight pressing me into the bed." Her hand dipped inward, her palm smoothing against his pecs then between them to his abdomen. "What if I don't want you to go slow?" Lower so her thumb drew a path just parallel to his sex and made it jerk with anticipation. "What if I want you to take me hard and fast now so we can take our time later?"

Fuck.

Moving fast, he caught her hand, rolled her to her back and pinned her hands on either side of her head. Her startled gasp and subsequent grin was every bit as exhilarating as the electrifying press of her body against his.

He couldn't rush this. Wouldn't. Tonight was too important. "You think you can draw me off point, *vozlyublennaya*?"

Her grin deepened to an unrepentant smile. "I can sure try."

The minx.

Part of him wanted to give her what she wanted just to encourage more of her assertive playfulness. But the other part of him—the man bristling for control and aching to make his mark—refused to give way. Needed to set the pace and claim his place.

"Try all you want then." With deliberate slowness, he lowered his head and teased her lips with his. "I'll just draw the moments out longer." He nipped her lower lip. "Make you wait while I build the ache." He licked the same spot. "Make it so you beg for release."

He sealed his mouth against hers. Let instinct and the carnal connection between them take over. Worshiped the sensitive spot where her neck and shoulder met. The delicate curve of her hip and the space just above each hipbone. Licked and suckled each straining nipple until her knees eagerly parted and she welcomed him to the cradle of her hips.

"I still remember the taste of you." He kissed his way lower, forcing himself not to rush. Funneled all of the waiting and frustration he'd wrestled into fueling her anticipation. "I craved it for days after you refused to see me." He nuzzled the top of her sex and let his warm breath whisper over her skin. "Wanted to hear those broken sounds you make when you come and lick up every drop."

"Kir." She fisted her hands in his hair and tried to urge him lower. "Please."

The scent of her surrounded him, the delicious musk of her arousal blending with her soft moans and mews. He slid his hands beneath her pert ass and lifted her hips toward his mouth. Sampled her swollen folds and indulged in her juices, but avoided the tight, distended bud peeking from beneath its hood.

"The ache is exquisite, isn't it?" he said between swipes of his tongue. "Your body trembling and straining for what it remembers, but missing the final piece to put it all together."

He flicked her clit with his tongue.

Her hips jerked, and a ragged groan ripped up her throat.

"I'm the one who'll give it to you." Another teasing lick, one with just a little more pressure that made her body bow in anticipation. "Only me."

Her grip tightened, the sharp sting against his scalp making his cock jerk and throb. "You're killing me."

His chuckle slipped out uncensored, pure male satisfaction even to his own ears. "No, *malyshka.* I'm not killing you." He circled her clit once. Then again. As lost as she was, he doubted a single word from his lips fully registered, but he shared the truth anyway. "I'm claiming you."

He closed his mouth around her. Worked his tongue against the sensitized nub as he suckled and gave her the pressure she wanted.

She bucked against him. Chased the path to pleasure he'd created and rode his mouth until her cry rang out, her pussy contracting and offering her succulent release for his feast. No inhibitions. No shyness. Just a gloriously hedonistic female taking and relishing in her pleasure.

And she was his.

If he'd had any doubts before this moment, they were gone now. Eradicated by the beauty of her vulnerability as she lay open and writhing from the ministrations of his mouth. Annihilated by the crackling connection between them and the promise of one even deeper. More powerful.

Only when the subtle roll of her hips subsided and the insistent pressure from her hands at the back of his head eased did he lift his head.

A soft smile tilted her lips, her features softened and relaxed. Her voice was like a steamy summer night—warm, sultry and dark. "Okay, maybe I was wrong."

The urge to unleash everything and let the beast free flayed him. Prodded him for action even as the hunter cautioned and reminded him of the ultimate prize. "Is that so?"

"Mmm-hmm."

He gently nipped the inside of one thigh. "What about?"

She opened her eyes, the weight of her eyelids that of a woman sated, yet eager for more. Wrapping her legs around his back, she pressed her heels beneath his shoulder blades and guided him upward. "Slow has its benefits."

"Indeed." He eased himself over her, taking time to rebuild her desire and keep his own in check with kisses and teasing caresses up the line of her belly. "Just wait until you see the benefits of what I have planned next."

"Yeah?" Her touch along his ribs and the sinuous stroke of her legs against his calves and thighs was a heady combination, but the brush of his cock against her sex was the ultimate temptation. A siren's most erotic weapon luring him to a place where thoughts and plans had no bearing. She stroked both hands up his torso and whispered against his lips. "Me first."

The sharp press of her palms against his pecs was unexpected. The strength behind the action even more so, the drunken haze and feral need he'd kept at bay too long leaving him off centered and unbalanced. He found himself on his back with Cassie kneeling between his legs and her head poised just above his cock in seconds.

She stroked from his knees toward his hips and smiled at him, delighted wickedness shining behind her eyes. With an excruciatingly tender touch, she coiled her fingers around the base of him. "Let's see…" She kept her gaze locked to his and leaned closer, her warm breath and the barely-there tickle of her lips along his shaft ripping all the air from his lungs. "I'm supposed to take my time, right?" She licked the tip and his cock jerked. "Drag things out as long as possible?"

The beast inside him roared and demanded he take control. To palm the back of her head and guide her kiss-swollen mouth down the length of him. Or better yet, throw her to her back and ram himself inside her.

But that wouldn't earn her trust. Wouldn't foster the

playful and sexy confidence demonstrated now, and he found he liked that side of her very, very much.

He folded his hands behind his head, cocked his knees and widened them. "By all means, *malyshka*. Take whatever time you need. Far be it from me to deny you any pleasure."

She chuckled at that, the smug pleasure of a woman all too aware of her feminine impact on a vulnerable man written all over her face. "Trust me. I won't be the only one feeling pleasure."

Warm, wet heat surrounded him. Wiped every shred of reality save the feel of her from existence. The tip of her tongue teasing the ridge beneath his cockhead. The slick glide of her lips around his shaft. The subtle vibration as she took him deep and moaned with pleasure.

He was lost.

Enraptured by the stretch of her lips around his girth and the candy pink of her tongue against his straining flesh. By the sheer devotion and concentration of each and every move. It wasn't a task for her. Not an obligatory function meant to reach an end goal, but a pleasure in the giving.

Release threatened all at once, the lower muscles in his belly fisting hard and his balls drawing tight. He cupped the side of her head. Marveled at the silky brush of her hair sweeping against his knuckles. Keeping his legs from shaking took everything in him. Fighting the growl in his voice impossible. "Cassie."

The little minx ignored him. Just bobbed her head again and again in a languid and sensual glide. He tightened his hold, his fingertips digging into her scalp. "Enough."

Her eyelids slowly opened, the blue-gray color behind them darkened to that of an incoming storm, and the silent rebuttal they offered unmistakable.

Not. Even. Close.

The beast snapped its leash.

He knifed upward, hooked his hands under her arms and yanked her toward him, spinning at the last moment so she landed on her back. A quick grip of her hips and he flipped her to her belly, jerked her to her knees—and then he was home.

Buried to the hilt in her tight, wet sheath with the sound of her pleasured cry floating in the air around him.

In the dimmest corners of his mind, caution raised its head. Flagged his impulse and gave him pause at their lack of protection.

Cassie's breath caught and she twisted to meet his gaze, the same comprehension flaring behind her wide eyes. "Kir... I'm not...this is risky."

"And I still want it." He rolled his hips. Reveled in the moan it drew past her lips. "Do not take this heaven from me."

Her hands fisted in the comforter and her lips trembled.

He braced, warring with the need to pump his shaft inside her. To show her how exquisitely they fit even as logic warned him of her likely denial.

But then her eyes slipped closed. Straightened and lifted her hips higher. Welcomed him deeper inside her. Undulated against him and matched each thrust eagerly. Head turned to one side against the mattress, her profile was pure rapture—lips parted on a drawn-out sigh and the peace of sweet surrender.

His fingers at her hips tightened, some dim place in his consciousness warning not to bruise her pale skin even as the beast growled his approval. Wanted the mark to remind her who'd given her pleasure. Who'd staked his claim and the fierceness with which he'd defend it.

He leaned into her, sliding his hands up her sides and under her torso to her breasts. "This is what you wanted isn't it, *malyshka*?" He licked and nipped the tender space behind one ear and teased her nipples. "To make me lose control and give you what you wanted."

"Yes." A bold admission offered on a breathless groan without a beat of hesitation. "I missed this."

He'd missed it, too. Had been lost without it. Confused and wounded.

But no more. He knew his focus. Had accepted and owned his fears. He lifted her upward, her ass cradled tight to his pelvis and her back flush against his chest as he pounded into her. Every slap of his hips against her perfect ass and the slick wet sounds as he shuttled in and out drew him deeper. Pushed the man farther and farther away and let the beast control all.

He wrapped his hand around her neck. Felt her pounding pulse against his fingertips. "I will be your protector. Your provider. In this. In everything."

She moaned, her fingers digging into his hips. "Kir."

God, he loved his name coming from her lips. Loved the huskiness of it when she was this lost. The need and the plea behind it. Keeping his hand at her throat, he played her clit with the other. Circled and teased until her body was drawn tight, her back bowed and her muscles around him quivering. "You are mine, Cassie. Mine in every way."

He firmed the pressure at her clit and angled his cock so it hit her deeper, nudging the sensitive spot along her

front wall. "Your body knows this already, *malyshka.*
Come for me, and let it show you."

Her voice rang out, the back of her head digging into
his shoulder while her pussy convulsed around his cock.

He tried to fight it. Squeezed his eyes shut and focused on drawing out her pleasure. But the pulsing vise
of her sex was too much. Too powerful for him to fight.

His own release jetted free. Filled her as his roar
ripped up the back of his throat.

His woman.

His chance to take what he thought he'd never have.

His promise, and his light.

He rolled his hips against hers, milking the sensations of her fluttering sex around his shaft with unhurried, leisurely undulations.

Beneath his palm at her throat, her pulse slowly
steadied and the pattern of her breathing eased, but
the feel of her in his arms—utterly replete with eyes
closed—that was heaven. A gift beyond measure.

He guided them down. Reverently caressed her belly,
shoulders and arms with all the gentleness in him and
skimmed tender kisses along the nape of her neck.

"That was…" She rolled her head to give him better access to the juncture where her neck and shoulders met. "Amazing." She shivered when he grazed the
spot with his teeth. "Seriously. It just gets better. Every
time."

He chuckled at that. A low, satisfied rumble so
loaded with masculine pride he had no prayer of hiding it. "I told you, *milaya.* Your body already knows and
accepts you're mine." He slid his hand from her belly
to their joined bodies, slicking his fingers through their
combined release. "And now I've marked you as such."

One heartbeat, and she jolted in his arms, the power

of her response nearly breaking them apart. She tried again to move away. To turn and face him.

But Kir held his arms tight around her. Kissed and crooned soft words she had no prayer of understanding until she settled, shaking, against him. "It will be all right. Shhh." Another kiss to her temple. To her cheek. "You have nothing to fear, Cassie. I have never once lain with a woman without protection, and I know for certain I have nothing I could transmit to you."

A fresh round of tremors rattled through her behind the husky admission. "Oh my God, I can't believe we did that."

"You are not on birth control?"

"No!"

No.

One single word, but it unveiled a whole new realm of possibilities he hadn't dared to consider. A life that both terrified and thrilled him.

She tried to wriggle free once more.

Rather than fight it, he used her momentum to flip her to her back and blanketed her body with his. When she tried to push him away, he captured her wrists and loosely pinned them to the bed. "You are right."

The admission stilled her struggles almost instantly, and her eyes widened with shock.

"It was impulsive," he said. "But I will not lie to you and say that I regret it. Not with you." He risked releasing one wrist and cupped the side of her face. "I want nothing between us. If you want tests to prove you have nothing to fear, we will get them." His voice caught trying to finish the rest. "If there is a child from tonight, it will be protected and cared for. By both of us. Always." The quaver in his thumb as he traced her lower lip should have embarrassed him, but he was too humbled by the thought to find any shame in it. "But I want nothing to block my connection to you."

"I can't have a kid yet, Kir. It's too much. Way too much, way too fast."

"Then we will get you protection." He stroked her hair away from her face. Skimmed his knuckles along her cheekbone and teased the shell of her ear.

All the while, she studied him, her gaze roaming his face as though she sought clues to guide her. "You know this is insanely fast, right? The kind of fast that should make a smart woman keep you at arm's length. Or flat out avoid you."

"That is what your logic says. What your American customs say. But what about you, Cassie? What do you want? What do you feel when you're with me? When you were with my family?"

She didn't answer, but her response was there, nonetheless. The longing in her eyes. The mysterious and inexplicable connection they'd had from the very beginning brighter than ever.

He clasped her hand resting on his shoulder and guided it to his lips. "I will not rush you." He pressed a tender kiss to one knuckle. "I will not force more than you are comfortable with." Then another. And another. "But I will ask for you to try." He squeezed her hand and held it tight. "Give me that, *malyshka*. Give me that, and I will give you everything."

Her answer was barely more than a whisper. "I can try."

He wanted to roar.

To sit back on his heels and shout out his triumph.

Instead, he sealed his lips to hers. A simple yet powerful kiss worthy of her willingness. Of the vulnerability she'd shown in trusting him. When he lifted his head, her features had softened, an easy acceptance settling into her expression.

"Beautiful." He kissed the tip of her nose, then rolled toward his side of the bed and stood. Carefully, he pulled the comforter and bedding out from beneath her and drew the covers over her beautiful body. "You will stay here, and I will see to you."

"See to me?"

"Yes." He padded to the kitchen and living room and turned off the lights.

Her voice carried down the hallway on his trek to the bathroom. "See to me how?"

He turned on the faucet and found a washcloth. "Stop worrying, Cassie. Part of trying means trusting me to handle things now and then."

When the water was warm enough, he wetted the cloth, wrung it out and returned to her.

She spied the washrag in an instant and threw back the covers. "Oh, I can get it. I'm—"

"No, you will not." He motioned her back to the bed. "Lie back."

"Seriously?"

"Yes. Seriously."

It took her a solid fifteen seconds before she moved, every one of them making him wonder if he'd have another debate on his hands. Finally, she stretched out on her back, one knee slightly cocked over her other leg. "I can't believe we're doing this."

He settled beside her and smoothed his hand from her ankle to her knee. "You gave me your body. A gift. What kind of man would I be if I didn't care for what I'd been given?"

Not giving her more opportunity to overthink it, he pushed her knee to one side and tenderly cleaned her still sensitive folds. By the time he straightened and met her gaze, her features were slack with wonder.

"I told you. Nothing between us." He squeezed her hip, leaned in and pressed a quick kiss to her lips. "Now, do you need anything before we sleep?"

"You're sleeping over?"

So sweet. How she could be so intensely sexual one moment and adorably innocent in the next, he couldn't fathom. "I think I've spent enough nights without you, *vozlyublennaya*. Tonight, we begin making up for lost time." He set the cloth aside and switched off the lamp. Stretching out beside her, he pulled the comforter over them both then tucked her close, guiding her head so it rested on his chest.

For long moments, tension riddled her body, every muscle poised as though uncertain how to proceed.

He caressed her spine. Her shoulder and arm. The nape of her neck. Waiting. Comforting her the only way he knew how.

Slowly, she uncurled her fist resting high on his belly and hesitantly drew an indecipherable pattern against his skin. "I'm not making this up, am I? You really want this."

More than he ever remembered wanting anything. More than was rational or reasonable. "Yes, Cassie. I want this. And when you're not thinking of all the reasons why you shouldn't, I think you want it, too." He kissed the top of her head and tightened his arm around her. "Now, sleep. Let go of your worries. We'll deal with tomorrow when it gets here. Tonight, we rest."

She nodded. An almost childlike motion that made him want to hide her behind the highest walls where nothing and no one could ever hurt her. An odd and slightly perplexing response he acknowledged wasn't at all logical and wasn't entirely sure how to contend with.

He stared through the darkness toward the ceiling, wondering at the fierceness behind his unexpected surge of protectiveness and savoring the feel of her next to him. How her body slowly eased and softened against his, and the way their legs entwined. Only when her breathing deepened to that of a person drifting into sleep and her head was weightless against his chest did he close his own eyes.

And let the promise born between them carry him into dreams of tomorrow.

Chapter Eleven

A ding. A pleasant, yet out of place sound in the realm of Cassie's dream-quiet mind that lifted her slowly upward. Not quite awake, but no longer asleep either.

Had she heard something? Or had she imagined it?

She shook the thoughts off. She felt too good to care. Relaxed. Content and warm. Safe and protected.

Kir.

It was his arms around her. The strength and warmth of his body blanketing her back, and the steady rise and fall of his breath creating an almost meditative cocoon. She didn't want to move. Didn't want to think about anything except this exact moment and everything about last night that had led them to it.

She was *so* in over her head. A baby lamb tottering on shaky legs alongside a full-grown lion. All she'd been able to hear on the drive home and while they'd talked was a cacophony in her parents' voices.

Are you insane?

Why are you standing here listening to this man?

He admitted he was mafiya.

You don't fraternize with dangerous people. You stay away from them.

This situation is dangerous.

Be smart.

Run.

Run.

Run.

But she didn't want to run. Didn't want to listen to the voices in her head anymore. Not even a little bit. She *liked* being with him. Had always felt a little more alive in his presence. More centered and aware. She'd marveled at the sensation even from the beginning. How easy everything from conversation to chemistry flowed with him. How even the simplest experience felt richer and more vibrant with him in the equation.

And then there was his family.

They'd been kind. Thoughtful. Inquisitive and accepting. Aside from that initial, piercing stare, even Sergei had seemed to lower his guard and allow her a glimpse into the man behind the stern exterior. Maybe it made her stupid or naive, but she wanted what they had. Wanted to be around people who didn't judge. Who didn't appear to give two figs about how successful she was, or offer incessant opinions on how she should or shouldn't be.

You and I will be.

He'd said it clearly. Unflinchingly.

And something inside her had whispered back a single *Yes.*

The ding sounded again. Definitely not her imagination, but the low sound of a text message coming from the living room.

Kir stirred behind her, drew in a long, sexy inhalation and nuzzled the spot just behind her ear. His low, sleep-sexy voice stoked all the memories of last night and promised more on the horizon. "Someone wants to talk to you quite badly, *vozlyublennaya.*"

"They've only texted twice. That's not urgent enough to make me move."

His rumbling chuckle and the languid press of his lips at the back of her neck sent a shiver down her spine. "You must have been sleeping quite deeply then because you missed the three that came before the last two."

No way. No one ever texted her that often. Not unless something major was going on at work, or Aunt Frieda was out with her girlfriends tying one on—the latter of which shouldn't be happening this early on a Monday morning.

With a groan, she shoved the covers aside and scooted out from the comfort of Kir's arms. "Figures. The one day I decide to sleep in and be lazy, something newsworthy decides to happen in New Orleans."

She padded to the bathroom and grabbed her short-yet-cozy blue chenille robe off the back of the door.

Kir watched her every step with unabashed delight, his sleepy smile only dimming when she pulled the sides of her robe around her and cinched the belt around her waist. "You know, you don't have to get out of bed. You could ignore your phone and stay here with me."

She aimed what she hoped was a stern look at him on the way out the door. "I have to work."

"But you're off on Mondays."

"Only if there's not an emergency." In the living room, she snatched her purse from the coffee table. "It's taken me two years to get to the point they call me first for big stories. No way I can ignore my phone, no matter how cozy I am."

"Ah, the life of a cutting-edge news reporter." Bedcovers shuffled and the soft swoosh of movement against the mattress followed. "I guess I'll have to save my next bout of seduction for after you're done sharing the latest developments with our city's fine citizens."

The phone's display lit up, and the device vibrated with another text just as she flipped it over for a look at the screen.

WHERE R U? I NEED DETAILS STAT.

Cassie reread the text from her Aunt Frieda then scanned the other equally urgent ones that had come in before it. "You've got to be kidding me."

Kir slipped his arms around her waist. "Is it the end of the world?"

"No. More like my aunt being nosey." She thumbed through the messages once more and noted each of them had come in ten minutes apart starting at seven thirty.

"Excellent news." Kir kissed the side of her neck, a lingering press of his lips that went a long way to wiping away Cassie's irritation with her aunt. "Tell her you had two exceptional orgasms and that, if she'll please excuse you, your man is going to give you more to start the day off right."

The swirl and tightening in her belly flared in an instant, the combination of his deep voice, his mouth and the words he'd chosen making her completely forget her aunt's demands for information.

Your man.

Her mother and father would say such words were childish. That they reeked of high school antics and spoke nothing of solid relationship values.

But wow they felt good. Possessive and primal.

"You're not typing anything, *milaya.* I've met your aunt, and she doesn't strike me as the type to give up easily. If you don't answer soon, she'll be at your door."

He gently scraped his teeth along the shell of her ear. "And if she's here, I can't see to those orgasms."

Type, Cassie.

NOW.

Somehow, her fingers got in gear.

Have company. Will call later. MUCH later.

The swoosh of a sent text had barely sounded when Kir took the phone from her hand, tossed it to the couch and slung her over his shoulder.

And Lordy, did she get the fast and dirty tango she'd wanted the night before, because thirty minutes later, she was out of breath, thoroughly sated and splayed on her back with a smugly smiling Russian stretched out on his side beside her. One who'd, thankfully, paused long enough to grab condoms this time around.

He coasted his fingers down her belly then teased the curls covering her sex, the languorous touch and the room's cool air against her sweat-misted skin fanning goose bumps out in all directions.

"Two orgasms before nine in the morning," he said, openly enjoying her naked body. "Will that be sufficient to satisfy your aunt's expectations? Or do we need a break for coffee and another round to guarantee earning her approval?"

She laughed without censure, one of those embarrassing as hell guffaws she usually hated with a passion, but that felt totally acceptable with him beside her. Still chuckling, she rolled to her side and caressed the hard planes of his chest. "You caught that she wanted details, huh?"

"I might have stolen a peek." His hand slid to the small of her back, and he pulled her flush against him.

"But I was prepared to angle for more even if the entire world had been on fire." He kissed the tip of her nose, a sweet and familiar gesture that warmed her clear to her toes. "Now, I'm going to forage through your meager kitchen and make us both coffee. How do you take it?"

"Black," she said before she gave him her own playful kiss. She pushed away and rolled off the bed. "But I'm making coffee. Knowing you, you drink it stout enough to keep me awake for three days."

She snatched her discarded robe from the floor and shrugged it on.

Propped on one arm, Kir watched her, that self-satisfied grin of his even bigger than usual. "Quite the contrary, actually. I take a good amount of cream and sugar in my coffee."

"Really?" She cinched the belt around her waist and ambled to the kitchen. "You'll drink vodka straight like it's water, but you need all the extras for coffee?"

"I'm Russian. Vodka *is* water. Coffee requires sugar and cream to even it out." He strolled into the kitchen clad only in his black boxer briefs just as she closed the refrigerator door.

Cassie paused with her coffee container in hand long enough to give every bit of his six-foot-two lean-muscled goodness a thorough once-over. "Well, there's a view I could get used to."

He hooked her around the waist and kissed the side of her neck. "A view you *will* get used to." Rather than make himself at home at the dining room table as she'd anticipated, he sprawled long-wise on the sofa so he had a line of sight view of her at work.

Doing her best to ignore the intensity behind the way he watched her, she measured out the coffee and poured water into the reservoir.

"I'd like you to accept the offer," he said matter of factly.

"What offer?"

"To photograph Lizzy and her band."

She punched the brew button and meandered in his direction. "I told you guys, I'm not a professional. She needs someone with experience."

Kir lifted his chin toward one of her favorite photographs mounted on the far wall—a cable car on Canal Street taken just before dusk. While the subject matter was popular tourist fodder, it was the coloring she'd most prided herself on capturing. The green of trees lining each side of the street. The soft glow of the old-fashioned streetlamps down the median and how the evening skies on one side blended into the sunset still lingering on the other. "From what I've seen, you're quite experienced."

"A few of my favorites doesn't make a portfolio."

He dipped his head, an acquiescent move typically reserved for polite negotiations. "You are correct. Show me more."

Well, shit.

Talking about photography was one thing. Actually showing someone her work was something else. No matter how many appreciative comments she got from her aunt or coworkers, she'd never been able to shake that perplexed expression on her father's face the first time she'd shown him an image she'd been excited about. "Seriously?"

He cocked an eyebrow.

"Oh, all right. Fine." She fished around the portfolio with her most recent work. "But remember—I'm more of a landscape and fixed image girl. Which is why I think I'd do horrible work for Lizzy."

He sat up and accepted the leather-bound volume. "Have you ever worked with people?"

"A little." She sat down next to him. "I've done okay with a few candid shots. I don't have a clue what to do when it comes to posing people, though."

He thumbed through the pages, lingering between each turn to fully assess what she'd captured. Halfway through, the picture she'd stashed of him slipped from between the pages and into his lap.

She tried to reach for it, but he beat her to it and held it well away from her. He studied it and wrapped his free arm around her shoulders, pulling her tight to his side. "What have we here?"

Her stomach clenched, and her lungs refused to do their job, the fear squeezing them too powerful to fight. "I…uh…"

What could she say? Not to give him a reason would only make him dig deeper, but to tell him the truth?

Be who you are and let Kir be him. The rest will take care of itself.

Evette's words. Wisdom earned from someone who'd not only earned the attention of a powerful man like Kir, but seemed beyond happy on the other side. Maybe the truth was the right answer. And if it wasn't, well wasn't it better to find out how he reacted now rather than later?

He set the photo aside and faced her, his expression open and not at all suspicious.

She let out a long exhale and swallowed around a sizable knot in her throat. "I was following you."

"Stalking me?" If the tone of his voice didn't give away his surprise, the shock on his face did.

She shrugged and eased from beneath his arm. "The stories were slowing down, and my editor had just nudged me for something new a few days before I took that picture."

Comprehension settled in his features. While there still didn't seem to be any anger, a healthy amount of caution and consideration settled behind his eyes. "And you thought I'd be able to help you find more."

"It was a lame move. I knew it when I saw you. Knew I'd treated you poorly." She nodded to the photo. "I was glad I got the picture, though. Even if it wasn't very good work."

Kir's gaze roamed her face, taking in every detail.

It was too much. Too painful to stomach such suspicious scrutiny after being the focus of his tenderness and appreciation for days.

She ducked her head and toyed with the plush chenille of her robe with her thumb. "I get it. I'd be mad, too. All I can tell you is, I'm sorry."

She expected him to leave. To stand, quietly dress and walk out the door with the same purposeful determination he'd walked in with the night before.

Instead he cupped the side of her neck and dragged in a long, deep inhalation. A deeply masculine sound that was sexy even in the uncomfortably tense moment. "Look at me, *malyshka*."

A command. One uttered in a low and patient voice, but a command, nonetheless.

She lifted her head, and her breath caught.

Never once had she seen such vehemence burning behind his blue eyes. Such unflinching force. This was the man her peers had warned her about. A man capable of as much violence as he was proficient at giving pleasure.

"You will not apologize again," he said. "You shared

your motive once. I accepted it. It is behind us and holds no bearing on where we go from here."

Of all the things he could have said, those were the last words she'd expected. "But you were mad."

"I was disappointed at the way you disparaged your work. The way you downplay and limit yourself on something that clearly is a passion."

"No, even before I talked about the quality of the picture, you got a funny look on your face. Like you weren't sure if you could trust me, or something."

As fast as his ferocious demeanor had dropped into place, it was gone again. Replaced with that wickedly charming grin that never failed to make her feel like a sixteen-year-old. "Or, perhaps, I was thinking to myself that, if it hadn't been for your pushy boss, I wouldn't have found myself sitting next to you this morning." He pulled her close and pressed a tender kiss to her lips. "Never assume with me, *vozlyublennaya*. I brood and get too deeply in my head from time to time for my expressions to be a reliable gauge. Trust my actions instead."

She nodded, the warm lightness mushrooming up from her chest, no doubt making her look like a love-struck goon from his perspective.

"Promise me," he prodded with an affectionate squeeze to the back of her neck.

"Promise."

"Good." He kissed her again, this time letting his mouth linger longer against hers before he lifted his head. "Now, since I'm the one who requires extra effort with my coffee, how about if I pour us each a cup while you gather more of your work for me to appreciate."

She wrinkled her nose and stood. "Fine. But only if you allow me a certain amount of latitude on moan-

ing and groaning while you look. Call it artistic flair
or whatever, but letting people see my work is hard."

"Fair enough."

They took their time. Chatted over two cups of coffee and worked their way through all of her portfolios
all the way back to high school. When they'd run out of
those, he insisted on seeing the raw work from her most
recent shoot. She nestled next to him on the sofa with
her feet propped on the coffee table as he filed through
the digital images one by one. "I think you should try
working with Lizzy."

He said it casually, but there was a bit of a dare behind it as well. A challenge that she'd have likely dis-
regarded entirely at the beginning of the morning, but
was hard-pressed to ignore after all the time he'd spent
studying her work. "But you saw for yourself—I don't
normally work with people."

"Not normally, no. But you had candid images
throughout, and I think that's what Lizzy's after."

"But this is her career. She won't want to trust that
to me."

"Trusting family is always wiser than trusting
strangers."

She opened her mouth to answer him, but he cut her
off before she could speak. "If you say you're not family
after last night, I'll have to introduce you to an entirely
different form of sexual play that requires me paddling
your adorable ass."

This time her mouth popped open for an entirely different reason. "You wouldn't."

He raised that imperious eyebrow that was both sexy
and infuriating. "You might like it."

Given the tightening low in her belly and the way
her thighs were clenched together, she was guessing she

probably would. But then, he could probably recite the alphabet and give her an orgasm if he put his mind to it.

The email program on her laptop chimed the arrival of a new message, and the notification bar flashed a subject line entitled *Who's Using Who?*

Odd.

And while the notification slid away before she could study the sender's name completely, it didn't look like one she recognized.

She pulled the laptop off of Kir's lap and flipped to her email. At the top of her unread messages, the mysteriously titled email sat with the sender *Vengeance-S33k3r@ymail.com*. The text in the preview window below was limited.

Such a cozy couple. I wonder—is Kir using you to do his dirty work? Or are you using him for yours?

Be careful. You know what happened to Stephen Alfonsi.

Beneath the words was a picture of Cassie with Kir. A blurry one that had definitely been taken in a rush, but unquestionably while they'd been walking out of *André's* the night before. She tried to zoom in for a better look, but before she could finish the motion, Kir pulled the computer from her lap.

"Who is this?" he demanded, scrolling from the top of the message to the image beneath.

"I have no idea. I've never received anything from anyone with that email address."

He scrolled back to the top, studied the words written for all of another ten seconds, then snapped the laptop shut and stood. "Get dressed."

"What? Why?" It was curiosity more than any desire that made her follow him to her bedroom. "Do you know them?"

He snagged his phone, punched a few options, then cradled the device between his ear and shoulder and started getting dressed. Whoever he was calling answered in less than two rings, but they couldn't be enjoying the call because the clipped string of Russian words flying out of his mouth didn't sound friendly at all. Pants, shirt and belt already on, he snatched his socks and shoes off the floor and sat on the edge of the bed. She couldn't tell what the party on the other end was saying, but Kir's gaze cut to her and he responded to them with a guttural *Nyet*.

Okay, so something was a very firm *no*. And from the determination etched on his face, she had a funny feeling her morning wasn't going to be as lazy and enjoyable as she'd expected it to be fifteen minutes ago.

Eyes still on her, he finished putting on his last shoe, nodded and muttered a final sentence in Russian. He ended the call and stood. "You will pack. Now."

She heard the words.

Comprehended them at the most basic level.

But for some reason, her brain couldn't quite generate an action or a response. At least it couldn't until he strode to her closet, opened the bifold doors and reached for her suitcase stashed on the top shelf. "What are you doing?"

"Assisting you." He opened the suitcase, scanned the room as though trying to determine where to start, then headed to her tiny dresser.

When he opened the top drawer and started reaching for her bras and panties, her body finally got in motion. "Hold up." She grabbed his wrist right before he pulled out a fistful. "Why am I packing, and where am I going?"

He frowned and faced her. "That email was a threat."

"Maybe. Maybe not."

"No *maybe*. Someone knows you've been helping me."

"Yes, but I don't know what I've been helping you with."

"Helping me find the person who killed one of my own. Now are you packing, or shall I?"

The world got scary silent, even her heart slowing to the point that a frightening nothingness filled her ears. "Killed one of your own?"

"One of my men. They were murdered as retribution for Sergei's actions against Alfonsi."

Murder.

Retribution.

Sergei's actions.

Simple words on their own, but strung together they were too startling to do anything other than leave her standing in one spot, gaping.

"Here you are unprotected," Kir said. "With my family, that will not be the case."

She shook her head and tried to clear the jumbled chaos in her head. "You want me to move in with you?"

"*Nyet.* My home does not have sufficient surveillance. I will move you to Sergei's house."

"I can't move in with Sergei."

"You can. You will." He turned back to the drawer, clearly intent on finishing what he'd started.

She yanked the clothes from his hand and threw them back in the drawer. "It was just an email. Who knows who sent it? It could just be a prank. Certainly nothing to make me move. And even if it was a threat, I can't just move in with people I barely know and bring that threat with me. He's got a family. A life. It's not right to intrude on that."

While his features were pinched with concern, he took a slow breath in as though mining for patience and lowered his voice. "You will not intrude. They have space for you. Sergei confirmed it." That unyielding determination she'd glimpsed earlier dropped into place, and his lips firmed. "Now you can either dress and pack, or I can take you as you are, and my men will come back and pack your belongings later. Your choice."

"You can't force me to move!"

"I can, and I will."

Not a dare. Not an idle threat. But a promise.

She paced away from him. Fisted her hair on the top of her head and tried to process it all. But it was like trying to put together a thousand-piece jigsaw puzzle in the middle of a hurricane. "That's…that's…crazy!"

She spun to make another lap and found him squarely in her path. His arm stole around her waist and yanked her flush against him. He cupped the side of her face, the urgency in his grip matching edge behind his words. "No, *malyshka*. That is what a man does to protect what is his. I told you last night—You. Are. *Mine*." He held her gaze for tense moments, whether to ascertain if he'd sufficiently delivered his message, or to gain his control, she wasn't sure.

He finally relaxed his hold, stepped back and smoothed his hand down the front of his shirt. "Now, are you changing into something else and choosing what you want to take with you? Or am I taking you dressed as you are and having your belongings packed later?"

He was serious.

One hundred percent deadly serious.

And something told her it would take nothing short of a nuclear warhead to get him to budge on his position.

The suitcase lay open on her bed, the rumpled sheets where so much pleasure and passion had been shared, beneath it.

You're gonna have to hold on for all you're worth, because he's gonna be a hell of a ride.

Man, Evette hadn't been kidding, had she? And more importantly, what if Kir was right and the email wasn't a joke? Someone had not only noted her with Kir and thought to snap a picture, but they'd found a way to track her personal email address to send the message. That meant they were invested. And if the sender truly was tied to the murder of one of Kir's men, then digging in her heels was utterly stupid.

With a fresh wave of fear rattling her nerves, she nodded and turned for the bathroom. "I'll change. Give me half an hour to pack."

Chapter Twelve

Clearly, Kir was lacking in the skills necessary to navigate a relationship. Protecting and providing for a woman he could do, and ensuring pleasure was… well, a pleasure. But finding his way through the mercenary terrain of a tight-lipped woman with clenched fists? That was something Sergei had failed to warn him about. How lost he'd feel, or for that matter, how terrifying making a misstep would be. He'd faced down dangerous men armed to the teeth more times than he could count, and never once felt this powerless.

Cassie stared out the windshield, her features pinched in concentration. If she noted the beautiful Creole and Victorian style mansions passing them by, she didn't show it. Just kept her gaze trained straight ahead and held her body locked solid.

He made the last turn onto Sergei's street then covered one of her fisted hands with his own. "Sergei texted while you were packing. Evette and Emerson are both looking forward to seeing you. The accommodations are quite comfortable. You'll see."

Slowly, she lowered her head and studied his hand on hers. A mix of bewilderment and strain colored her soft voice. "It's not where I'm staying. It's not being around Evette or anyone else in your family."

"Then what is it?"

She lifted her head. Raw fear and uncertainty burned behind her beautiful eyes. "I plan things. I'm methodical. Logical. I've been raised to be that way since I can remember. But in the last three weeks, my life has gone from routine days at work and take-out dinners, to romance with a man who doesn't do subtle or slow, a world I have no clue how to navigate and a possible murderer nosing into my life. It's a lot, Kir, and I don't know how to handle it."

She had a point. Several of them, actually. And if he hadn't been so focused on logistics and his own fears, he might have seen them for himself. "You are right." He released her hand and turned into Sergei's driveway.

"I am?"

He nodded, put the car in park and faced her. "I cannot change who I am and the way I was raised any more than you. I will not ignore the threat to you and will ask that, where your safety is concerned, you will exercise patience, but I will endeavor to give you time to adjust to our relationship."

Her frown would have been comical if the topic at hand didn't have him so vexed. "You say that like we'd agreed to marry each other last night. We're dating. Not marching down a path to matrimony."

Oh, yes, they were. It might have taken some verbal bludgeoning from Sergei and Roman to get him to realize what a good thing he'd found, but now that he'd acknowledged it, he wasn't letting her go.

Still, he wasn't stupid. "You are the first relationship I've entered into. I would not take such an action lightly."

Her eyebrows hopped high. "I'm your first girlfriend?"

Girlfriend? Such a paltry representation for what he wanted from her. For what he envisioned for them both. "Yes, *malyshka*. You are my first."

And my last.

The admission seemed not only to calm her, but painted her features with an open wonder. "That's…" Her gaze roamed his face. "How is that even possible?"

Because he'd never allowed himself to consider such emotional exposure. Because he'd never met a woman worth the risk, and certainly had never experienced even a tenth of the connection he shared with her with anyone else. He cupped the side of her face and traced the line of her cheekbone. "That's a long story better shared another time."

"But you'll share it with me?"

He didn't want to. Didn't want to relive the details himself, let alone share it with a woman whose opinion of him mattered so much. But a partnership built without trust was no partnership at all. "Yes, *vozlyublennaya*. After you're settled."

He helped her from the car, the tense preoccupation that had gripped her the whole drive replaced with a keen awareness of her surroundings. A thorough study of the men who gathered her luggage from his car. Noting the men stationed around the grounds and appreciating the splendor of the estate itself. Nothing escaped her scrutiny. Though, when he guided her to the carriage house rather than the main building, he did seem to catch her off guard.

"This isn't a garage?" she said.

"Quite the contrary. The carriage house was renovated along with the house before Sergei bought it. Evette and Emerson lived here briefly before Evette accepted Sergei's marriage proposal." He nodded to the guard stationed closest to them, opened the main door and motioned her inside. "As I said, you staying here will be no inconvenience for them at all, and they are happy to know you are protected."

Inside, he guided her through the simple layout. The living and kitchen area downstairs with its open design, soaring ceilings and contemporary farmhouse décor, and the two luxurious bedrooms on the second story separated by a catwalk with wrought iron railings.

He waited by the door of the master suite and watched her slowly taking in the surroundings. While the red and turquoise pillows and gold silk comforter weren't as bold as the colors that filled her own home, her gaze still lingered on them in open appreciation. "It was much less colorful before Evette lived here. More of a monochromatic scheme with little personality."

"It's lovely." She peeked inside the spacious bath and shook her head. "Way more than anything I'm used to."

She'd adjust. Not just to being here, but to not doing without ever again.

The door downstairs opened and the hushed voices of his men carrying in her things drifted from over the catwalk. A few moments later they filed in and carefully laid her bags at the foot of the bed.

Kir snatched the key to Cassie's house from his pant pocket and handed it to Sam, one of the first and sharpest men he'd brought on his team since relocating to New Orleans. "You have her address, yes?"

"Yes, sir."

"Good. I want a full sweep. Look for any signs of tampering with doors or windows."

"Of course." Sam jerked a quick nod and started to leave, the other two men tight on his heels.

Kir stopped them a few steps mid-departure. "One

moment." He wrapped an arm around Cassie's waist and introduced them. "Cassie, these are the men who'll be watching over you when you're away from the estate. Sam, Patrick and Abel. Sam will lead the team and is who you'll coordinate with when you need to go somewhere."

Patrick and Abel kept their silence, but offered polite acknowledgment with a dip of their heads. Sam stepped forward and offered his hand. "It's nice to have you with us, Miss McClintock. Don't worry. We'll take good care of you."

Cassie aimed a wide-eyed look at Kir, then shook Sam's hand and offered a tremulous smile. "I didn't realize I was going to have guards." She smiled at the other two men, then stepped back and clasped her hands in front of her. "Is it awful if I say I hope this turns out to be the most boring job ever?"

The quip drew a chuckle out of each of his men, but Kir had to fight the urge to preen like a proud peacock. By her own admission, her life had been thrown on its head in the most dramatic fashion, and yet she still handled each surprise with class and a personable touch. "I suspect keeping up with you will be anything but boring." He hugged her tighter to his side and motioned the men to the doorway behind them with a lift of his chin. "I'll check in with you in an hour. If you find something sooner, let me know."

The men left as quickly as they'd arrived, but Cassie only made it until their footsteps sounded on the hardwood floors downstairs before she faced him. "Do I really need guards?"

"Do you want to go to work?"

"I have to go to work. It's my job."

"Then, yes. You need men to watch over you. Your

station has security, so they'll give you distance after they walk you inside, but when you leave the estate, they will be with you."

"For how long?"

"Until I'm certain there is no risk to you."

She paced to the bed and stared down at her suitcases like the contents inside might hold the answers her mind couldn't find. Her head snapped his direction. "You really think someone might have put bugs in my house?"

"It depends on who we're dealing with and the extent of their capabilities or resources. We will know soon enough, and we'll determine the best actions from there." He paused for a moment to give her time to process what he'd said before he laid on the rest. "I'll need your computer, your phone and any other devices you have as well."

"Why?"

"Because if they've been compromised in terms of access or tracking devices, we'll want to either clean or replace them."

She sat on the edge of the bed with a heavy sigh, a mix of weariness and reluctant humor drawing her mouth to the side in a wry mew. She dug her laptop from her briefcase and her phone from her purse then held them out to him. "You understand I'm supposed to be the one reporting on stories like this. Not the one featured in them."

He set the devices aside, sat beside her and smoothed his hand down her spine. "This will not last forever, *milaya*. The email you received is a strong lead for us, and I have significant resources to research it."

"A strong lead because you think whoever sent it is the same person who killed your guy?"

"Most likely, yes. Or an accomplice."

She sat with that a moment, and her gaze narrowed. "Tell me about your man. The one that was killed."

The memory of his soldier's pale body and sightless eyes aimed toward the ceiling flashed unwelcoming in his mind's eye. While the weeks that had passed had helped him focus and hone his anger, the fire still smoldered in his belly. Waiting. Poised and ready to strike. His muscles tightened, and the need to stand and pace crawled beneath his skin. "His name was Kevin. He was twenty-five."

She swallowed hard. "Same age as me."

"Yes. Too young to die and underserving of what happened. He was not like Sam or the other men. He worked on computers. Did research and specialized cyber activity."

Her eyebrows lifted in that pragmatic cut-to-the-chase way she had about her. "You mean he was a hacker."

The fact that she could draw even the faintest smile from him in such a moment was testament to how much he appreciated her candor and her clever mind. "Yes. Not as experienced as myself or other people I know, but insatiably curious and eager to learn." He paused a moment, weighed what he should and shouldn't share for her protection. "He helped me in tracking information about Alfonsi. When we found Kevin, we also found that his computer had been completely wiped—a fail-safe he had in place should someone ever try to access the data on it without the right credentials. That tells me whoever this was wanted information."

"But they didn't get in?"

"No."

"But why kill him to get to his computer? Why not just break in and try to access it when he wasn't there?"

"Kevin had security at his home. Cameras as well. Whoever got to him would have had to be exceptionally skilled with extensive resources to get past them."

"And the recordings?"

"Weren't captured. We found him stabbed in his bed with no sign of struggle."

"So, whoever it was, Kevin was expecting them."

"Exactly."

She thought on that for a moment. "Just because they tried to access his computer doesn't mean his death has anything to do with you or Sergei. Or Alfonsi for that matter. I mean, did he only work for you? If he did any side work for other people, they could have been looking for information for someone else. Or it could have been another client who didn't want Kevin sharing embarrassing information he'd learned."

"Except that the killer left a printed web article you wrote about Alfonsi with a candid picture of Sergei at the top."

Cold reality settled behind her gaze. "One of mine?"

He nodded, hating what he had to share next. "I thought it only coincidence before, but with the email you received this morning, I cannot be sure. What I do know is, it's a message. They know who brought Alfonsi down, and they want someone to pay."

For long moments, she held his stare, a vulnerability etched on her face that left him feeling inadequate and powerless. "Did you call the police?"

It was the last question he'd expected. And yet, it highlighted the most significant hurdle they'd face together. The one that had been the downfall for his mother and father. "*Nyet.* This is family business and will be dealt with as such."

Her stare shot to the carpet. To her clenched hands in

her lap. To the suitcases beside her on the bed. A frantic visual leapfrog that no doubt mimicked the internal debate going on inside her head.

With a frustrated huff, she stood and paced to the window. "So, how am I supposed to navigate all of this at work? With the men following me around, I mean."

The knot in his gut unwound, and his lungs surged on the first decent breath he'd taken since he'd pulled away from the curb in front of her house. Logistics he could deal with. Emotions and blending his unconventional life with a woman who'd been raised ultra-conventional were an entirely different proposition. "The men are accustomed to maintaining a low or shadow profile when necessary. They will remain at a distance when you're with people from work unless you're approached by someone suspicious."

Staring at the beautifully landscaped backyard and pool below, she seemed to consider what he'd shared, her profile pinched with thought as though inwardly imagining what such a scenario would look like. She spun a moment later, a fresh level of panic in her voice. "What about Aunt Frieda? And my family? If whoever this is has been listening, they'd know about them, too. Do you think whoever it is would do something to hurt them?"

"Frieda is a possibility. I can assign men to watch over her if you like. Or you can invite her to join you here. She can have the guest room and use the time to get familiar with the rest of us. The rest of your family is in Houston, yes?"

She padded closer to the bed. "Houston Heights, technically, but yes."

"Then we will take measures to ensure their safety as well."

"Without them knowing, right?"

He nodded. "If that is what you want, yes. Though, I suspect the person, or people, we're looking for don't have sufficient reach to take action in Houston. If they did, their response would have been much timelier and more direct." Namely, with a pointed assault at Sergei, Roman, or Kir himself, but he wasn't going to share such a detail at this juncture. "And what would you like to do about your aunt?"

Her gaze slid sideways and she worried her lower lip. As was her decisive nature, her focus sharpened quickly on Kir. "I'd feel better if she was here."

"Then we'll arrange it."

Downstairs, the front door *kachunked* opened. Footsteps and Evette's bright laughter rolled in right behind it. "Kir? Cassie?"

"The men said they are here," Olga grumbled, every word thick with her unapologetic Russian accent.

The crisp rattle of paper grocery bags being juggled then unloaded onto the kitchen counter sounded, then Emerson added, "Uncle Kir's probably upstairs bein' all lovey-dovey like he was last night."

"Uncle Kir can hear you." Kir stood and lowered his voice for Cassie alone. "Do you want company? Or would you rather have time alone?"

"We brought some groceries," Evette said from the kitchen below. "None of us knew what kind of comfort food you'd want, so we got everything from fruit to vodka."

"The vodka was Olga's idea," Emerson added helpfully.

"Who's Olga?" Cassie nearly whispered.

"Sergei's cook," Kir said equally quiet. "Though, she would be an efficient bodyguard as well should anyone threaten one of her chicks. Now—" he moved in close and hugged her to him "—what would you prefer?"

Between the opening and closing of the refrigerator door, Evette chuckled and said, "I'm startin' to think you're right on the lovey-dovey, kid. Maybe we should unload and come back in a bit."

Cassie rested her forehead on Kir's chest, but her torso shook on silent laughter. "No, no lovey-dovey," she called out to the trio below. "Just unpacking and mentally readjusting to a bizarre morning."

"You want some help?" Evette said. "Unpacking's kind of a no-brainer, and I've got ice cream to help with everything else."

One corner of Cassie's mouth lifted in a crooked smile. "They sound like my aunt."

"Well, then she'll fit in here with you just fine." He kissed her forehead, stepped away long enough to retrieve her laptop and phone, then urged her toward the hallway. "Come. See what they've brought you. Enjoy their company for a little while, and I'll handle the rest."

"What about Frieda?"

"Call her from Evette's phone. It's secured and will give the two of you a way to communicate until I can clean or replace yours. Tell her whatever you feel she needs to know, and let her know a man will be at her address within a half hour."

They reached the bottom of the stairs and Evette said, "Who's Frieda?"

"Cassie's aunt," Kir answered. "We're moving her here as well just to be safe."

"Sweet!" Evette said. "Maybe we should call Dorothy, too. The women can all camp over here and drown in comfort food while the men go beat on their chests."

Emerson spun from putting a monstrous box of Lucky Charms in the cupboard. "Where am I gonna go?"

Evette cocked an eyebrow. "You can be the guys' ambassador with free travel back and forth, but you have to promise not to share any girl secrets."

He shrugged and dug into the grocery bag on the floor beside him for whatever else was inside. "I can work with that."

Giggling like she truly was hosting a girls' sleepover instead of dealing with the fallout from a personal threat, Evette wrapped Cassie up at the waist with one arm and shooed Kir toward the door. "Go. Sergei and Roman are in Sergei's office waiting for you. Do whatever it is you badasses do, and we'll hold the fort down here."

From the fatigued, yet bewildered look on Cassie's face, the mix of slapstick hilarity and female companionship was probably just what she needed to get through the hours ahead. Leaving her, though, proved more difficult than he'd expected. "If you need me, they all have my number."

He forced one foot in front of the other—out the front door and along the meandering flagstone path through the beautiful backyard to the main house, making calls to his men with instructions to pick up Cassie's aunt. He nodded to the man stationed closest to the back door and strode through the quiet kitchen. Past the formal living area with its adjacent living room, and up the stairs to Sergei's office. Unlike the carriage house's more updated look, the landmark estate had been primarily restored with a nod to its heritage, complete with crystal chandeliers, custom rugs and silk drapes covering nine-foot windows. A mix of French Creole flair from days gone by offset by the most enviable modern conveniences.

He found Roman comfortably seated in front of Sergei's desk, his phone to one ear and his scowl aimed at Kir as he came through the door. "Start at 7:30 and watch until 10:30. All three camera angles available in the bar."

Sergei sat with one ankle perched across his knee, his elbows resting on the arms of his thick leather chair, and his fingers steepled in front of his chest.

Kir stalked toward the seat next to Roman. "Who's he talking to?" he said to Sergei.

"The manager on duty last night at *André's*," he answered low enough so as not to disrupt Roman's conversation. "We've pulled security tapes."

"I don't care how many hours it takes." Where Roman's voice had been commanding before, now it was all hard edge and cold warning. "You will sit with the man I've provided to help you, and you will capture pictures of any individuals who appear to be using their phone."

He waited for an agreement, then added, "Good. And this does not leave your office. Is that clear?"

Another pause. When he'd heard what he wanted, he ended the call and refocused on Kir. "It will take some time, but we should have photos for Cassie to review soon."

"And the email?" Kir asked.

"I called Knox," Sergei said. "Your skills are superior, but leveraging his industry connections will get us information more quickly than any trace might provide."

It was a valid point, and if it meant ensuring Cassie's safety and finding Kevin's killer, he was more than willing to swallow his pride and let someone else drive. He nodded and added his own plans. "I've sent Sam, Patrick and Abel to Cassie's house. They'll sweep for bugs and signs of forced entry."

Sergei inclined his head toward the devices in his lap. "And those?"

"Powered off. I'll screen them myself and will get her a new phone if they're compromised." He hesitated only a moment, then added, "I've sent my men to retrieve her aunt and bring her to the carriage house as well."

Roman shifted in his seat.

Sergei cocked one eyebrow.

"Her aunt is special to her," Kir added. "The only family member she is close to, and she was afraid for her safety."

"An appropriate action," Sergei said, surprising Kir. Even more surprising was the dry humor in his voice and the smug smile that came with it. "Though, I must confess, I don't envy you dancing around the questions posed by not just one woman, but two."

He wasn't wrong. To the degree he was able to share information, Cassie deserved to know the truth of who he was and what he did in the same way Evette did. But beyond that, the lines with family grew tricky. "I've met her once. I take her as a very no-nonsense woman with street smarts and common sense. My hope is that she will read between the lines and offer Cassie the support she needs without requiring specifics."

Sergei nodded. "Fair enough. So long as she is loyal to the family, there are no concerns from me." He volleyed his gaze between Kir and Roman. "What else?"

"Cassie's family is in Houston," Kir said. "I don't see whoever is behind this having that far of a reach, but leveraging them is a possibility."

"Not likely," Roman said, "but possible. We could engage other family connections in Texas."

Sergei shook his head. "Keep ties to us limited. Contact Beckett in Dallas. Ask him for security options in Houston, and hire them privately."

"Done," Kir said. "I will also upgrade security at my home so that Cassie can relocate there."

Roman chuckled and shared a sly grin with Sergei. "Note how quickly our brother seizes the opportunity to move his woman into his home?"

"Clever," Sergei said. "Though, I suspect he'll have a hard time moving her out of the carriage house with Evette playing interference. She likes having another woman close by."

Whether it was the razzing from his brothers, or the highs and lows of the day that made him snap, he couldn't say, but he spoke without censure. "She belongs with me."

Silence stretched in the wake of his clipped words, Roman and Sergei trading shocked and uncertain looks between each other.

Kir shifted in his chair and lowered his gaze. Of all the people who deserved his short-temper, Sergei wasn't among them. Not when he'd been one of the few people to stand by his side through the years. "My apologies. I meant no disrespect."

"No disrespect was taken," Sergei said. "Quite the contrary, I'm encouraged by the level of your commitment." He leaned forward, bracing his forearms on his desk and clasping his hands together. "I assume with the measures you've taken today, Cassie now knows the reasons behind your search?"

The question felt like a test. A trap like so many others that had been thrown before him growing up to see if he'd put his *bratva* in front of everyone else, or make the same poor choices as his father.

But Sergei wasn't like other *vors*. He was a true brother-in-arms. As fair as he was lethal. "Until this morning, she was unaware. But once the email came in and I demanded she move, I felt she deserved to know. Without it, she would not fully understand the risk."

Sergei didn't miss a beat. "Good." He looked to Roman, then back to Kir. "Then unless there's anything else, I think it's time to execute."

"Agreed." Kir stood, more than ready to engage in tangible actions after a morning of holding himself in check. He paused beside his chair only long enough to meet each brother's stare and added, "The sooner we find who's behind the email, the sooner we make them pay for what they've done."

Chapter Thirteen

One definite upside to having bodyguards that drove you everywhere—someone else had to deal with rush hour traffic on I-10. Add to that, Sergei—or Kir, or whoever it was in charge of security—didn't scrimp on cars, because the Mercedes they'd been carting her around in the last four days kept her comfortably isolated from the chaos outside.

Another thing she'd learned? Sam, Patrick and Abel were not only great at being stealthy, but had a decent sense of humor when Kir wasn't around. Only once had one of her camera guys asked about Abel watching them, and that had only been because a drunk at a festival had made the hugely unwise decision to try and pick her up.

She stared out the passenger window, noting all the unknown people from all walks of life going about their normal days not giving her the slightest attention. She should be happy. Or at least relieved that nothing else had happened. God knew, every single person in Kir's family had gone out of their way to make her feel comfortable. At home and relaxed. And, for the most part, she was. Especially, when it was just her, Kir and Frieda at the carriage house at night.

But something was off. Something that kept her feeling like there was a barrier between her and everyone else, and she was the only one aware of it.

Finally off the highway and making inroads to the Garden District, Sam met her gaze in the rearview mirror. "Same schedule tomorrow, Miss McClintock?"

"It's Cassie. Miss McClintock makes me feel weird. But yes, I won't work the later shift until Saturday and Sunday when I'm on set."

"I bet that's cool," Patrick said from the front passenger's seat. "I saw a story one time where they explained how the weathermen use a green wall for the maps. Is it really like that?"

"Pretty much. If you want, maybe on a weekend, you guys could come and watch one of the newscasts."

"They'd let you do that?" Sam said.

"Sure. Lots of people bring family and friends in."

Sam glanced at Patrick then focused on the road ahead. "Maybe after things calm down. I noticed your boss checking us out in the front parking lot tonight before you came out. Probably better to keep things low key for now."

Great. Dodging questions from her cameramen was one thing. Skirting questions from her editor would be a whole different terrain riddled with land mines.

Sam pulled into the drive, and Patrick hopped out and opened her back door out as soon as the gearshift was in park. "Any plans for you or your aunt tonight?"

"Definitely not for me. I got enough of humanity covering the Caribbean Festival this afternoon in near 100-degree heat." Cassie spied her aunt sitting sideways in the wingback on the other side of the carriage house's front picture window, her legs thrown over the arm and every scrap of her attention lasered on Cassie's arrival. She motioned toward her aunt. "Now, for her—there's

no telling. She's known far and wide for her spontane-
ity, so you'll just have to be prepared to wing it."

Patrick chuckled at that, as if he'd already learned as
much about Frieda. "We'll handle whatever she throws
at us." His steps slowed to give her distance as she
neared the carriage house. "Have a good night, Miss
McClintock."

"It's Cassie," she fired back the same way she always did, but added a friendly smile along with it as
she opened the door. "And you, too."

Settled in Frieda's lap was a clear Tupperware bowl
full of red grapes. She popped one into her mouth, not
bothering to take her eyes off Sam and Patrick strolling
toward the patio behind the main house. "Where in the
world does Kir find these guys?"

"Is that all you do all day while I'm gone? Ogle the
guys?"

"Hey, I've got loads of vacation time coming to me
and a prime, smorgasbord view. Don't deprive an old
woman of her pleasures." Her gaze shifted again, and
she nabbed another grape.

"I know twenty-year-olds that act older than you."
Free of her briefcase and purse, Cassie meandered over
to study the view from Frieda's perspective. "Hmm.
Maxwell. Kir said he's newer to the crew, but I'll
admit—he is a hottie."

"Girl, you're *not* kidding. All that dark hair, muscle
and swagger? Mmm-mmm-mmm." She spun, put her
feet on the floor and grinned up at Cassie. "You know,
I never thought I'd say I was a fan of drama, but this
whole murder debacle has its benefits."

"Ha!" Cassie kicked off the black flats she'd paired
with her khaki capris and black station polo shirt and
padded to the kitchen. "You're always a fan of drama."

"No, I'm not."

"Aunt Frieda, I called you four days ago and told you you had to leave your house because I'd caught the eye of a killer, and you responded like I'd invited you to take a weeklong vacation on the Riviera. By the time you walked through the door, you were practically dancing and flirting with Patrick. If that's not a love for drama I don't know what it is." She jerked open the refrigerator door and studied the multitude of leftovers stored inside.

Frieda stood and headed her way. "So, I've got an adventurous spirit. What's wrong with that? Plus, you know I'm a huge buttinsky with your love life. Do you really think I'm going to pass up an opportunity to get a front row seat while my future nephew-by-marriage sweeps my niece off her feet?" She slid in front of Cassie, grabbed an already opened bottle of white wine and shut the door before Cassie could grab anything. "By the way, no snacking. Dinner's in the main house in thirty minutes."

"Again? And drop it with the marriage stuff. We just started dating."

"Trust me, kiddo. You're way past dating." Frieda snagged a stemless wineglass from the cabinet and un-plugged the cork from the wine bottle. "And yes, din-ner every night at six thirty is a standing engagement around here. Olga's doing Mexican tonight. Enchilada casseroles—beef and chicken—*frijoles á la charra* and Spanish rice. I helped her practice on the *churros* for dessert this morning. Turns out they make for great breakfast snacks, too." She turned and lifted her glass in salute. "The woman can cook."

Cassie snatched Frieda's wine before she could pull it out of reach, dragged a chair from the kitchen table and settled in. "You two are awfully chummy these days."

Frieda harrumphed, turned for another glass and went about pouring another for herself. "What's not to get chummy about? You wouldn't believe some of the stories she tells. Chefs she's worked with. Mob bosses she's cooked for. Stuff she's seen, but pretended not to." She turned and leaned one hip against the counter. "Makes my time in New Orleans look like a trip to pre-K."

It hit her all at once. A huge, weighted deluge of emotion that poured over her like cold molasses. Maybe it was the aftereffects of spending four hours in the afternoon heat, or just the cumulative stress of holding her shit together for more days than she could count, but suddenly she was just too tired for everything.

She shook her head, sighed and stared at her glass atop the table's whitewash surface. "I don't know how you do it."

"Do what?"

Cassie lifted her head. "It's all so easy for you. Adjusting. Sliding into a new environment. Fitting in." A sharp bark of laughter filled with an embarrassing amount of bitterness hopped out. "You've been here four days, and you're completely at home. I'm dating— or as you would have it, near to matrimony—with Kir and I feel like a weird imposter that can't quite catch the same vibe as everyone else. Like… I don't know…"

Frieda carefully set her glass aside and lowered her voice. "Keep going. Like what?"

She didn't want it to come out. Didn't want to hear the tirade building inside her or the childlike words that came with it. The emotion behind it was too powerful. Too threatening and dangerous for her to process.

It rushed out anyway. "Like everyone here is in a whole different reality. A make-believe world where everyone's happy and supportive and actually enjoys each other's company. Half the time, I expect little cartoon forest creatures to sweep in and start tidying the house. But then I remember—*Oh, no. This is absolutely real because mixed in with it all is the reality that my boyfriend is a mobster and someone may, or may not, want me dead.* Do you realize how insane that all sounds? I mean, seriously. The Mad Hatter could walk through that door right now and I wouldn't be the least bit surprised. But I'm pretty sure you'd ask him to dance."

Her aunt stared back at her, the dumbfounded expression on her face one Cassie had never once seen before.

Heat crept up Cassie's neck, and her belly roiled in a grossly unpleasant spin. All her life, her aunt was the only one who'd shown her comfort. Made her laugh and accepted her no matter what. And yet, she'd spewed all over her like some petulant shrew. She stood, her legs shaking from a mix of adrenaline and fatigue. "Aunt Frieda, I'm sorry."

Frieda closed her gaping mouth and swept Cassie with a head-to-toe assessment. "Don't be."

"But I yelled at you. I made it sound like you were whack-a-doodle when it's me who's the odd man out."

Frieda pushed off the counter and strode toward her. "You are *not* whack-a-doodle. You're doing the best you can with the tools you have to work with." She gripped Cassie by both shoulders and held her tight. "That also wasn't yelling. It was a whole lot of emotion that's probably been brewing a while finally finding an outlet." She pulled her in for a fierce hug.

Cassie readily accepted it. Closed her eyes and let the love, comfort and relief her aunt's embrace offered soak into every cell. "I don't like losing control like that. I don't like hurting you, and I don't like feeling like the person sitting on the sidelines in the middle of a big party."

"Well, first—you didn't hurt me. Not in the slightest. Startled me, maybe. But you're going to have to learn to actually yell and throw in some choice obscenities before you have a chance at getting under my skin." She backed away only enough to meet Cassie's eyes and rubbed her hands up and down Cassie's arms. "And I know this new situation you've found yourself in is frightening. Not just because of the email or the person behind it, but because life's thrown you in a situation full of healthy, happy, loving people who won't let you keep them at a distance. They *like* you, Cassie. They think you're smart. They think you're funny. They think you're worthy. *Just like I do.*" She squeezed Cassie's shoulders and lowered her voice. "You're the only person keeping yourself on the sidelines. We're all here. Waiting. Ready for you to join in. All you have to do is stand up and step into it."

The pressure behind Cassie's chest pushed higher, wedging like a swelling knot at the base of her throat. Tears burned along the bridge of her nose. "I want to," she whispered. "I see them laughing. How easily they joke with each other and support one another." She swallowed. Or tried to. "What if I don't fit in? What if I let go, and they find out I'm not the person they thought I was?"

A soft, sad smile curved her aunt's lips. "Oh, sweet girl." She tenderly cupped the side of Cassie's face. "Are we talking about Kir's family? Or are we talking about yours?"

Two gently spoken questions, but they pierced straight to the heart of her. Wedged through the cracks Kir had started and pried past all the stones of disappointment she'd carried around for years. Was it really that simple? Was she holding herself apart from people she genuinely liked and wanted to be with based on the childlike need to fit in with the family she'd been born to?

A tear slipped free and spilled down her cheek. Then another. And another. With each one, more weight slipped free, and the knot inside her throat loosened. Her lips trembled as she spoke. "What kind of daughter am I? They're my blood. They raised me. But being with them—even talking to them—makes me feel so inadequate. Out of place."

"But being here?"

Her body shook on a half laugh, half cry as the truth came out. "Feels nice. A relief. Light and free. And then, as soon as I realize it, I feel guilty that I can't feel the same thing with my own family."

"It feels like you're being disloyal."

"Yes!"

"Oh, kiddo." Frieda sighed and pulled her in for another hug. Stroked her back and held her while the tears and sobs ran free. A complete and utter ugly cry, the likes of which she hadn't had since she was a preteen.

Only when the tears slowed did Frieda speak again, still holding her tight. "There are two kinds of family in this world, Cassie. Those we're born into and those we choose. We can't change who our parents are, or what we like and dislike, but we *can* choose happiness. Taking that step doesn't make you disloyal. It makes you healthy."

A ragged and somewhat broken chuckle slipped free as Cassie pulled from her aunt's embrace. "I'm not sure Mom and Dad would agree with you."

"Well, they don't have to agree with me. Just because they've both got PhD's doesn't mean they know everything. Accept them for who they are. Love them as they are. Then move on and make yourself happy. That's all any of us can do."

Cassie swiped her cheeks with the back of one hand and sniffled, the lightness in the wake of her crying jag blending with an awkward amount of mortification. "How'd you get so smart about this stuff, anyway? You sure you don't have a counseling degree somewhere you're not telling me about?"

"Nope." Frieda sashayed to the sofa's end table and plucked a few tissues from the colorful dispenser. "Life's been enough of an educator for me, thank you very much." She handed over the tissues and crossed her arms over her chest. "Feel better?"

Cassie wiped the rest of her tears and blew her nose. "More like I watched a four-day marathon of weepy chick flicks, but I don't think I'll go off on anyone at dinner."

"Good, then my job here is done." She waved Cassie toward the stairs. "How about if you go take a minute to unwind and get your face put back together. If the last few days are anything to go by, your guy is gonna show here in another fifteen to get us both to dinner. I'll stall for an extra ten or so."

God, she loved her aunt. Loved that, just like the people in Kir's family, there wasn't an ounce of pretense to her. What you saw with Frieda Shalaway was 100% what you got and that made being with her all the more sweet.

"Thanks, Aunt Frieda." She pressed a shaky kiss to her aunt's cheek. "Not sure what I'd do without you."

Frieda scoffed and trounced back to her wingback.

"You'd be bored, probably. Or maybe pursuing a degree as a neurosurgeon."

"Eww."

"I know, right?" She grabbed a battered paperback romance novel off the table beside her and cozied in. "Now skootch. I'm gonna get a good part in to take the edge off before your man gets here."

"Right." Cassie headed up the stairs.

"And put a cold compress on your eyes before you fix your makeup," Frieda added. "Kir's a charmer, but I don't think I'd like being around him if he thinks I'm the one that made you cry."

She wasn't wrong on that score. If Kir had demonstrated nothing else in the last three weeks, it was that he was the fiercest of protectors. "Duly noted."

Chapter Fourteen

It was hours later, the lively conversation that always surrounded dinner winding down, the delicious Mexican food heavy in Cassie's belly and the *churros'* lingering cinnamon and sugar still on her tongue when Evette asked, "Long day at work, Cassie? You seem tired tonight."

Kir had said the same thing when he'd come to retrieve her from her bedroom for dinner. He'd also paired it with a long, suspicious study of her face, but had let her have her space rather than dig for details.

The truth of the matter was, she felt lighter than she had in a very long time. Free of the rigid restrictions she'd kept herself bounded with for years and strangely open and more receptive to the people around her— even if the sensations were overwhelming. Much like taking noise-cancelling earphones off after a long flight, or exposing winter-protected skin to the first rays of summer.

She doubted anyone around the table would get such an explanation, though, so she gave Evette the same answer she'd given Kir. "I think it was the heat this afternoon. The Caribbean Festival starts tomorrow, and my crew was in the field for four hours talking to organizers and vendors."

"Cool! Mom, can we go?" Emerson said.

Evette looked to Sergei, who seemed to consider the request for a moment, then dipped a single nod. "I guess so," Evette said. "Assuming you get your chores done. But we'll go after dinner so it's not so hot." She stood, grabbed her plate, then Emerson's and headed for the kitchen. "How about you run up and get your shower done for the night. I think your daddy wants to talk to Aunt Cassie about some stuff."

Aunt Cassie.

When had that happened?

And more importantly, why would Sergei want to talk to her?

Unlike most kids who might have balked and whined about not being privy to conversations, Emerson just bobbed his head, hopped off his chair and made his rounds with goodnights in the forms of hugs and high fives. The last thing she'd expected was for him to stop at her chair and give her a hug of her own. "If you're not too tired after work," he said, "maybe you and Uncle Kir can go with us. If they've got games, he can win you a stuffed animal. He got me two of them at the state fair in Shreveport last year."

"We will see," Kir said before Cassie could answer. "Cassie works on weekends, and if she covers the festival again tomorrow, she may be too tired."

"I can rally," she said to Emerson, surprising herself. "I haven't really been to a festival just for fun since I was your age."

"Why not? They're a blast."

Across the table, Aunt Frieda subtly cocked one eyebrow. A silent dare for her to finish what she'd started.

Cassie wrinkled her nose, but focused on Emerson. "My parents weren't big on festivals. They thought it was a waste of money and didn't care for the noise or the people. They were miserable, so I quit asking to go."

Emerson shook his head like she'd just told him she didn't believe in Santa Claus. "That's crazy. Who'd pass up the chance for funnel cakes?"

"You will," Evette cut in, "if you don't go take your shower and get into bed."

"Ugh," he said to his mom with a good-natured frown. "Okay, I'm going. Night, everyone."

A round of goodnights and wishes for sweet dreams followed in his wake, but more than a few gazes lingered on her, unspoken questions and open curiosity behind their eyes.

Evette wasn't content to hold her questions, though. "You really haven't been to a festival since you were his age?"

Cassie shrugged and tried to downplay what she'd shared, uncomfortable with the attention. "I've been to some since I moved here."

"She means outside covering one for a station," Frieda said. She shifted her attention to Evette. "I did manage to get her to Mardi Gras the first year. I thought her eyes were gonna bug out of her head the first time a guy begged her to flash her boobs."

"That will not happen to her again," Kir stated matter-of-factly then sipped his coffee.

Sergei grinned.

Roman chuckled.

Frieda and Evette both cackled, but it was Frieda who rounded off the topic. "Yeah, well, I'm not too worried about you having to keep her from hearing the suggestion again. We left about two minutes after it happened, and I haven't been able to get her to go back since."

"We'll get her there," Evette said. "You can't spend

time around the lot of us and not have a little wild side rub off on ya." She winked at Cassie and took a drink of her iced tea.

Frieda's smile softened and a knowing tone slipped into her voice. "I'm counting on it."

Kir must have sensed the byplay behind her aunt's words, because his gaze shot to Frieda, then to Cassie. For a moment, he looked as if he might start digging in with questions.

Sergei intervened before he could. "If we are to make it a family outing tomorrow, then perhaps it would be best for Kir to review what we've learned so Cassie can get some rest."

A silent look passed between the three men at the table. Kir looked conflicted at best, but Roman and Sergei appeared utterly resolved. Given the clueless expressions on Frieda and Evette's faces, the silent communication moving between them was as indecipherable to them as it was to Cassie.

Kir nodded to Sergei, stood and retrieved a folder from the antique buffet table behind them. "We've traced the email Cassie received Sunday morning. It was sent from an IP address originating from the public library. The computer address appears to be one of the public computers provided by the library." He sat back in his seat beside Cassie. "One of Axel McKee's brothers in Dallas is a very skilled hacker. Knox Torren. He's been known to assist the government and has extensive connections in the cyber industry."

"His wife, Darya, is the one I told you about from Russia," Evette added. "She and Sergei knew each other, which is how our family ended up tied to them. They helped each other out when a loon from Russia was after Darya."

Cassie's head snapped back, and she blurted, "Was after her for what?"

"Unspeakable things that could not be allowed," Sergei answered with a cold finality that said whoever the loon from Russia was, he probably wasn't breathing anymore.

Cassie sucked in a slow breath and opted to leave that story alone for the time being. "Okay, so this Knox guy is really good."

"Very good," Kir said. "He used connections and found that the sender account was created only minutes before the email was sent from the same IP address."

"The library has security cameras," Roman said. "We've pulled their footage and compiled snapshots of everyone using public computers during the timeframe the account was created and the email sent."

Kir opened the folder and slid it in front of her. "We pulled footage from *André's* Saturday night as well. Any individual noted with a phone in their hand was captured in a still photo for you to review. Facial recognition did not compile any matches, but the camera angles from the library do not provide clean shots of all people in the computer area."

Cassie's heart kicked to a higher pace, and whatever remnants from her early crying jag remained scattered on a wave of adrenaline. There were two stacks bound by clips—one with color pictures and a background that was unmistakably from the bar area at *André's*, and another in grainy black and white in an office-type environment. She flipped through the library pictures first. A woman with two children in tow. A balding heavyset man. A person wearing sweats and a ball cap that she was pretty sure was a woman, but couldn't be positive. A teenage boy toting a backpack that looked like it weighed a ton.

She studied the next three behind it, then went back to the top of the stack. "There aren't very many from the library."

"The library opened at 10 a.m. that morning," Roman said. "The email was sent at 10:30 a.m. Those were the only people there during that time period."

Cassie hesitated at the picture of the woman in the ball cap. "I can't make a face out on this one at all."

"They only have one camera in the computer room," Kir said. "None of the other angles from other rooms gave us any more detail."

With a sigh, Cassie shifted to the pictures from *André's*. "Well, you had a lot more to choose from here."

Frieda leaned in for a peek and chuckled. "That's because people can't do without their phones anymore. I remember refusing to go someplace with my mom and dad because I was waiting for a boy to call and didn't want to miss it."

"No way," Evette said.

Cassie flipped to the last photo—a blurred profile image of the woman she'd seen at the bar that night tucking her phone into her purse.

"Way," Frieda said. "When call waiting became a thing and you could actually buy an answering machine, it was as revolutionary as a cordless phone."

The whole table, save Cassie, laughed.

Kir must have noted her attention rooted on the photo in front of her, because his laughter died off and he leaned closer. "You know this person?"

"No, but I remember seeing her at the restaurant when Evette and I were coming out of the bathroom."

Evette stood and came around to look over Cassie's shoulder. "I don't know her."

"I don't think I do either, but she seemed familiar to me that night." She went back to the top of the stack. "Any chance I could study the live videos? Maybe if I see them in motion it'll trigger something?"

Roman looked to Kir, a silent question on his face.

Kir nodded. "Of course. I'll upload them and provide you with a link so you can study them as you have time."

She tucked the pictures back inside the folder. The reporter in her wanted to ask questions. To dig and claw her way into every action Kir, Sergei and Roman had taken.

But another, more quiet and gentle instinct urged her to relax. To let go and trust. An odd and foreign sensation to be sure, but also a huge relief. "So, does that mean we're at a dead end?"

"There is no such thing as a dead end," Sergei said, pulling his wife closer to his side and wrapping his arm around her waist. "Whoever this is wants vengeance for a wrong they feel has been done to them. Enough to take another's life. Motive and anger will win out over cleverness and patience, eventually. Until then, we remain vigilant and ready."

Kir covered Cassie's hand on the table with his own and gave a gentle squeeze. "We will keep you safe, *malyshka*. This level of security will not always be necessary."

This *level* of security.

Not that the security would go away after they found whoever they were after.

A minor nuance to be sure, but one her mind latched

onto. Much the same way her parents would have jumped in to add their own censure.

We can't change who our parents are, or what we like and dislike, but we can choose happiness.

Did *she* really mind having someone watching over her? Evette dealt with it every day and didn't seem to mind. Emerson, too. And Sam, Patrick and Abel had been anything but a burden the last several days. More of a security blanket than a hindrance. Who cared about details like that if it meant time with Kir? If it meant enjoying family dinners like tonight and trips to festivals with people who knew how to enjoy themselves?

"I don't mind the security," she said. "I'm adjusting, even if it is a little weird."

"Good." He palmed the back of her neck and pulled her in for a quick kiss. "Then, how about if we get you back to the carriage house so you can rest?"

"Sure." She stood, picked up her plate and reached for Kir's. "I'll just help Evette clean up first."

"Oh, no." Frieda hopped up, hustled around the table and took both the plates from Cassie. "You two go and take a load off. I'll help Evette, then I'm gonna hit Olga up about seeing a movie."

The comment earned her aunt more than one surprised look.

Cassie opened her mouth to ask when those plans had come about, but her aunt shot her a *don't-even-think-about-it* look.

Ah.

Ever the sneaky one, her aunt was either in matchmaker mode, or flat-out consorting with Kir to give them some alone time. Not that he'd let Aunt Frieda's presence be a deterrent for sleeping in her bed the last four nights. He'd also proven himself adept at using hands-on sexual attention to ensure the recent changes in Cassie's life didn't impact how soundly she slept.

"Well, okay then." She stood and looked to Kir whose smirk clearly indicated he was aware of what her aunt was up to. "Looks like I'm all yours."

"That, *vozlyublennaya*, has never been in question." He stood, kissed the back of her hand and offered the table at large a semi-bow. "If you'll excuse us?"

The walk along the meandering flagstone path was quiet, only a few cicadas filling the summer night with their songs and the dwindling hum of cars winding through the neighborhood. Kir ambled beside her, his gait unhurried. He covered her hand notched in the crook of his elbow with his free one as if he had all the time and patience in the world.

Inside the carriage house, only a single lamp near the front window was lit. Rather than turn on any others, Kir led her straight to the stairs and up to the master bedroom.

She stopped at the foot of the bed and faced him. "You're quiet tonight."

Kir flipped on the bedside lamp, then emptied his pockets of his cell phone and wallet and set them on the nightstand. "One could say the same of you." He padded to the oversized chair in the corner, shrugged off his suit jacket and toed off his shoes.

"The heat zapped me."

"Is that so?" His belt went next. Then his button-down. "I'll have to talk to the men about paying more attention to you in the heat."

Well, shit. "There's no need to talk to them. It's on me to pay attention to my health, not them. And besides, it didn't really hit me until I got home. Probably doesn't help that Frieda keeps it like a refrigerator in here."

"Mmm-hmm." Clad only in black boxer briefs, he strolled toward her, his demeanor as relaxed and unthreatening as it had been on the walk over. Only this time she had the added benefit of the dim lights and shadows playing across each defined muscle on his body. A body she could no more pretend not to notice than she could hide her own body's shivering response. He knew how his touch impacted her. Seemed to mirror the same soul-rattling sensation anytime they were skin to skin. And while a part of her acknowledged he was likely leveraging their connection to bind her closer to him, she couldn't quite find the will to fight it. Didn't want to deny herself the pleasure any more than she wanted to stop breathing.

He halted right in front of her. "Shoes off, Cassie."

"We don't normally go straight to bed. You like to Netflix a little after dinner."

"I like to Netflix when your aunt is here and I'm trying not to make it blatantly obvious I want you in our bed."

Our bed.

Not her bed.

Or his bed.

"Your aunt isn't here tonight," he said, "so I don't have to wait. Except for you to take off your shoes so that I can undress you at my leisure."

Oh, boy.

It was bad enough that he had a way with words, but paired with his accent and the sexy rumble of his voice, physical foreplay was a bonus more than a necessity.

Who are you kidding, Cassie? All the man has to do is look at you and crook one of those grins, and you're hot, bothered and ready to go.

She shook off the mental byplay that was suspi-

ciously carried on her aunt's voice and stepped out of
her sandals. "You're telling me I'm not going to see the
end of *Mad Men* season three tonight?"

He slid one of the straps from the pretty gold sundress she'd put on before dinner over her shoulder, then
repeated the move with the other. "I'm telling you the
likelihood of you having the energy or desire to do anything but fall asleep naked next to me once I'm done
is negligible at best." One tug of the cotton fabric and
the dress slid to her waist, barely clinging to her hips.

His eyes locked on her exposed breasts, and a low,
appreciative rumble rolled up his throat. "You weren't
wearing a bra at dinner, *milaya*."

"I'm barely a 34C, Kir, and the jump from a B to
a C cup is more wishful thinking than anything. Unless I'm sporting a fitted T-shirt, planning on vigorous
exercise, or hanging out in Antarctica, I can get away
without wearing bras just about anywhere."

"Perhaps." He slipped his fingers beneath the fabric at her hips and pushed her dress to the floor. "But
now that I know the possibility exists, I'll be wondering if other men notice and will have to fight the urge to
murder anyone who so much as glances at your chest."

"You wouldn't."

Slowly sinking to his heels in front of her, he teased
his fingers over the silky surface of her boy shorts.
His breath when he spoke whispered against her inner
thighs. "Perhaps I wouldn't murder them." He hooked
his fingers in the waistband of her panties, languidly
pulled them toward her ankles, then looked up. "But I
assure you, they would never again dare to covet what's
mine."

Lost.

Found.

Possessed.

He was crouched before her. An undeniably submissive pose on anyone else, but there was no mistaking who was in charge in that moment. Who was the hunter, and who was the hunted.

She gloried in it. Let what was left of her worries and the need for control slip like an invisible cloak from her shoulders and embraced the promise behind his eyes as he stood. Surrendered to the magic of his touch against her exposed skin. Luxuriated in his kiss until the only thing that existed was the press of his body against hers and their connection.

From the very beginning, it had been this way with them. A unique bond her mind struggled to understand, but that a deeper, more instinctual part of herself not only accepted, but craved. A natural flow. A grounding the same as electricity seeking contact with the earth. Her energy rooted itself in him. Found indescribable silence, peace and pleasure within his arms.

He maneuvered them both to the bed. Leisurely tossed aside pillows and peeled the silky comforter from beneath her until they lay beside each other in a tangle of arms and legs. Sensation was all she knew. All she needed. The cool crisp sheets. Kir's taut hot skin. The taste of him. The scent of him. The brush of his fingertips along the curve of her hip, and the teasing path he drew along the top and lower swells of her breasts.

It was heaven. An indulgence she was content to ride as he slowly built her pleasure. Trusted and let him guide her at the pace he'd chosen.

She stroked his upper arms. His shoulders. His chest and each defined indentation along his belly, savoring the strength of him and the way his muscles moved beneath her palms. So lost in her exploration and the demand of his lips, the brush of his boxer briefs against her fingertips was a shock. She pulled away from his mouth only enough to meet his gaze and hooked her fingers in the waistband. "Why are these on?"

Before she could gain any ground at pulling the briefs off, he caught her wrist, rolled her to her back and pinned her hands on either side of her head. "Because I want to talk to you before I love you, and my cock gets greedy and overrides good sense when you're naked and next to me."

She grinned up at him and rolled her hips against his, his shaft a delicious press against her aching center. "On this issue, I'm afraid I'm going to have to agree with your cock. Now is not the time for conversation."

His groan and the frustration glimpsed before his eyelids slipped shut was supremely gratifying. But the stern press of his lips when he opened them again and his tightened grip on her wrists dampened her hope for goading him into action. "Now is exactly the time for conversation."

"Why?"

He held her gaze for a moment, studying her features intently. "Because we're alone. Because you're naked beneath me where I can hold you the way you need to be held when you tell me what happened today."

"Nothing happened today."

"Ah, *malyshka*." He relinquished one of her wrists and cupped the side of her face. "You and I both know the days since you moved here have been a struggle for you. You've been tense. Withdrawn, but watchful.

"But today was different. I knew it the minute I saw you. Felt it at dinner and after as we walked together."

The rising passion and need he'd built collided with

the vulnerable moment. Left her exposed and trembling despite the heat radiating off him.

His voice softened. Shifted to a subtle croon as reverent as his touch. "I understand the fear in sharing. Meeting you has forced me to face my own in many ways and will no doubt bring more to light. But how can I help you face yours if you do not share them with me?"

Not a demand for information.

Not censure, or a lecture on what she should or shouldn't do.

But a desire to help. A partner demonstrating awareness and a willingness to stand beside her.

And the truth of it was—he was right. If she wanted to choose happiness, the first step was owning her truth. No matter how foolish or childlike it sounded inside her own head.

She splayed her hands against his pecs. Centered herself in the steady rhythm of his heart beneath her palm and pulled in a deep, stabilizing breath. "Your family is big. Loud. Expressive and funny."

He nodded, his focus solely on the words she said.

"Mine wasn't like that at all. Dinners were…awkward. So quiet it was almost oppressive. And when there was conversation, it was stilted and bland."

"And you are having a hard time adjusting?"

She couldn't stop the sharp bark of laughter. "No. Quite the opposite."

His frown was subtle, one geared toward trying to comprehend more than anger.

She swallowed. Or at least tried to. No easy feat considering how defenseless she felt in that moment. "I like it."

A spark of comprehension settled behind his eyes, but he held his silence.

"Being with your family—seeing how they interact and how open and supportive they are to each other—I wanted to be a part of it, but at the same time, I feel like I'm giving up on my own family."

"And if you give up the family you were born to and the struggles that come with it, then what are you left with?" he finished for her.

"Exactly," she said. "It's like being an office worker and waking up one day to find someone's replaced all your staplers and file folders for camping gear, toys and surfing equipment. It's all shiny, fascinating stuff with lots of potential to enjoy, but you don't have a clue what to do with it all. And more than that, you're afraid whoever it was that owned the office stuff is going to walk in at any moment and bust you for goofing off."

He smiled down at her. "That's an unusual analogy, but a very effective one." He traced the line of her cheek, the tenderness in his gaze beyond anything she'd thought possible from a man as hard and unyielding as Kir. "Thank you for sharing with me, *malyshka*."

"You don't think it's stupid?"

Something behind his gaze shifted, pain peeking out from behind his sky-blue eyes then disappearing behind a soft smile. "No. My family was not like yours, but they left their mark on me as well. It took me many years before I trusted Sergei. Even more before I trusted Roman. That you faced your past in a matter of days is something to be proud of."

She wrapped her arms around his neck and toyed with his hair where it touched the nape of his neck. "Tell me about them."

"*Nyet*. Not tonight." A softly spoken refusal, but unbending all the same. He skimmed his mouth against hers. "My woman has had enough words and revelations for one day." His tongue teased the seam of her lips as he rolled his hips against hers. "I think she's earned my undivided attention and devotion."

A simple change in focus.

The mere hint of a kiss paired with the wicked promise in his eyes, and she was ready. Willing and eager to set everything aside save the erotic haven he offered. She traced the waistband of his briefs. "Well, then we'd better get rid of these."

His smile deepened, a bit of playfulness mingling with the devilish glint in his eyes. "As you wish, *milaya*." He rolled to his back and shed himself of his briefs, but rather than slide back between her legs, he pulled her across him.

"Whoa!" She straddled his hips and braced her hands on his chest. "What happened to getting undivided attention and devotion?"

He chuckled, but the sound was that of a deeply satisfied male. He caressed her hips. Up her sides and inward to tease the lower swells of her breasts. "Oh, believe me, beautiful. With this view, nothing will distract me."

Her eyes slipped closed, the delicious warmth and rasp of his fingertips against her hardened nipples making the muscles at her core clench. She tried for a sassy quip, but it came out breathless and distracted. "So, this isn't just a ploy for me to do all the work?"

He gently pinched her nipples. Tugged and rolled them in unhurried pulls. "Does it feel like you're doing the work?"

Nope. Not even a little bit. If anything, being astride him rather than beneath him was freeing. As liberating as the rest of the night had been. She shook her head and opened her eyes. "No."

"Good." He lifted his hips and pressed his shaft

against her clit. "Because I'm going to give you my cock just like this." He undulated again, the slickness between her folds letting him glide easily against her. "Going to pet and tease you over and over until you beg me to let you come."

Was he kidding? She was already ready to beg, her hips eagerly matching the rhythm he'd set.

She widened her knees, angling for more pressure on her clit.

Kir shifted his hips before she could. *"Nyet."* Before she could protest, the head of him nudged her entrance. "You're not supposed to do the work, remember?"

A whimper slipped up her throat, every ounce of her attention focused on the promise of having him inside her. Filling her. Stretching and connecting him to her. She tried to push backward to gain more of him, but he stopped her with hands at her hips.

She wriggled again. "Stop teasing me."

"I'm not teasing you, *vozlyublennaya.*" He pressed inside her. Infinitesimally slow increments that maddened her even as his leisurely advance sent her need reeling. "I'm loving you. Giving your body what it needs." Only once he was seated fully inside her, did he begin to truly move. To pump his hips over and over, the cadence slowly escalating with the pace of her heart.

God, he felt good. Not just the hard length of him shuttling in and out of her, but the commanding feel of his hands at her hips. Each press of his pelvis against hers, and the flex of his muscles as he moved.

He shifted beneath her, took one nipple his mouth and suckled deep.

Pleasure shot straight between her legs, each flick of his tongue against the sensitive tip catapulting her higher. Blending with the drag of his cockhead inside her until she couldn't breathe. Could only feel. Want. Pray for release.

"Kir." It was a whisper at best. A plea paired with the press of her hand against the back of his head. "Please."

His growl as he switched from one breast to the other was every bit as intoxicating as the rest of him. A reminder of the primal man beneath the refined exterior he showed the rest of the world. He licked her other nipple. "Please what?"

The question wouldn't compute. Couldn't be processed amongst the sensations bombarding her body. The wet heat of his mouth. The slick glide of his cock. The sheer power of his body, and the feel of them joined together.

He nipped her distended nipple and locked his eyes on hers. "You want to come, yes?"

Want was too insignificant. She *needed* to come. Craved it desperately. "Yes. Please."

His hand at her hip slid inward and he slicked his thumb through the wetness coating her sex. "I need it, too, *malyshka*." He circled her swollen clit, the pressure colliding with the tightening pressure in her belly. "Need to feel your sweet pussy fisting me so I can mark you as mine."

Oh, hell.

It was right there. So close.

He slid the hand between her shoulder blades upward and fisted the hair at the back of her head. "Come, beautiful." He pressed his thumb harder and tightened his fist in her hair. "Come and show me you're mine."

Fuck.

Her sex contracted. Pulsed around his shaft with the same unyielding grip he held on her hair and stole her breath. Made her legs tremble and her heart stutter.

His hips slammed against hers—once, twice, three times—and his cock jerked inside her. Sent a fresh new rippling wave of aftershocks powering through her even as his grip on her hair eased.

He cupped the back of her neck. Stroked the curve of her hip and slowly pumped his shaft inside her, guiding them both through the cresting sensations and down from the peak.

Bit by bit, his muscles eased, and her breath steadied. A string of words murmured in Russian fell from his lips, and he pulled her flush against him.

She was more than content to comply, the lethargy from her release quickly sinking into her muscles and dissipating what stress lingered from the day. She sighed and settled her head atop his chest. "What did that mean?"

The comforting stroke of his hand up and down her spine faltered for a moment. He palmed the back of her head and wrapped his other arm around her waist. "I said that this is where you belong. With me. With my family."

You're the only person keeping yourself on the sidelines. We're all here. Waiting. Ready for you to join in.

We can choose happiness.

She'd already taken the biggest step. Had not only found her truth, but had shared it with Kir. Could she let all of her fears go? Release the self-judgment and simply enjoy the gift she'd been given?

She focused on the steady beat of his heart beneath her ear. Let her eyes slip closed and went with the moment. "I'm done fighting it. This is where I want to be." She lifted her head and met his eyes. "Especially with you."

His smile was instant, soft and understanding even

as it seemed to hold a thread of satisfaction. He cupped the back of her head and lifted his own to press a tender kiss to her lips. "That's good, *milaya*." He guided her head back to his chest and wrapped her up tight. "Because I have no intention of letting you get away."

Chapter Fifteen

Good things definitely came in odd packages. If someone had told Cassie a year ago that she'd not only find an attractive, successful and attentive boyfriend, but a supportive and happy family to boot by means of a murder, she'd have outright laughed in their face.

But that was exactly what life had handed her. Granted, her *attentive* boyfriend often strayed into possessive territory, but after having been mostly ignored her whole life, sometimes his overbearing side was an exquisite comfort. And when she felt the need to push back and gain some room, he usually acquiesced.

Usually.

Except when it came to her safety.

She stared out the back window of the Mercedes, her stupid grin in the reflection blending with the Sunday midmorning sun as it glinted off the buildings lining I-10. The last few days had been perfect. The festival outing on Friday full of laughter, noise, junk food and a little silliness. The Saturday night dinner with his family relaxed, and the surprise trip to the opera Kir took her on afterward an utter delight. Who knew a badass mobster would have a thing for opera? Or that she'd actually enjoy it?

Sam exited the highway and navigated the near-empty streets.

That was another funny thing. Usually, she'd catch herself holding her breath and clenching her hands around the steering wheel on the drive in to work. A focus and a tension that made her think of nothing else but gaining ground in her career. Not what the weather was like. Not what was going on around her—unless, of course, it was newsworthy. Definitely not what she'd be doing when she got home.

But the last three days? Zero tension. Nada. Sure, in the back of her mind she was thinking of new angles or stories she might pursue, but mostly she'd just handled whatever assignments were given to her and taken things moment to moment. And through it all, she'd texted with Kir and Evette and looked forward to what was lined up after she clocked off for the night. Talk about your novel developments.

The Mercedes glided to a stop in front of the station, pulling her from her happy thoughts.

"Same time tonight, Miss McClintock?" Sam said as Patrick alighted from the front passenger seat and opened her door.

"You're really not gonna drop the Miss McClintock thing are you?" she said.

Sam chuckled. "If Mr. Vasilek was your boss, would you?"

"Good point." She took the hand Patrick offered, slid out of the back seat and ducked down for eye contact with Sam. "And yes, I should be out around 10:45 tonight. If I need to leave the building, I'll let you know."

"Hey, girl," Bonnie said the second Cassie hit the lobby, but her googly eyes were all for watching Patrick still waiting by the car to ensure Cassie made it in safely. "You ever going to tell me who those two look-ers are?"

"Just some guys my new boyfriend hired to pick me up and drop me off at work. He's got a protective streak and thinks me being a television reporter makes me a target for crazy people."

Not a huge stretch from the truth, considering you had to be crazy to take someone's life in cold blood.

"A protective streak and loaded," Bonnie said. She grinned at Cassie and added, "Any chance the new boy-friend is the hot dude in the suit you went to El Torro with a few weeks back?"

"That's the one."

"Does he have any brothers?"

Oh, now *that* was an intriguing idea. Roman and Bonnie? She and Bonnie weren't BFFs by any stretch, but Cassie had talked to her enough over the last few weeks to surmise Bonnie could absolutely use her own Cinderella story with a Russian prince. "Actually, he does. But he's not really the suit type like Kir unless there's a bona fide reason to wear one. He's more the T-shirt and jeans fella."

"I like T-shirts and jeans." She waggled the piece of paper pinched between her fingers in the air—an in-voice of some kind by the looks of it. "I just don't like it when they can't hold down a job, charge up my only credit card and disappear out of nowhere."

"Oh, no."

"Oh, yes." She shook her head, sighed and folded the paper up. "Doesn't matter. He was a loser anyway. Bet-ter for me to focus on Pops and get his bills paid off."

"Is he doing any better?"

Her lips curved in a tight smile, but there wasn't

much hope in the gesture. "'Bout as good as we can hope for unless they find him a donor."

"I'm sure they will. You just need to hang in there long enough for it to happen."

Bonnie gave her a look that said she'd believe such an eventuality only once she won the lottery. "Funny thing about livers and the people who figure out who's gonna get 'em. They tend to go to the people who haven't run the ones they were born with into the ground with drugs and alcohol. My dad thinks a fifth of whiskey falls under good hydration habits and is probably going to die with a cigarette between his fingers. He's not high on their list."

Yep. Bonnie definitely needed a prince. Or at least a steady full-time job with benefits and to only have to take care of herself for a change.

Before Cassie could come up with something comforting or encouraging to say, Bonnie shifted gears and jerked her head toward the door that led to the newsroom. "By the way, a friendly heads-up. The green-eyed monster is in today."

"What?" The code name they'd come up with for Lizbet during one of their talks sent Cassie's gaze darting for the door. Turns out, Bonnie wasn't any fonder of her nemesis than Cassie was. "She's supposed to be off today."

"That's what I thought, too, but she showed about ten minutes before you. A little more out of breath than normal, but all gussied up and ready for action."

Well, shit. She and Lizbet hadn't had any direct runins for the last few weeks, but just the thought of her kind of put a damper on Cassie's good mood.

Why do you care? It doesn't have to be a competition. You've got zero reason to try and prove yourself.

Wow. She really was on the happy path of acceptance these days if she could string all those thoughts
together. She'd have to text Aunt Frieda ASAP and share
the good news.

She shrugged and headed for the door, enjoying the
lightness that came in the wake of her thoughts. "Oh,
well. Maybe there's something unexpected they needed
her to cover."

"Not your problem, sister. You're prime time and on
the camera today."

Exactly.

Life was good. All she had to do was enjoy it and be
grateful. She swiped her badge, pulled the door open
and waved to Bonnie. "See you at lunchtime."

"Deal."

Inside the bullpen where the reporters' desks were
lined up, it was mostly quiet. One of her male colleagues
tap-tap-tapped away at his keyboard, the epitome of
professional focus. Another one had his chin propped
on one hand, his eyes halfway closed. Lizbet's desk
was empty.

"Hey, Tom," she said to the first man, then rapped
her knuckles on the second one's desk as she passed.
"Long night, Jerry?"

"Something like that," he said, barely stirring.

She unloaded her briefcase, docked her laptop and
settled herself behind her desk. The upside to getting in
a little early meant she'd have some extra time to give
a second look to the *André's* security footage, even if
she wasn't very hopeful of finding anything new. The
first pass through she'd taken pains to study the woman
she'd originally recognized, but nothing had triggered
her memory. And, if the woman had actually managed
to take a picture of Cassie and Kir with her phone, she

had to have done it during one of the many passes the bartender had made in front of her.

Look. Fast forward. Pause. Rewind. Look again.

After thirty minutes, she was pretty sure she looked as interested in the images on her screen as Jerry was looking at his.

Her desk phone rang, a sharp, technical sound that visibly startled everyone in the room.

The readout showed her editor, Ed, calling from his office.

Odd. He rarely came in on the weekends unless a big story was brewing, or he'd had a roaring fight with his wife.

"Sorry," Cassie murmured to Jerry and Tom, then picked up the phone. "Yes, sir?"

"Need you to come up." On the bright side, he sounded distracted more than mad. A plus for whatever he wanted to talk about.

"Sure, let me grab something to write on. Or do I need to bring my computer?"

"Just yourself."

An uncomfortable, prickling awareness whispered across her shoulders. As if someone had cracked a non-existent window in the middle of a winter storm. "Okay. I'll be right there."

Through the hall and past the studio, everything and everyone carried on as she'd expect them to, but the sense that something was different—off-kilter or happening as an alternate reality—clung to every step. She took the stairs to the second floor where the managers' offices were located. Just as she opened the stairwell door and stepped out, the elevator down the hall dinged and the doors swooshed open.

A flash of red registered in her peripheral vision, but

the elevator doors slipped shut before she reached them. Her editor's door snapped open just as she reached it.

"Hey, Cassie." He smoothed his hand down the front of his T-shirt the way he would've if he'd been wearing a tie. "Come on in and have a seat."

"Is something big going on?" She sat in one of the two chairs angled in front of his desk. "I didn't see any special news being reported when I got ready this morning."

"Hmm?" He looked up from the distracted frown he'd aimed at his desk and shook his head. "Oh, no. No special coverage needed. We just…" He looked to the side as though searching for the right words, then refocused on her. "We have a situation we need to deal with."

"A situation."

"Yes."

Not good. Not good at all considering the uncertainty behind Ed's eyes. He was a good man. Direct. To the point on both praise and criticism. So, if he was stalling and struggling to put words behind what needed to be said, something was seriously wrong.

She cleared her throat and straightened her spine. "Well, then, maybe the best thing to do is just get it out there."

He studied her a moment, his mouth pinched tight. "Right." He splayed his hands on the desk, focused on them for a good three heartbeats, then lifted his head and pinned his gaze on her. "We received information last night that you're directly involved with a local mafia organization and that you've been leveraging the station's resources to further their interests."

The chill that had chased her every step upstairs settled iceberg hard against her skin, and if she hadn't been sitting down, the dizziness that hit her would have knocked her over. "I'm sorry…what?"

He huffed out an awkward chuckle and clasped his hands together. "That was my reaction, too, but the allegation is a pretty serious one, and one of the higher-ups insisted it was a legitimate claim we needed to address."

"Address how?"

"Well, that all depends. I told my boss the odds of it being true were slim, but then I remembered the men in the fancy car who've been picking you up lately. When I talked to one of your video guys, they said they'd spotted men following your crew while you're working, too. So, I thought it best I follow up immediately."

Shit.

Shit, shit, shit.

Her heart took off at a sprint, and a cold sweat broke out along the back of her neck. "I hope you don't mind my asking, but where did this tip come from?"

"One of the execs. They were at some big fund-raiser last night. The Midsummer Masquerade."

"And you're calling into question my ethics on a casual comment?"

He shook his head. "It wasn't casual. It was quite pointed. The person they spoke to said you're presently involved in a relationship with a man by the name of Kir Vasilek and that this Vasilek person works for Sergei Petrovyh—who's rumored to be tied to Stephen Alfonsi's disappearance. A fact you well know since you've done a good number of stories on Alfonsi in the past eight months."

"Every single one of those stories were not only solid, but corroborated by a number of witnesses."

His expression shifted, sadness settling behind his soft brown eyes. "That isn't what I asked, Cassie. Are you, or aren't you, romantically involved with a man who's allegedly involved in a mafia organization?"

The question came out of her boss's mouth, but it registered in her head as though her father had voiced it.

She'd known it would come to this. Had kept her distance from Kir as soon as she'd learned about him for a very pragmatic reason.

And yet, she couldn't find it in her to deny him. Couldn't see past the smiles he'd given her. The passion and the connection that came with being with him, or the happiness that had her all but floating for the last four days.

Four days, Cassie. Are you really willing to trade your career on the whim of four days?

No, that was her mother talking. Not her own feelings or good sense. She didn't have to make decisions based on what her parents thought. Or what Kir thought. Only what felt right to her.

She moistened her lips and tried to steady her voice. "The last time I checked, suspected doesn't mean guilty. You yourself just used the term *rumored*."

"This isn't a courtroom Cassie. It's a news station. Even if your previous stories were corroborated, there's no way you can assure they were objective. Let alone maintain that objectivity going forward. And if it got out that one of our reporters was involved in a relationship with a man suspected of being part of a mafia organization, we'd lose all credibility." He paused long enough to draw in a long breath. "Now, please answer the question."

A part of her wanted to deny it. To cling to what she knew. What she'd fought so hard for, even if it wasn't the real dream she'd wanted for herself.

But that was the old her. The frightened part of

her trying to gain approval from people who simply couldn't understand who she was. "The answer is yes. I'm in a relationship with Kir Vasilek. I'd only just met him when I first aired the stories about Alfonsi and didn't begin a relationship with him until earlier this month, but I can absolutely say that neither Kir, nor Sergei Petrovyh, deserve the title of *mafiya*."

Her boss must've caught the nuance in using the Russian form of the word versus the more traditionally used *mafia*, because his expression turned to one of defeat. "You and I both know it doesn't work that way. Perception is reality, and your reality will have a negative impact on this station." He paused long enough to sigh, then added, "I'm sorry, but this is a conflict of interest, pure and simple."

"But I'm scheduled to anchor today."

He shook his head. "Not anymore you're not. I called Lizbet in to back you up just in case. I told her to be prepared to step in after we talked." He rubbed his hands awkwardly back and forth, a nervous gesture either fueled by the difficult situation he'd been put in, or the fact that he'd waded into uncomfortable territory with the girlfriend of a mobster. "I'm sorry, Cassie, but you have to go."

Chapter Sixteen

Dangerous men with zero conscience. Situations where Kir and those with him had been grossly outnumbered. Guns, knives and a good number of other weapons intended for his demise. Kir had faced them all and then some since the day he'd last seen his mother, but not one of them left him feeling as powerless as the last half hour. He'd been far east of the city dealing with construction crew issues when Sam had called and told him that Cassie had been fired, but couldn't offer any other details. Cassie hadn't answered her phone. Neither had Evette. If Sergei hadn't answered his and assured him Evette and Cassie's aunt were inside the carriage house with her, Kir would have likely blown well past the speed limit and had a string of policemen on his ass with sirens blazing the whole way home.

He pulled into the drive more aggressively than was wise and found Sergei and Roman milling just outside the carriage house door. Sam and Patrick were there as well. All four eyed him as though he were an unpredictable threat.

The strikes of his Italian dress shoes against the concrete were louder than his voice. "How is she?"

"Past tears and on to fury." Roman glanced through

the four-square windows that topped the front door. "Most of it aimed at the television."

"She has a competitor at work. Lizbet Montlake." He looked to Sam and Patrick. "Is she the one behind this?"

Patrick shook his head, but it was Sam who spoke. "She didn't give us any details. Only asked us to take her home and tried not to cry while we drove."

"It was us," Sergei said. "Evette couldn't tell me much by way of text, but someone told an executive that she was intimate with you. And, by way of that relationship, was using station resources to further *mafiya* interests. Namely, mine."

His fault.

Perhaps nothing he'd done directly beyond being who he was, but his fault all the same. At least that was the way Cassie probably saw it. "I need to talk to her."

Sergei cocked an eyebrow. "By that, I take it you're asking me to risk life and limb to extract my bride?"

"And Cassie's aunt."

The smile on Sergei's face was slight, but also held deep understanding. "You ask much, *moy brat*, but I will try."

Roman cast them a sidelong look that said he thought they were both crazy and jerked his head toward his men gathered outside the main house. "Good luck. I'll be with them."

Sergei chuckled and reached for the doorknob. "Enjoy it, brother. One day you'll have your own reckoning and escape won't be so simple."

Inside, Cassie sat dead-center of the flannel sofa, her stare locked on the television. She'd changed from the professional attire she'd left in this morning to a simple tank, the loose cotton pants she preferred when watching TV, and bare feet. Her lips were pressed so tightly together, Kir had no doubt her jaws would ache tomorrow, and her hands were clenched between her knees. She glanced at Sergei. Then Kir. Then went right back to glaring at the screen.

Standing behind the sofa, Evette grimaced and aimed a silent plea toward Sergei.

Aunt Frieda, sitting to Cassie's left, patted her niece's leg. "Baby, it's not gonna help you any to sit there and watch her. You said yourself, you didn't think she had anything to do with this."

"Perhaps," Kir said, wading into the tension-riddled room, "another option would be for me to have some time with Cassie so that I can understand, in full, what's happened."

Cassie let out a harsh exhale, snatched the remote off the coffee table and punched the off button with unnecessary roughness. "Nothing I shouldn't have expected to happen." She tossed the remote back to its place, the harsh clatter against the wood overloud in the room's quiet. She looked to Frieda then Evette. "It's okay. You can go. I'm not going to do anything stupid. Except maybe eat all that ice cream Evette brought me in one sitting."

Proving his calm under pressure, Sergei rebutted as if the situation at large was no major event at all. "My bride tells me it cures all. I've since given Olga orders to keep the freezer stocked at all costs."

Surprisingly, the humor worked, drawing a slight, yet fatigued smile from Cassie. "Guess that explains how she's able to get it here so quickly." Her shoulders sagged and she dipped her head forward, stretching the muscles in the back of her neck. "Really, girls. It's okay." She lifted her head and finally met Kir's stare. "I need to tell him what happened."

Frieda offered Kir a look that begged him to show patience.

Evette volleyed her gaze from Sergei to Cassie as though she wasn't sure what to do.

Sergei closed the distance between him and his wife and nudged her off the fence. "Come, love. If you leave our son unattended with Olga and her desserts much longer, you'll have no prayer of getting him to sleep before midnight." He let Frieda exit first, guided his wife across the threshold, then shot Kir a sympathetic smile. "We are close if you need us."

And then it was quiet. A gaping chasm of tension and churning hopelessness that left the air between them too thick and uncomfortable to breathe.

He shed himself of his jacket, took the space Frieda had vacated and pulled Cassie into his arms so her torso lay cradled against his chest. "Tell me."

She laid it out. From the moment she'd arrived and learned Lizbet had been called in when it should have been her day off, to the final words her boss had uttered before he'd walked her to the bullpen and on to the front door. Every detail came out as though she'd replayed them a hundred times in her head, her voice drained and defeated until it finally cracked at the end. "It was mortifying. Lizbet was right there. She kept her head down the whole time, but everyone else watched every single detail."

The tips of her fingers idly pushed and pulled against the fabric of his button-down, an absent, yet vulnerable motion that made him long to feel someone's waning pulse beneath his fingertips. He covered her hand instead and pressed her palm against his heart. "I am sorry, *milaya*."

Her chuckle was ripe with bitterness. "Why? You

didn't do anything. All someone had to do was specu-
late about what you do for a living, and the rest took
care of itself."

That was the part that grated at him. Plucked at his
instincts the way a sound out of place in the dead of
night warned him to be alert. "This tip—who did it
come from?"

"I don't know. An executive talked to someone at
the Midsummer Masquerade last night and boom, I'm
toast."

Kir sucked in a deep breath, the possibilities the new
development opened up for finding Kevin's killer re-
kindling his optimism. "We will find out who they are.
Whoever it is may have ties to Kevin's death and the
email you were sent."

"Maybe. Maybe not." She pushed upright and twisted
so one of her knees lay bent on the cushion. "The fact
is, Kir, this could have been any random person I've
pissed off with a story. Either way, I'm out of a job."

He sat up and cupped the side of her face. "You know
you have nothing to worry about, Cassie. You will be
cared for. All of your needs provided for."

The last thing he expected was a frown, but that
was exactly what he got, paired with an agitated tone.
"I don't want to be taken care of. I want to take care of
myself. I want to be able to stand on my own two feet."
She shoved upright and paced toward the kitchen. "Even
more than that, I want to clear my reputation. I didn't
do anything wrong."

Kir stood as well and faced her, the frustration and
helplessness he'd wrestled with since receiving Sam's
call billowing larger. "Why do you care what they
think? Reporting isn't what you love. You're good at
it, yes, but photography is what you really enjoy. You

only kept with the reporting because it gained at least *some* acknowledgment from your family."

She spun and threw her arms out wide as if he'd proven her point. "And now my family is going to find out I've been fired because I'm hooked up with a mobster."

There it was.

The blame for today, and the conflict that had stretched long and taunting between them since the first day they'd met. The man who lived by his own law, and the woman who made a living reporting on those who went against the status quo.

That's not what's really bugging you, though, is it?

He strode to the window with a bird's-eye view of the main house, wishing he could ignore the question every bit as much as he wanted to ignore Cassie's situation. Wanted to pretend the ugliest truth of all wasn't right there dancing square in the middle of his conscience.

He was *glad* the conflict was gone. Had nursed a secret hope on the drive home that this would be the beginning of something deeper between them. A chance for them to be true partners where he never had to hide or couch his words in her presence.

What if he told her how he felt? What if he shared his fears and his past and let her make her decisions from there?

You are worth another's love and trust as well, brother. Don't let your parents' past rob you of it.

Sergei was right. Leveling with her was a risk—one he wished his father had taken with his mother and saved them all heartache. But if he didn't come clean, how was he any better? How could he possibly hope for a different outcome?

He faced her.

Whatever she'd been thinking before, the expression on his face wiped the consternation and frustration from hers in a second. "What's wrong?"

He nodded to the sofa. "Sit. Please."

For a moment, her gaze shuttled between him and the door—not so much as if she sought to escape, but more that she seemed to consider calling for backup. Instead, she padded to the sofa, perched on the edge and gripped her hands in her lap, her concerned gaze locked on him.

For the life of him, he had no clue how to start. How to put into words all the wrongs and distrust that had formed his life. "My father was *bratva*. His father was *bratva*."

Comprehension settled behind her beautiful eyes and her expression softened. "If you're going to tell me about your family, could you do it a little closer?"

He studied the distance between them, finding the courage to close the gap more difficult than any steps he'd taken to date in his life. Sharing his past was hard enough. Being close enough to feel her pity wasn't something he was confident he could stomach.

He forced one foot in front of the other and sat beside her, his elbows on his knees and his hands clasped in front of him. "I've told you that Sergei's family is different than most. He is ruthless in business, yes, and does not limit his investments or activities to what the government says he can or cannot do, but he does not extort from those who have not chosen his way. He does not blackmail innocents. And he protects his investments and those he considers his with formidable strength. There is no action he will not take if it means keeping those within his world safe."

He pulled in a slow stabilizing breath and turned his

head to meet her gaze. "But the family I was born into was different. More in line with Alfonsi's actions and what you see in movies. Perhaps worse."

She waited. No signs of revulsion or terror showed on her face. Just patience and openness.

He sat up and allowed himself to sink into the thick cushions behind him. "My father and mother met and married quickly. He loved her deeply. Adored her. But he never shared with her about the life he'd chosen."

"Why not?"

An ironic huff pushed from his chest. "Because to share what happened within the brotherhood wasn't done. Many men would not take brides to avoid the conflict." The memories of his youth rushed up to greet him. The idyllic life he'd thought he'd had until reality came crashing down around him. "He kept her in the dark on everything. Even made up false details about what he did for a living. Came home every night for dinner with a briefcase in hand and talked about business affairs that had nothing to do with how he'd spent his day."

"And then she found out."

Kir nodded. "A mistress of one of his brothers. A jaded woman who saw nothing of selling drugs or weapons save as a lucrative industry that allowed her man to provide her every luxury."

From the look on her face, she already suspected what would follow in his story, but she asked the question anyway. "What happened?"

"My mother got greedy. Realized the power her husband could leverage and the spoils that could become hers. She pushed my father. Demanded more and more of him—none of which he would deny her."

He thought of her twirling in the fur his father had

given her for her birthday. The new house he'd moved them to shortly after. Then he remembered the tightness behind his father's eyes. The fear in them. "My father was a soldier. And while they do not suffer financially, there is only so much they can make without skimming from their *vor*."

"Oh, shit," Cassie murmured.

Kir nodded. "Oh, shit indeed. The government kept close tabs on my father's organization. They saw my mother's excesses and my father's troubles. They cornered my mother and let her know how close her husband was to being found out."

He met Cassie's gaze, all the disgust and anger he'd had to navigate alone as a child rushing up and lodging in his throat. "They used her. Manipulated her fear. Said the best way to save him from certain death was to give them enough evidence against him to warrant an arrest so that he would be safe. Said that the alternative would be for her to be implicated as well and suffer similar consequences."

"She betrayed her own husband?"

"Worse." Kir tried to swallow, for all the good it did him. "Once he was arrested, she worked him incessantly. Begged him to give the authorities the information they wanted to incriminate the whole family so that the three of us could escape and live a luxurious life."

"I've never heard of anyone escaping such a life."

His shrewd woman. Always wise and seeing things even before they would be apparent to others. "With Sergei? He would release me, wish me the best and do everything in his power to see to my success so long as I kept my silence. That's who he is."

"But your father's family wasn't like that."

Kir shook his head and stared at the coffee table in

front of him. "*Nyet*. They were powerful. Ruthless and deadly. My father knew it and fought it as long as he could." He met Cassie's gaze. "But as I said, he loved her and would deny her nothing."

Cassie voice dropped to a whisper. "What happened to him?"

Saying it out loud even now cut deep. Brought all the pain and agony of those initial moments when he'd learned the truth back to the surface as though they'd never abated. "He was dead before he could share a word. My mother and I were captured and brought to the *vor* before his body was cold."

He remembered every moment. His father's blood. His mother's screams. The terrifying silence, and the way the men in the car stared at him throughout the long drive.

"She sold me to them," he said. "She was given money to disappear in exchange for my service to the family. Everything she'd ever wanted."

"Oh my God. And she took it?"

His sweet Cassie. So genuine and forthright. Had she been put in the same position, he had no doubt she'd have fought tooth and nail to free herself and her son. "In truth, she had no choice. I would be theirs either way. She could walk away from me and live, or insist on keeping me and die. It was that simple."

He gave himself a moment to let the emotions pass, wiping his palms along the outer edges of his thighs. "Sergei helped me keep tabs on her until she died five years ago. She was a husk of a woman. Went through her money in very little time and died mostly alone."

"And what about you?"

"I was a part of a family—the same as Sergei's led by a man named Anton—but I was never allowed into the inner circle. My father's betrayal was a stain I could not erase." The peace that always came when he thought of his brothers settled inside his chest. "But then Sergei befriended me. He, too, was a misfit. Was brought into Anton's family when he was very young and withstood many trials from others who'd been born into the life. He stood by me when most would not trust me."

"That's why you came here with him?"

"Yes. And for what he has done for me, he has my complete loyalty."

She studied him for long moments, those insightful, curious eyes of hers processing any number of thoughts and theories. "Why are you telling me this? Not the story, but why are you telling me today?"

There it was. The opening he'd created. An opportunity to change the past and share his own truth.

He stood, took her hand and guided her to her feet. Let the feel of her tiny grip in his ground him. "Today, when you owned our relationship, you chose honor. Even when it meant the loss of your job."

She ducked her head, but he guided her face back to his with a gentle nudge beneath her chin. "I understand you're hurt. I understand not liking the way you went out, or wondering what people will think. But what difference do they make in our life? The life of a reporter will always be in conflict with how we live. You are happy with our family. With us. You have a chance to do what you really love." He cupped the side of her face. "Let me give you that. Let go of what was and take what's right in front of you."

He studied her face. Searched her gaze and prayed his words would take root. "Choose me, Cassie. Take the risk. Accept me. Accept us all. Be mine and all that comes with it."

Chapter Seventeen

She couldn't have heard him right. Couldn't possibly be drawing the right correlation between the words he'd spoken and the meaning her mind calculated in its wake.

Cassie shook her head. Blinked her eyes a few times and rewound what he'd said one more time in her head, but the sincerity on his face didn't waver. Didn't flinch or show a single sign of humor. She licked her lips, the effort woefully inadequate for how dry her mouth had gone. "I'm not sure I understand what you're asking me."

"You know what I want. What I've wanted since the night I picked you up for dinner. I have no intention of changing my mind." He slid his hand from the side of her neck to the back of her head, his grip implacably holding her in place for his steely stare. "Be mine. Only mine. My wife."

Holy hell.

As proposals went, it was completely unapologetic. An alpha's open declaration of pursuit and verbal claim wrapped up in the guise of a request.

But he wanted her agreement. Her acquiescence and complete surrender. Not just a personal surrender, but of life as she'd known it—her career included. The stark determination was written in every feature—

in the harsh press of his lips, the sharp angles of his cheeks and jaw and the unyielding resolve behind his ice-blue eyes.

It would be so easy. Too easy after the day she'd had. But rash decisions seldom paid off. Particularly when made in the aftermath of sudden change. Hell, she'd had a month of sudden changes.

She eased into him. Stroked her hands from his elbows to his shoulders and savored the strength of him beneath the cool, crisp fabric of his fine shirt. "I won't lie to you. I want to say yes. Want to give you what you want and drown myself in the promise of some idyllic happily ever after."

"Then do it."

"It's not that easy, Kir. Everything has changed for me since I met you. My day-to-day routine. My home. Twice. How I'm looking at my life, and what I want from it. Not to mention losing the job I'd fought so hard to build and finding myself in the middle of a murder." She wrapped her arms around his neck. "I didn't just choose honor today. I followed my conscience and the future I think the two of us can have together. The future I want for us to have. But I need for you to give me time to make sure I can commit at the level you want. Time to make sure my answer isn't driven on wanting an escape, but on a real belief we can make it. That we'd be happy with each other for the long haul."

"You know we will be."

"I *think* we will be. But I'm reeling right now. My emotions are all over the board. Definitely not a frame of mind suited to making life-altering decisions like marriage. You deserve an answer I feel in my gut as well as my heart and my head. We both do."

His lips pinched tighter, and a muscle at the back of his jaw twitched.

She caressed the spot with her thumb and lowered her voice. "That's not a *no*. That's just me saying I need some time to tune out all the chaos. To forget today's pain. To get a little more practice letting go of all the old things that used to drive me and let the idea of trying on a new career settle in my head."

His fingers in her hair tightened against her scalp, and his voice was a broken growl. "They hurt you."

"Only whoever it was that shared the information. My boss and his boss were just protecting themselves. But it will pass. Tonight, I just want to forget. About everything. My parents and their expectations. Jobs. Killers. All of it." She teased her fingers through the loose curls at his temple. "Everything except you."

The light behind his eyes changed in an instant, the spark of inspiration honed by laser-focused tenacity. "I can make you forget."

The swirl in her belly and pleasure spearing to her sex shouldn't have been possible. Not with everything else that had happened.

But this was Kir.

A man who resonated with her physically, emotionally and mentally unlike anyone else. Who seemed attuned to her needs and responses at the most primal level. Maybe she couldn't give him the answer he wanted right this moment, but she could give him all that she was right now. Let go of her worries and pride and yield to his comfort and strength. "I'd like that. Very much."

She waited. Anticipated the tightening of his arms around her as the dominant in him rose to the surface. The confident play of his mouth against hers and the sweet peace his kiss created. The mastery he employed with each touch.

The predator was right there in front of her. Bristling with energy and an unbending resolve she couldn't wait to feel unleashed on her overwrought senses.

But he held completely still. Studied her with a keenness that cautioned the old and structured part of herself to run. To reconsider the door she'd just opened and what might lie on the other side. When he spoke, his voice roiled with the power of thunder in the distance—a warning and a vow of what was to come. "You have no idea of the lengths I would go to for you."

A tremor snaked down her spine, and goose bumps that had nothing to do with the room's chilled temperature fanned along her shoulders and arms. "The way you say that, I'm not sure me knowing is wise."

His mouth crooked on one side, the grin of a mildly amused pirate that did little to dissipate the intensity of the moment. "My actions will never hurt you." He skimmed his calloused palms from her bare shoulders up to her wrists. "But I will be your protector." He peeled her arms from around his neck. "Your provider." He held her stare and kissed the palm of one hand, his voice pure velvet. "In all things."

There he was.

The wolf free of his cage. Hungry, focused and poised to take what he wanted.

Keeping his fingers manacled around one of her wrists, he inched backward and tugged her arm. "Come."

If he kept looking at her like that and talking in that low, throaty voice, coming wouldn't be a verb that entailed walking. Her feet got on board despite the ache quickly building between her thighs, and she followed him up the stairs.

Sun slanted through the master suite's wide window, the boldness of the early evening rays bleaching the blue from the skies beyond and painting the horizon with hints of gold. Before she could get her bearings, Kir veered to the bathroom, led her inside and spun her so her hips pressed against the vanity's ledge. Not pausing, he turned, padded to the glass-fronted shower and cranked all three showerheads to life.

Her brain tried to keep up. Struggled to match his actions with the libidinous weight of his stare as he approached her. "What are we doing?"

He lifted the hem of the soft cotton tank she'd donned shortly after her early return home and peeled it over her head. "You want to forget, yes?"

She nodded. Or tried to. Between the wanton promise in his expression and the erotic sweep of the room's chilled air against her bared breasts, anything more was impossible.

"Then I will wash it all away." He slipped his fingertips in the waistband of her cotton pants and pushed them past her hips until gravity took over and made them pool around her ankles. "Drown the day with my touch. My kiss. My body." He stepped back and raked her naked body with a long and covetous perusal. Only once he'd taken his fill did his eyes lock onto hers once more and he began to undress himself. "All you will know is us. All you will need is us. And when you fall asleep, you will do it beside me. Where you belong. Free from worry. Relaxed and drifting from the pleasure delivered by the man who will give you everything."

All too quickly, the story of his mother and father

leapt to the front of her thoughts. "I'm not asking for everything, Kir. Only you. As you are."

Steam from the shower drifted from the open glass door and coiled near his feet. He pushed his boxer briefs to the floor, stepped free of them and prowled toward her, his shaft fully erect and straining toward his belly. "*Nyet*. You are not my mother. You are wise, Grounded in the ways of the world and driven by a good heart." The weight of his hands at her hips was a godsend. An anchor to keep her steady as his words rushed over her. "But I understand my father's actions now. Knew when I heard the pain and frustration in your voice downstairs that there is nothing I would not do to give you what you need." He pressed his body against her, his cock an insistent rod above her mound, and his lips a whisper that teased her mouth. "My heart is hard and unskilled in love. But it is yours."

He'd barely touched her. Had only undressed them both and let her feel the crackling skin-to-skin connection between them. But his humble words undid her. Cracked open what was left of her resistance and left her as bare and vulnerable inside as out.

She squeezed her eyes shut and gripped his shoulders, need, want and all the emotions of the day crashing through her in an all-consuming wave. "Please." She didn't know what it meant. Only knew that she trusted him to find the way. To help her across the shaky bridge of emotions to the haven of just the two of them in this moment.

"I've got you, *malyshka*." He lifted her. Cradled her against his chest and skimmed his lips against her forehead as he moved. "No more thinking. No more reality." The warmth and heaviness of the steam embraced her as he carefully lowered her feet to the tile floor. "Only pleasure."

He eased her backward with hands at her hips, and water from the rainshower faucet overhead gently spilled from her crown to her shoulders and back. She closed her eyes, tipped her head back and savored the heat. The internal sigh as her muscles responded and released the day's tension. Releasing her hold on his shoulders, she sluiced the water through her hair.

The sharp snip of plastic on plastic and the coconut scent of her shampoo floating through the steam drew her head up and her eyes open.

Kir poured a good amount of the pearlescent shampoo on one palm, set the bottle back on the inset tile shelf and rubbed his hands together.

"What are you doing?"

He grinned, smoothed his coated palms atop her drenched hair and carefully worked his strong fingers against her scalp. "What does it look like I'm doing?"

It was such a simple thing. A task she handled every day on her own in the most perfunctory manner.

But this was something else entirely. A level of intimacy beyond anything they'd done before. An act that spoke of love and care more than sexual contact.

He was showing her. Demonstrating with his actions that his words were anything but empty. This unbending, powerful man accustomed to leading many who expected absolutely loyalty was serving her. Relinquishing his power to give and provide exactly as he'd promised in the simplest of gestures.

Odd, how hard it was to let go. To let him work the thick lather in a slow, but purposeful massage. To guide her back into the water, rinse each strand clean and repeat it all once more with her conditioner. With every movement—every moment—her certainty solidified. Her trust deepened.

His heart really *was* hers, and he would undoubtedly move mountains if it meant seeing to her happiness.

She skimmed her fingertips over his taut pecs, eager to give him the same experience. "My turn?"

He shook his head and reached for the shower gel. "*Nyet*. Tonight is for you."

The almondy goodness of the gel filled the shower, but its scent was nothing compared to the feel of his hands along her shoulders and neck. The sensuous massage he worked into each stroke, and the erotic glide of the gel and water against her skin.

He took his time. Gave ample attention to every place he touched. Her arms. Her back. Her breasts and ass. Her thighs and shins. Sitting on the built-in bench against the shower's back wall, he guided her hands to his shoulders for balance and lifted one foot.

An involuntary moan slipped free of her lips, the throaty sound of it reverberating against the glass and tile walls as he worked the arch with utmost devotion.

"I love that sound." His head was down, but the longing behind his words echoed the desire building inside her. "Love the way your body comes alive beneath my hands. The taste of your kiss and the scent of your skin on mine."

He eased her foot to the floor and repeated his massage on the other. With every second the mood shifted. A sexual awareness creeping into the moment and permeating the thick steam around them. Deepening the bond between them.

His gaze drifted from her foot to her sex, and his fingers hesitated.

Oh, dear God.

If the ravenous hunger on his face matched even a tenth of the determination behind his eyes, she was done for. A pagan offering left standing before a starving heathen god.

He guided her foot to the bench outside his thigh, never once shifting his stare. The hand closest to her anchored leg skimmed up her shin and over her bent knee. His thumb dragged a wicked path along her inner thigh and traced teasing circles just shy of her sex.

"I should not." He added his other hand to her standing leg. Skimmed his thumb just a hair's breadth from the seam at the top. "I wanted to give. Not take." He lifted his head, the clawing lust that drove him setting the icy blue of his eyes on fire.

He'd deny himself. Cheat them both of the gratification that waited if she so much as balked at the idea.

Could she be this bold? Grab on to the instant and take what he freely offered—the physical and what lay beyond it?

You know the truth. Would never have acknowledged who he was to you today if you didn't.

She trailed her fingers from one shoulder to his neck. Combed her fingers through the loose, damp curls at the side of his head and surrendered to what lay ahead. "Then make it a gift."

A low rumble rolled from his chest. His fingers squeezed her thighs and his gaze sharpened. An alpha unleashed from his cage. "My beauty." He lowered his head and kissed the inside of one thigh. "My prize." He rolled to his knees and nuzzled her swollen clit. "My heart."

His tongue slicked through her folds. Sampled and savored every inch. Every drop of the desire he'd created. Worked her sex with his mouth until all she could do was cling to the back of his head and shoulder and pray the oncoming explosion would leave her standing.

He circled her sex with his tongue. Flicked the base with an increasing pressure while he pressed two fingers deep. His growl vibrated through her, the demand behind his words absolute. "Give me what's mine."

His lips surrounded her clit and he stroked the sweet spot along her front wall.

Release.

Sweet, unrelenting release. Each pulse greedily grasping his thrusting fingers as her hips rolled against his mouth. Her legs quaked. Teetered on the edge of collapse.

But he anchored her to him. Kept one steely arm coiled around her hips while he drank his fill.

The connection was huge. Beautiful. Altering on so many levels it defied reason or comprehension.

But it wasn't enough. Didn't satisfy what her body insisted she needed. What they both needed.

She forced her eyes open, and a fresh spasm rocketed through her pussy, the alluring sight of him kneeling between her legs and his face buried between her thighs permanently marking itself in her memory.

"Kir." When he refused to meet her gaze, she grasped his hair at the back of his head. "Please."

Either the bold move or the plea in her voice captured his attention, and he lifted his head, a savage wildness burning in his eyes. A beast interrupted from his feast.

Her body trembled. "I need you."

Three simple words, but they brought an almost frightening focus to his gaze. He squeezed her hips. Slowly stood and caressed her water-slick body as he rose. He cupped her breasts. Swept her pebbled nip-

Rhenna Morgan 263

ples with his thumbs and growled his pleasure when she whimpered.

"You want my cock?" He backed her against the shower wall, all pretense of gentleness knocked aside by the wolf she'd released. "Need your man to fuck you? To show you the truth? To bind you to him?"

Yes.

Yes, yes, yes and then some. Crude or not, his words rang true. Matched the primitive need raging inside her.

She moaned in lieu of an answer and dug her nails into his shoulders. Tilted her head to the side to give his questing mouth and tongue more room to work.

"You *will* be mine," he murmured against her skin. He dipped slightly and captured one leg, hooking her knee over his arm. "You will take me." He repeated the act with the other, leaving her spread and vulnerable, her back pressed to the hard tile and her pussy fully exposed. "You will accept me." His teeth scraped the tender flesh where her neck and shoulders met, and his straining cock nudged her entrance. "Mine."

He thrust inside. Filled her completely in one delicious surge. Claimed her. Demanded and took what he wanted. What they both wanted.

It was perfect. Powerful. The sweetest assault, and the ultimate surrender. His and hers.

He pumped inside her. Drove them both higher and higher and forged a connection she had no prayer of breaking.

The muscles inside her sex fluttered. Whispered of the promise just ahead. Of the climax that would rearrange everything. That would seal her fate. Her future.

She clung to him. Let the steam, his strength and the power of the moment wash over her as she opened her eyes.

The mirror opposite the shower was foggy at the edges, but the visual in the center was staggering. Kir blanketing her. The muscles in his shoulders and arms bunched tightly as he held her in place. Her legs spread wide. His hips pounding into her and his ass flexing with each undulation.

His strangled voice rumbled near her ear, the desperation behind it mingling with the image. "Let go, *malyshka*. Accept where you belong."

Release rang through her. Sent her body soaring and her pussy grasping his hard shaft.

His own shout rang out. Agony. Relief. Triumph and gratitude. So much emotion coiling around her. Every bit of it as strong and powerful as the man who held her.

She couldn't go back from this. Didn't want to. And the truth of it shook her to her very core. Frightening as it was, he seemed meant for her. Always had. And as much as she'd tried to fight it—had been afraid of the connection—she couldn't refuse it anymore.

Her arms shook, and her body shuddered, the wake of their combined release making the warm water seem cool in comparison.

The rhythm of his hips slowed. A languid, easy pace overtaking the wildness and guiding them both back to earth. To now and the new reality she'd accepted even if she hadn't spoken it out loud.

Gingerly, he eased one of her feet to the cool tile. Then the other. His hands against her skin were a constant comfort. Each skim of his lips against her cheek—her eyes and temples—a show of devotion. A demonstration of love and connection without a single word spoken.

He rested his forehead against hers, and his voice

was little more than a shaky whisper. "Taking you was not my intent."

So honest. Open and vulnerable. More so than she imagined he'd ever been with anyone.

She trailed her fingers along the back of his neck. "Well, it was my gift. You can't take it back."

He lifted his head and met her stare, the depth of solemnity behind his gaze staggering. "How could I? I am lost to you."

Her beautiful man.

Hers.

Completely.

The depth of the realization must have played across her face, because he ducked his head, a shyness she'd never have expected driving his actions as he eased away and turned off the faucets.

Without his body to keep away the chill or their connection to keep her grounded, she shivered.

He snatched the towel hanging just outside the glass and quickly wrapped it around her, drying her with careful gentleness. Only when he was certain the cold would no longer cause her discomfort did he grab another towel and see to himself in quick, perfunctory movements. He tossed his towel aside, gathered her in his arms and padded to the bedroom.

While sunset was still an hour or more away, the sun had slipped behind neighboring trees and cast an easy shade on the room, shadows and the promise of night matching the languor of her muscles.

Kir settled her beneath the bedsheets, crawled in beside her and nestled her in the crook of his arm. Beneath her ear, his heart hammered a steady rhythm. A cadence that helped her own pulse find steadiness.

Wrapping his arms around her, he caressed her back

and kissed the top of her head. "We'll see to it your reputation is cleared." He paused a moment as though searching for the right words. "Just promise me you'll consider what I've asked."

At first, his words made no sense. Not after what she'd felt and realized in the last hour.

But she hadn't spoken those feelings aloud. Hadn't spoken her truth even if she'd accepted it clear to her soul.

She snuggled closer to him. Reveled in the scent of his skin and the protective way he held her. Marveled at the gift she'd been given. She smiled to herself and toyed with the faint dusting of hair between his pecs. "There's nothing to consider. Not anymore."

He froze beneath her, every muscle in his torso drawn tight and pensive.

She pressed herself up enough to meet his eyes, prayed her smile conveyed her certainty as deeply as she felt it and laid herself bare. "I choose you, Kir Vasilek. You and your family and all that comes with it."

Chapter Eighteen

Another Monday morning. Usually, it would be the first day of Cassie's "weekend," but the view from this particular Monday was different. The first day of a whole new world.

Her new reality.

She rolled onto her side, the cool crisp sheets whispering in the silence as she grabbed Kir's pillow and hugged it tight. While he'd showered and kissed her goodbye a good hour ago, the light woods and citrus scent of his cologne still lingered. Coiled around her and promised that yesterday hadn't been a dream.

He loved her.

He hadn't said it in those words, but she'd felt them. And the truth was, she loved him, too. Felt as though a part of her had always known him and recognized him as the one for her. Good or bad, she was committed to giving her new life a try and doing what she loved for a living versus something logical.

Okay, so are you gonna lie around in bed all day? Or are you gonna get your butt up and actually do something to get this new life of yours in motion?

She smiled into Kir's pillow and let out a low chuckle. She might have finally chosen to leave her parents' ideals behind and strike her own path, but her mother's drive didn't appear to be quieting down in her head anytime soon.

Propping herself up on one arm, she grabbed her phone from the nightstand.

8:12 a.m.

So, she hadn't fallen into complete sloth territory yet. That was a bonus. And from how quiet the house was, Frieda hadn't rolled out of bed yet either. That meant she'd have at least a little time to herself to enjoy some coffee and figure out her next steps.

Teeth brushed and a comfy T-shirt and fresh cotton pants donned, she meandered downstairs and fired up the fancy one-cup brewer gadget. Outside the kitchen window was a straight view to the back of the main house and the luxurious pool behind it. Per usual, two men sat outside the back door, both of them dressed somewhat casually in jeans and button-downs. No doubt, Sam, Abel or Patrick were somewhere near her front door as well.

Would her life always be like this? If they had children, would they have guards the same as Emerson?

The machine hissed and gurgled the end of its routine, and the coffee's rich nutty goodness filled the kitchen. She pulled the mug free of the machine's base and blew across the steaming surface. God, how spoiled she'd become in such a tiny amount of time. State of the art everything. Loads of room to move around. Fashionable furniture and details. She'd gone from boho to Better Homes and Gardens in days and hadn't even flinched.

Which begged the question—if she and Kir were really going all in together, where would they live? For the life of her, she couldn't imagine Kir puttering around her little 500-square-foot hut, but getting out of her lease wouldn't be easy.

Seriously? You're worried about getting out of a lease when your significant other is Kir?

Hmm. Good point.

And he'd mentioned that he had a home of his own, so maybe they'd live there.

You've agreed to marry and rely on a man whose home you've never seen. Do you realize how insane that sounds?

Nope. She wasn't listening to that crap anymore. The negativity was yesterday. This was today. Fresh and positive.

She padded to the kitchen table, stood beside it and sipped her coffee. Boxes full of her portfolios, cameras and accessories sat neatly stacked along the far wall of the living room. Her favorite images that had been hung in her house were there as well, turned so they couldn't be seen.

Funny. That was how she'd always treated her work. A passion kept boxed up and facing away from the real world except for rare occurrences where she allowed herself to indulge. Maybe the first step was to fix that and get her gear and dreams out into the light.

Two-thirds through unpacking boxes, three sharp knocks sounded on the front door. Evette smiled and waved through the windows, then opened the door and poked her head in. "Up for a visit?"

Cassie carefully unrolled yet another lens from its packing paper. "Sure, if you don't mind being surrounded by a little chaos."

With an indelicate snort, Evette shut the door and ambled inside. "I have an eight-year-old. Chaos is all I know." She paused with her hands on her hips and surveyed all the gear and albums stacked on the coffee table, end tables and chairs. "I'd say this looks promising— so long as it's because you're planning on using all this stuff and aren't planning an estate sale."

Cassie stood and stretched out her back. "No. Not selling anything. Just trying to figure out what I've got to work with and what I might need."

"For?"

Rubbing her hand across her stomach, Cassie tried to still the roiling sensation in her belly.

Just say it. Put words behind it.

"I'm going to give the whole photography thing a go."

"Really?"

Cassie nodded her head and enjoyed the rush of excitement just voicing the words created. "Looks like it. I mean, I'm officially no longer employed, right? No better time to start than now. Though, I've got no clue where I'm gonna start."

"Oh! You could do a gallery. Get one of those trendy places in Jackson Square, or something."

The response that no one started out with a gallery hovered on her tongue, but she shook the words loose and tried for something more positive. More open. "Maybe. I think the first thing I have to do is figure out what my specialty is, and then I'll know where to go." She grabbed her now empty mug and headed for the kitchen. "You want some coffee?"

"Nope. None for me. I already had two cups with Sergei this morning before he headed out for meetings." She followed Cassie to the kitchen and leaned one hip on the counter. "Actually, I was worried you'd be bored out of your mind and was gonna see if you wanted to come with me and Emerson for a lunch thing."

Waiting for the coffee machine to do its magic, Cassie snagged a granola bar from the pantry. "What kind of lunch thing?"

"An invite from a costume designer. We've got a big Mardi Gras charity event planned for the church next year. This bigwig costume designer who does all the parades and events around town called me a few weeks ago and volunteered to donate her time doing the costumes for it, so I'm meeting with her today. I decided I'd take Emerson along because she apparently does superhero costumes, too. Figured I'd take the easy way out this Halloween."

"Mmm. Livin' the highlife."

"Girl, you're not kidding. Every year, I hold my breath waiting to see what my boy's gonna come up with for his Halloween plans. This year, I'm like *bring it on*." She cocked her head. "So, what do you think? Wanna come along?"

Cassie took a bite of the bar, but her gaze drifted to the boxes and gear scattered through the living room. Now that she'd started, she was too pumped to walk away. Besides, the shower in Aunt Frieda's suite upstairs had turned on ten minutes before Evette had shown up, and she was kind of eager to get her aunt's take on where things were headed.

She shook her head. "It sounds like fun, but I think I'll pass today. I want to dig into my stuff a little more and see if I can't map out some kind of plan on what to do next."

Another woman might have pouted or given Cassie a hard time, but Evette smiled huge and pushed away from the counter. "Sounds like a damned fine plan to me." She pulled Cassie in for a hug.

It was awkward at first, Cassie's initial response to

keep distance between them as she had last week firing hard. But then she let it go, shoved her resistance away and wrapped her arms around Evette in kind. "Thank you. For everything."

Evette's smile was still in place when she pulled away, but it was softer and thick with understanding. "No need to thank me. We're family. It's what we do." She turned and offered a backward wave. "I'll stop by when me and Emerson get home to hear how the plan's moving along."

"Deal."

Pausing with the door open and one foot past the threshold, Evette added, "A friendly hint. If you want peace and quiet, you'd be smart to go see Olga sometime this morning." She dipped her head toward the granola bar pinched between Cassie's fingers. "Maybe grab a real breakfast. I heard her grumbling something about bringing you a food care package if she didn't see you before noon."

More proof she was part of a family now. A real one that operated on caring rather than an outlet for educational advancement. "Duly noted."

She got back to work, sorting through her equipment and making note of the things she might need depending on the direction she took things. Stills and landscapes were her comfort zone, but if she truly wanted to make a go of things, she'd need to stretch herself more. Consider live work and candid opportunities like the one Lizzy had offered her.

Snatching her most recent portfolio, she settled onto the middle of the cozy couch, crossed her legs and rested the heavy album on her thighs.

Frieda's steps sounded on the stairs behind her. "One

definite benefit to you being home is the smell of coffee being the first thing that greats me in the mo—"

At the sharp cutoff of Frieda's words, Cassie twisted to see what was wrong.

Frieda stood two steps from the bottom of the staircase, her hands braced on the thick railing and her mouth ajar. "What's going on?"

Cassie scanned her things stacked this way and that. "I'm working on a plan."

"As in a plan for a fire sale?"

Turning once more, Cassie frowned up at her aunt. "Why does everyone keep asking me that?"

"Because you're too stubborn to consider things that are good for you, and you never *ever* take out more than the absolute essentials when you go out for a shoot." With that, she took the final two steps down the stairs.

Cassie shifted her attention back to her album. "Well, I took 'em all out today. And not for a fire sale." She flipped the page and considered the work she'd saved.

"So, what kind of plan are we talking about?" Frieda said as she started her own morning brew.

Hmm. Where should she start? With just the professional stuff, or the whole kahuna?

Cassie worried her finger on the edge of one page. "Well, I'm out of a job, and everyone keeps telling me I should give the whole photography thing a try, so I'm trying to figure out how to do that." She cleared her throat and added, "And it looks like Kir and I are in it for the long haul."

The sputtering hiss of the coffee machine matched the sounds coming out of Frieda's mouth. "What?"

Resting her head on the back of the couch, Cassie rolled her head toward her aunt. "Which part?"

"Both," she said, marching toward the living room

with coffee in hand. "With *a lot* more details." She settled right next to Cassie, drew her knees in close to her chest and cradled her mug in both hands as though ready for a juicy story. "Start with the long-haul part and work your way up from there."

It figured she'd start with the relationship stuff. Frieda was nothing if not a romantic.

Cassie started with the events from last night, sprinkled in with discussions she'd had with Kir in the weeks before it, but carefully avoiding the physical aspects—a fact Frieda indicated her displeasure of with more than a few scowls. She wrapped it up with Kir's insistence that he was not only willing and able to support her while she found her groove in a new business, but that he wouldn't let up until she did.

She shrugged and motioned to the album in her lap. "So, here I am, trying to figure out what options I've got and which way I want to go from there. Kir thinks I ought to consider the candid work like Lizzy offered, but I'm not really convinced that's my thing."

Frieda leaned in and looked at the images on the exposed pages. "Well, have you really tried? I mean, if all you've got to go on are the stills you intentionally photographed, then maybe you're making a decision without enough data."

"I've got some candids." Cassie turned the page. Then another. "They're scattered in between everything else, but Kir likes them."

She turned another page and the unmounted image she'd taken of Kir that day at Bacchanal slid into her lap. She held it up and grinned. He'd surprised her that morning when he'd reviewed all of her work. Had shown amazing support, even from the beginning.

"That's a candid one," Frieda said, "and it's fabulous."

"Well, it's of Kir," Cassie fired back with a roll of her eyes. "The guys on GQ covers look boring compared to him."

"Mmm. True." Frieda sipped her coffee, but kept her gaze on the picture. "You gotta admit though, it shows promise. What were you thinking about when you took it?"

How relaxed he seemed in the moment. How he owned the space around him and naturally drew attention wherever he went. Not just with women, but with everyone. The same way beasts in the forest took note of a wolf prowling through their habitat.

Her attention shifted to a woman near the edge of the image. The hat she wore was one of those long-brimmed Southern types reserved for ladies who loved afternoon tea no matter how hot it was, and her skirt and jacket were almost vintage Jackie O.

Kind of an odd outfit for Bacchanal, now that she thought about it. Not out of place really, but a little much for the time of day she'd taken the picture.

Wait a minute.

She drew the image closer and studied the woman's profile.

"What?" Frieda said, leaning closer.

"I know that profile. I've seen it somewhere."

Frieda narrowed her gaze. "You know, now that you say that, I think so, too. She's got a little upturned nose. One of those that's cute so you never really forget it."

The nose.

It was the same as the woman she'd glimpsed that night at *André's*. And she could have sworn the girl she'd seen at the coffee shop had a similar profile, but she'd had different-colored hair.

Cassie handed the picture to Frieda. "But you recognize her, too?"

"Yeah. I can't quite say why, though. Not with only a profile to go on."

A profile.

Black and white.

Cassie surged upright, slid the album on the coffee table and grabbed her empty coffee cup. "The interview we watched together. The one with the Pro Domme, or whatever you call them."

"The kinky lady?" Frieda kept her seat, but twisted to follow Cassie's progress. "What about her?"

"That's where we saw her." Cassie plunked her mug in the sink and darted up the stairs.

"Whoa, whoa, whoa." Frieda stood and planted her hands on her hips. "Where in the world are you going?"

Cassie kept going, taking the stairs two at a time. "To get dressed."

"Why?"

Because Kir needed a name and, if her gut was right, she had the means to get him one. She leaned over the balcony and met her aunt's stare. "I've got to talk to Lizbet."

Chapter Nineteen

Three months into having his own office and Kir still wasn't used to such a luxury. Built into the back of one of the newly built *André's* locations, it gave him a secured and private place to run his crew and mirrored the setup given to Roman at the second *André's* expansion.

And it wasn't a hole in the wall either. Not a warehouse full of dust and outdated furnishings like *avtoritets* he'd worked under in Russia, or a bland sea of gray and white baseline furnishings like so many cheap office buildings he'd visited in America. It was all class. An extension of the gleaming black furniture that graced the restaurant in front with glass, steel and crimson accents.

The gift was an honor. A demonstration of trust on Sergei's part that had caught both Kir and Roman off guard, and a level of prestige Kir still hadn't gotten used to. Even more disconcerting was seeing his boss casually seated opposite his desk rather than the other way around.

Sergei flipped to the first page of the 300 plus guest list Kir had hacked from the Midsummer Masquerade's online site. "New Orleanians do love their galas and masquerades."

Seated beside Sergei, Roman grunted his agreement.

"Wealthy New Orleanians. The lowest ticket price was five thousand per couple."

"I've noted the attendees Roman and I recognize or can get connections to," Kir said. "Unless there are names you'd rather approach yourself, we will start working through them and see if any might have ties to Alfonsi."

"And the others? The ones you don't know?" Sergei said.

One corner of Roman's mouth twitched, but he kept his silence.

"I called Knox this morning," Kir said.

Sergei cocked an eyebrow, obviously as surprised by Kir's action as Roman had been when he'd shared the news earlier this morning.

"With Kevin gone," Kir said, "I am the only one with sufficient skills and experience to research those we don't know. I cannot do both tasks, and time is of the essence."

This time Sergei smiled, a knowing grin that spoke of satisfaction. "A wise move. They can be trusted."

"It's not a matter of trust. It's a matter of habit." And pride, if he was honest. "Anton would have never outsourced sensitive matters beyond family."

"Anton's family is generations old with vast resources. Ours is no less strong, but young. We build as we go and leverage the trustworthy connections we have as needed." Sergei shrugged. "And besides, they are family."

"We still have a resource issue," Roman cautioned. "We need local technological expertise beyond Kir. He cannot lead behind a computer."

"Agreed." Sergei shifted his attention to Kir. "And what of Cassie?"

A quiet peace settled inside him. A lightness he hadn't expected. Odd, how just the mention of her name could settle him.

Roman smirked. "Now you've made him lose his focus again. Twice this morning, he put our work on hold to direct the men installing security in his home."

"She cannot stay at Sergei's indefinitely," Kir said. "Her safety is my responsibility."

"Not solely yours," Sergei corrected. "The responsibility falls to us all, and there is no rush."

But there was a rush. Identifying the why of it had eluded him all day, but he'd known the moment he woke that he wanted her in his space. In his bed. Wanted to begin their life together in the truest sense possible without haste. "Everything will be in place by week's end. Frieda's home is being updated as well." He paused a moment and met each man's gaze one at a time. "She will not continue her career as a reporter. Once we find the person responsible for Kevin's murder, she will explore a future in photography."

Sergei settled deeper in his chair. "It seems you had an eventful discussion last night."

Eventful barely scratched the surface of the night they'd shared. With her acceptance, he'd woken altered. Grounded, yet also driven to demonstrate his worthiness at a level that defied description. "She will be my bride."

Roman's eyebrows hopped high, open surprise reflected on his face.

Even Sergei, who'd long ago mastered the art of masking his reactions, seemed caught off guard. He schooled his features almost instantly. "And will there be a wedding to celebrate this decision? Or have the two of you opted for a more contemporary arrangement?"

Oh, there would be a wedding. Now that she'd chosen him, he had every intention of binding her to him in every way possible. "She will have my name, but we have not discussed details. She's had enough thrown at her. When we've found and dealt with Kevin's killer and she is in my home, then we will make plans."

Sergei looked to Roman. "Wisdom and patience demonstrated inside one day. It seems our brother has found a new path."

"Yes," Roman said, "but another wedding means the rest of us have to be patient as well."

The quip earned a surprising bark of laughter from Sergei. No doubt because he remembered all too well how quickly the mothers from Dallas had descended on New Orleans at the promise of nuptial planning. For days after their arrival, it had been chaos on Sergei's estate, but Kir had to admit, he'd enjoyed it. More than that, he found himself looking forward to sharing a similar experience with Cassie.

His phone vibrated inside his suit jacket. Still chuckling with the other two men, he pulled it out, noted Sam's number on the display and answered. "I thought you were off rotation today."

An awkward silence stretched for two heartbeats before Sam responded. "Well, I was. I mean, I am. But Miss McClintock called about a half hour ago and said she was going out."

"Out is good. How is she?"

Another pause. "Very…focused."

Focused.

An odd word that didn't seem as troubling as the uncertainty voiced behind it. "Where did she want to go?"

"She said she needed to be taken to the television station, but when Abel and Patrick picked her up, she wasn't dressed like she normally is when she goes in. Had on a T-shirt and jeans. I wasn't sure if that was something you needed to know about."

The station?

It made no sense. Not after the things they'd talked about and the path they'd set.

Unless she'd changed her mind.

He clenched the arm of his chair, the action mild compared to the tension that settled in his stomach. "Did she say anything else?"

"No. Only said that she didn't think she'd be long and that Abel and Patrick should plan to wait on her."

The levity that had colored Roman and Sergei's expressions seconds before was now gone, replaced with the same laser focus Kir felt.

He needed to say something. Give some kind of direction to his men, but his thoughts were too erratic. Spinning like a compass incapable of finding north. "It was wise to call me. Have them stay close to her and text me the minute she's back in the car."

"Yes, sir."

Kir ended the call and slid his phone back into his jacket's interior pocket.

"Where is she?" Sergei said.

He forced himself to take a steady breath. Then another. "She went to the station."

"To what purpose?"

"She didn't say. Only told the men she wouldn't be long, and that they should wait for her."

Roman volleyed a look between Sergei and Kir. "Doesn't sound like anything serious. Maybe she just forgot something."

Possible. But walking away from a career overnight

wasn't something many people would do lightly. Someone as driven to succeed as Cassie even less so.

"Whatever you're thinking," Sergei said, "do not
make assumptions."

"Nyet," Roman added. "She would not say one thing
and act differently only hours later."

They were right. She might have allowed the opinions of others to sway her once upon a time, but she'd
owned her relationship with him when confronted by
her boss. She was opening up to who she was. What
she wanted. She was smart. Clever. Never once tried
to manipulate him the way his mother had his father.

He nodded more to himself than to the men across
from him and straightened in his chair. "You are right.
Whatever she's doing, she'll have a reason for it." He
stood, picking up his copy of the guest list as he did.

Sergei and Roman stood as well, but it was Sergei
who spoke. "And?"

"And Roman and I have work to do." Kir rounded the
desk and buttoned his jacket. Cassie trusted him. Had
chosen him for her future despite what she was giving
up to do so. She deserved the same trust from him in
return. "In the meantime, I will give her space to do
whatever it is that needs to be done."

Chapter Twenty

You've reached the voice mail for Lizbet Montlake. At the tone, leave your message and a number where I can return your call.

"Shit." Cassie punched the end button on her phone before Lizbet's voice mail could kick in and scowled out the Mercedes's back window. A week ago, hell would have frozen over before she'd have called her former colleague four times inside a one-hour time period. Now, she'd give a lot just to have her on the phone for five minutes.

Maybe she was busy.

Maybe she was avoiding talking to Cassie to steer clear of any awkwardness or taint by association.

It didn't matter. In another ten minutes, the only way she'd be able to avoid Cassie would be if she was out of the office on assignment.

She flipped open the thick folder full of contacts she'd snatched on her way out of the house. Six months' worth of interviews, every one of them conducted in painstaking thoroughness and carefully documented.

Using station resources to promote mafiya *activities, my ass.*

One-third of the way through the stack, she found the notes from the interview she'd done with Alfonsi's bodyguard. Cassie punched the mobile number scratched on the top right corner into her phone.

One ring.

Another.

And another.

She tapped an impatient rhythm on the side of the folder in her lap and chewed her lip.

"Yo!" Not exactly the most professional way to answer a phone, but definitely a voice that matched the man she'd interviewed before.

"Mr. Hofster?"

"Yeah, that's me. Who's this?" Defensive and a little suspicious, but understandable if he hadn't recognized her number.

"This is Cassie McClintock. We talked several months ago about Stephen Alfonsi."

An irritated huff sounded before he answered. "Yeah, I remember. Look, miss, I don't mean to be an ass. You're pretty and nice and all, but I told you everything I knew back then. Alfonsi's gone. Everyone's forgotten about him. Maybe you should do the same, yeah?"

God, she wished. Alfonsi and talking to people who had no desire to talk and fighting for every single step forward in her career.

The unfiltered thought startled her. Enough so that Hofster started talking again before she could. "Hey, I'm sorry. I didn't mean to bite your head off. I'm just over the whole ordeal, ya know?"

"Yes, absolutely. I am, too. I just had something come up yesterday and needed to tie off one topic we talked about. Can I ask you a quick question?"

Either she'd caught him at an optimal time, or he was

processing a lot of guilt for the way he'd spoken to her, because he sighed and said, "Yeah, sure. What is it?"

"When we talked, you mentioned that there were times Alfonsi didn't want anyone watching over him. I just wondered—is it possible he was seeing someone? Maybe had a mistress, or something?"

"Lady, Alfonsi had an eye for pretty women, and his son was just like him."

"But he didn't have a particular favorite, or one you saw him with more than once?"

Hofster hesitated. Not a sizable silence, but one still marked enough to make her instincts spark. "He was real careful about who he was seen with."

"Careful enough he wouldn't want any of you with him if he was seeing someone regularly besides his wife?"

Another pause. "That'd be a possibility, yeah. He was damned sure happier on the mornings when he drove himself in. Not the short-tempered asshole he sometimes was."

"Was there anyone closer to him he might have shared details with? Another bodyguard, maybe?"

"The only person he shared details with was Junior and, my guess, he's not gonna be talkin' any sooner than his daddy is."

Not the answer she was hoping for, but more than she'd expected. "Okay. If you think of someone, can you give them my number and ask them to call?"

His chuckle was one reserved for lost causes and half-mad people. "Yeah. Sure. Good luck."

With that, the line went dead.

Cassie pulled up the browser on her phone and typed *Pro Domme* into the search bar.

...specializing in BDSM sexual services with male or female clients for commercial gain.

Lizbet had asked the interviewee if she'd made a living at it.

"I didn't have to for a very long time. Now...it helps."

There'd been pain behind her voice. An aggravated edge that Cassie had originally chalked up to the woman being caught unaware by the question. But what if there was more to it?

She was so focused inward, Sam's turn onto the street in front of the station sent her listing to one side. She caught herself with one hand and scanned the employee parking. "Hold up, Sam."

Almost instantly, Sam eased up on the accelerator.

"Everything all right, Miss McClintock?" This from Abel, who sounded more than a little concerned.

"Yeah, fine." She sat a little taller in her seat. At 11:30 in the morning, a lot of employees were already headed out for lunch, so the parking lot wasn't as thick as it could have been, but the tall iron fence that surrounded the lot didn't make looking any easier. "Just trying to see who all is here."

There. The snappy little red Chevy Spark that Lizbet had been so happy about buying just a few months ago.

"I'm good." She waved Sam on to the guest parking lot in front of the building. "If you'll drop me off there, I'll just run in and get what I need."

She hustled down the long sidewalk, a power walk just shy of a jog, and heaved open one of the tinted double doors.

Bonnie was the last person she'd expected to see manning the front desk, and given the surprise on Bonnie's face, Cassie was the last person she'd expected to see today, too. "Cassie! Please Jesus, tell me the big dogs came to their senses and brought you back."

"No. No call backs. But if you're here on a Monday, does that mean you're full-time now?"

"Nah. The weekday girl's got some kind of cooties, so I got lucky. What are you doin' here?"

"I need to talk to Lizbet. Have you seen her?"

"Yeah. She was in the break room about an hour ago." She picked up the phone. "You want me to call her and get her up here?"

"No!" Cassie lurched forward and waved the receiver back toward its cradle. "God, no. I think she's avoiding me as it is. If I'm gonna talk to her, it's gotta be a sneak attack."

A shit-eating grin crept onto Bonnie's face, and she gently put the phone back in place. "Oh, this sounds like a juicy story in the making. How can I help?"

Talk about fortuitous opportunities. If it'd been the regular girl, management would have been notified of Cassie's arrival two seconds inside the front door. "Any chance you can buzz me through?"

Bonnie frowned. "If I do that and someone sees you go through, they'll be able to check the logs and see it was me that let you in."

Right. And Bonnie needed this job in a seriously bad way. "It's okay. Maybe I can wait outside and follow her when she leaves."

"No." Bonnie shook her head a little and her gaze drifted sideways, distant. A second later, she pulled out her keyboard and narrowed her attention on the screen in front of her. "There might be another way, though."

Her fingers flew over the keys, the muted clacks the only sound in the otherwise silent lobby. She hit the enter key and waited. "Hmm."

"Hmm what?"

"Just…hang on." The transformation in her demeanor was shocking. On the surface, Bonnie acted like a girl who was more comfortable working a beer tap and waiting tables than working a computer, but seeing the level of concentration on her face and the confidence in each keystroke made it seem like she was born with a screen in front of her.

"Yep. There it is." She zeroed in on Cassie. "I found the security database. I'll punch you through then wipe the transaction."

"You can do that?"

A weird look crept across her face. Part guilt, part consternation. "My brother's got a thing for computers. I've picked a few things up from him."

"Oh, that sounds like another story. One that requires drinks."

The playful rebuttal worked and drew a wry smile back to Bonnie's face. "Someday. Maybe when I'm not holding down three part-time jobs."

"Deal." Cassie glanced at the security camera mounted in the corner. "What about that thing?"

Bonnie cleared her throat and fiddled with the pen on her desk. "That database has the security recordings, too, so…"

Oh, yeah. They were definitely getting drinks, and unemployed or not, Cassie was footing the tab. "You sure?"

"Hell, yeah. Haven't had this much fun at a job since a fight broke out over DC versus Marvel comics at the bar I was tending." She pulled up something on her computer. "You ready?"

This was it. Once she went through that door, she was really in it.

She wiped her sweaty palms on her hips and nodded. "Absolutely."

The buzzer rattled like an amplified bee and the door clicked open. Voices from men in the studio echoed off the hallway's industrial white tile, but no one showed in her immediate line of sight. With a quick wave to Bonnie over her shoulder, she let the door snick shut and crept toward the bullpen.

Her arms and legs trembled, and the best her lungs seemed capable of were shallow short breaths.

Footsteps sounded from the side hallway behind her, and her heart jolted.

She ducked into the women's bathroom, huddled next to the door as it closed and waited for the person with the quick heavy footsteps to pass. Not that hearing anything over her pounding pulse in her ears was an easy feat. Sneaking into a TV station was certifiably insane. Definitely *not* the kind of work she was cut out for.

The footsteps passed, leaving only the quiet of the lounge that separated the bathroom from the exit in their wake.

"Cassie?"

No. Freaking. Way.

Cassie straightened away from the door and slowly turned. "Well, if it isn't the girl I snuck in to see. Why aren't you answering your phone?"

"Um." Lizbet motioned to the bullpen. "I do have a job to do." As soon as she said it, she seemed to remember the same was no longer true for Cassie and flinched. "Sorry."

Cassie waved it off. "Don't be. But I need to talk to you. *Now.*"

She checked beneath the stalls in the main part of the restroom, gripped Lizbet by her suit-clad arm and

tugged her toward the two padded slip chairs in the corner. "You know that BDSM novelty piece you did a few
weeks ago? The one with the Pro Domme?"

Lizbet demurely took the seat next to Cassie and
smoothed her scarlet red pencil skirt toward her knees,
a mildly incensed frown on her face. "That wasn't a
novelty piece. It was the start of a series. And the online comments were triple that of any other stories done
this month."

Cassie shook her head. "Sorry. I didn't mean it as
a dig. I'm sure it did great. But I need to know about
your source. The lady whose identity you kept hidden."

The incensed expression shifted to wariness, and
Lizbet edged away from Cassie as though uncertain
who or what she was dealing with. "What about her?"

Now for the tricky part. Getting any reporter to
share their source was iffy at best. If she shared that
the Domme was a possible murderer that might get
Lizbet off the fence, but would open a whole different
can of worms. Kir had trusted her with family knowledge. She wasn't about to break that confidence now.
"I think she's the person who told the execs about my
relationship with Kir, and I think she shared it because
she was somehow tied to Alfonsi."

"So?"

"So, why would she want to shut me up? *A reporter?*"

The shift in Lizbet's features was subtle, but it was
there—the slow dawning of comprehension.

"There's something there," Cassie said. "Something
she doesn't want me to know. Either because I'm a reporter, or because I'm tied to Kir."

"And why would you want to know? You don't have
an outlet to report whatever you learn."

"Because Ed accused me of using station resources

for Kir's benefit. Implied I haven't been objective. Neither of those things are true. And while I get they have to think about station credibility and all that, I want a chance to clear my name and prove the work I did while I was here was solid. Wouldn't you want to do the same?"

Lizbet pinched her lips together. Whether it was because she thought Cassie was crazy and was trying to hold the opinion in, or she agreed with Cassie's motive and was too afraid to voice it, Cassie couldn't say.

Either way, Cassie wasn't giving up. "Do you think I deserved the action they took? Really?"

Gaze sliding to the floor, Lizbet let out a sharp huff. "No." She straightened her spine and squared her shoulders almost as fast as she'd offered her agreement. "But, be that as it may, I don't see how this involves me, or why I should tell you anything about my source."

Inspiration struck. One of those glorious moments of intuition that blossomed in her gut. "Because if what I'm thinking is going on, I'll give you the story. Everything. All the details and full credit."

Lizbet's head snapped back. "Why?"

"Because I'm done with reporting. I don't need the story, but I *do* want to clear my name. The best way for me to do that is for the management team to realize they've been caught up in a scheme and we were both pawns."

"You're done with reporting?"

"Completely. I'm going to do something I really love. Take some time and explore my options."

The way Lizbet studied her, one would think she'd just grown two heads. "And this Kir guy...does he have anything to do with you being able to take your time?"

Hell, yes, he did. He had everything to do with her

life. With her future. "Kir believes in me. He knows I'm good at reporting and he's proud of what I've accomplished, but he also knows I'm in the business for all the wrong reasons. He wants me to do something I love and be happy."

In the time she'd known Lizbet, Cassie had seen many sides of her colleague. Focused. Angry. Coy and professional. But in that moment, a soft appreciation settled in her features. She smiled, the gesture marked with sad envy. "You're a lucky girl. Not all of us get that kind of a chance."

She regarded Cassie for another moment, then nodded, stood and straightened her jacket. "When Ed called me in the day they let you go, he told me what had happened. He said the tip came from someone at the Midsummer Masquerade."

An odd shift in topic, and not exactly the response she'd been hoping for, but Cassie went with it. "Yes. Someone shared the information with one of the executives."

"Hmm." Lizbet kept fiddling with her suit, tugging on each sleeve of her jacket and delicately flicking her fingers over the fabric as though ensuring no lint had dared to touch it. "That's a big event. It'll be hard to narrow down who might have said it. And that's only if you can get your hands on the guest list."

She snapped to attention and zeroed in on Cassie as though she'd been jolted by a thought. "You know, now that you've got a man with deep pockets, maybe you can afford a trip to the lady who makes my custom suits. She's a costume designer like the ones who work those masquerade balls. I'll bet she could even make a skinny thing like you look like you've got curves." She winked then sauntered toward the door, full of attitude. Opening the door, she paused for a last look at Cassie, a silent message behind her eyes. "Good luck."

The wink.

It hadn't been a sassy one, but a *pay attention* one.

She's a costume designer like the ones who work those masquerade balls.

And she'd made sure to bring up the Midnight Masquerade. If a costume designer did a ton of work on a masquerade, surely they'd be included on the guest list.

Cassie slipped her phone from her back pocket and opened her browser.

Costume Designers in New Orleans

Cassie clicked the first one—a man located near downtown. She hit the back arrow and tried the next.

A carousel of images featuring all manner of parties and costumes took up the bulk of the home page, but the address at the bottom showed Canal Street.

Fell on hard times and had to branch out or something. She's over on Canal Street.

Yes!

She punched the Bio link in the top right-hand corner and the designer's image filled the screen. Behind her, a multitude of colorful costumes lined the wall on prime display, but those full lips and turned up nose were unmistakable.

It was Lizbet's source. And the woman she'd seen in the coffee shop. And at *André's*. The only difference between the three were hairstyles and clothes, but as a designer she'd know all kinds of ways to alter her appearance.

In the corner of the image, a slick blue and red costume stood out among the others. Not something you'd expect at Mardi Gras or a formal masquerade, but more in line with a superhero movie.

No.

One resounding thought that ricocheted through Cassie's head and made her blood turn cold. Evette and Emerson were going to a designer at noon—one who Evette had hoped to have make Emerson a Halloween costume and who'd specifically reached out to them and volunteered her work.

Bolting from her seat, Cassie jerked the bathroom door wide and took off at a run down the hallway.

Her editor ambled from the side hallway and right into her path, his shirtsleeves rolled up to his forearms and his glasses perched on the end of his nose. He looked up and jerked with recognition just as Cassie passed him. "Hey, what are you doing here?"

"Just stopped by to say hi to Lizbet." She punched the release button on the door and didn't look back. "See ya."

Bonnie lurched straighter in her chair the second she laid eyes on Cassie. "Whoa, you okay?"

"Perfect," she huffed without breaking step. "And we're definitely having drinks soon."

She shoved one of the doors wide and opened up to a full sprint for the parking lot. She made it all of three strides before Abel and Patrick hopped out of the car and started her way. She waved them back and opened her own car door. "Quick. Get in the car. We gotta get ahold of Kir."

Chapter Twenty-One

Kir exited the Pontchartrain Expressway into the heart of New Orleans's Warehouse District and tried to ignore the weight of his phone in his jacket. It'd been well over an hour since Sam had called him. An hour he and Roman had spent casually feeling out a potential suspect from the guest list when what he really wanted was drive to the station and make sure Cassie was okay.

"You're overthinking it, *moy brat*." Seated in the passenger seat, Roman perused the passing landscape outside Kir's Audi like he hadn't just poked a sleeping bear.

"I'm not overthinking anything."

Roman swiveled his head and nailed Kir with a droll look. "And yet, you've made no observations about the next person on our list, and we're only a mile away."

Kir grunted. He could try and argue, but the truth was Roman knew him well. "Something feels off. She should have called by now."

Roman shrugged. "Then call one of her men. Ask them for an update."

He was tempted.

Sorely tempted.

But trust was a skill he'd left far too underdeveloped with women for too long, and he refused to jeopardize their long-term future for short-term comfort.

He shook his head, gripped the steering wheel a little more firmly and forced himself to focus on the task at hand. "The next name is one of your contacts. How do you want to play the conversation?"

Roman huffed out a smug chuckle and started to reply, but the subtle electronic ring of an incoming call cut him off.

Cassie's number flashed on the display.

Cocking one eyebrow, Roman dipped his head toward the dash. "Perhaps now you'll be able to concentrate."

Kir glared at Roman, but punched the answer button rather than argue and feigned a tone much lighter than the tension in his gut. "Hello, *vozlyublennaya*. I was wondering when I'd hear from you."

Cassie's labored breathing filling the car's interior, her voice sharp and hurried. "I think Evette and Emerson are in trouble. Someone needs to call the police and send them to 2940 Canal Street."

Roman's gaze snapped to Kir's, the same shock Kir felt like a living current beneath his skin reflected in his brother's expression.

On the side of the street were two open parallel parking spots. Kir checked over his shoulder, then whipped his car into the slots and demanded, "What's going on?"

"I know who tipped off the execs at the station. It's a woman and she works at that address. She's a costume designer and her name is Via Ricci, and I think she's the same person who took a picture of us at *André's*. The things is, Evette told me this morning that she and Emerson were going to see a costume designer about volunteer work for an upcoming fund-raiser. I think it's the same woman and I think Evette was set up."

"I'm calling her guards," Roman said, taking out his phone.

Kir kept his focus on Cassie. "What do you mean you think it's a setup?"

"Do you want details, or are you going to check on Evette and Emerson?" she bit back with an edge he'd never heard before.

He took the none too subtle jab, though, glanced over his shoulder and U-turned out of the parking space. "I'm driving. Roman's calling her men. Now talk."

Her sigh was one short on patience. "Short version— I've seen women while we've been out together I thought I recognized, but nothing ever triggered for me because they all looked different. Different hairstyles and hair colors. Different clothes. This morning, it all clicked— they're all the *same woman*. She's just wearing different disguises."

"And you figured this out how?"

"Because once I pointed it out, Aunt Frieda recognized it, too, and it's the same woman Lizbet interviewed for a special interest piece. I went to the station to see if Lizbet would share her source. I told her I thought her source was somehow tied to Alfonsi and had intentionally leaked my relationship to you as a means to shut me up and keep me from stumbling onto something I shouldn't know."

Pride blossomed behind his chest and the invisible fist gripping his lungs eased just a fraction. Rather than put the family at risk by sharing Kevin's murder, she'd cleverly spun the truth to give her request more credence. "Did she give you her name?"

"No. But after I told her I'd give her the story if what I suspected panned out, she gave me enough clues to figure it out on my own. Her name is Via Ricci and she's a costume designer. One who does a lot of stuff for Mardi Gras and masquerades."

And the anonymous tip that had cost Cassie her job had come from the Midsummer Masquerade. The connection made sense.

Roman barked something low at whoever was on the other end of his call and frowned.

Not good.

"And the tie to Evette?"

"She came to the carriage house this morning and invited me to visit a costume designer with her. She said the lady called her a few weeks ago about volunteering her time for an upcoming charity event Evette is overseeing. If I'm a person who's out to get revenge on Sergei, *who are the top two people in this world you'd target?*"

Roman ended his call and interrupted. "The guards were waiting for Evette and Emerson outside. They broke into the shop—there's no sign of anyone, but Evette's purse and Emerson's phone are in the workshop. I'm calling Sergei."

"You need to call the police," Cassie said.

Roman already had his phone to his ear.

Dead ahead, the stoplight turned yellow.

Kir pushed the car faster and hung a hard left. "Cassie, repeat the address."

"Kir, please listen to me. I know you want to handle this your own way, but I think you should call the police. If Via's got Emerson and Evette, it's a clear case of kidnapping. The police have more resources, and it'll show Sergei being on the up and up and working with authorities. It's also the last thing Via would expect from Sergei. That might make her panic and screw up whatever plans she's got. It's a win-win all the way around."

Emotions clashed inside of him. The driving compulsion to stay focused and protect his *vor's* beloved bride. The lightness that came from hearing Cassie think and act in the best interest of the family. The humbling gratitude that she'd gone to the station not for her name or her job, but to aid them all.

The buildings on either side of the street flew by, and Roman growled information into his phone, each word spoken in Russian. But his own voice was calm, grounded despite the tension of the moment by the woman listening on the other end of the line. "You underestimate me, *malyshka*. Certain things might be kept within family confines, but that does not mean we don't leverage other assets when warranted."

"You do?"

"Yes. We do." He checked over one shoulder and shifted lanes for the upcoming turn.

Beside him, Roman hung up the phone, the tension in his expression indicative of how the conversation with Sergei had gone.

"I need to focus," Kir said to Cassie. "You will go to the carriage house and wait for me there."

"No, I want to meet you on Canal Street. Evette might need me."

"Evette will need you at home and waiting for her when we get there." He took the turn as quickly as he dared and lowered his voice. "This is what I do, Cassie. Trust me to handle it. Wait for me where I know you're safe."

She hesitated, but only for a moment. "You'll call me when you find her?"

"The second we have her."

"And you'll be safe?"

Roman's gaze slid to the display with Cassie's name

emblazoned on it, and his mouth crooked in a wry grin despite his grim focus.

"Yes, *milaya*," Kir said. "I will be safe." He disengaged the call before she could change her mind, steeled his resolve to keep his promise and looked to Roman. "Call our contact at the downtown precinct."

Chapter Twenty-Two

Waiting wasn't Cassie's strong suit. For as long as she could remember, she'd been taught to make things happen. To get up and dive headfirst into whatever needed doing. Not sit and wait and twiddle her fingers, which was exactly what she was doing plunked right in the middle of the living room couch.

Aunt Frieda paced from the kitchen to the living room's picture window. She planted her hands on her hips, scanned the drive and the two men standing guard outside the carriage house door and harrumphed. "Where the hell are they?"

Well, at least Cassie wasn't the only one fighting impatience. "No clue." She checked her phone again, the only text on the display the one Kir had sent an hour ago that simply said They're safe. Working out details. Be home soon.

Of course, it'd taken three hours of absolute, tension-riddled silence before they'd gotten that much. At least now they knew everyone would be coming home, which should have made the waiting a little easier. But after four years of working jobs where she was always in the know, being in the dark sucked.

She snatched the remote off the coffee table and

thumbed through the local stations for any breaking stories.

Ellen DeGeneres.

Dr. Phil.

Jeopardy.

Judge Judy.

Zero news.

Not the most surprising outcome. You had to have something pretty major happen before you interrupted regular programming. Even with impending hurricanes, people didn't much appreciate it if you robbed them of their routine.

She punched up her old station. Only five more minutes and the regular five o'clock newscast would start.

Frieda dropped onto the cushion next to her. "Surely, they'll have something about it on the lineup."

"Maybe. Maybe not." Cassie upped the volume just enough to follow Ellen's closing remarks, but not so much it would overpower her phone's ringer. "After what Via said to the execs, they might be gun-shy about covering anything to do with Sergei."

She handed off the remote to Frieda and took her own turn glaring out the front window. If she had a dollar for every time she'd been tempted to pick up the phone and demand information from Kir, she'd be able to fund the launch of her business without any outside help. Seriously. How hard was it for a guy to pick up the phone and knock out just a few more details? Maybe at least an ETA?

This is what I do, Cassie. Trust me to handle it. Wait for me where I know you're safe.

Doing the dangerous stuff wasn't all he did. She knew from the discussions they'd shared since moving into the carriage house that he was more of an overseeing manager these days than an enforcer. A by-product of the type of family Sergei was determined to create.

But he was also capable of actions no ordinary man would ever take on. Had gone well beyond the shades of gray some might dabble in and had welcomed the dark.

Most of the time he masked it. Presented himself as an affable and carefree bachelor with a penchant for fashion and more money than he knew what to do with. But every now and then, the hard edges he'd honed him bled through, and her heart ached at the past that had shaped him. So, if he wanted her to sit and twiddle her thumbs so he could focus, then she'd by God sit, twiddle her thumbs and wait.

The five o'clock newscast music kicked in and the male anchor's customary light delivery droned the standard welcoming spiel she'd done herself in one form or fashion. His female counterpart was a whole lot more no-nonsense when she spoke, cutting right to the chase.

In breaking news, a kidnapping and ransom attempt involving the wife and child of local businessman and philanthropist Sergei Petrovyh, was foiled tonight by local authorities. Live on the scene at Bucktown Harbor with all the latest is Lizbet Montlake.

Cassie spun and slid back into her spot next to Frieda who'd already upped the volume and was leaning in with both elbows on her knees.

Behind Lizbet, the east horizon was already darkening to an early evening shade of blue, but the setting sun shimmered off the harbor waters. Her scarlet dress suit was still as immaculate as it'd been earlier, and not a single hair was out of place even with the heat, but there was obvious fatigue on her face.

"Earlier this afternoon, local authorities received information indicating that one of New Orleans's most

sought-after costume designers was suspected of abducting Evette Petrovyh and her minor son. Using GPS tracking, police tracked and apprehended Via Ricci at Bucktown Harbor just before she managed to smuggle her victims onto a private yacht kept at Bucktown's marina.

"Upon further search of the yacht, investigators found a drafted email on Ricci's computer addressed to Sergei Petrovyh, demanding ten million dollars in exchange for his wife and child's safe return. Authorities also arrested the man hired to pilot the boat who later advised authorities of Ricci's plan to sail to the southernmost Texas border and pass into Mexico.

"I spoke to the lead investigator in the case just after Ricci and her pilot were apprehended and questioned, and here's what he had to say."

The live scene cut to a bold afternoon sky and a swarm of police cruisers and ambulances crowding the edge of the parking lot closest to the marina.

Before Lizbet could ask the officer her first question, movement through the living room window caught her eye. Guards hustled toward the driveway and a second later, the throaty hum of more than one car rose above Lizbet's handoff back to the station.

Cassie abandoned Lizbet's segment and beelined it for the door. "They're home."

By the time she made it outside, a small crew was already gathered. Four guards from the main house surrounding Sergei's BMW. Abel, Patrick and Sam approaching Kir and Roman as they alighted from his Audi behind the BMW. Olga pushing her way through all the men and, of course, Evette and Emerson at the middle of it all. Sergei stood between Evette and Emerson, his hands planted on each of their shoulders as though he didn't dare risk letting either of them go.

Cassie hesitated just beyond the threshold, an awkwardness she couldn't quite name holding her feet in place.

Frieda paused just two steps ahead of her and looked back. "Cassie, baby. What's wrong?"

It was surreal, memories of coming home from school each afternoon and trips she'd made back to Houston to visit her parents layering themselves on the current moment. She'd always been an outsider before. Had fortified herself with a shield of emotional indifference just to walk through her parents' front door. Pretended she was someone she wasn't or steer clear of her interests to avoid censure.

But she didn't have to anymore. Those old survival skills no longer held value. Were not just unnecessary, but unwanted.

Kir strode into full view, his jacket gone, his shirtsleeves rolled to his forearms and his resolute gaze locked on her.

Her lungs surged on a full breath of air, and her feet got in motion. In less than four strides his arms were around her and the steady thrum of his heart beneath her ear. His woodsy scent was a balm to her senses. His warmth and strength a comfort that unwound the afternoon's tension in an instant. "You're okay."

"I promised you I would be." An utterly arrogant statement that might have rankled and started an argument if she hadn't been so overcome with relief, but there was appreciation in his voice, too. A loving lilt that said he found her concern as heartwarming as it had been for her to lay eyes on him again.

He kissed the top of her head. "I'm sorry I couldn't

call you. There was much to deal with, and Sergei wanted to get Evette and Emerson home."

She shook her head against his chest and hugged him tighter. "No. You did what you needed to."

Footsteps sounded on the pavement, growing closer. Kir slid his hands up her arms and squeezed her shoulders. "You have company."

Evette.

Seeing Kir she'd forgotten everything except the need to feel him against her.

She straightened on a jolt and found not just Frieda, Sergei, Evette and Emerson closing in on her, but Olga, the guards and Roman as well. She wrapped Evette up in a hug that would have been foreign to her even a month ago and squeezed her eyes shut. "I was so worried about you two."

Evette's arms shook, but the strength of her response was no less powerful than Cassie's. While there was still an indomitable spunk and spirt in her voice, there was a solemnness to it as well. "Yeah, well, Emerson and I would be almost to Mexico by now if it hadn't been for you."

Cassie pulled away enough to grip her shoulders and scan Evette and Emerson head to toe. "I just caught Lizbet talking about it on the news." She looked to Sergei. Then Kir. "Does anyone know what her motive was?"

"Money," Kir said. "And revenge." He cast an almost bewildered expression at Sergei and Roman before he shared the rest. As if he couldn't quite yet fathom the story himself. "Via Ricci was Alfonsi's mistress."

"I knew it!" Cassie said. "I asked one of his bodyguards if he might have had one, but he couldn't give me any specifics."

"Well, that's because Via wasn't just his mistress," Evette said. "She was his Dominatrix, too."

"His what?" Frieda said, scanning the entire group as though she wasn't sure she'd heard right.

It all came together for Cassie in a single *whoosh*. "He was a submissive. A male submissive—especially one doing what Alfonsi did for a living—couldn't withstand that kind of information getting out."

"Ricci kept his secret for years," Roman said. "In exchange, he paid for all of her needs."

"And when Alfonsi went poof, so did all of his support," Frieda said, finally piecing the last of the information together.

Kir dipped his head in a slow nod. "Correct. And she blamed Sergei for the situation, so she decided to use Evette to extort the money she needed to make up for the loss."

"Holy crap. It's almost too crazy to believe." Cassie shook her head, still reeling from the unexpected turn of events. She scanned Evette and Emerson once more. "What do you two need? A punching bag? A bath? Ice cream?"

"I want ice cream," Emerson said, looking up at his dad.

Olga, who'd braced herself behind her young charge, tapped his shoulder. "You will have ice cream. And cake. And anything else you want."

Evette smiled down at her son and ruffled his hair. "Probably for dinner and all three meals tomorrow. For both of us." She faced Cassie and her expression sobered. "Seriously. Thank you. I don't know what would have happened if you hadn't figured things out and tracked down that lady's name. She was batshit crazy."

"It wasn't just me. Lizbet had a hand in it, too. But

yeah. I'm glad it all came together, too." She looked to Kir then Sergei. "What happened to Via?"

Where the mood had been thick with fatigue and relief before, a chilling darkness swept in. A sinister pall weighted by deeds too dark to be spoken.

Sergei looked to Kir, a silent communication moving between them she had no hope of translating.

Kir's voice dropped, but rather than resonate with its usual warmth there was a brutal finality to it. "At the moment, she is in custody, but I had an opportunity to…talk with her before she was taken away."

"And?"

He hesitated only a beat. "And she eagerly admitted to taking Kevin's life."

And she will pay.

He didn't say the last part out loud, but the message hung in the air as sure as the strike of a judge's gavel.

Cassie cleared her throat, nodded and shifted her attention to Emerson who looked like he could either pass out on the spot, or run laps around the pool. "You should all rest. Or dig into the ice cream at least."

"God, yes." Evette said moving back into the curve of Sergei's arm. "You should come over and have some with us."

It was tempting. Feeling the unbending protection of those around her and their warmth was a welcome sensation, but she needed Kir more.

She shook her head. "No." Beside Evette, Sergei stood rock solid. His hard expression no doubt hiding all the pain and panic he'd felt throughout the afternoon. Cassie smiled at him and shifted her attention back to Evette. "I think your guy needs some alone time with you and Emerson. And frankly," she said laying her hand on Kir's where it rested on her hip, "it's going to take an hour or two before my adrenaline tapers off."

Standing slightly to Sergei's right, Roman chuckled and shot Kir a knowing look. "I suspect my brother would be more than willing to help you with that."

Apparently, Evette had the same idea because her laughter was just as wicked. "Yeah, that might be on Sergei's agenda, too. Right after ice cream."

Emerson frowned as if confused at what everyone was talking about.

Sergei released Evette, stepped forward and gripped Cassie by both shoulders. The hardened mask he'd kept in place slipped, revealing a man who'd fought many fears over the last hours and wrestled with terrible outcomes.

Kir squeezed his hand on Cassie's hip, and the group got frighteningly quiet. Even the cicadas stopped singing and the wind rustling the leaves overhead seemed to still. "You saved my bride and my son. Both halves of my heart. I am in your debt."

Cassie couldn't move, the strength of Sergei's hold and the reverent sincerity in his words leaving her mind and her body utterly dumbfounded. To some degree, he'd always been the one she felt least confident with. The most hesitant to approach. But in that second— hearing the tenderness he'd so openly expressed for those he loved in front of others and seeing the depth of emotion play across his face—she wasn't afraid at all.

"Family doesn't have debts," she said. "They just look out for one another."

He smiled at that. A soft one she suspected was usually reserved for only Emerson and Evette. He cupped the side of her face and shined the tenderness she'd heard in his voice down on her. "This is true. And you are family. In every way."

Releasing her, he stepped back, wrapped Evette close to his side and laid a hand on Emerson's shoulder. His gaze shuttled to Kir and a string of Russian words flew past his lips, delivered on a low and somber pitch.

Kir dipped his head in what looked like formal acknowledgment and blanketed Cassie's back, his hand at her hip wrapping around her waist. *"Spaseeba."*

Sergei smirked, kissed Evette on her temple and steered his family toward the main house. "Come. It's time to forget this day and plan for tomorrow."

The crowd dissipated quickly, the guards moving back to their stations, and Olga and Frieda hustling toward the kitchen well ahead of Sergei, Emerson and Evette.

"You know," Cassie said, "as tight as Frieda's gotten with Olga the last few weeks, you might have a hard time moving her out of here."

Kir chuckled, kissed the top of her head and steered her toward the carriage house. He held the front door open for her. "It would not matter. Sergei would begrudge them nothing, and it is no hardship for her to live here." He followed her inside and shut the door behind him. "Besides, you will be moving in with me."

"I will?"

"Did you have any doubt?"

No. She really hadn't. But she'd been so preoccupied with all the ups and downs of late that the actual logistics hadn't had enough priority in her head. "What about my lease?"

Kir ambled to the living room window and casually shut the curtains. "It has been dealt with."

"When?"

While she couldn't see his face, there was a smile in his voice. "The day I moved you here. The rest of your things were carefully packed and moved to my house for safekeeping."

Sneaky man. "So, your plan the entire time was to move me to your place."

"Yes." No hesitation. No pretense. Just the God's honest truth.

She could have given him a hard time. Probably should have just to keep his possessive tendencies in check. But the truth of it was, his certainty felt wonderful. Made her not only feel protected and cared for but wanted. "And this move to your place—when should I plan for it?"

He turned and prowled toward her. "Tomorrow. Tonight, I believe I've been tasked with relieving you of unwanted tension and anxiety." He smoothed his hands over her hips to her waist and skimmed his lips across the sensitive spot she loved just below her ear. His voice was pure velvet, his accent making his words that much more erotic. "And you know how I value my work."

A delicious shiver rippled through her, the warmth of his breath against her skin and the promise of feeling him against her heady enough to eradicate anything else.

Until her phone on the coffee table let out a sharp ring.

Kir pulled away enough to eyeball the device then cocked an eyebrow at her.

Cassie sighed. "I know Frieda's safe, but after the day we've had, I should check."

She answered on the third ring. "Cassie McClintock."

"Cassie, this is Ed. I don't suppose you watched tonight's newscast?"

No way.

Would the day's surprises never end? She covered the phone's microphone with her hand and whispered to Kir, "It's my editor."

The same amazement and curiosity she'd felt upon hearing Ed's voice reflected in his expression, but there was suspicion, too.

She put the call on speaker, laid the phone on the coffee table and sat in the center of the couch. "You mean the story about Sergei's wife and son? Yes, I saw it. I thought Lizbet did a good job." Which was another thing she was going to have to ask her man about.

"She did. But the story itself actually calls to attention how our executives were clearly fed information intended to result in your dismissal. When Lizbet came to us with the story this afternoon, she pointed out that Miss Ricci had likely taken the action she did to keep you from finding her connection to Alfonsi."

"It does seem that way, doesn't it?"

Beside her, Kir stood and listened, his face giving her no indication of his thoughts.

"Yes, well…" Ed cleared his throat. "In light of this information, I feel like we owe you an apology."

Kir held completely still, his gaze anchored on the phone.

Silly man. Their relationship would still be a point of contention with the station. And even if an apology turned into an offer to reinstate, she'd never been the type of person to retrace her steps. "I appreciate it, Ed. More than you know. But I'm also glad things happened like they did. It really made me think about what I want."

Kir shifted his gaze to hers, a silent question in his eyes.

She lifted the phone, stood and wrapped her arm around Kir's waist. "I've decided I'm going to move in with Kir and give some dreams I've put on hold a try. See if I can do something with my photography instead."

"No more reporting?"

She shook her head, even if Ed couldn't see it. "No. I'm good at working stories, but I've got a chance to make a living doing something I love instead. But I appreciate you calling. It means a lot knowing you don't think I acted inappropriately with station resources and my work was solid."

While she couldn't see her editor's face, there was enough shuffling in the background to imagine his fluster at the mistake they'd made. "Yes, well. You're a bright girl. Whatever it is you do, I've got a feeling you'll nail it. If you need any personal help—connections getting your work out or references, just let me know."

"Will do. Thanks for calling, Ed."

Ending the call, she muted the phone and slid it back to the tabletop. "About Lizbet…" She straightened and smoothed her hands along his pecs. "You're the one who called her, aren't you?"

"You made her a promise. I merely ensured it was fulfilled on your behalf."

Of course he had. And no doubt had done it despite the other chaos swirling around him. And how amazing was that? Not just to have a man who would do whatever it took to have a woman in his life, but would champion and help fulfill the things that were important to her.

She pressed herself flush against him and wrapped her arms around his neck. "And that other task you had to take care of...the one about ensuring I'm free from tension and worry...when do you plan to see to it?"

His grin was delightfully wicked. The purpose behind his eyes and the confidence in his touch as he palmed the back of her head even more so. He brushed his lips against hers. "Right now. And every day that comes next."

Epilogue

Cassie's biggest freaking shoot since she'd struck out on her own, and she was going to be late. Fan-freaking-tastic.

She hurried out of the over-the-top studio Kir had commissioned for her at the back of the shotgun-style house she now shared with her husband-to-be and jogged down the stairs. With every step, her equipment bags bounced against her legs and her shoulders protested that maybe she'd overdone it packing for Lizzy's concert.

Sun streamed from the living room's two floor-to-ceiling windows at the front of the house, the garnet velvet drapes that lined either side of them pooling against the oak floors. Beyond the windows, a riot of wildflowers and the fluffy plumes of pampas grass in the front flowerbeds danced on the late September breeze. From the first day Kir had brought her here, she'd been enchanted by his home. Every inch of it was brand-spanking new, but the builder had stayed true to the old homes that had inspired it. From the veranda with a porch swing, to the thick round pillars in white that accented the home's carnelian siding, and wrought iron accents from the stair railing to the balcony outside the master suite, the place was vintage New Orleans.

She grabbed her purse off the side table in the entryway, dug out her phone and tapped out a quick note to Kir.

Just now leaving. Tell Lizzy I swear I'll make it up to her for being late.

She rushed out the front door, hit send on the text and scampered down the brick-laid sidewalk to Sam and Abel waiting by the Mercedes in the street.

Abel met her before she made it to the iron fence lining the property and quickly divested her of her bags. "You should have called me, Mrs. Vasilek. I'd have hauled those out for you."

"Well, I just now finished packing, and I'm late already, so calling for help when I could carry them just fine didn't make sense." She slid into the back seat and aimed a playfully exaggerated look at her guard. "And PS—I'm not married yet."

Already behind the wheel, Sam chuckled and waited for Abel to take his place in the passenger's seat. "Mr. Vasilek was very clear that an engagement was as good as married and we could use the practice."

"Did he now?" The words might have been suited for a woman warming up for a fight, but the truth was, she thought it was sweet.

Her phone chirped and vibrated in her palm.

Kir: Lizzy says fashionably late is a requirement in the music business. Take your time.

The little bubbles that indicated another text was on the way rolled beneath Kir's last message, then a new one popped up.

Kir: I should probably warn you. There are some people here to meet you.

Cassie: Who?

Nothing happened for a long time. No bubbles. No text. No nothing. Then all of a sudden...

Kir: The women from Dallas.

Holy crap. All freaking day long she'd managed to keep her nerves in check, but all of a sudden, her body hummed like she'd firmly stuck her finger in a light socket. In the last three months, she'd heard all kinds of stories about Sylvie, Ninette and the rest of the women from Evette.

Cassie: Which ones?

Kir: All of them.

Shit.
Boyfriend jeans rolled up to her shins, a loose pink T-shirt and simple tan flats might've been a good choice for bending, stooping and kneeling to get the right shot, but they made a lame first impression.

Cassie: The mothers, too?

Kir: They were off the plane first.

Eek! Seeing Lizzy perform live, her first real live action shoot and meeting a good chunk of her extended family all in one night. Kind of made her old reporting gig look tame in comparison. But then, every single day since she'd apologized to Kir at Bacchanal had been a sublime whirlwind. A life not just worth enjoying, but celebrating.

Cassie: Is Frieda there yet?

Kir: Already has on her all-access pass and is making eyes at the stage manager.

Well now, that wasn't exactly a shock. Though, her aunt better get her flirting in early, because as Cassie's one and only employee, Frieda was going to have her work cut out for her juggling camera equipment and keeping up with Cassie once the show started.

She typed out a quick response that she was twenty minutes out, tucked her phone back in the side pocket of her purse and rifled through the main compartment for her notes. Since moving into Kir's house, she'd done a lot of experimenting with different types of photography. Mixing images with graphic alterations for a unique blend of modern art had proven to be unexpectedly gratifying. Especially when Evette had turned around and sold a few of her pieces at a charity event for an impressive sum.

But the biggest surprise? She really did have a thing for live work. And hallelujah for having a family who not only supported her passion, but was patient while she'd honed her skills through weekend outings and too many rowdy dinners to count. Emerson, in particular, had proven to be quite the clown when there was a camera in close proximity.

Last-minute cramming completed, she stuffed her notepad back where she'd stowed it earlier and eyed

New Orleans's Central Business District to one side of the Pontchartrain Expressway. Traffic on the highway wasn't much, but wow, had the people congregated around the Smoothie King Center for the show. Not surprising, given how the arena could hold nearly 18,000 people, but watching the masses stream in to watch someone she not only knew, but had exclusive rights to photograph was a rush.

Sam drove to the back of the arena, past at least a dozen matching semis with red cabs and gleaming silver trailers, to the iron gate where the die-hard fans were camped out in hopes of a Lizzy sighting.

The gate trundled open, and the guards at either side crowded close to keep the fans well behind them. Up ahead, four pimped-out Prevost buses sat side by side, every one of them painted in glossy black with sweeping gold and silver swirls. Impressive as they were, they only held her gaze for a minute, because the sight of her man strolling from the loading area was far more appealing.

And Lordy, was he a sight. He'd forgone his usual suit and donned jeans and a black Lizzy Hemming concert shirt that fit his torso perfectly. Seriously, if Lizzy needed a marketing vehicle to up concert T-shirt sales, having her guy stroll past the merchandise booths would be the way to do it.

The Mercedes rolled to a stop, and Kir opened her door before Abel could even get one foot on the pavement. He held out his hand and helped her from the car.

On the street side of the gate, the crowd let out a swell of cheers—right up until they realized it wasn't Lizzy getting out, but some blonde chick in unremarkable attire.

Cassie wrinkled her nose at Kir. "I think they're disappointed."

"I'm not." As was his penchant these days, he wrapped his arms around her waist and gave her a sweet, yet lingering kiss. "Are you ready?"

Funny. All he'd done was give her a simple kiss, and all of the anxiousness that had built in the hours before this moment vanished. She smoothed her hands atop his pecs and practically purred. "I'm not sure. I might need a minute or two alone with you to appreciate this shift in attire."

His grin was pure mischief. "It seemed fitting to show my support. I take it you approve?"

"I not only approve, but herby motion to make all Saturday nights casual wear."

He chuckled at that, stepped away enough to capture her hand in his and motioned the men toward the loading door. "Come. We'll introduce you to everyone, then give you time to familiarize yourself with the stadium."

Her guards fell in on either side of them, each one carrying one of her equipment bags. Shadows surrounded them the minute the door banged shut, only laughter from somewhere beyond, shouts from the roadies hustling in all directions and the low murmur of the crowd in the arena filling the void.

Kir unerringly found his way past stacks of black boxes meant for heavy traveling and down a long hallway with a closed door at the end. The light when he opened it was blinding, but the cheerful greetings that welcomed them even more overwhelming. Bit by bit, her eyes adjusted to the posh backstage lounge with its bold décor—gold walls, elegant black moldings, cougar print carpets and crushed velvet gold and black settees and sofas.

The real eye-opener in the room, though, were all the people smiling at her with even more laughter in their eyes.

Kir splayed his hand low on her back and addressed the group at large. "Everyone, my fiancée, Cassie Mc-Clintock."

Cassie wiped her suddenly sweaty hands on her hips. "Wow. Kir said I was going to get to meet more of the family. I didn't think I'd get to meet all of them."

And by *all*, it appeared the women weren't the only ones who'd made the trip, but their men as well.

One of the women chuckled and strode her direction. She might have been older than the other women in attendance, but with glamorous silver hair halfway down her back and a lithe, graceful body, Cassie bet she could still crook her finger and draw any number of willing men to her side. Rather than offer a handshake, she wrapped Cassie up and gave her a hug. "We don't normally travel en masse, but it's Lizzy's last show until she drops another album, so we figured we'd all fly in for the event."

She backed away, but kept one hand on Cassie's shoulder. "I'm Ninette." She motioned to a man with dark hair pulled back in a ponytail, a goatee and nearly black eyes in the corner. Unlike Kir, he seemed the type who'd been born wearing a T-shirt and jeans.

"That's my boy Jace." She hooked her arm in Cassie's and guided her toward him. "Next to him is his wife, Viv."

Cassie nodded and started to say hello, but Ninette kept going, introducing every couple in the room. Trevor, who seemed to be the down-home country boy type, his wife Natalie and their son, Levi. Knox and Darya, who she'd heard a ton about from Kir and Sergei. Beckett and Gia, who seemed to be equal parts gorgeous and badass. And finally, Zeke and Gabe, who looked like they could be the poster children for an all-American perfect couple.

"You know," Ninette said, "Gabe's a photographer, too. Takes the pictures and then does all kinds of killer stuff to 'em after she's done. You two should totally talk shop at the after-party."

"You do?" Cassie said to Gabe.

Gabe blushed, but nodded. "Yeah. Nowhere near as advanced as the stuff you do, but I enjoy it."

Cassie glanced at Kir who'd meandered up beside her, but couldn't glean any clarification from his smug expression. "You've seen my stuff?" she said to Gabe.

A few of the women cleared their throats and avoided eye contact, but Darya beamed a huge smile. "Oh, yes," she said, her Russian accent nowhere nearly as thick as Kir's. "Evette told me she sold some of your work at a charity event, so I asked her to send us copies." She motioned to Jace and Vivienne. "Jace has many connections in the art world, and Vivienne does a lot of their event planning, so they passed them on to a few contemporary galleries."

"My pictures are in galleries?"

"Well," Vivienne said. "A few of them are. I made a few calls on the flight here, and all but two have sold."

Jace grinned at Kir and twirled the toothpick wedged in the corner of his mouth. "Supply and demand, brother. Better stop hogging your woman and give her time to get more work in."

Holy crap.

Her pictures were selling.

Like real art.

How freaking crazy was that?

She turned to Kir. "You knew?"

His smile deepened and his voice dropped to that husky pitch she loved. "Of course, I knew. I have a vested interest in my woman being happy in her new career."

"Now there's a sign of a smart man," Ninette said, looking around the room like she'd lost a stray duckling. "I'd introduce you to Sylvie, but I don't know where in the hell she ran off to."

"She's giving the New Orleans crew a tour," Natalie said. "Though, if you want to know the truth, I think she and Frieda were comparing notes on which of the men on the stage crew had the most potential."

As if they'd staged their arrival for just that moment, the door swung open and Evette's, Frieda's and Sylvie's laughter rolled into the room ahead of them.

Evette locked eyes with Cassie almost instantly. She rushed forward and wrapped her up in a hug as everyone else strolled in. "You made it!"

"You sold more of my pictures!" Timing wise, it probably wasn't the right response, but Cassie couldn't help it. Her insides were still reeling from the news and doing their darnedest to keep up.

Evette leaned back, eyes wide with mock chagrin. "Oops?"

Laughter filled the room, and Sergei aimed an amused yet adoring look on his wife. He rested one hand on his son's shoulder and shifted his attention to Cassie. "It's what family does. You will forgive her, yes?"

"Well, of course. But I hadn't printed any new ones since the last set you asked for. How'd you get them?"

Frieda rolled her lips inward, but her face turned a bright red and the smile behind her eyes was pure mischief. "She might have had an inside track with your only employee."

Of course, she'd been the one to smuggle out the goods. Frieda was nothing if not a busybody—not that Cassie had any complaints.

The older woman with dark cherry-colored hair and enviable curves who'd walked in with her crew saun-tered toward Cassie. When she spoke, her words were thick with a Scottish accent. "Well, then. Now that we got all that out in the open, I'm Sylvie," she said, wrap-ping her arms around Cassie with the same familiarity Evette had. "Welcome to the family, lass."

Wow.

Just. Freaking. Wow.

Not just a big night.

A phenomenal one.

The stuff of dreams and happily ever afters. Her man by her side. Loads of happy, unpretentious, kind and giving people around her. A blooming career she hadn't seen coming.

And she hadn't even taken her camera out of her bag yet.

"Well." Axel's big booming voice came from the hallway at the back of the room and carried the same accent as Sylvie's only much, much lighter. "I see no one's scared off the new girl yet. Always a miracle."

"Um," Gia said. "Pretty sure it's the guys who usu-ally scare us off and the women who find a way to sweet-talk us back on your behalf."

"Mmm-hmm," Natalie echoed.

Sylvie released Cassie and aimed a superior look at her son. "Ye see? The women know the truth of it."

Lizzy, who'd walked in beside Axel and still had

her hand in his, shook her head. "You're diggin' a hole, Handsome."

Axel didn't seem to care. There was too much laughter in his eyes and the presence of a man who had it all and then some. He winked at Cassie and asked, "So, you've met the clan, yeah?"

Cassie nodded, the most she could muster considering how much she'd taken in over such a short time.

"Well, all right then." He clapped his hands together, rubbed them like someone had just wheeled in a cartful of beer or Scotch, then wrapped his arm around Lizzy's back. "Let's get this show on the road. Everyone get their seats, and we'll get Cassie set up."

Everyone stood, making their way toward the door and the hallway beyond.

Roman patted her shoulder, dipped his head to her ear and murmured, "Good luck," before following the crowd.

Sergei nodded in a show of encouragement and guided Emerson and Evette behind Roman, but Evette winked and wiggled her fingers in farewell over one shoulder.

In less than a minute it was just Cassie, Frieda, Kir, Axel and Lizzie remaining, but it was Kir who was closest. Her rock. Her champion. Her man.

He pulled her in close and cupped one side of her face? "Are you ready?"

She was more than ready. She was happy. Living a dream and loving every second of it. All because of the man holding her. "Absolutely. Let's do this."

* * * * *

Acknowledgments

I am tremendously blessed by the people in my life—some of them family by blood, some of them family by choice, and some of them business partners I'm damned glad to have. Together, they keep me sane, focused, and energized to keep chasing this craft and profession I love so much.

For the Carina Press & Harlequin crew, especially Kerri Buckley, thank you for your time, your patience, and your enthusiastic support. Even through transitions and uncertainty, you've done everything possible to keep the runway smooth and comfortable. That means more than I can possibly convey in words.

Cori Deyoe, Lucy Beshara, Jennifer Mathews, Juliette Cross and Dena Garson—what in the ever-lovin' world would I do without you guys? You've talked me off ledges more times than I can count and haven't once let me catch you rolling your eyes. Thank you for being my trusted friends and mentors.

And I don't dare let an opportunity pass without giving thanks for my beloved family. For my dad, my sister, my beautiful girls—Abegayle and Addison—and the love of my life, Joe Crivelli. My days wouldn't be anywhere near as bright and vibrant without each of you in them.

About the Author

Rhenna Morgan is a happily-ever-after addict—hot men, smart women, and scorching chemistry required. A triple-A personality with a thing for lists, Rhenna's a mom to two beautiful daughters who constantly keep her dancing, laughing and simply happy to be alive.

When she's not neck deep in writing, she's probably driving with the windows down and the music up loud, plotting her next hero and heroine's adventure. (Though trolling online for man-candy inspiration on Pinterest comes in a close second.)

She'd love to share her antics and bizarre since of humor with you and get to know you a little better in the process. You can sign up for her newsletter and gain access to exclusive snippets, upcoming releases, fun giveaways, and social media outlets at *www.rhennamorgan.com*.

Read on for a sneak preview of
Mine to Keep, *the next book in*
Rhenna Morgan's NOLA Knights series.

The good thing about public transportation was that it ran more reliably than Bonnie's beat-up Ford Focus.

The bad thing?

New Orleans's Transit Authority didn't run on demand. Which was going to make for a slow getaway on her return trip home later this afternoon. Definitely not ideal when you were trying to escape the nightmare neighborhood you grew up in.

Bonnie leaned against the bus's hard plastic seatback, crossed one jean-clad leg over the other and took a good gander at her fellow travelers. At mid-afternoon on a Monday, Line 80 didn't have a ton of passengers, but the ones it did have looked like they all needed three solid days of nothing but sleep.

Well, everyone but the guy in the dirty gray coveralls at the back of the bus. He'd been stretched across three seats and out cold since she'd gotten on near her apartment in Tremé. Whether he was drunk or just hiding from the quick January cold snap that had hit their fine city yesterday was a toss-up. But so far, nothing had made him budge. Not even the painful screech of the bus's brakes at every single stop.

Twelve of them, to be exact.

At this rate, Bonnie was going to have permanent hearing loss before she got where she was going.

As if the bus driver had heard her snide thoughts and taken them as a personal attack, he hit the brakes and sent another fresh squeal ringing from under the chassis. The passengers had barely righted themselves from the sharp forward jolt when the he opened the doors and droned into the microphone, "Louisa and Abundance Streets."

Bonnie sighed and stood. "Home, sweet home."

She'd murmured the snarky comment under her breath, but the middle-aged woman who'd been trying to keep two energetic young boys in line piped up before Bonnie could make the front door. "Look at it this way. From here, anywhere you go is up."

With a sharp laugh, Bonnie made her way to the pavement and readjusted her backpack on her shoulder. The lady wasn't wrong. For a neighborhood called Desire, it was a long, long way from what anyone would consider desirable. More like a country town that had been forgotten and left idling in the seventies. A few tiny houses dotted what had once been a fully populated area—some mostly well kept and surrounded by chain-link fence and others falling apart. In between many of them were empty lots, the homes that had once stood in the decent-sized plots now well overgrown with weeds big enough to rival trees. The only new structure in sight was a decent-sized church surrounded by baby crepe myrtles.

The driver revved the engine and the bus trundled away, leaving Bonnie two blocks and a fruitless conversation away from her escape. Crossing the street, she ducked her chin deep in the collar of her jean jacket and forged into the crisp wind. "I have got to get my car fixed."

The walk to Clouet Street was over in no time, and the sight that greeted her was the same as it always was—Dad's Chevy parked a little off the tiny driveway, the gate to the chain-link fence left open and the trash can that never left the front curb close to overflowing. The house itself was basically a double-wide that had taken on permanent airs and was painted in the drabbest tan known to man. Once upon a time, the oak trees in the front and backyard had added a homey feel to their lot, but these days they'd gone so long without trimming they all but hid the house from plain view.

She rounded her brother's Triumph motorcycle blocking the sidewalk, jogged up the cement stoop and—sure enough—the front door was unlocked.

Inside, the living room was all shadows and disarray, the blinds drawn tight against the clouds outside and all kinds of bills and junk mail scattered over the coffee table and couch. No lights were on in the kitchen either, but at least a little light streamed through one uncovered window. She headed in that direction and opened her mouth to call out a hello, but stopped dead in her tracks when her dad's voice bellowed from his room at the end of the hallway.

"Boy, you've got shit for brains! What the hell were you thinking?"

Well, guess that answered where everyone was.

She changed directions and started clearing a pile of motorcycle magazines off the couch.

Her brother Kevin's response wasn't intelligible from the living room, but the tone behind it was reminiscent of all the other lectures her brother had endured over the years. She'd bet his hands were jammed in the pockets of his jeans, a scowl on his face and his face flushed just like all the times before, too.

The irony of those lectures was that Dad was often just as guilty of doing whatever it was Kevin had done (and then some). Hence, the reason Kevin had to fight so hard to keep from blowing a gasket.

Ah, the joy of family.

She plopped onto the couch, unzipped her backpack and dug out the stack of medical bills she'd spent the last week juggling and pleading over. Might as well settle in and get her ducks in a row while the two of them duked out whatever needed duking. Better that than getting in between them. She'd learned that lesson the hard way when she'd tried to referee a drunken fistfight shortly after her mom had died.

"Enough!" Kevin's shout was loud enough someone could've heard it from the street. "You can call me whatever the hell you want, but if you think Bonnie's gonna have enough to bail you out with Pauley, you're out of your mind."

Bonnie's head whipped up from the stack of bills in her lap so fast her spine cracked. Pauley? As is Pauley Mitchell?

She tossed the bills on top of all the other trash on the coffee table and stalked to her dad's room. She hadn't even fully reached the end of the hall before she interrupted whatever Dad was saying to Kevin. "Do not tell me you're racking up a balance with that shark again. Do you have any idea how long it took me to get your last debt paid off?"

Both men whipped their attention toward Bonnie, eyes wide and jaws slack.

Translation: They were both guilty as hell about something.

Her dad recovered first, shook his head and took on that blustering bullshit demeanor he used whenever he wanted to sweep something under the rug. "Got nothin' going on with Pauley you need to know about, little girl." He aimed a warning look at Kevin, then waddled toward her in that painful- looking gait that plagued him these days. He palmed her shoulder when he got close enough and steered her down the hall. "Come on. I'm so damned tired of this bedroom I can't see straight. Let's get you settled and you can tell me what you're here for."

As if he didn't know. The only thing her brother and father wanted to talk to her about these days was money. Not surprising since she was the only one who could hold a job for more than a few months at a time. Or, in Bonnie's case, two or three jobs.

Still, one didn't throw snark in the face of a dying man, so she pretended to fall for the nicety and sat her ass back on the sofa.

Her dad wasn't quite as quick getting settled, the swollen gut that came as a byproduct of his failing liver just one of the sad realities he had to face. "Now," he said once he was in his recliner with his feet up. "Tell me what brings you here."

Seriously? They were going to dance around this? Usually he was all get-in-and-get-out with money business so he could get back to sipping his whiskey on the sly. "Um, bills?"

Her dad—or Buzz as his buddies called him, since he was always on the search for a good high—waved her comment off and smiled. "No talk of bills. Without a transplant, I'm gonna kick it soon, and those high and mighty assholes have said they're not giving me one. So, no point in either one of us bailing water with a thimble anymore. Now…tell me how that new job is coming."

New job?

Which one? Answering phones at the TV station, or the dive bar where the owner had practically handed over managing the business Sunday through Wednesday every week? And how the heck he'd call either one of those new considering she'd been doing both for over six months was a stumper.

"Well, uh…" She dared a glance at Kevin, who'd lifted one of the blinds and had taken to staring out at the empty lot on one side of the house like all the answers to the universe were gonna start rolling in any second. "The TV station is good. I sit on my butt, answer the phone, and don't let crazy people through the front door. It's easy money so long as I don't lose my shit with anyone."

Her dad laughed. Or tried to. It came out as a mix of a cackle and one hell of a smoker's cough. "Public relations. You were always good keepin' people in line. That's why people lean on you."

Lean on her? From her side of the coin she'd call it taking advantage of her. But hey—she'd never found the courage to tell anyone in her family no, so who was she to complain? "Yeah, they don't call it public relations. They call it a receptionist. But it's inside and I haven't had a fight break out yet. Can't say that for most nights at the Dusty Dog."

"Oh, yeah." From the look on her dad's face he'd forgotten all about the bar gig. "How's that place doin' anyway? Last I heard, that rusty old bastard who bought the place was about to go belly up."

Okay. Something was seriously wrong. Dad wasn't the conversational type. Not unless he was trying to sugar someone up for a con.

Bonnie gave up pretending and aimed her attention on Kevin. "You wanna tell me what's going on?"

Kevin shot their dad a nasty look then bit out, "Like he said. Nothing."

Nothing her ample white ass. She was just about to say as much out loud when Kevin muttered something she couldn't quite make out under his breath and stalked to his coat thrown across the well-worn club chair. He reached underneath it and pulled out a slim, shiny laptop. "Here. I brought your computer back."

"Hallelujah and praise the Lord!" She was on her feet and cradling the hand-me-down MacBook Pro Cassie had given her several months ago in less than a heartbeat. "I was starting to think you'd pawned it."

Kevin scoffed at that, moved his jacket out of the way and dropped into the seat. "You gonna pile on and give me shit, too?"

"I don't know," Bonnie fired back, easy-as-pie. "Depends on what Dad was giving you shit for."

"Nothin' you're gonna get involved in," her dad answered before Kevin could. "If the two of you were smart, you'd steer clear of all that techno mumbo jumbo. It's all gonna backfire on the lot of us one of these days and then what are you gonna do?"

Bonnie ducked her head to hide her smile and smoothed her hand over the top of the computer. Prepping for Armageddon or just a good old-fashioned technological revolution had been her dad's favorite pulpit topic since Kevin had first shown him the internet. That said, he'd never put one iota of effort behind his prepper ideas.

Rather than give her dad any more to chew on, she focused on Kevin. "I still don't get why you needed a

Mac. What was wrong with that new Windows machine you got last year?"

Her dad grunted and wiggled in his recliner.

Kevin cleared his throat. "I just thought I'd try my hand at doin' some app front ends. Lots of demand for people who can do that kind of work—especially, stuff that goes on an iPhone. Can't do that with a Windows machine."

"Yeah? How'd it go?"

Kevin rubbed the back of his hand across his nose and aimed his answer at the coffee table. "Not my kinda gig, apparently. Gonna have to stick to networks and databases, I guess."

"Or you could stay the hell out of all that nonsense and get yourself a real job like your sister," their dad said.

Kevin clearly wasn't done with the arguing. "Just because I don't clock in and out of some dead-end, boring-ass corporate gig doesn't make it nonsense."

"Oh, right," Dad said. "It's not nonsense. It's the thing that's always landing you in deep shit with more people than we can count."

Mmm. Fair point. What Kevin called networks and database work, most other people referred to as hacking.

Clearly, Kevin knew his dad had hit close to the truth because he shrugged the comment off, focused on Bonnie and changed the subject. "A word to the wise—I turned location services off on your computer. If you're smart, you'll keep it that way."

"What the hell's location services?" Dad said.

Bonnie chimed in before the two of them could start going at it again. "It helps you find your computer if you lose it or someone steals it."

Dad snapped his attention to Kevin. "That true?"

"Hell, yeah, it's true. Phones, too. It's the way things work today."

"Well, that's bullshit." Dad flicked his hand toward her computer. "You do what your brother says and keep that location thing off. Government's got no business messing in your affairs."

Bonnie raised both hands in surrender. "Fine. Fine. I'll leave it off. Now can we focus on these damned bills so I can get back home and enjoy my one day off?"

Her dad crossed his hands across his swollen belly. "Already told ya. Not gonna worry about bills and medicine and doctor's appointments anymore. Gonna live my life the way I wanna live it with the time I have left. So, don't go giving me any grief about it."

His stare slid to Kevin and he added, "Not either of ya. Understand?"

No. She didn't. Not even a little bit. She'd already lost her mom because of booze and partying. Just sitting back and accepting her dad giving up wasn't even remotely in the cards.

Outside, the muted rumble of an engine pulling up and idling in front of the house made its way through the thin living room window. With their house being the last one on the dead-end street, that meant her dad's buddies were rolling in early to help him get his drink on.

"Are you kidding me?" Bonnie said, twisting for a peek behind the blinds. "It's barely after three o'clock in the afternoon."

Before she could get a glimpse, Kevin shot to his feet, knocked her hand aside and looked for himself. He straightened and shot their dad a look that was all business. "It's them."

"God damn it, boy. I told you this wouldn't be good."

He folded down his footrest the way a gunslinger stowed his gun, stood as quick as he could and waved toward the hallway. "Get Bonnie out of here."

"She can't leave. If they see her, she's fucked."

"Then get her to my room. Put her in the gun closet. I'll stall."

"Are both of you out of your mind?" Bonnie interjected.

Rather than answer, Kevin snagged her laptop, shoved it in her backpack and manhandled her down the hallway. He lowered his voice as they neared her dad's room. "You gotta be quiet, Bonnie. No fucking around, all right? Not a single fucking word no matter what."

"Are you for real right now?" Bonnie twisted as much as his pushing allowed and tried to look in his eyes. "What the hell is going on?"

"Nothing you need to know about." He jerked open the closet's bifold doors, slid the clothes aside and opened up the hidey-hole where her dad once kept his illegal firearms. It was a simple unfinished cabinet with now empty gun racks, but the outside blended with all the rest of the paneling in the room. Kevin shoved her inside and paused only a moment. "Promise me."

A knock sounded on the front door, and Kevin's already pale face blanched a deeper shade of white. In all the years she'd known her brother and through all the crazy trouble he'd gotten himself into, she'd never once seen so much fear in his eyes.

Bonnie swallowed hard and pulled her backpack tight against her chest. "O-Okay."

Lips mashed tight together, Kev gave her a sharp nod and closed the door.

The hangers scraped across the metal rod and the bifold doors whispered back into place.

What the ever-lovin'-hell were the two of them up to?

What they're always up to, her conscience whispered back to her. Doing things outside the way the rest of the world lives and then ending up with their asses in one sling or another.

Voices sounded in the living room, but her heart pounded too hard for her to hear. A sickly sweat built along the back of her neck and her spine.

God, she was sick of this crap. Her whole damned life she'd done her best to stay in the shadows and out of the messes her family created. Why they couldn't just have normal jobs, pay taxes and lead calm lives like everyone else was beyond her. Everything had to be a party. A scheme, or the next great con.

The voices grew louder, her dad's gruff take-no-shit tone volleying back and forth with another one she didn't recognize.

A second later, something cracked. A heavy thud against wood followed by scuffling and grunts. The clatter of the metal screen door against its frame.

Then quiet.

Painfully terrifying quiet.

But she kept her promise and waited.

And waited.

Her legs trembled with the need to move, and her forearms ached where she clutched her backpack tight.

Where the hell were they? She had to have been in the cramped space at least thirty minutes. Maybe more. It sure as shit felt like more. If whoever it was was gone, why didn't they come give her the all-clear?

What if they can't come get you?

All too easily, the grunts and scuffles she'd heard replayed in her head.

If you think Bonnie's gonna have enough to bail you out with Pauley, you're out of your mind.

No way.

Pauley and his goons weren't the types to bust heads. More like B-grade loan sharks who annoyed you into paying outstanding debts.

Unless Pauley was out of options and was tired of her dad's crap. Yeah, Kevin might be able to hold his own with someone out to rough him up, but Dad didn't have a prayer.

One thing was for sure—someone was going to have to stick their neck out and figure out what to do next. Per usual, no one else was showing up for the job.

With a deep inhale and a slow exhalation, she eased her backpack out of the way enough to feel for the release latch in the dark. The cold metal was a welcome brush against her fingertips, but the tiny click that came as she slid it aside felt gunshot loud.

She paused and listened, the air from her father's bedroom swooshing through the tiny crack she'd created and gently stirring whips of hair against her face and neck.

But other than that—nothing. No movement. No voices. Just an absolute void of activity.

She nudged the door just wide enough to slip free and ducked beneath her father's clothes. One painstaking step after the other, she rounded the unmade bed to the open bedroom door. A peek down the hallway showed absolutely nothing but the tan shag carpet that should've been replaced five years ago and a beam of overcast light from the side window Kevin had uncovered.

Sticking close to the wall, she tiptoed forward, pausing at the two bedrooms along the way to glance inside. Her heart pounded and her lungs clamored for air as if she'd sprinted a mile. At the corner where the hallway opened up to the living room, she hesitated, closed her eyes and braced. Whatever was on the other side, she could handle. She'd had more than ample training dealing with crap like this her whole life. This was just another drop in the bucket.

She pressed one hand to the wall and leaned forward...

Nothing.

Not a single soul.

But the bills and junk mail that had littered the coffee table were all over the floor and her dad's recliner was turned at an odd angle. The front door had been left open just a crack with only the screen door keeping the cool January air at bay.

So, what? They just left her here? Forgot she was hiding in the closet?

No, her family was crazy and unreliable as hell, but they weren't so callous as to leave her hiding in a cramped space. Not unless they were drunk, anyway. Which had been known to happen a time or two growing up, especially when a special school event had clashed with a roaring party.

With a sharp huff, she slid her backpack off her shoulder, sat it in front of the end table and went to shut the front door. The last thing she needed was someone else unexpected showing up while she tried to figure out what the heck was going on.

She shoved the door flush with the jamb—and froze.

Was that blood?

Reopening the door to let in the light, she shifted for a better look.

It was blood. A decent-sized streak of it that carried

across the doorjamb at standing height. A quick check outside showed two fat drops on the stoop as well.

Her stomach lurched and a mangled cry lodged in her throat. She slammed the door shut once more, threw the bolt and scrambled well out of reach.

This was bad.

Very bad.

Wiping her hands on her hips, she paced to the open side window, scanned the street outside and pulled the blind back down.

Okay. She just needed to think things through. Figure out the right thing to do.

"The cops," she said to the empty room. "Everyone calls the cops." She hustled for her phone in her backpack, pulled it out and fired up the screen.

Um. Tiny problem there, hot rod. This is your dad and Kevin we're talking about. You call the cops and there's no telling what trouble you'll bring down on them.

She stared at the phone a beat longer, punched the button to put it back to sleep and dropped to the spot she'd cleared out for herself on the sofa. Even if she did risk it and call the cops, they'd probably rope her into the mess as well—guilty until proven innocent and all that.

Hell of a predicament when you couldn't call the people who handled shit like this for a living. Talk about your damned if you do / damned if you don't situations.

Jaw clenched, she planted her elbows on her knees and glared down at the bag lying between her feet. Cops weren't an option. Kevin's buddies weren't an option. Neither were her dad's. The only people she knew outside her family's friends were good law-abiding people who'd be scared to death to step foot in this neighborhood.

She let out a slow, steady breath and forced the muscles in her shoulders and neck to relax. Between the open zipper of her backpack the corner of the laptop Cassie had given her peeked out, the brushed aluminum an almost space-aged touch compared to everything else in the room.

Hold up.

Maybe there was a non-law-abiding option.

Not Cassie. She was as good and sweet as they came. But Cassie's new man, Kir—and the freakishly hot badasses he ran around with all the time—were rumored to be mobsters. Russian ones at that. Surely one of them would know what to do in a situation like this.

Of course, she'd have to call Cassie to get one of them to help, and calling Cassie meant exposing the ugly side of her life. Not an ideal plan considering how far she'd gone to hide it from her new friend. Even if she dared to let Cassie see where she hailed from, didn't calling on the mob always end with a debt being owed?

She stood, paced to one side of the living room and back, all the while eyeballing the blood smeared on the ivory paint around the door. There had to be another option. Something that fell between bringing cops into the equation and making deals with mobsters.

Stopping mid-path, she planted her hands on her hips and glared at the bloodstain. Really, the only other options were to walk away completely and leave her family to fate, or to venture out on her own to figure out what happened—neither of which were likely to generate results.

She can't leave. If they see her, she's fucked.

Right. Another problem if someone was watching the house.

Her gaze slid back to the MacBook.

Funny. The slick device Cassie had gifted her with after her man had hooked her up with a newer and more powerful one to further her photography work was probably the most valuable possession Bonnie owned.

Including her broken-down car.

Cassie hadn't asked for a single thing in return. Had just said she liked hanging out with Bonnie and wanted to pass some goodness along to a friend.

No strings.

No agendas.

Just a smile and a hug before she'd gone off to a photo shoot.

Of all the people you know, she's the least likely to judge.

Part of her wanted to believe the thought. Part of her was too tainted by the two-faced people who'd marched in and out of her life.

The fact of the matter was, the only family she had left was missing. And, from the looks of things, they hadn't gone peaceably.

She palmed her phone once more.

A knot lodged at the base of her throat, and her blood buzzed like she'd had nothing but caffeine for days. She scrolled to Cassie's number and tried to ignore the way her thumb shook over the keypad. She hit the call button, lifted the phone to her ear and muttered to the room, "Swear to God, if my fucked-up family ruins the one good friendship I've got, I'm gonna kill 'em both myself."

Don't miss Mine to Keep *by Rhenna Morgan,*
Available October 2020
wherever Carina Press ebooks are sold.
www.CarinaPress.com